Not Another Wish

S.P. Wilcox

ISBN: 0615726097
ISBN-13: 978-0615726090

DEDICATION

In honor of my mother who still tells me she loves me every day and my sister who lifts me up when I am down.

In memory of my father, I didn't inherit your wicked math skills but I did inherit your crazy bigger than life imagination!

CHAPTER 1

"Welcome aboard Flight 225 with non-stop service to Denver International Airport, our flying time today will be approximately two hours and fifteen minutes. Please sit back and enjoy your flight." The pilot announced over the intercom.

Leaning forward with my elbows on my knees, and my fingertips rubbing my forehead, my head was hurting. My mind is overwhelmed by the events of the last 12 hours. It is New Year's Day and I am on a plane to Colorado to see Grant. What am I doing... am I crazy? I have barely gotten any sleep, after having a marathon phone call with him.

The evening began somewhat normally, getting ready for the New Year's Eve Party at the country club and texting Heather; well at least I thought I had been texting Heather. Quite a few drinks, dancing, black jack, and the fortune teller. Oh God the fortune teller. I am replaying the evening over and over in my mind. The fortune teller telling me the only one to cure my broken heart is the one who broke it in the first place. How did she know about that and the phone call from Grant at midnight, begging me for forgiveness?

I can hear Grant's voice perfectly in my mind, "I don't want to kiss Curt at midnight- I want to kiss you. I want to hold you...Oh, God, Sydney... I miss you so much, I am so sorry."

I just stood there listening to him speak. I didn't say anything, I couldn't breathe, and I was starting to hyperventilate.

"Sydney are you there, tell me what did the fortune teller say when you asked her about me? Are you going to say anything? I can hear you breathing," he said, his voice laced with concern.

My mind was racing, why… why is he calling me? It had been four months since I heard his voice, not counting when he was on speaker phone with his mom, but I wasn't counting that time.

"How did you know about the fortune teller and why are you calling me on Heather's phone?" I squeaked out.

"She forgot her phone when they left to go out tonight, and I knew you wouldn't answer if you saw my number."

"Oh…God… that was you texting me tonight? When I was texting Heather it…it was you? What do you want? Why are you doing this to me?" I asked him.

I didn't know what to do; I wanted to yell at him, I wanted to kiss him, I wanted to hang up on him, shit I am confused. The tears are coming, I could feel them… this was all threatening my sanity.

"Grant, I just…"

"Sydney, tell me something- do you love him?"

"Who?" I asked completely lost by his question.

"Jason, do you love him?"

"No, I don't love him. Why do you care? You moved on a long time ago… I can't do this, I just can't, I have to go," I said.

I was standing on the patio of the country club walking in circles, tears coming down my face, completely torn apart. After all these months why does he decide to call, why now?

He was begging me, "Please don't hang up… Sydney… I am so sorry. I know you hate me for the things I said to you, for not trusting you when it was all in my mind. I just…I can't bear the thought of not having you in my life. The last few months of not being able to talk to you or touch you has been awful, there are no words for me to describe how badly I feel inside without you in my life."

Our conversation kept replaying in my mind during the flight to Colorado.

"Grant, I have to go," I told him.

"No, please talk to me, will you talk to me… tell me how you feel."

I am dying right here on the patio.

"What do you want me to tell you, that all is forgiven and we can be together?"

2

"Is that an option?" he asked me. I laughed a little.

"It is going to take more than one phone call asking for me to forgive you for it to be an option," I told him.

My hands were shaking, I was nervous, and the cold evening air was making me shiver.

"Come to see me in Vail."

"What are you nuts? I can't come to Vail."

"Yes you can, come here so I can tell you in person how much you mean to me, how you fill my heart with love, how without you in my life I am empty inside and only going through the motions to get by," he cried to me.

"You telling me all those things in person, or on the phone, won't change the facts. You are incapable of trust. You decided in your mind I was doing something to betray you, with no facts you just let your imagination run wild."

There was silence, no response, did we lose the connection? I looked at the phone, shows a connection.

"Grant?"

"Yeah, I am here."

"Do you want to respond to what I said?"

"You're right," was his only response.

"Come to Vail?" He asked me again. "I don't want to talk about this over the phone. I should have done this a long time ago. Come to Vail so we can resolve this in person, so I can see the look on your face when you are yelling at me."

My parents walked out on to the patio looking for me, it was late, I put one finger up to tell them one minute.

"Grant I have to go, my parents are waiting for me. Can I call you back in a little while?"

"Yes, you promise to call back?"

"Yes." I said.

I remember the drive home, which is only 5 minutes, taking forever. My mom was desperate to know who I was talking with on the phone.

"Don't ask Mom, don't ask!" Was all I said to her.

The car wasn't even in 'park' and I was bolting into the house, running to my room. I grabbed my phone out of my purse and called Grant back on his phone this time. Lying on my bed, I looked at the time 1:15 am.

"Hi," he answered on the first ring.

My heart was racing when I heard his voice again. God, I have missed him, the ache in my heart even more intense.

"Hi," I said.

"So, are you coming? I have a ticket booked for you leaving LAX at noon today. It is already paid for, all you have to do is show ID and board the plane," he stated.

I am smiling, not that he could see me, but I really want to go.

"How did you manage to do that so quickly?" I asked him.

"I've had the ticket since before your birthday, it was your birthday present from my parents, I just had the airline re-issue it for today."

I was stunned, my tears beginning to fall again. I was lying on my back, holding my pillow for moral support.

"So, will you come...Sydney, will you come to me?"

I was silent; afraid of what might happen if I didn't go to him, never knowing if our love was true and strong enough to survive. If I went could we work our problems out? Is he truly sorry for his behavior, there is only one sure fire way to find out.

I quietly said, "Yes, yes I will come... but Grant, I can't make you any promises."

He was silent; I could hear him breathing, his voice cracking as he spoke.

"Sydney, I am just glad you are willing to come to me, don't give up on us, you're my soul mate."

He gave me all the flight information. It was late or early, however you want to look at it. I need to leave for the airport by 9:30 am, which gave me a few hours to sleep and get ready.

When I told my mom my plans, she smiled and surprisingly said, "It is about time you two worked this out!"

She kissed my forehead and said, "Sydney, give him a chance, let him explain himself before you go all crazy on him, ok?"

I didn't say anything. The smile on my face was huge, telling her my answer. I couldn't wait to get to Colorado. My parents drove me to the airport. My dad muttering the entire way to the airport about how ridiculous this is, flying off to see some guy on a couple hours notice. My mom telling him to be quiet and think of all crazy stuff they did when they first fell in love.

"That was different," he said. She just laughed at him.

I must have fallen asleep on the plane because the next thing I know the captain was announcing our arrival.

"Thank you for flying with us today, have a safe trip in Denver or wherever your final destination may be," the pilot stated as the plane taxied to the gate.

As the plane taxied down the runway, I could see a light snow falling to the ground and the wind blowing. It took forever to get off the plane. I was wearing my UGG boots, jeans, long sleeved blue henley and had my sweatshirt in my arms. Grant would be waiting for me by the baggage claim. I stopped in the restroom really fast, checked my hair, fixed my make-up and put on some lip gloss. I wonder what he will say about my hair. I looked one last time at myself in the mirror...I look good!

I followed the signs through the airport leading me to the trams which take you to the baggage claim. My heart was beating super, super fast on the tram ride to get my luggage. After exiting the tram and walking to the carousel, I could see him waiting for me, I swallowed really hard, my smile coming across my face. I couldn't have stopped smiling if I tried. I started to blush when I saw his face, God he is gorgeous. His hair a little longer, his skin not as tan, his eyes twinkling with excitement and his grin wide. He was wearing faded jeans, which made him look delicious, boots and his Yale sweatshirt. He was holding a sign, *SYDNEY STANTON*. I laughed as I got off the escalator, he grabbed my carry-on bag and pulled me into him, wrapping his arms around me, hugging me, my heart filling with happiness, this was the right decision.

He whispered, "I am so happy you are here, so happy!"

I could feel my tears of joy coming down. He was slowly rolling his thumb across my bottom lip.

He leaned down and asked, "Can I kiss you?"

I didn't answer I just looked up at him and he could see the answer in my eyes. The kiss- it was-heart stopping, the lightning bolt went shooting between us and when we finished the kiss, we both laughed. I bit my bottom lip, I could feel my lip a little swollen from the long kiss he had given me. He took my hand and we went to get my luggage from the carousel.

We walked to the car hand in hand, not talking, just looking at each other smiling. The snow was falling softly around us as we walked. He put my bag into the back of a black Range Rover, opened the door for me, and buckled me in, giving me another heart stopping kiss. Then he walked around to get into the driver's seat.

"We have a two hour drive to Vail, we can talk the whole way to the hotel, or we can wait and talk after we go to our room, it is up to you," Grant said.

I was looking out the window, he grabbed my hand, "Sydney, are you alright?"

I turned and looked at him my smile still huge on my face, "Yes, I am good, thank you. Hotel I thought we were going to the Wilders' house?"

He smiled, "I thought it would be nice to have some privacy, to discuss our situation without having to worry about everyone listening, and I don't want to share you with anyone for a few days. I hope that is okay with you?"

I didn't say anything I squeezed his hand and smiled. My heart was filling, I think I can feel the pieces coming back together.

"Do you want to yell at me or can I tell you everything I have wanted to say for months?"

I looked at him, "I think I will yell at you for a few minutes and then you can talk," I said laughing a little but not too much.

"Okay, I am ready, go ahead, kick the shit out of me," he said.

I looked out the window as Grant pulled out on to the highway and I turned to look at him, wanting to see his facial expressions. He is massaging the back of my neck with his right hand and playing with the back of my short hair. "I like your hair, why did you cut it?"

I shrugged, "I just needed a change, to make me feel better about myself I guess."

"Oh… I am sorry," he said his voice low with remorse.

"I just don't understand, why you didn't trust me, when you asked me to be your girl last summer, I was so happy, I never even thought about another guy and then when we got back to Arizona, you…you changed. You just assumed the worst, I told you before Rush even started I wouldn't be available, but you didn't believe me and you just acted like an ass! We weren't even apart a week. How do you think we are going to fix this… if you are incapable of trusting me?" The words just kept coming out of my mouth, I couldn't stop even if I tried.

He didn't say anything he just looked at me. I was starting to get mad, my blood pressure rising. I am trying to remain in control, without becoming a complete basketcase.

"Before you left you were so mean, saying the vilest things to me that night at the Fraternity House. You didn't even fight for us, you took off for New York, you didn't call, you didn't even try! Not once did you call, text, or email me. Nothing!"

I took a deep breath, to keep my composure. I felt chilled, I put on my sweatshirt, which was really Grant's Arizona State sweatshirt. I could see him watching me and the smile come across his face when he saw me putting on his sweatshirt, but he didn't say anything. He is driving calmly, but I could also see the tension in his face.

I took another calming breath, "Look I have thought a million times about everything I would say to you if we were ever in this position. Why did you leave me? Why did you walk away so easily? I thought you really loved me, and your words telling me you didn't ripped my heart out. I cried every day, until one day I just couldn't cry anymore. I started running whenever I felt bad. With every stride I felt better to the point I could make it through the day without crying about you."

I was rambling on, but I needed to tell him how I felt the past months. How his words and actions destroyed me.

"I was really feeling better, when I went home for Thanksgiving weekend."

I see him tense at this moment. He must know what is coming.

"I cut my hair, relaxed, and decided to come back to school with a new attitude and stop feeling like a widow. When I returned to Arizona, I was walking through the airport, I could feel you, somewhere near me. It was an odd queasy feeling, but still I knew you were close. That is when I saw you with her- with Ashley."

I started to cry, I couldn't hold it in any longer, I am crying and yelling at him, "How could you go to her? How could you touch her? It made me sick, it still makes me sick! Why…why did you go to her, why?"

Grant didn't say anything for a while, he hand both hands on the steering wheel. His knuckles were white from his grip. The lines around his jaw were tight and his eyes and forehead were scrunched up. I turned to look out the window at the snow is still falling. I could feel tears rolling down my face. I didn't want him to see me crying. I wiped the tears away with the back of my hand.

Finally, he started to speak, his voice cracking at first, "Sydney, no matter what I say, will you please let me finish before you comment? I will tell you everything. I don't know where to begin. Uh…when I took you back to school it was so much harder than I ever thought it would be. I was so jealous not seeing you every day- not that I had any reason to be jealous, because I most definitely had no basis for my jealousy. When I took you to the Sorority House it just had the worst memories for me. I know you don't understand why… it was because Ashley was in your sorority."

My head whipped around so fast to look at him. "OH MY GOD!" I was screaming inside my head, my eyes had daggers in them now. I was staring at him with hatred, how could he not have told me this? This is a big deal! I didn't open my mouth I just let him continue. I am so angry my hands are balled into fists in my lap. Why didn't I know this girl? Well if you have ever been in a sorority you would know that the senior girls don't usually come around as much, they may participate in Rush or not. May go to the parties or not. They are not usually as involved as the younger girls. They live off campus and don't come to the house as much. As a Pledge, which I was, I wouldn't have been at the meetings for active members only Pledge meetings.

"I can see you are fuming at me, I see it in your eyes," he swallowed really hard and took a breath. "I know I should have told you last summer, I didn't think it made a difference, but I was wrong-it did. I flipped out on you and it wasn't your fault. I know it wasn't your fault. I never truly dealt with the situation Ashley created; I drank and partied the pain away, but the emotional pain I never really resolved."

He took his right hand and grabbed my left hand and kissed my knuckles, sending my emotions into a tailspin. How could I be so mad at him and still feel the lightning bolt?

"I didn't know you saw me with Ashley in the airport. Not until you told Heather in your text message. I went to her, wanting her to explain what happened, so I could finally have closure on it. We met at a restaurant, there was wine… too much wine, but I didn't mean to sleep with her, I swear to you Sydney, I didn't mean for it to happen," he declared.

I couldn't hold my tongue anymore, I yelled at him, "You are a *LIAR*. I don't believe you. Why would you lie about this? I know you wanted to have sex with her, if you didn't want it, you would have never had her at the airport with you, she was sitting on your lap, playing with your hair and kissing you! All of those are such intimate gestures, you are a fucking liar, take me back to the airport, I hate you…pull this car over at the next stop so I can get out!"

He is crying now. I am screaming at him incoherently. This is a disaster.

"This was a terrible idea. You still can't come clean with me, I HATE YOU, I HATE YOU! How could you go to her after everything she did to you and you let her touch you? I loved you so much and you left me and went back to her... I can't do this!"

My heart was aching. Why did I agree to come here? This is awful, worse than I could have predicted. I knew before I got here about him sleeping with Ashley, but it was so much more real now. I was clenching my stomach, I could feel the bile rising in my throat.

"I feel sick, pull over, I think I am going to be sick," I gasped to him.

He pulled the car over and I jumped out of the car and walked to the embankment, leaning over the guard rail, completely sick.

Grant jumped out of the car yelling at me, "Sydney, be careful, the ground is slippery."

Grant was rubbing my back, saying, "God, I am so sorry, it didn't mean anything to me, I just got caught up in the need... the need to be touched and then it just got out of control. I told her I didn't want anything from her, that there would never be anything between her and me again, and that I am in love with someone else."

I looked up at him and I didn't say anything; I climbed back in the car, shut the door, put my seat belt on and just stared out the window. He didn't take me back to the airport; we drove the rest of the way to Vail in silence.

When we arrived at the hotel it was gorgeous of course, the sun was beginning to set and it looked beautiful, the blue sky and bright orange sun setting behind it. I was exhausted from lack of sleep and the emotional roller coaster that had become my life. I couldn't even look at him, I didn't want him to touch me. I just wanted to take a shower and lay down for a few minutes. Grant checked in to the hotel before picking me up at the airport so we just went straight to our room. We are standing in the elevator, I could see my reflection in the mirror- I look awful, pale, and tired. I could see Grant as well, he looks defeated.

We finally made it to our room. Still not talking, after he put my bag down I grabbed some stuff from it and went into the bathroom. I turned on the shower to let the water heat up, I brushed my teeth, and washed my face. I just stood looking at myself in the mirror, muttering, did you really think you'd resolve everything in a two hour car ride, you knew he slept with her? This is not new information. If you really love him, you will keep trying to get your relationship back. I feel awful, my stomach is in knots and my heart feels more broken than ever before. I took a deep breath, I need to find a way back from this, I will have to put my own pride to the side and forgive him for his mistake. I stripped out of my clothes which, I think had some throw-up on them, and got into the shower.

A few minutes later, I could hear the bathroom door open, "Sydney, I brought you the fluffy robe from the closet, I will hang it out here," he said with an uneasy tone in his voice.

I could hear him taking a deep breath. He sat down in the chair at the vanity. I looked out at him; he was leaning down with his head in his hand, rubbing the back of his neck.

"I don't know what to do, I seriously never thought I would have another chance with you, I am not excusing my behavior- I was a wreck. I let our love and you slip through my fingers, and I fear that is still true. I started seeing a therapist in New York after the incident over Thanksgiving," he shared with me.

I was still in the shower, I was done, I just didn't want to get out yet. The water is so soothing as it rains down on me.

"Are you still seeing the therapist, is it helping?"

"I believe it is, I feel less anxious about things, I understand why I behaved so badly to you and how wrong I was to treat you like that."

I finally turned off the shower, "Can you hand me a towel and the robe," I asked him.

He handed me both, I wrapped myself up in the robe, put my hair in the towel and stepped out of the shower. I could hear his breath quicken and a small gasp come out of his mouth when he saw me. I pulled the towel off my head and ran my hands through my short hair, shaking my head at the same time.

"I feel a lot better now. Maybe we could go downstairs have something to eat together?" I asked him.

He jumped up, "Yes, oh that sounds good, are you sure you are okay to eat, I mean you did get sick not too long ago?"

I looked up at him from under my eyelashes, "I think I will be fine."

My mind is up to no good, I am going to make him squirm. I moved past him in the bathroom, just barely brushing against his stomach. I stopped to put on a little make-up and fiddle with my hair. I could feel him watching me. I walked out of the bathroom and took some clean clothes out of my bag. I laid out my clothes on the couch; jeans, socks, turtleneck, and a warm yellow sweater. No underwear. I have ample breasts but with two layers of clothes plus a jacket I could get a way without wearing a bra. Grant was leaning on the door frame of the bathroom watching me. My back was to him.

I let the robe drop to the floor, I purposely leaned over to put my jeans on, and I could hear him start to moan those little manly noises he does when he is hot for me. I grabbed my perfume and sprayed just a small squirt on my chest. I pulled the turtle neck on over my head, not putting on a bra first, and then the sweater. I didn't turn around, because the smirk on my face would have given my plan away. I put on my socks and then my UGG boots.

Grabbed my jacket and turned around, "Ready?" I said walking to the door.

He took a very long deep breath, walking up to me, and opening the door for me. We got in to the elevator, which is filled with other guests. I could feel Grant's eyes on me, I pulled my lip gloss from my pocket and seductively glazed my lips making them shiny, puckering, and smacking them methodically.

He placed his left hand on my lower back and whispered in my ear, "You are mean."

I smiled and let out a small laugh.

We went to the steak house in the hotel, it was cold outside - too cold for me. We sat inside by the window, the view was out of this world, I could see the mountains lit up by lights for night skiing. The restaurant was lovely, white tablecloths on all the tables with small candles in the middle. The wait staff wore white long- sleeved shirts, black pants with black aprons. I ordered an iced tea to drink and Grant ordered a beer. The waitress told us about the evening's specials and then we sat in silence looking at the menu. I was smirking behind my menu and Grant... well he was squirming in his seat.

"What are you going to have to eat?" I asked him.

"Hmmm...I think steak, baked potato, salad and you?"

I raised my eyebrows at him, "Well, the soup sounds good, I think I will have a bowl of soup and maybe you will share a few bites of your steak with the woman you love," I said smiling.

I waited for him to respond to my comment.

"It seems the woman I love has a very bad temper and can be extremely mean to the man she loves." Grant said to me making my smile grow wider.

I know we still had to work out our issues, but I didn't want to fight anymore, well at least not now.

The waitress returned with our drinks and we placed our order. She came back with a basket of bread. The restaurant was busy with tourists, and the bar attached to the restaurant was very busy. He was staring at me as I put butter on a piece of bread.

"What? Why are you staring at me?" I said my eyebrows furrowed at him.

"You have changed since August, not just your hair, which is very nice, but your body, damn, what have you been up to? Your body was hot before, but now well… it is fucking hot," he said and not in a whisper.

"Grant Montgomery, be quiet, people will hear you," I said.

"I don't care… it is true," he said tipping his beer back for a long drink.

"I run 3 or 4 miles, three or four times a week," I told him.

"Well, it does your body good," he said licking his lips at me.

I could feel my body- it was in full overdrive for him. I tried not to show the desire burning through my body, but he knew. His eyes danced with desire.

I put my finger up, pointing at him, "No, I am hungry and so are you, let's get through this meal and take a walk after dinner, maybe sit outside by the fire pit," I said.

The waitress came with our food and it was delicious, the soup was yummy but the steak Grant ordered was maybe the best steak I had ever tasted. We finished our dinner and shared Crème Brule for dessert. I ordered a cup of coffee, because I knew this would be a long night.

Once we finished dinner Grant took me on a nice walk around the grounds of the hotel. We held hands and he told me about his classes, apartment, and how rude people are in New York.

"People don't smile there, they are in a perpetual state of annoyance," he said.

I laughed at his comment about New Yorkers.

"Then maybe you should transfer back," I deadpan.

He didn't respond, I knew he wouldn't do that, it was his dream to attend Yale.

"I am just kidding, you will be done before you know it," I told him.

We made our way to the fire pit which is outside the bar, music was pumped outside for guests on the balcony to hear. We found a small love seat to snuggle on by the fire. A waitress came up and asked if we wanted a drink or to make s'mores.

I smiled up at Grant, "Can we please make s'mores?"

"Yes, of course." We ordered our s'mores kit and some beers, and I cuddled up to him on the small couch.

He was in the corner of the couch and I was wrapped under his left arm. We just fit together so perfectly. I got up on my knees and turned to him, so we were looking at each other.

"Grant, I don't want to fight, I don't want to rehash the past few months, I want to move forward with our relationship. But I don't want to have to worry about you being jealous or making assumptions that just aren't true. What do you think?"

His smile was beaming, the twinkle in his eyes earth- shattering. I could feel my heart continuing to mend by the look on his face. The fortune teller was right!

"I love you Sydney, and I will spend the rest of my life showing you how important you are to me." Pulling me into him, Grant gave me a big kiss and hug. I am so comfortable in his embrace; I hadn't realized how much I missed his touch. Our waitress brought out our s'mores kit and we went to town, I burned my first marshmallow and of course Grant made his perfectly. He gave me his and made a new one for himself. We laughed and giggled. We were talking endlessly about everything, I told him about my job at the bookstore. I showed him pictures on my phone from Pledge Presents. He frowned a little, realizing he missed a formal with me and seeing me in my black dress. I was running my fingers down his arms across his thighs and then back up again. Grant was squirming.

"Can you please stop doing that, I am barely keeping myself from taking you on this couch, so unless you want an audience, I suggest you either stop or we go to our room?"

I looked up at him, not saying a word; the expression of pure lust across my face had him jumping from his seat. We were in the elevator, impatiently waiting to reach our floor.

CHAPTER 2

We are barely in the door to our room and I am pinning him up on the wall, I couldn't wait to get my hands all over him. My breathing is hard, not able to form any thought except to get his clothes off, and my hands on his hard abs and erection. I could feel his length bulging in his jeans. I am grinding on him. He is unbelievably gorgeous, and my attraction to him hasn't changed over the time we were apart.

I love putting my hands in his hair and tugging on the ends. He pulled my hands from his hair, "No, I am not making love to you on the wall after not having had you in months."

He picked me up and carried me to the king size bed. Panting with desire, my body was aching for him. He pulled my sweater off over my head, and grabbed my breasts through the turtleneck I still had on, my nipples hardened by his touch.

I let out a moan, "Oh, mmm."

He pushed his hands under my shirt, raising the shirt up to expose my breasts. My body releasing all kinds of sounds of desire from the sensations coursing through me.

"That was very mean what you did to me earlier, dropping your towel and dressing in front of me, not putting on a bra or panties. I couldn't get your naked body out of my head- you were eating your soup naked in my mind," he said with a wicked laugh.

I didn't say anything, he was licking my nipples, pulling them in between his teeth. He sucked so hard on each breast. Suddenly, I felt sick to my stomach, not the "I ate something bad or I have the flu sick", the kind of sick you feel when you know you are not ready for this step. I pulled away from Grant and sat up in the bed. I pulled my knees up to my chest. Grant's eyes were locked on mine.

"What's wrong? He asked me, while moving up the bed to be next to me. "I thought you wanted this?" He said moving his hand back and forth between us.

I can't breathe, I feel like the oxygen is being sucked from my lungs.

"I...I...feel sick, every time I close my eyes, I see her hands on you, and her lips on your neck. Maybe I was wrong...maybe I am not able to put this behind me." My lips were quivering as I spoke.

Grant tried to wrap his arms around me to comfort me, but I pulled my body away from his embrace.

"Sydney, I don't know how to make you feel better. I messed up... I know that doesn't make you feel any better. Tell me what to do? I am sorry for what happened." Grant's face was grim.

I didn't know what to tell him. I don't know what is going to make me feel better, or make me forget what I saw in the airport that day.

"Will you let me hold you?" He asked cautiously.

I nodded my head yes. He wrapped his arms around me as I leaned my head on his chest. He was stroking my hair and kissing the top of my head.

"I need to know why Ashley was at the airport with you. You said you got drunk and that is why you had sex with her, I can somewhat understand what took place. But you were not drunk at the airport. What was she doing there with you?"

I needed to know why he allowed her to touch him like that, how he allowed her to be so forward if it is not what he wanted?

Grant took a deep breath, continuing to hold me tight against his chest.

"My dad dropped me off at the airport that day. I didn't ask her to come with me. I didn't ask her to meet me at the airport. She just showed up. She was trying to convince me to get back together with her. She wanted me to take her back and she was trying everything in her power to do so. What you saw was her trying to prove to me that she is the right woman for me. I didn't want her touching me... it was actually make my skin crawl." His whole body shivered for a second.

"What you apparently didn't see, was me moving her to the seat next to me. Me telling her being with her was a mistake. You didn't hear me tell her that I am in love with someone else. That I am happy she is out of my life because I would have never found my true soul mate if she and I had stayed together." His voice was fortified with passion and sorrow.

His words kept playing over and over in my head. I fell asleep with his arms wrapped around me and my head resting on his chest. It is the most wonderful feeling; I am completely surrounded by his body, warming my aching heart, and southing my overactive imagination.

When I woke up in the morning, I tried to quietly escape his grasp to use the bathroom, but he woke up. He grabbed for my hand.

"I am just going to the bathroom," I said and then my stomach growled.

He looked at me with raised eyebrows, "Hungry?"

I laughed, "Well soup only goes so far."

We both got up, I showered first and then Grant showered. He did attempt to get into the shower with me, but I am not quite ready to take that step with him again. We headed downstairs for breakfast.

"Do you want to go snowboarding, snowmobiling, or tubing, today, my lady?"

I rolled my eyes at his comment, "Snowmobiling sounds fun, you drive and I hold on to you, or I drive and you hold on to me?"

He waggled his eyebrows at me, "Umm, we can do that in the room you know?" he said almost spitting out his food as he laughed.

I gave him a funny look as if to say, "Not so fast."

After snowmobiling we headed back to the room. We both changed and were sitting in captains' chairs in front of the television in our room, relaxing. I was spinning back and forth in my chair. I had my feet up on Grant's chair in between his legs. He was rubbing my toes. Today had been fun, we took turns driving the snowmobile and decided next time we would each have our own to drive. Though I think he was just humoring me.

I got up from my chair and went to sit on Grant's lap. I slowly began kissing his neck, swirling my tongue around his ear lobe, lightly biting on it.

"Hungry are you? You missed me, my love," he rasped to me.

"I want you so badly, if you don't make love to me I think I might explode," I moaned to him.

"Take your clothes off and we will see how badly you want me," he said.

At the same time he was cupping my sex with his hand from the outside of my jeans, I groaned from the pressure of his fingers pressing on my oversensitive mound. I couldn't have moved faster as I ripped off my turtleneck and tossed it across the room. When I went to take off my jeans, he grabbed my hands moving them to the side. I was boiling from the inside out, I could feel the wetness between my legs. He stood me up in front of him popping open the top button on my jeans, pulling the zipper down at a ridiculously slow pace, and pushing his hand down my pants. I gasped from the feel of his touch he pulled out his hand and pulled my jeans off.

He took off his shirt and I watched him remove his jeans and take off his boxer briefs, releasing his erection, which was by all means gloriously standing at attention. My breathing hitched as I stood in front of him, leisurely taking in the sight of him.

"I want you now. I want to feel you inside of me please," I whimpered.

I knew he was ready. He dropped down, lifting my leg over his shoulder, and put his head in between my legs, immediately using his tongue to enter me. He took a long lick from top to bottom moving my folds and blowing softly on me. I was reeling from the pleasure he was giving me. He stood back up, kissing me.

"Damn Sydney, you taste so good, I missed your taste on my tongue. One more lick and we both get what we want," he whispered in my ear.

I could feel his tongue touch every part of me. It wasn't one more lick, but I didn't care because the orgasm he gave me was out of this world. I began screaming for more. He quickly moved us to the bed and climbed on top of me entering me slowly, stretching me to fit his massive erection. The feeling was beyond wonderful. With each thrust I took him further into me, as far as I could get him. I wanted him deep inside me, marking me.

"Harder, don't stop," I moaned.

"You are the only one for me, we are so good together," he said through clenched teeth.

The electricity between us was ignited into a full blown wildfire. We were sweating and gasping for breath. I was pulling him into me trying to get us as close as possible. With each thrust of his hips, his tongue thrust into my mouth, giving me deep kisses.

"Come inside me," I said, "I can't hold on," and with that I was gone, bursts of bright lights were around me and he was groaning. His body shuddering from his release.

He dropped to my side, holding me, I could see tears in his eyes.

"I have missed you- I never thought I would hold you again. I love you. Please don't leave me." Grant sweetly said.

"I won't leave you, you are my one and only," I said.

We both fell asleep wrapped together after making love. When I woke, I found Grant staring down at me caressing my face.

"You're finally awake. Did you have a nice nap?"

I stretched my body, "Yes, I haven't taken this good of a nap in…" I started to count on my fingers back to August. "Well, not in five months." I laughed giving him a quick peck on the lips before getting up to go to the restroom.

"Come right back… I have something for you."

I looked at him and then down to the erection, which was puffing up the sheet like a tent. I laughed and then went to the restroom. I was parched and drank a bottle of water before returning to the bed with another bottle of water in hand. He was sitting up leaning against the pillows and I shared my water with him. Before I could get back under the covers he grabbed me, removing the sheet, lowering me down on his very hard erection.

"You're always so ready for me…you feel so good. I can't get enough of you," he said, taking one breast into his mouth.

I am riding him, moving my hips back and forth; it is so good, feeling him inside me. I leaned down and kissed him with sheer passion.

"I…umm…you feel so…oh, yeah," I said my words not forming a complete thought.

He was rubbing his thumb over my sensitive spot. I was heading over the edge, I could feel my climax. My breathing is sporadic… my eyes closed… my head leaning back at how wonderful he feels inside me.

"Not yet…don't let go yet," he said, I was barely able to breath.

He flipped me over onto my back without us coming apart. He is pounding into me, we are coming at the same time I could feel his body tensing and his final thrusts as we feel over the edge of ecstasy together. I am buried under him when we finish, relishing the feel of his body on mine.

He is still inside of me not moving, holding my face in both hands, "Sydney, I love you." He said looking directly into my eyes. The ache in my heart I have been feeling all these months is finally gone and my heart feels whole again.

"I love you, Grant Montgomery."

We lay together for quite some time, when our breathing finally returned to normal, I rolled on top of him and looked in his eyes.

"What do you want to do tonight?"

He gave me a salacious smile.

"No, we are not staying in bed all night," I said.

"Why not we haven't seen, or been together, in months, I could do this with you all night." He said kissing my forehead.

"Today was fun, did you enjoy yourself?" I said attempting to change the subject.

"I did. My favorite part was when you had your arms wrapped around my waist and had your thighs like a vise grip on my legs. Were you scared?"

"You drive that snowmobile like a mad man!" I said to Grant. "So, hell yes, I was scared."

"You have a sunburn… or snow burn. Do you want to put some aloe on your face?"

"Yeah, in a minute… can we going dancing tonight? Maybe see if Curt and Heather will meet us?" I asked him and he smiled back at me.

"Sure, I will text Curt and see what they are up to, but I thought you would want to spend the night alone, since we will be going back to my aunt and uncles' house tomorrow?"

We moved to the chairs by the TV, I laughed and kept moving my chair back and forth. Thinking- we have some issues to discuss before we move on from here.

"I do want to be alone with you. But I would like to go out tonight too. Can we please discuss how we are going to make this…I mean you and me, work? You know the long distance thing?"

He looked at me with apprehension. I wasn't looking at him in the eyes, not wanting to meet his gaze, not sure what his response is going to be. Not to mention, I still need to end things with Jason.

"Well, we never even tried. How about we make a plan to call, no texting unless it is just to say hi, miss you or I love you," he said with a big smile.

"I agree, texting can get so impersonal and calling is better, how about Skype? Can we try to Skype, so we can see each other when we are talking?" I raised my eyebrows, wiggling them up and down.

"What is that about?" He wagged his eyebrows back at me laughing.

"I was thinking using Skype could make... well...you know...phone sex so interesting, what do you think?"

He started to move closer to me, coming off his chair. He came across the floor on his knees, putting his upper body in between my legs and moving in for a kiss. I could feel my heart start pounding in my chest the closer he came to me. The lightning rod igniting... oh how much, I have missed this man.

"Sydney, you have made me so happy. Coming here, working things out so we can be together. Don't let me be an ass again!" He took my face in his hands and gave me a kiss, pushing his tongue in my mouth, I could feel his tongue and mine dancing and my body melt against his.

"I can't keep you from being an ass, you're a man you have to control your insecurities." I kissed him this time. Wanting to get as close to him as possible. I was covered only by the hotel robe. Pressing my breast into his chest.

"Why don't I help you out of this robe?"

"Wait, let's finish our discussion and then you can have your way with me, ok caveman?" I smiled at him wickedly.

"What else is there to discuss?"

"What about vacations, flying to see each other, and formals?"

"Formals?" He looked all confused.

I tilted my head to one side and raised my eyebrows again at him. He is so clueless sometimes. I mean he has only been out of college since June.

"You know, you already missed Pledge Presents, I want you to come with me to my spring formal. Will you come?"

"Yes, will you wear the black dress?"

"No, but I will get a new dress, for the spring formal. I will let you know the date as soon as I have it, but it is important to me that you take me to it, okay? So don't flake out!"

"Okay, make it a sexy dress, something I can take off of you without much effort, are we done?" He laughed, smiling wickedly.

"No… okay, so just to confirm, phone calls, Skyping, and texting for loving messages only, with much effort to listen and communicate. No jumping to conclusions and this is monogamous-nobody else, correct?"

"Yes, everything you said, Sydney. What about Jason? Don't you need to put an end to that relationship?" He said, as he was kissing my neck. But I could hear the annoyed tone in his question.

"You know I really like this short hair, I have better access to your sexy neck." I was giggling and trying to finish the discussion.

"Stop, I will take care of Jason and yes… now, we are done discussing, happy?"

"No!"

"Why… not?"

"I want to hear you call this Jason character and end it." He is still in between my legs, looking right into my eyes. I want to hear you tell him you are back together with me.

"You want me to call him right know?" My voice was kind of high and uneasy.

"Yes, is this a problem for you? I can call him for you." He said laughing.

He was already kissing his way down my neck and moving my robe to expose my nipples. I could feel his tongue brushing against my now very hard nipples. I took a deep breath, to steady the ache growing inside me.

"Yes, fine, I will call him right now… let me up and I will get my phone." Grant moved out of the way so I could get my phone from my bag. I saw him grab his phone and then sit down in the chair I had been in so he could text Curt.

This was going to be a very awkward conversation. What am I going to say to Jason? I shouldn't be too worried; I mean we only went out a couple of times.

I sat down on the edge of the bed not facing Grant. I found his number in my phone and hit the send button. It was ringing. My stomach was rolling a little bit.

"Hey gorgeous, how are you?" Jason said. I took a deep breath.

"I am good… umm…actually…I am in Colorado."

"What, you never said anything about going to Colorado over break, when did you get there?"

"Well it is a very long story. But listen Jason, I need to tell you… umm…I came here to see Grant, my ex-boyfriend." You could hear dead silence on the other end of the phone. "We have decided to try to work things out and see if we can make our relationship work. So, I wanted to let you know what was going on with me. I would like it if we could still be friends."

I looked over at Grant, he was sitting in the chair, with his arms crossed and a scowl on his face, shaking his head no at me.

I turned around so Grant couldn't see my face.

"Sydney, I can't say I am happy about your decision, but I hope it works out for you guys. If it doesn't maybe we can go out again and Sydney, remember, a tiger never changes his stripes."

"What do you mean by that?" I said with a nasty tone in my voice.

"It means, don't be surprised when he breaks your heart… again. Good luck."

Jason hung up after that, he was just bitter, though his comment will be stuck in my mind.

"Happy now?" I said putting my phone down.

"Extremely!"

He is smiling, happy with himself. He got up from his chair crossing the room to me. He was standing in front of me, with his hands on his hips and a very determined look on his face, his ripped stomach and his more than muscular oblique's causing me to let out a sigh, and a small noise escaped from my throat.

"Are you drooling at me Miss Stanton?"

I just smiled and put my hands on his stomach, following the outlines of his muscles. I could feel my body tingling with anticipation of him touching me again. He pushed me down on the bed. Looking up into his eyes, which had grown dark, filled with love and lust. I started to scoot backwards up the bed.

"Where are you going?" He said as he pulled me back by my feet.

"Escaping whatever it is you have planned for me, anyways don't we need to get ready? Aren't we meeting Curt and Heather in a few minutes?"

"Yes, we are meeting them but not for a while, so I do believe we have time for me to have my way with you," the sound of his voice laced with desire was more than I could take.

"Why fight the inevitable?" I thought to myself, but I think I will make him work for it a little. I jumped off the other side of the bed to see if he could catch me. I shrieked each time he tried to catch me. Eventually he had me cornered, I had no escape route. He leaned his forehead on mine, with his hunky arms pressed on the wall, his elbows almost resting on my shoulders. I smiled coyly at him, thinking I might still get away.

"Sydney, since you made me chase you around the room, I will have no pity on you when you are begging for me to make love to you."

"We'll see about that." I said.

I reached my hands out and followed the lines of his body down to top of his boxer briefs. Running my fingers along the inside, I rubbed the palm of my hand over his bulging penis and smiled up at him, licking my lips. I removed his boxer briefs releasing his erection, stroking it back and forth. Licking my way down his stomach, and lowering myself to my knees, I filled my mouth with the full length of him.

"Your mouth... mhmm." Grant moaned.

Grant was moving his hands in my hair, holding me still. Rocking his hips back and forth, deep sounds were emanating from his core. I could feel him tensing and grasping my head tighter in his hands.

"Don't stop, use your tongue...Oh...Sydney." He was coming in my mouth. After his final shudder, he picked me up and threw me on the bed. Looking me up and down, I could feel him undressing me with his eyes. I couldn't wait for him to come over me with his powerful body taking total control of my needs. As he watched me, I began taking off my robe, never letting my eyes leave his. I heard his breathing quicken and more manly groans.

"Come take what is yours," I said, urging him to come to me with the wave of my hand.

"I am, my eyes are feasting on you, you are so gorgeous, and you're mine, I am a lucky man." He said smiling and crawling over me.

"Yes, you are a lucky man, so take me before I self-combust!"

I just want him to make love to me- no foreplay, I was hot enough after giving him a rock your world blow job. He could probably just touch me and I would have an orgasm.

"You know how I want it, give it to me," I told him.

He was still moving over my body, touching me slowly methodically. Then suddenly he got up off the bed and went to turn on the music channel, flipping through the stations. I dropped my head back on the pillow and let out a long sigh. Seriously, he was being so mean. I sat up on my elbows and looked at him.

I yelled at him across the room, "Are you kidding me, forget the TV, get your hot ass over her and give me what I want."

Smiling at me from ear to ear, licking his lips and touching himself… taunting me. I got up from the bed. I walked over to him and put the remote to the TV down on the small table in front of the captains' chairs. I took his hands; I put one on my ass, one on one breast, and pulled his head down to give him a fierce kiss.

"Wow, when you want me you really know how to show it," he said through the side of his mouth as I continued my attack.

"Now, stop this and come take me to bed."

We were so caught up in each other we lost track of time and we were supposed to be downstairs in the bar 30 minutes ago. I was running around our hotel room getting dressed. My hair was out of control, I used my flat iron to settle it down and fixed my make-up. Finally we…well I, was ready. Grant pulled on jeans and a shirt, fixed his perfect hair by running his hands through it, and then watched me continue to run around the room.

"Sydney, you look beautiful all the time, why are you making such a fuss? It is only Heather and Curt, would you come on all ready? I am going to leave you." He barked at me.

"Not all of us look perfect after having sex all afternoon!"

He grabbed my wrist, pulling me close, "You look radiant -your skin is glowing and your smile is beaming, let's go!"

"Fine, I can't wait to see Heather."

We finally made it downstairs, into the very packed bar. The place was crowded and the music was blaring. We found Heather and Curt sitting in a back booth cuddled up all cute, having a drink.

As soon as Heather saw me coming, she was jumping out of the booth, hugging and screaming at me over the loud music.

"I am so excited you are here, I have missed you so much!" She said giving me an exuberant hug.

"I can't believe I am here, I am glad I came," My smile beaming at her.

"Really, have you two worked things out, are you back together?"

We finally broke our embrace. I gave a really big smile to her and then looked at Grant and smiled.

"Yes, we are going to try, I think we have come to an understanding. Hopefully we can make the long distance thing work for us."

Heather smiled at me, giving me another warm hug. We sat down and talked. The waitress came over and took our order. One round of shots and a couple of beers later I was feeling no pain.

"You know, I found some interesting messages on my phone the other night," Heather commented.

Grant was looking uneasy in his seat. I turned and looked at him, he was looking all over the bar, everywhere except at Heather and me.

"There was this whole conversation between you and I, I mean I know I was drinking on New Year's Eve, but I can't recall texting those messages to you," She said. Heather is laughing and Curt, not wanting to get in the middle, elbowed her to stop.

"Heather, knock it off, don't cause problems," Curt said.

"I know, you were so weird that night…it was almost like it wasn't you," I said. Of course we all knew it had been Grant. I scooted as close to Grant as possible without sitting on his lap. I put my hand on his inner thigh.

"That was a very sneaky move, why did you do that?" I asked him.

He was smiling shyly. His face was actually a little flushed, and sweat was beading on his forehead. My man was embarrassed, unbelievable. I was giggling at the well-deserved torture Heather and I were inflicting.

Grant cleared his throat and took a long drink of his beer. He looked right into my eyes, "If Heather had remembered her phone, you wouldn't be here right now. So, I think that should be enough of an answer for you." I raised my eyebrows at him and squeezed his thigh.

"Although, you are correct, that is side stepping the question," Heather said.

"I didn't even notice your phone on the table until it beeped, and wel,l I couldn't resist. I grabbed the phone…subconsciously hoping it would be Sydney. And when it was…no one was around, so I pretended to be you. You would never have answered the questions I asked if you knew it was me asking them." He took a deep breath and another drink. "I wanted to know if you still cared and after my mom mentioned you were seeing someone, well I just needed to know. I wanted some contact with you. Even if you thought I was Heather."

I was still very close to him; he leaned down and gave me a swift kiss. "I don't regret doing it, I would do it again in a heartbeat."

He was right, if he hadn't used Heather's phone to text me and call me, I would be at home and we would not be together. He put his hand on mine, rubbing his thumb across my fingers.

"Sydney, don't drink too much, the altitude here is different, and the alcohol will affect you faster," Grant advised.

I was already feeling good, I wish he would have warned me about that first.

"You could have told me that before the shot and beers. Want to dance with me?"

"Anything for you my lady, now move it hot stuff!" He said and hit my ass to make me get out on the dance floor.

I shot him a look, but went happily to dance with him.

The dance floor was packed, we started to move, his hands on my hips as the music played. "Turn Me On" by Nicki Minaj and David Guetta was rocking the place. Grant and I are so close we might as well be having sex on the dance floor. By the time the song was over, his hands are on my ass, my chest pressed against his, and my hands are latched around his neck. We danced inseparably for the next three songs until we were sweaty and dying of thirst.

We grabbed some waters and headed back to the table, the four us falling into our seats.

"So, you guys are coming to the house tomorrow right?" Curt asked.

"Yes, we will be there after breakfast or maybe lunch, depends how we feel in the morning." Grant said and gave me a look like "don't even plan on getting out early because I am going to rock your world all night baby". I smiled lovingly back with "a bring it on" expression.

"Well, we are going to say good night, I have been without my man for far too long. I want to show him how much I have missed him." Grant was startled by my announcement, but was happy to indulge me. Heather and Curt just smiled at us and waved good-bye.

CHAPTER 3

Our time together in Colorado was great. I learned to snowboard, not that I was super successful, but I was able to go down the runs by myself. Even so, Grant was a nervous wreck, thinking I was going to break my neck. His parents were very happy we worked out our differences. I had to promise to have lunch or dinner with his parents at least once a month. Grant went back to New York from Colorado. I went home to pick up my stuff and my parents were letting me take my car back to school. So Kendall and I caravanned back a few days later.

Our plan was to Skype at least one time a day, no texting except for loving messages, and talking on the phone as much as possible. I had a harder schedule this term, classes every day, working at the bookstore, and getting elected to be Philanthropic Chairman for my sorority. I am still running three to four times a week. Hopefully, not running into Jason.

Tonight after dinner would be our first attempt to Skype. At 7:00 pm, which was 10:00 pm for Grant, I logged on to my computer and turned on Skype. So far, so good. I called his number and he answered, this was great; I could see him and talk at the same time. Technology can be so grand.

"Hi, how was your trip back?"

"Good, it is snowing here and people are still grumpy. Did you drive your car back? Did you have any problems?"

"Yes, I have my car. I am happy to have my car and no- no problems with the drive."

Seriously, can he be more overprotective!

"Do you want to see what my room looks like? I will spin the camera around so you can see it."

I picked up my laptop, turning it around my room so he could see; the room is a long rectangle, with a large window covered by curtains, beds on opposite sides of the room, two desks, two dressers, and a long closet. My desk is next to my bed. I have pictures of Grant and me in frames on my desk, and shots of him surfing stuck up on the walls.

When I was finished giving Grant the tour of my room, he said, "Nice, are those photos of me surfing on your wall? Where is Kendall?"

"Kendall is at Matt's, you should know that, and yes that is you on my wall!"

"I didn't realize you were taking photos of me surfing, I thought you were always sleeping on those early mornings."

I was laughing, because I did sleep most mornings in my chair on the beach while watching Grant surf. "I did sleep, but I took a lot of photos of you in the mornings and afternoons."

"So, what time is your first class tomorrow? Do you still have a four day weekend?"

"Well, I learned my lesson, no early classes, so my first class is at 10:00 and unfortunately no more four day weekends for Sydney. Although, my only class on Fridays is over by noon. So, technically, I could get out of town early on a Friday. Why- ready to make plans for me to visit you?"

Grant looked so adorable, I could see him sitting at his desk, twisting in his chair, the stubble on his chin had grown from the day, and his hair was a mess. A sexy mess of course.

"Yes, let's make plans for your first visit to see me. We'll make plans at the end of this week of classes, so I'll know how my semester is going to be. Now, let me give you a tour of my room." He said, picking up his laptop. He slowly spun around in his desk chair holding up his laptop. I could see plain white walls, a double bed on the far wall, with a blue comforter (of course), no nightstands, a dresser with crap all over it, what looks like an open door (bathroom?), and his duffle bag on the floor.

He put the laptop back down on his desk, seeing his handsome face coming back into view. "Your room is very plain," I said. "Do you plan on brightening up your space at all and how come I didn't see any pictures of me up?" I asked with some hesitation in my voice.

"You didn't see the photo of you and me from the concert, taped on the mirror on the closet?"

"No, I must have missed the closet and the mirror, since your room is so exciting, so many things to see," I laughed.

"Hold, on." He said.

He picked up his laptop again and began to walk with it to toward the closet.

"Do you see your picture? That was a fun night...oh crap." He blurted out.

"What, do you have to go?" I said with worry.

"No, no, in a few minutes, but I wanted to give you back your necklace. Seeing it in the photo from the concert reminded me. Um, the necklace is at my parents' house. Shoot, okay, I know what I am going to do. My first class is at 8:00, baby, so, I need to get to bed."

"Okay, so we will talk tomorrow night? Wait, I have a class 6:00 tomorrow night, so, what if we talk in the middle of the day? Because by the time I get home, it will be late for you." I said to him.

"Well, I have classes all day and I am not sure what time I will be back in my apartment. I will call you in between classes, okay?" His big smile warming my heart.

"Great, I love you, sweet dreams."

"Miss you, good luck tomorrow, love you too." He said.

And with that we had survived our first night of long distance love. Maybe this could work- maybe my wishes can come true. It was early for me, I flipped on my TV to watch whatever was on, and unpack my bags. I need to get my work schedule so when I am done unpacking, I will check the bookstore website for my schedule. The book store is very accommodating working around all of the employee's class schedules.

The first week back in school with new classes flew by; Grant and I spoke everyday either by phone or on Skype. My heart was full of happiness and love. I kept up my running schedule, fitting it in at least three times a week, sometimes early in the morning, or in the late afternoon after class. It was Friday night; I sent Grant a text to see if he was home for a Skype call. Figuring he might already be out for the evening.

I turned on my computer, turning on Skype, dialing his number and went to wash my face. I could hear him, "Hey, are you there or is your computer calling me all on its own?"

I yelled back, "Yes, hold on..."

I flopped on my bed. My face was flushed and my hair was plastered to my head. My hair had grown out since Thanksgiving and was almost at my shoulders.

"Hi, how was your week, classes good, you're not out tonight?" I asked him three questions at once.

"Wow, you look flushed, what are you doing? What... are you wearing?" Grant asked me I could see his eyebrows raised and an aroused look on his face.

"I just got back from a run, only 2 miles today, I am exhausted."

"Is that what you wear when you run?"

"Yeah, why...you don't like it?" I said spinning around so he could see the whole thing. I was wearing a bright yellow and black long tank top with a sports bra underneath and matching running pants.

"No, I love it, but geez, Sydney, it shows off your amazing body and you know I don't like to share! I wish I was there to help you out of it and into the shower."

My breathing grew fast again and just the thought of him touching me had me squeezing my thighs together.

"Stop, I don't even want to go there, and you are not sharing, people can look they just can't touch," I said laughing.

"Hmmm...I don't even want them looking." He was licking his lips at me. "Sydney are you alright, you seem out of sorts?"

"Grant, you are 3000 miles away and you are turning me on."

He was laughing at me. But I could see his smile it was a very come hither smile.

"I can tell...your nipples are hard!" I quickly crossed my arms over my breasts to cover myself.

"Hey, don't... that is not nice, I want to see you...all of you." He said in his seductive voice.

I could hear a knock at his door. He turned in his chair.

"Hold on baby, someone is at my door, don't hang up."

I sat on my bed, drinking some water, trying to regain my composure. I could hear him talking, "Give me two minutes, I am Skyping with Sydney." Finally he came back into sight. But this time someone was with him.

"Hey, Syd, this is my friend Craig, he lives in my building and we have a few classes together." Craig was shorter than Grant, darker skin, dark eyes, dark hair and were those earrings in his ears? Oh, lord, who is my man hanging out with?

"Hi, nice to meet you Craig." I said, smiling trying not to jump to any conclusions about this friend of Grants.

"Hi Sydney, nice to finally meet you. I have seen your pictures but, wow, you are too cute for this guy! How about you dump him and hang with me?" Grant punched Craig in the arm and said "Shut up dude!"

I just laughed. I didn't respond.

"So, what are you and Kendall up to tonight?"

"We are going to the movies tonight with some of the girls, quiet night, tomorrow we have a philanthropy event and an exchange in the evening. What are you guys up to this weekend?" I said fast hoping he wouldn't freak out.

"I think we are going out for some drinks, this week was rough, classes- I mean and then studying all weekend." Phew, I think, I am in the clear. "So, do I need to worry about you tomorrow night, you're not going to drink too much right?"

"Do you think I have a drinking problem or something?" I said sarcastically.

"No, but I know how those exchanges are, too much drink makes girls a little less inhibited. I don't want you to get yourself in trouble."

I rolled my eyes at him. I let out a deep breath.

"Seriously…anyways it is with your House, so I will be under the watchful eye of your fraternity brothers. Happier now?"

"Very. Okay, baby have a fun night and we will talk tomorrow, love you."

"Okay, you guys have fun, be careful with your friend, he seems to be a wild one. Love you too."

Saturday was turning out to be super busy day packed with a required philanthropy event for the house, which ended up taking the entire day. By the time we got back to the house it was dinnertime and then time to get ready for our exchange. The house was always a buzz, but on the night of an exchange, it was worse. Girls, running up and down the halls trying on clothes, make-up, hair, and giggling. I never understand why it is called an "exchange" when it is just a party, usually two sororities and two fraternities all together at one of the fraternity houses. There is always some theme, tonight it is "Vegas Style."

I took my shower and called Grant. I decided not to Skype because I needed to get ready and the sight of me in my towel, then just a bra and panties getting ready, would push Grant over the edge! I called him from my cell and put the phone on speaker so I could do my make-up and finish my hair. Not to mention Kendall was getting ready too and I didn't want Grant seeing her au natural.

"Hey, this is Grant, you know what to do." Shit his voice mail.

"Hi boyfriend, hope you are having a great weekend. Kendall and I are getting ready to go out for the evening, so I will be in my room for about 30 more minutes, give me a call back, otherwise I will talk with you tomorrow, love you," I said and then sealed the call with a smack of my lips.

Grant didn't call back before we left. I was sad, but I wasn't going to sit in my room all night waiting for him to call back, I have a life. We were ready to go, I put my phone in my back pocket. We headed over to the exchange with a bunch of our friends and prepared for a good time.

The next morning was well, bitter sweet, we had a good time at the party but both Kendall and I woke up with headaches. Actually, I was surprised Kendall had come home with me at all, usually she spends the night with Matt.

"So, what happened with you and Matt last night?" I asked her while we brushed our teeth.

"Ugh, he was being an ass last night, I don't know what his problem was, I just didn't feel like dealing with him."

"Maybe he drank too much?"

"Probably, I don't want to talk about him. Let's go get some breakfast, do you want to walk or ride bikes?"

"Bikes, then we can ride around campus and burn off the beers we drank last night." I said with a big smile. Kendall, not always up for a workout smiled, and nodded her head yes.

We finished breakfast and headed out on our bikes. I could feel my phone vibrating in my pocket.

"Hey, Kendall stop, let me get this call- it is Grant." We pulled over to the side of the siedewalk we were riding down.

I answered the phone, "Go for Sydney Stanton."

"I will go for Sydney Stanton 24/7," the voice on the other end said.

I started giggling with a ridiculous smile on my face. "Hi, sweetheart, how are you?"

"I am great now that we are talking. I am sorry I missed your call, we went to grab some pizza after our study group. Did you have fun last night? Not too much fun I hope."

"We did, Kendall and I had headaches this morning, but we are out on a bike ride, which is making us feel much better. You don't have to worry, I only have eyes for you even after a few drinks- my eyes are only for you." I could see Kendall rolling her eyes and sticking her finger in her mouth like she was going to make herself throw-up. I laughed out loud and told her to stop.

"What are you laughing about?" Grant asked me.

"Kendall is making fun of us, as if she and Matt are not all sappy together. They are the King and Queen of sappy," I said. "Are you going to be around in about an hour? I want to finish our ride, take a shower, and then call you back before we head to the library."

"Wow, you are such the workout enthusiast now, and did you say library…?"

"Not funny, I think you are benefiting from my workouts, and yes I did say library."

"Who are you?" He was laughing at me, because I had never been much for studying or exercising.

"Not funny," I said again. "I am just trying to keep up with my overachieving boyfriend with the hot body that makes me weak in the knees! I will call you in about an hour, love you."

"K, love you too," he said and we disconnected the call.

Kendall and I continued our ride and stopped after about 30 minutes to take a break. We sat down on the grass in front of the Performing Arts Center. I lay back on the cool grass, catching my breath.

"Well, it seems you two are making this work," Kendall said smiling at me.

I knew the months would be long and hard in between visits, but with one week under our belts, I was happier than I had been since the summer. Maybe tonight Grant and I would plan some trips to see each other.

"It seems okay so far. I mean, I miss him terribly and wish I could see him in person every day, but at least we see each other using Skype, that really helps."

"It will all work out. It may not be the ideal situation, but you two love each other enough, it will come together in the end."

"From your mouth to God's ears, I hope it is not just another wish." I said with an air of skepticism in my tone. Kendall was looking at me, knowing I was scared things wouldn't work out.

"Let's head back so we can study, you know how excited I am to study." She said, throwing her head back and laughing.

CHAPTER 4

Grant and I were doing really well- we had planned for me to go visit him in a few weeks for a long weekend. Our spring breaks were at different times, so we decided I would fly to New York for mine, and he would come to his parents' house in Arizona for his. This way we would have two weeks together. Not 24/7 together, but at least seeing each other every day. Then Grant would come back in May for my spring formal, and then he would be out of school for the summer by the time Jade's wedding rolled around. Things were looking good.

I was super busy with classes, working, and sorority. Who knew being part of a sorority would take up as much time as going to class? I have been shadowing the current chair of my position all semester, learning what I need to do to be in charge of philanthropy. It is a lot but I was up to the challenge, it kept me busy and out of trouble.

I am supposed to be studying in my room for a test in the morning. But my eyes keep moving over to look at the photos on my wall of my very gorgeous, hot bodied boyfriend, who is currently 3000 miles away from me. I shook my head as I could feel the ache in my heart and between my legs for him. Only one more day and I was off to New York for a long weekend- bringing an out of this world smile to my face and a long sigh.

Kendall looked up from her book, "What are you sighing about over there? We have a huge test tomorrow."

"Nothing," I said making an annoyed face at her.

She rolled her eyes at me, "Stop thinking about Grant, you will be with him at this time tomorrow. You have to keep your GPA up if you want to be on the PanHellenic Counsel next year, so get studying! When are you going to tell Grant you are planning to stay out here this summer for summer school, and because of your position in the house?"

"Ugh...I hate this class, who cares what happened in England in the 1800's, why do they have so many people with the same names it is very confusing? I am going to tell him when I am in New York this weekend." I said, making grunting noises.

"Don't put it off. Tell him as soon as possible. If you keep putting it off, the harder it will be. It is like a band-aid just do it fast!"

"Nice analogy, I will do it, stop nagging me about it."

Presidents' Day weekend was here. I was out of Arizona and on my way to New York, the weather is pretty cold so I had to break out my real winter gear. I was leaving right after my exam on Friday, my flight was supposed to land at JFK at 11:00ish pm New York time. Hopefully the flight will be on time, it is a long enough flight to begin with. I was restless on the plane, I couldn't get comfortable, the seats are so close together and the lady next to me was asking fifty questions about my trip. I really need to find out about frequent flyer miles, so I can get upgrades to first class. Finally I fell asleep for the remainder of the flight, only waking up when my ears starting popping because of the descent.

My stomach was doing flip-flops, not from the flight but from my excitement. I have never been to New York without my family. I am excited to be staying in the city, walking out the front door of his apartment building with the city at our fingertips is very appealing.

It took forever to taxi to the gate, then waiting to get off the plane was torture, I wanted to scream, "What is wrong with you people, move your asses!" I packed light, only a rolling carry-on bag. Anything I forgot, I could buy or borrow from Grant. After an eternity, I was finally off the plane. It is freezing here! I stopped and put on my jacket. I am tired. I hope it is not a long ride to his apartment.

"Sydney, over here..." I could hear Grant's voice yelling to me, but I couldn't see him. I was looking around completely lost.

"Sydney, walk to the curb towards the taxi cabs." I kept walking until the sound of his voice got louder and louder. The crowds of people clearing, I could see Grant leaning on a yellow taxi cab, bundled up in a sweatshirt and jacket. Grant is standing by a taxi cab waiting for me to come out. I must have looked frazzled and out of sorts. He was waving and smiling. My feet couldn't move fast enough, I was running to him. I jumped into his arms, hugging and kissing his face.

"God, I thought I would never find you, do these people know what time it is, I mean it this place always so busy?"

"Yes, always this busy. Can we go? I am freezing and I want to get you home." He said with a salacious grin.

"Oh yeah, let's go. Do you have any food at your place I am starving?"

"We can stop down the street from my place, there is a deli or pizza place, what do you want?"

"Deli sounds good."

"I am so happy you are here; let me tell the cab driver where to go," Grant said, holding my hand.

While he was giving him the address, I was looking out the window, I had been so tired before, but now my adrenaline has kicked in and I could be up for hours- hopefully hours it would be.

"Okay, we should be at the Deli in a little while, I can't believe you are here, I did all my studying this week so we will be able to spend all of our time together, with no interruptions." He was smiling, holding my hand on my thigh.

"What do you want to do while I am here? I mean, we will make it out of your apartment?" I asked, knowing full well what his plans were.

"Why would we need to leave my apartment?" He said with his head cocked to one side and his wicked smile across his face. "Every restaurant in town delivers, so we will have no need to leave at all!" He was laughing at the look on my face.

"Maybe we will get snowed in and you will have to stay longer." I was biting my bottom lip as he spoke to me. My eyes were completely focused on his mouth. The anticipation of his wet lips and strong hands all over my body had we making soft little noises.

"Well my dear, maybe we should skip the deli and go directly home, based on the look on your face and sounds you're making."

I started to laugh, "No, sustenance first, then home." I said.

My stomach was growling when we finally reached the deli. It was really late but it was very busy. The deli was full of people. As we entered the scent was mouthwatering. We sat down in a booth, smooth red seats, and Formica tables. I grabbed the menus and handed one to Grant.

"I think I am going to have pancakes, with lots of syrup." I told him

"Yummy…but I think I will have a cheeseburger and fries, power food," He said raising one eyebrow to me. I rolled my eyes at him.

We talked until our food came. When we were done eating Grant paid the bill and we headed home. We only had to walk a few blocks to his apartment building. He used a key to open the front door. Then another key to open the inner door. I was making funny sounds about all the doors. He looked at me as if to say this is the way it is here. No elevator, so we walked up three, yes three, flights of stairs. Thank goodness I have been running or I would be exhausted already. One more key into a door, to get us on to his floor. We walked down a long hall, turning once.

We made it to his door, Apartment 3C. He opened the door, and put his hand on my back to lead me in. It was very small. A small narrow entry way, we took a few steps and there was a small galley kitchen on our right. Grant kept me moving into the apartment. We turned to the left and there was a small living area with two doors at the far right side. The living room has a small brown couch with a matching reclining chair. There was a light attached to the wall, a rectangular cocktail table in front of the couch, and a flat screen TV hanging on the wall across from the couch.

"It is … small but comfortable. How did you find this place?" I said turning to look at him.

"Through the housing office, it is a sub-let, it came furnished and as apartments go in NYC, this place is considered big- and a steal." He led me to his bedroom, opening the door for me and putting my bag down on the floor of his room.

I looked around the room, it looked just like it did when he showed it to me on his laptop. I sat down on his bed and flopped on to my back. I was starting to get tired again, now that my belly was full.

"Sydney are you tired?"

"A little." I sat up on my elbows yawning. Grant came and sat next to me on the bed. I took off my boots, stretching out my toes, and stretched my arms up high above my head arching my back.

A strong, "mmm…" came out of Grants throat. I laughed and threw myself on top of him. He was still sitting on the end of his bed and I was straddling his lap. He put his hand on my hips and started nibbling my neck.

"Your hair is getting long again, are you going to keep it long?" He asked pulling it all to one side.

"That is my plan." I said, but my mind was relishing the feel of his lips on my neck and my hips are starting to respond to his touch. I took a deep breath as his hands started moving up and down my back and over my bottom. He reached over to his dresser and turned on his iPod, "One More Night" by Maroon 5 came on, and music filled the room. He loves music on in the background.

It wasn't long before our pace picked up and we were rolling on the bed. The weeks of separation and not touching were quickly released. We were panting, slowly undressing each other, savoring every touch. He would caress my face and make small noises with every touch.

We feel asleep in each other's arms after making love. I couldn't have been happier.

We woke late the next morning, sleeping-in together was wonderful. We cuddled into each other. My back pressed against his chest with his arm resting over my hip.

Grant was running his fingers up and down my arm, giving me goose bumps, which was very relaxing, I loved it. He is nibbling my ear, sucking on the lobe. I am smiling so happy, my heart is bursting with happiness, I am in heaven. I turned my head to look at his face. He is so handsome, his facial growth rough against my chin.

"What?" He said softly as he held me.

"Nothing…I enjoy looking at you, and in to your dark eyes."

He lightly kissed my lips.

"That was nice, this is nice. I wish we could do this every day." He said. I could feel my emotions kicking in and a small tear free itself rolling down my cheek.

"I have something for you." Grant moved from our embrace, reaching under the bed. He grabbed something and handed me a black bag. I sat up, taking the bag in my hand.

"What is this?" He didn't say anything. He just smiled and leaned back, putting his hands behind his head, leaning on the headboard.

I opened the bag, turned it upside down, and let the contents fall into my other hand. Quickly turning to look at him as my smile came across my face, meeting my eyes. I jumped on top of him.

"My necklace! I thought you said it was at your parents" house?"

"It was. I had my Dad send it to me so I could give it to you when you got here. Would you like me to put it on you?"

My heart is pounding, the necklace represents everything I mean to him and not having it around my neck for so long always left me with an ache in my soul. I nodded my head up and down. He took the necklace from my open hands, placing it around my neck. I ran my fingers along the infinity symbols. Now my heart is complete, no pieces are missing, life is perfect!

"Thank you." I said.

"For what, giving you back what has always been yours, you don't need to thank me. I am so happy you are here and we are together, I love you." Grant kissed me and we made love.

I am not sure what time it was when we actually left his apartment. We could walk almost everywhere he wanted to take me. We stopped at a local coffee shop for breakfast or lunch, not sure which, but it was our first meal of the day. We looked at each other with loving smiles all day long. Walking hand in hand, we went in and out of all kinds of stores and checked out the vendors peddling their goods along the streets.

We came upon a small farmers market, which Grant didn't even know they had every Saturday. We picked up some fresh fruit and he bought me a bouquet of beautiful flowers. Eventually, we had weaved his way around all the streets which were unfamiliar to me but were second nature to him. We were standing in front of his school. He walked me around the campus, pointing out different buildings, the library, student union. I was losing steam.

"I am kind of tired, can we head back to your apartment?"

"Sure baby." He said kissing my forehead.

"Do you want to work out later? We can go to my gym, they have an indoor pool, racket ball, treadmills."

"That sounds good. I was wondering how you were staying in such good shape." I said to him, eyeing his body up and down.

"Stop objectifying me woman!" Grant started laughing at his own statement. I smacked his arm.

We finally made it back to his apartment; I put the fruit in his fridge, noticing there was nothing in it but containers from restaurants from all over the city, and beer. I looked over at him.

"What?" He said looking a little guilty.

"Do you eat out for every meal?" I asked him. "I mean you don't even have milk."

"It is just me here, I can run to the corner market if I need something. There is no point to waste money on groceries, I am hardly ever here. I am either at school or studying somewhere."

I rolled my eyes at him and then walked over to sit next to him on the couch. My heart was starting to speed up. I needed to talk to him about the summer. I am nervous. I hope this will not ruin our weekend. He is relaxing with his feet up on the cocktail table, his head is leaning against the couch and his eyes are closed. I laid down on my back, resting the back of my head on his thigh, with his right arm coming down onto my stomach. I am playing with his fingers.

"I need to tell you something." My voice trembling a little. I was looking up at him, I could see him open one eye.

"Yes…"

"Well, you know, I am in the Philanthropic Chairman for next year?"

"Yeah, I know and…"

Really quickly I spat out, "I have to stay at school for the summer because of it, and I am going to go to summer school." My shoulders are hunched and my eyes are closed waiting for his reaction.

I hadn't noticed but Grant was holding his breath. He let out a long sigh and leaned down to kiss me. I was completely shocked by his response. I was pleasantly surprised.

"Okay," He said. "I understand… were you scared to tell me?" He is playing with my hair and running his fingers along my forehead.

"Yeah, I figured you would be mad at me not coming to the beach for the summer." I had worked myself up into panic mode thinking he would be upset.

"I am not mad, I am happy for you. You enjoy being at school and doing all the sorority stuff. Where are you going to live, still in the house?"

"No, the bathrooms are being remodeled this summer. I think Kendall and I are going to get an apartment not far from school, so we are close enough to ride our bikes to campus. What do you think?" I looked up at him, his smile warming me.

"I like it, then I can stay with you when I come to visit, are you going to go back to the house at the end of the summer, or stay in the apartment?"

I hadn't even thought about not living in the house in the fall. That is a good idea.

"I don't know... I will have to talk to Kendall about that." Grant looked odd for a moment.

"Since we are on the subject of the summer, I have something to share with you too." He said.

My heart started to pound again.

"I have the opportunity to have this really great internship here in New York. But if I take it, it means me not coming home for the summer. What do you think?" He is asking me my opinion, I am honored.

I smiled up at him with loving eyes and adoration. There is no way I am going to tell him not to stay here. I wanted to be selfish and have him closer to me but I wasn't going to tell him that information.

"You should take it, if it is what you want to be doing, you should grab it!" I said elated for him. "I would not want to come between you and your dreams." I told him.

Once again, he leaned down and kissed me, not a soft kiss, but a kiss filled with love and passion. My heart rate kicked into high gear and my hands went right into his hair, tugging at the ends. When we finally stopped we were both flushed with desire.

"Sydney, thank you, you surprise me at every turn. First flying to Colorado, forgiving me, and allowing me to pursue my dreams. I am blessed to have you in my life."

I just smiled up at him and pulled him down for some more of the kissing- the kissing is soo good!

"So, will you be able to get time off during your internship, do you think we will get to spend at least the 4th of July together?" I asked him.

"I am not sure, I hope so, I will have to talk with the human resources people at the company."

"What kind of company is it? What will you be doing?"

Grant was animated starting to talk about the internship. "I am not sure exactly what I will be doing but it is a hotel management company like my dad's. This company has international properties, whereas my dads are only in California and Arizona. So hopefully it will give me some insight and information to help me when I go to work for dear old Dad." He said laughing.

He was very excited about everything. He kept on about the company, I tried to listen but my mind was wandering off and my eyes were heavy. I must have fallen asleep. It seemed like I was asleep on his lap forever, I woke to him whispering my name and giving me butterfly kisses.

"Welcome back, sleepy head."

"I am so sorry, I didn't mean to fall asleep on you."

"It is okay, the time difference, don't worry about it, you were tired. I am glad you got a little nap in. Do you want to go to the gym, I could do with a swim or run?"

"I didn't bring a swimsuit, so I can run while you swim, do they have an indoor track or only treadmills, I am not much for treadmills."

"They do, there is an indoor track on the floor above the pool. You can look down at the pool from the track."

"Do you get ready here or at the gym?"

"At the gym, it is too cold to walk around in a suit here."

"Okay, let me get my workout clothes and running shoes."

I grabbed all my stuff and put it in a small bag, along with my iPod and earphones.

"I am ready," I told him as he was getting his gym bag, with a surprised look on his face.

"Okay, that was quick I will sign you in as my guest. We can walk to the gym. It is only a few blocks from here."

He took my hand and we set out for the gym. Seriously, how does he live here, it is so cold, windy, and people are not very nice. The cab drivers are always honking, people are yelling at each other. I just don't get it.

Grant walked me to the women's locker room and pointed to the stairs which lead to the indoor track. I usually run for about an hour, so I will just run until he is done swimming.

I went into the locker room and changed. I had a hot pink sports bra, a short navy running shirt and navy running pants with hot pink stripes down the side. My new running shoes are navy with bright yellow laces. I put my bag in a locker and tied the key to my laces. I put my hair up in a high pony tail and checked myself in the mirror. There were a few women in the locker room, who eyed me oddly.

I headed up the stairs, putting my headphones on and turning on my iPod which was attached to my upper left arm. I leaned over the railing to look for Grant. He was walking over to the pool. Yummy, was all I could think when I saw him. I had a smile on my face, he must have felt me looking at him because he looked up and saw me staring. His eyes met mine and I could feel him looking me up and down, taking in my attire. He nodded his head and winked. I winked back. I did some stretching and started my run. I have never run on an inside track, it was different, the floor has some kind of cushioning in it. I feel as if I have an extra spring to my stride because of it. There were only a few people running or walking.

My music was pumping in my ears and I am lost in time as I go about my workout. I hadn't noticed Grant standing in the corner watching me run. Sweat was dripping down my neck and back as I was in my own world. My thoughts drifting to the trip to Colorado, thinking about how great our relationship was going, and worrying a little about the summer. I came around the corner and I noticed him sitting on a bench, a towel wrapped around his waist. I smiled and put up one finger, making a swirling motion. Indicating I needed one more lap. He smiled and nodded his head up and down.

I slowed my pace on the last lap to cool down. I stopped just before the bench he was sitting on. I was breathing hard and my chest and stomach were glistening with sweat. I put my hands on my knees and dropped my head a little to catch my breath.

"Wow, you really like to run. You sing along with the songs or were you talking to yourself as you ran?" He asked me. His eyes were wide as he looked at me.

I laughed, "Maybe a little of both, depending on what I am thinking about at that moment!" I said as I attempted to catch my breath.

He pulled me towards him, holding me by my hips, his face level with my chest. He took a deep breath. I put my hands in his hair which was still wet from the pool.

"What were you doing today, singing or talking to yourself?"

"Singing, usually I only talk to myself if I am upset! Singing, definitely singing!"

He continued to hold me and we stood looking at each other for a few more minutes.

"You are sweaty, do you want to shower here, or head back and shower together at my apartment?"

"Well, Mr. Montgomery since you asked so nicely, I think I will choose the latter." I leaned forward to give him a kiss on his forehead. He grabbed my hand and we went down stairs.

"You have two minutes, grab your stuff and put on your jacket, I don't want you getting sick while you are here, since you are running around in that skimpy outfit."

I shook my head at him. I ran into the locker room and grabbed my bag and met him at the door where he was waiting for me. A few people waved to him as we left.

"Do you know those people?" I asked.

He looked back, "Um, yeah, I work out sometimes with those guys, you know- encouraging each other to bench press more weights and stuff. They are nice, we have hung out a few times."

"Oh good, glad to know you have some friends here," I said.

He was walking ridiculously fast, pulling me behind him. The cold air was whipping around my face and I was chilled. I sneezed and stopped.

"Oh crap, you are getting sick."

"I only sneezed, I am not getting sick, I haven't even been here 24 hours, how could you think I am getting sick?" I looked at him, he was grimacing at me. I sneezed again.

"I have never heard you sneeze before, you must be getting sick." I rolled my eyes at him and kept walking. I was pulling him now. Not that I know where I am going.

"Sydney, do you even know where you are going?"

"No, but I figured you would steer me in the right direction, you always get me going in the right direction." I said with an inference that had nothing to do with maps.

Grant started laughing and picked up his pace.

"I like the way your mind works, hot stuff!" he smacked my ass and I jumped.

I didn't like when he did that but I didn't want him to stop either.

We ran up the three flights of stairs to his apartment, which only made my heart rate go faster. We were stripping out of our clothes while the water was warming up in the shower. Between the cold weather, and chill of my body from the sweat and wind, I was really looking forward to a hot shower, with my hot guy.

Grant was licking my neck.

"Salty," he said with a drawl in his voice.

I giggled.

He is touching me so seductively and my body is loving it. We climbed into the shower, grabbing the shower gel and squeezing some in his hands and then in mine, we each began washing each other. Then he washed my hair, it was so relaxing his strong hands massaging my head. I moved under the shower head to rinse my hair, leaning my head back. Grant was in front of me, I could feel his eyes on me and his intense stare. I kept my eyes closed and made some gratuitous sounds of pleasure as the water came down on me.

Hoping this would entice his fingers, sure enough, I felt his hand on my hip and the other hand on my sex. With a quick thrust he put one finger inside me and I gasped at the unexpected feeling. His finger was moving inside me while the palm of his hand was rubbing against my hot spot. Then another finger and I gasped again, he is teasing me making me so hot for him.

I brought my mouth to his and took his tongue deep inside my mouth, sucking on it as he continued to move his fingers inside me. My pulse was in overdrive and I grabbed his dick in one hand, stroking it back and forth. He let out a few toe- curling sounds which pushed me into a mind numbing orgasm. When I was done, he pushed me up against the shower wall, lifting me a little and penetrating me slowly with his more than eager erection. I am clawing his shoulders, his hips are moving fast and I am more than happy to meet him, thrust for thrust. He leaned in and sucked on my collar bone, I am sure there will be a mark there when he is done. He is mumbling something, but I was flying into a second climax.

"Hold on… not yet, open your eyes, so I can see your eyes dilate when you come for me. Look at me," he gasped to me, in between hard breaths.

"Grant…" was all I could get out and he was saying my name as he came, our eyes locked together as we reached our pinnacle as one.

We finished our shower, wrapping up in towels and putting on some comfy clothes to relax in for a while.

We were sitting on the couch together and my head began to thump and my body began aching. I knew he was right, I am getting sick, damn him he is always one step ahead of me.

"Do you have any Tylenol?" I asked him. He looked suspiciously at me, he let out a breath, and got up to look in the medicine chest, and then the kitchen.

"I told you… you were getting sick, you never listen to me."

Not wanting to give in to him, "I just have a headache, relax."

Grant came over to me and kissed my forehead like my mom would do to see if I had a temperature.

"Sydney you are burning up, geez. I will go to the pharmacy and get you some medicine." He said making his way to the door.

"I only need the Tylenol, it is good for a fever."

"Your nose is running and you're sneezing, you won't get any sleep tonight if you are congested. I will get you some decongestant. I will be right back." He gave me a kiss and put a blanket on me, tucking me into the couch.

I must have fallen asleep on the couch while he was gone. When I woke up he was sitting with my feet across his lap watching a movie. My head was still hurting and my body was super achy.

"How long was I asleep?" I asked him my voice kind of hoarse.

"You were asleep when I got back from the store, maybe two hours. Are you feeling better?"

I shook my head no.

"I feel worse, I am sorry." I said tears glistening in my eyes.

Really, I just wanted to close my eyes and sleep. He was rubbing my legs. He got up and went into the kitchen and came back with some medicine. He poured some medicine in one of the little measuring cups that come with it and handed it to me with some water. I took a whiff and wrinkled my nose at it.

"Drink it." He said sternly. "I am not sending you back if you are sick, your parents will be pissed at me if you catch pneumonia and miss classes."

I made an awful face as I swallowed the worst tasting medicine I have ever had, and chased it with the entire glass of water.

"That was awful, did you buy the most disgusting medicine on purpose to torture me?"

He laughed, "How about some chicken soup? I picked some up from the deli, it is fresh, no canned soup for my girl." He said lovingly. This I can get used to, him taking care of me this way is wonderful. "Or hot tea, what can I get you?"

I smiled at him, "The soup sounds good, I think I will use the bathroom, can I eat on the couch?"

He helped me get up and walk to the bathroom, because I was feeling a tad wobbly. When I came out Grant was leaning on the wall waiting for me. He took my hand and helped me back to the couch. He had my soup set up on the coffee table with some crackers and hot tea. I looked at him with a smile on my face.

I sat down on the couch, he handed me the bowl of soup and sat down next to me. The soup smelled delicious. I took a few spoonfuls of the soup, it was very good, but I have no appetite.

"Sydney, are you okay, you look very pale?" There was concern all over Grant's face. He put his hands on my forehead.

"God, you are burning up and all clammy." He got up and went into the kitchen, he came back with a wet paper towel and thermometer. He set the food on to the table and I lay back down on the couch. He placed the wet towel on my head and I kicked off the blanket, I was so hot.

"What are you doing? Keep the blanket on you, you are going to get cold." He scowled at me.

"I am hot, if I have a temperature, then keeping the blanket on me will just incubate the fever, making me hotter." I told him.

He looked at me kind of funny and pulled out his iPad and started typing something. Then he laughed.

"Fine, you are right. I was going to call my Mom, and ask her but I didn't want her worrying about you." I smiled at him and let out a little laugh.

"You are a worrywart, I can't imagine what you will be like as a father." I wanted to shoot myself after the words left my mouth.

He didn't say anything, he just looked at me and smiled. What an idiot, why did I say that?

"Get some rest, the medicine should kick in and you will probably fall asleep again." He went to get another wet towel and replaced the one on my head. He stuck the thermometer in my mouth. I wanted to roll my eyes at him, but refrained, not wanting to hurt his feelings. It finally beeped and he grabbed it out of my mouth before I could look at it.

"Shit, you have a very high fever," he said with a worried look on his face.

"What... how high?"

"102! Were you getting sick before you left to come see me?"

I squinted my eyes at him and crossed my arms over my chest like a child about to have a tantrum.

"No I felt fine, maybe I got it from someone on the plane, you know how many people are on there and the air is recycled." I huffed at him and he huffed at me.

"It is not as if I planned this you know, do you think I like being sick?"

"I know, I didn't mean to infer anything or make you feel bad. Is it okay if I sit with you and watch TV, anything you want to watch?" He asked nicely trying to make me feel better.

"No, I am good, I am just happy to have you next to me. I am so sorry I am sick, you need to take some vitamin C, so you don't get it too."

He said he had already taken some and would rest with me on the couch in case I needed anything. I fell into a deep sleep not hearing anything around me for the rest of the night. I did wake up at some point to go to the bathroom. Grant must have carried me to his bed because I woke up completely disorientated.

"Are you okay?" He asked gruffly from his slumber.

"Yes, you are sweet, I am just going to the bathroom."

He laid his head back down and fell right to sleep.

I spent the rest of my visit in bed or on the couch feeling awful. I felt guilty, Grant was waiting on me hand and foot, which was wonderful. But this was not how I imagined our weekend together. He wanted me to stay until Tuesday to make sure I was all better. I couldn't change my flight and still make it to class on time Tuesday afternoon. He was not happy with my decision to head back to school still not feeling well.

"I have to go back and my fever is gone, I will be okay. I will call you when I land." I told him as we said good-bye at the airport. I kissed his cheek and thanked him for all his amazing nursing skills.

"I will miss you so much, I love you, and we will be together in a few weeks when you come back for your spring break, right?" He asked me, tears coming to his eyes.

My hunk of a guy was really going to miss me. I love it.

"I will be back, I will make my flight arrangements this week, and you need to make yours as well," I reminded him.

We kissed one more time before I went into the terminal.

CHAPTER 5

After my eventful visit to see Grant in New York where I spent the whole time sleeping because I was sick, life was back to the usual pace. School, work, sorority, Skyping, phone calls, loving text messages. Every day, every week, seemed to get easier. Grant and I fell into a great pattern of managing our time between our lives apart and our lives together. We discussed openly our feelings, insecurities, and sometimes lack of understanding for what we were each going through.

I spent my spring break in New York, and a week later Grant came to Arizona for his break. We were inseparable. I would drive to his parents' house everyday after my classes or work, spend the night, and get up early to drive back for school or work. This went on for a week. When he went back to New York, I was exhausted from all the running back and forth. We had a great time on both breaks. We were racking up frequent flyer miles and getting really good at assimilating into each other's lives.

Next trip it was Grant's turn to come out for my spring formal. I am excited to get all dressed up for him. The formal is in a couple of weeks. So I still have time to go look for a dress. Kendall and I headed out shopping early Saturday morning, we had no sorority stuff this weekend so we were free for the whole day. We walked into the mall, looked at each other and laughed.

"Where should we go first?" I asked Kendall.

"Hmmm…little stores or big?"

"Big stores, let's start with Nordstrom and work our way around the mall, k?"

Kendall and I love to shop, we could go all day as long as we have Diet Coke and some lunch, we will be in good shape. I want something amazing to wear for Grant. We were looking in the dress department. We found a few dresses each and had the salesgirl open the dressing rooms for us. I was changing into one of my dresses, Kendall was in the dressing room next to me. I could hear two young woman talking. One of the voices sounded familiar but I couldn't place it, the other I did not recognize.

They were talking about whoever they were dating or used to date I couldn't tell. I was trying on dresses not really liking anything, maybe I should have called Corinne to meet us. I should have, she would have loved to shop with me, maybe tomorrow if I don't find anything today.

"Hey, are you done trying on your dresses?" Kendall was standing outside the dressing room I was in.

"Almost I have one more, but so far I don't like any of them. Did you find any…" I was cut off when someone approached Kendall.

"Hey Kendall, what are you doing here?" The voice said.

"Oh my, hi Elizabeth, nice to see you, oh umm we are shopping for dresses for the formal."

I was inside my dressing room not saying anything just listening. I wanted to finish dressing and move on to the next store I didn't want to end up having a 30 minute visit with Elizabeth.

"Kendall, this is Ashley St. James, she graduated in June, she was in our house, or is in our house, whatever, you know what I mean." Elizabeth said. Kendall was silent for a minute.

I was having a panic attack inside the dressing room. My mind was swirling, holy shit, it was *the* Ashley. I seriously never thought I would be this close to her, let alone meet her. I didn't move, I was fully dressed, standing listening intently to their conversation. I think I felt my stomach flip over, which made me nauseous.

Kendall lightly knocked on the door, "Are you coming out of there, Elizabeth is here with um… Ashley St. James, you should come out," She said to me. I took a deep breath, I am going to kill Kendall for this.

"Hi, it is nice to meet you Ashley, so what are you doing now that you have graduated?" Kendall never afraid to just get right to the point.

I was still in the dressing room, taking my time coming out.

"Nice to meet you too, oh, I am deciding what to do with my life, but I am working for a pharmaceutical company in sales." Ashley responded.

I finally decided to brave the impossible situation outside my dressing room. Thank goodness I had showered and put on my make-up today. I have a very cute outfit on, I put on my "I am overly confident face" as I opened the dressing room door. Kendall's eyes were huge, when I came out and the look on her face was sheer panic.

"Hi Elizabeth." I said.

"Sydney, I didn't know you were in there, Kendall you didn't say you were shopping with anyone today." Elizabeth gave me a big hug.

"Sydney- this Ashley." Elizabeth introduced us.

Ashley was thin, tall, long blonde hair and blue eyes, but nothing about her looks bowled- me over she was just average. This made me feel much better.

I put my hand out, "Nice to meet you," I said.

I was very uncomfortable, hoping no one would pick up on my feelings except Kendall. I don't think she knows anything about me, hopefully not.

"Well, it was nice to see you Elizabeth and meet you Ashley, but Kendall and I are on a mission, so will have to catch up with you later." I said. I looked over at Kendall. "Ready?" I said to her so we could escape the drama which might unfold in front of us if Ashley knew I was the girl Grant was in love with. Maybe I should say something like. "Oh, Grant is going to love this dress." Or "Do you think Grant will like this dress?" I shook the thoughts from my brain. Why stir the pot up and cause a scene when he is all mine. No need to prove anything to anyone, especially not Ashley.

We were walking silently away as fast as possible, without being obvious of our intent to escape. When we were out in the mall I almost fainted into the railing. Not really, but that is how I felt. I think Kendall was more freaked out then me, and was about to hyperventilate.

"That was so weird, right?" Kendall said looking at me. "Are you alright?"

"I cannot believe that just happened, do you think Ashley has any clue about me and Grant? I don't know if he told her about me, or if he only said there was someone else."

I tried to push the incident out of my mind so we could concentrate on shopping. I did spend the rest of my day looking over my shoulder to see if they were around. Luckily we didn't see them again and we had a very unsuccessful day shopping, argh.

Later in the evening I called Grant via Skype. He picked up, "Hi gorgeous, I wasn't expecting to hear from you tonight since we spoke this morning, but I am happy to see your beautiful face."

"Nice, what did you do wrong… you are being super sweet," I said, laughing at him.

"Can't a guy just be happy to see his girl?" He said his eyebrows raised and a big smile, which made my heart melt.

"Well, yes he can, but I need to share something with you. Nothing bad just something odd happened today."

"Shoot," he said.

"So, Kendall and I went shopping today for dresses for the formal and well…"

"Well what? Did you find something, was it expensive, what is the problem?" He was lost having no clue where I was going with this conversation.

"No, I didn't find anything. That is not it. We were trying on dresses in Nordstrom and we ran into, well we ran into umm…Elizabeth and Ashley, I met Ashley today."

The look on Grant's face was not what I had anticipated. I thought he would freak out, but he was cool as a cucumber like always. Completely unaffected by what I thought was a terrifying experience.

"So, do you have any response?" I asked him.

"What do you want me to say? I am sorry you met her or ran into her. She doesn't mean anything to me, she is my past. I was a different person with her and you are my heart and my future. It doesn't bother me in the least and it shouldn't bother you either." He was very calm, always Mister Confident about everything.

"Were you upset by meeting her? Did she say or do anything to offend you?"

"No, she was polite, it was probably less than a minute before Kendall and I left them. I just thought you would want to know."

"Well, I am glad you shared your day with me, but I am more upset that you didn't find that sexy dress!" He said laughing.

I was much more relaxed knowing I shared this information with him. "I was thinking of calling your mom to go shopping with me, is that okay with you?"

"Of course, you know my mom adores you and loves to shop, so you would combine two of her favorite things together. You have her number?" He asked me.

"Yes, I will give her a call when we are done. How is your weekend going?"

"Good, you know studying and more studying! I am sure you will have more fun than me this weekend."

"Well this is it for us, we are staying in, we rented a movie and we are going to watch it downstairs in the Chapter Room. So, I'd better go, thanks for listening, I love you."

"Sydney, I love you too."

We both signed off at the same time. I love him so much, my heart aches for him when we are apart but things have gone way better than I could have predicted. I wiped away a few tears from my eyes before heading downstairs.

Oh, I need to call Corinne, I did that too, before watching the movie.

Like I predicted, I had a successful shopping trip with Grant's mom a few days later. She found the perfect dress for me to wear. We had a lovely day together. She shared funny stories with me about Grant and his brothers, and told me how she and Mr. Montgomery met. But my favorite part was when she touched my hand and told me how important I was to her and to Grant, and that she knew once we worked it out we would be back together just as she had foretold. My life was on track; I would be graduating in two years, Grant would be back from New York in a year, and maybe our lives would finally be together in the same city.

Grant flew out for my spring formal in April, we stayed at the hotel where the formal was being held, for the entire weekend. It was a magical, having him with me, dancing, being with my friends, was more than I could have imagined. But as always Sunday came with the blink of an eye, and I was driving Grant back to the airport. Tears stinging my eyes, we held hands the whole way and before I dropped him off and gave him yet another agonizing good-bye hug and kiss, I held him so close as if it would be so long in between visits.

"Sydney, we will be together again in June for Jade's wedding. Why are you so upset, you don't usually get this upset when it is time say good-bye, what's up?"

I didn't know why I was so upset my heart was aching for him. I didn't want him to leave, I was tired of the back and forth, the marathon phone calls, I wanted him every day next to me.

"I will be fine, I just I miss you so much, and having you here this weekend just reminds me of how much longer we have to be apart, and summer, and… I don't know. Just go, you don't want to miss your flight. I will be fine, call me when you get home, don't forget." I wiped away my tears and gave him another hug and a long kiss.

He smiled at me one more time before he turned and was lost in the sea of people in the airport terminal.

Chapter 6

It was the beginning of May and finals were upon us. Kendall and I found an apartment and we were moving our stuff in during finals week. Everyone had to be out of the Sorority House by Friday so construction on the bathrooms could start right away.

As soon as we were done with finals, we were out of the House and feeling quite good to have some privacy at our new place. It was, to say the least, very quiet. The apartment was on the first floor. It had covered parking and we had two reserved spaces. There were two bedrooms, each with its own bathroom, the kitchen was off to the left and the family room was quite large. The best part, we have our own washer and dryer so no lugging dirty clothes and detergent to a laundromat, oh and the pool, can't forget about the pool. The apartment came furnished so all we needed was new bedding, in the Sorority House we had single beds, and the apartment had double beds.

We plopped down on the couch and looked at each other. We both started giggling.

"Who would have thought two years ago we would be sitting in our own apartment, away from our families, and in love with two of the most amazing guys on the planet!" Kendall was grinning with her profound statement.

"Well, I would never have guessed we would be here right now. But I am so happy we are. Our friendship means more to me than anything, and having shared so much together I know we will be friends forever, even when we are old living in the senior home together." I had tears in my eyes, Kendall squeezed my hand and gave me a hug.

"Sydney, why are you crying you should be happy? We are on our own, this is our dream- things will be great this summer. I know you miss what you and Grant had last summer, but everything is going good with you guys, and he adores you. Change doesn't mean bad, it just means different. Come on, lets go check out the pool."

We walked to find the pool and mail boxes. We also found the trash dumpsters. We headed back to the apartment and decided to go grocery shopping, which was probably a bad idea. We came home with a lot of junk food; frozen pizzas, chips, all the good stuff. We did get fruit and yogurt too.

"I am going to call Grant." I said, and headed to my bedroom.

I had picked out a blue comforter with a yellow paisley design. I was looking a little haggard so I decided to call him instead of Skype. His voice mail came on, hmmm, wonder where he could be? I left him a sweet message.

"Hi handsome, wanted to say hello and let you know we are all moved in to our new place, give me a call, miss you, love you."

I came out of my room and Kendall was on the phone with Matt. She looked up at me, "Hold on I will ask her," she said to Matt.

"Syd, when is your sister's wedding?"

"First weekend in June."

"Ok," Kendall turned her attention back to her phone conversation with Matt.

I was sitting on the couch, maybe I will go for a swim. I made a swimming motion to her with my arms. She shook her head no and I went to change, and headed to the pool. I took my iPod and headphones with me. I was lying on a lounge chair listening to music, it wouldn't be long before I was hot and jumping into the pool. I could feel my body heating up from the sun. Maybe five minutes later I jumped in and started swimming laps. There was no one even here, so weird.

I was about half way through what was turning out to be a small workout for me, when I heard someone jump in the pool. I stopped mid stride to see who it was, but they were under the water. I continued my swim. Slowly I could feel someone swimming beside me, I didn't look, it is a community pool so anyone can swim in it.

I was shaken and unnerved, when two big hands pulled me by my waist and hugged me uncontrollably. When I came up from under the water, Grant's deep dark eyes were fixed on mine. My heart raced with excitement. I kissed him with fierce exuberance.

"Holy shit…what are you doing here, you scared the crap out of me?" I was holding on to him for dear life. Is this a dream, was he really wrapped around me in the pool?

"I missed you and you were so upset when I left last month…I knew we couldn't go another four weeks without being together."

"Grant, I am so happy you are here." I was kissing his neck. "I love you so much…this was the sweetest thing you have ever done…I have missed you so much."

We made out in the pool and swam, and eventually walked back to my new apartment. I couldn't be happier at this moment, but I had a feeling I would be much happier in about 10 minutes.

"First night in your new apartment, I can't wait to christen your new bed," he said with his wickedly sexy smile.

He is only wearing board shorts and flip-flops- not even a towel. His muscles so defined you can see the V leading down to his… best part. His hair is short, he must have had a haircut before coming to surprise me. My hunky man is the best.

"I love the way your mind automatically goes to sex the minute you see me, is that the only reason you love me?" I asked him giving him a shy smile.

"Where is Kendall?"

I looked around the apartment for her, found a note posted on the TV. She left to give us some privacy. Such a good friend.

"Looks like she has left us alone, she is a good friend… knows when to make herself scarce." Grant said.

"Did she help you arrange this surprise?" I asked him.

I walked over to him, he was sitting on the edge of my bed. He pulled me to him by my hips, I leaned down giving him a long passionate kiss. Grant brought me down onto the bed, he had a strange look on his face almost as if he was hiding something from me. I looked up at him, grabbed his face again, and brought his lips down to mine. I could feel his need in his kiss and heard small moans escaping him.

He pressed his forehead on mine, "I have something important to talk to you about, I know you are going to be upset with me."

I had already been upset lately about our relationship constantly feeling as if at any moment things would begin to break down, separating us. Not that anything had happened, just some inner part of my brain and heart knew time was running out.

I didn't say anything, the look in my eyes said it all, he knew I was scared.

"My internship, well it is starting soon, and…"

I could feel the lump in my throat getting bigger and tears welling in my eyes. I wanted to yell at him to "spit it out already." I didn't say anything.

Grant continued, "I am not going to be able to go with you to Jade's wedding." He said it very softly, sorrow in his voice. He was looking at me, straight in the eyes.

I sat up and pushed him away from me. I didn't know what to say, I was furious, I was sad, and I was terribly hurt. I could feel the ache in my heart returning and the tears start coming down my face. This is why he came out to see me this weekend, it was to pacify me, knowing we wouldn't be together in June.

"What… why… didn't you ask for the time off?" I asked my voice laced with sadness.

"I did, but they said there was a new project starting and I would be a part of the team handling it. Sydney, there is more I need to tell you."

I was standing with my back to him, while he was still sitting on my bed. The ache in my heart, weakening me. "God, what else?" is all I thought.

Not turning to look at him, quietly, I asked, "What is it Grant, just tell me."

"The project it is…it is not in New York…it is overseas."

Quickly, I turned to look at him, tears in my eyes, my hands hanging at my side, "What does "overseas" mean?" I asked, putting the word overseas in air quotations.

"It means, I will be out of the country for most of the summer, it is a great opportunity for me, especially as an intern, it could mean a job for me when I graduate."

"I am not asking you not to go, I understand. I would never keep you from following your dreams, I have told you that so many times. But the whole summer and not being with me at Jade's wedding? I am so disappointed, there are no words for me to describe the pain I am feeling right now," I told him. My voice was low and very calm, not my normal overreacting head strong self.

"I knew you would be upset, but it is only a couple of months. We can still Skype and call- it will be okay." He came up to me and held me, but I didn't hold him back, I couldn't. "Sydney, I am here with you now. Please don't be upset with me. We have four days together, I don't have to be back in New York until next week," he tipped my chin up to him so are I eyes could met.

I was beyond upset, I was emotionless, "Is this a pity visit, so you can leave and go away not feeling guilty?" I asked him, the words left my mouth in a vicious tone.

Grant pushed me back from him while holding my shoulders, he continued to look directly in my eyes, I am not sure what he saw, but what I was feeling was emptiness.

"God Sydney, no. I would never do that, or feel that way about you, you are my life, I can't imagine the future without you in it."

My vicious tone still spurting from my mouth, I asked, "Why do you need a job offer in New York, when you have your father's company waiting for you?"

Grant dropped his head and his hands from me, "Sydney, this is an opportunity for me to thrive and be more than just Kevin Montgomery's son. Don't you see it is a chance for me to make my name stand out from my families, without their help?"

I understood all of it and I didn't like it, as a matter of fact, I hated it! This was going to be so much harder.

I went into my closet and put on my running clothes, hot pink running bra, short running shorts, shoes, and grabbed my iPod. Grant was standing in the middle of my room, just watching me move around like a small tornado.

"I am going for a run!" I said to Grant without looking at him.

I left in a huff and wasn't even sure I wanted to return to him; I was so mad, upset, betrayed. He was leaving the country for the entire summer, going overseas. I was running as fast as I could, muttering under my breath, music blasting in my ears. His words played over in my head, "I am not going with you to Jade's wedding. I am leaving the country for the summer." I tried to push the sound of his voice from my brain. Finally, after I don't know how long during my run, the words started to fade.

The ache in my heart was making me feel so sad. Our relationship had worked for the past months with him 3000 miles away, what would happen when he was in another country? He never even said which country. My mind was filling with crazy thoughts, hotels, woman, what happens on the road, stays on the road. I stopped running when I got to campus and sat down in the grass by the Student Union building, it was quiet as most students were gone for the summer and it was late in the day.

I lay back in the grass and I could feel the tears coming like a wild storm, buckets and buckets of tears. My heart was breaking not because he didn't love me but because I knew I had to let go of him to let him pursue his dreams. My tears eventually stopped and I began to run back to my apartment.

Before I opened the door to my apartment I took a few deep breaths, stabilizing myself for what was to come with Grant. He was sitting on the couch watching TV and drinking a beer. We didn't have any beer, so I surmised he had taken my car to the store, which of course was fine. I was glad he wasn't sitting with a bottle of tequila on his lap.

He looked at me with sad eyes when I came in the door. I was more than sweaty and my eyes were red from my tears. Grant smiled at me but I couldn't even muster a smile back. I walked to the kitchen to grab some ice water. I stood with my palms down, leaning against the counter for support. Grant came into the kitchen, leaning against the opposite counter.

"Sydney are we going to talk about this, figure it out together? I know you are hurt and obviously very sad, but it doesn't change what we have." He was moving closer to me, he put his arms around my waist turning me to face him. His warm hands caressing my face, his thumb gliding along my bottom lip. He came down to give me a kiss, it was gentle and warming to my soul. I threw my arms around him and my sobs started again. I am not sure how long we stood in the kitchen before he calmed my crying.

He led me into my room and we lay down on the bed, he was holding me, whispering wonderful things in my ear. About how much he loves me, adores me, and how nothing will change. Unfortunately, my heart already knew better. So I played along wanting to savor every moment with him.

"I will be okay, just let me have some time to digest all the information you have told me today. What I don't know is, what country you will be in, do you know?" I asked him.

"Well, it is not just one country, we will be travelling to different hotels which the company manages, all over Europe."

"Oh." Was all I could say in response.

I tried to make the best of our time together, I put on a happy face for him but my insides were tied in knots. Grant was super sweet with me during his visit, reassuring me as much as possible of his love for me. I believed every word he said, I held on to everything he said, wanting to savor every moment we had together, holding on to every memory. Making a mental note of the look on his face when he kissed me, when he made love to me, and said good-bye to me.

The day I took him to the airport I nearly had a meltdown, I held it together not wanting him to see me completely loose it. I gave him as many kisses and said I love you as much as possible, during the short ride to the airport. But when he waved his final good-bye, I lost it.

CHAPTER 7

I was sitting on the couch, alone in our new apartment, tissue box in my lap, with used tissues on the floor in front of me, staring straight forward in a trance. The front door flew open, the light blinding me- Kendall storming in with a duffle bag on her arm and fume coming out of her ears.

My eyes got wide, she was furious. A small laugh escaped my throat.

"Wow…I thought I was miserable, but you look like you are ready to kill someone, what is wrong?" I asked.

Kendall slammed the front door, threw her bag into her room and stalked to the couch. She sat down next to me crossing her arms and muttering under her breath. She looked at my face, then to the tissues, and up to the TV which was off, then back to my face.

"What is wrong with you?" She asked.

"I asked you first, spill?"

Kendall took a deep, and hopefully, soothing breath.

"Matt, he can be such a butthead!" Did she say butthead, I laughed a little again.

"Sorry…butthead? What did he do?"

"Well, Matt has decided our relationship has been moving too fast and wants to slow things down for a while. I was so pissed. I picked up all my things and put them in my bag and left. After, I finished yelling at him of course!"

"Of course, so are you broken up, or are you guys just slowing it down, and what does slowing it down mean?"

She grabbed a tissue and wiped the tears which had started escaping her eyes. I was rubbing her back.

"Kendall it will be okay, maybe it is too much for him, the love he feels for you. I see the way he looks at you. Maybe he is overwhelmed, give him some time."

"I don't know, this is so out of the blue. I thought we were happy. Now he wants basically just to be friends for the summer and see what happens when school starts."

I looked at her with a puzzled look on my face, "That sounds like a break up not slowing it down, is that your feeling too?"

"Exactly!"

I didn't want to ask, but I did anyway, "Do you think he is seeing someone else?"

Kendall looked at me with huge eyes, tears streaming down her face, "I don't know, maybe, but when would he have time, I mean we are together almost 24/7."

"Hmmm…maybe it isn't anyone else, maybe he is feeling smothered."

Kendall and I talked for a long time about our current situations. I told her all about my time with Grant and his announcement about leaving the country for the summer, and my belief that our relationship would never sustain the long separation.

"Sydney, I understand why you feel this way, but only time will tell," Kendall advised.

Kendall and I spent the next two days feeling sorry for ourselves and having a pity party in our apartment together. Finally, I came out of my room on the third day of our pity party, stormed into her bedroom, and made a grand proclamation:

"Kendall Martin, you and I are not going to sit here all summer feeling sorry for ourselves because our supposed boyfriends have flown the coop for the summer. It is summer, we are young, and beautiful. So, let's get our summer on!"

Kendall looked at me like I was crazy. I pulled her out of her bed.

"Get your bathing suit on, we are going to go swimming. Next, out to lunch, and tonight we go out; first to our favorite bar, and then dancing. Do you hear me? Get up, I am not going to feel sorry for us anymore."

We lay in the sun for hours and swam until we were cooled off. Our skin was glowing golden when we went out for the evening. We had a determination for fun this evening. Of course, at our favorite bar were a few of Matt's friends, which made Kendall tense.

"Don't worry even if he comes in, we are on a girl's night out and he should see that you are not sitting home waiting for him to come to his senses."

Kendall smiled and agreed with me. We finished our pitcher of beer and headed out on our bikes to our favorite dance club, The Barrelhead. The evenings in Arizona barely cooled down to a normal temperature. We were dressed in short jean shorts, tank tops, and light short sleeved blouses. Our hair is long and flowing as we ride our bikes down the street. It was a quick ride over to The Barrelhead.

We locked up our bikes and showed our ID's at the door. For a summer night the club was pretty full. We found some of our friends and joined them at their table. I had my phone in my back pocket, I put it on vibrate in case I got a call. Grant and I have barely talked since his departure a few days ago. I tried not to think about him, he was leaving for Europe in a day and was completely focused on preparing for his trip. Kendall refused to return Matt's messages.

We went up to the bar to order some drinks because we had no patience to wait for the waitress to come to our table. Kendall and I were waiting to order from the bartender when we were pleasantly surprised when he approached us with two shots of tequila, and two beers.

"Hi, the gentlemen at the other end of the bar, sent these over for you two!" The bartender said. He was pointing to two very fine looking guys with cowboy hats on, nice tans and well, smiles to die for.

Kendall and I looked at each other giggled a little, and mouthed thank you to the guys. We raised our shots towards them and slammed them. We took our beers and cheered each other.

Kendall with a huge smile on her face and said to me, "Summer is on!" I laughed. My head tilting back as I took a long drink of my ice cold beer.

"We should go meet the very nice gentlemen who have sent over the drinks?" Kendall announced.

I know this would not sit well with Grant, that we were out drinking and flirting with boys, but you know, I just want to have fun and forget the pain aching inside of me. What is wrong with dancing and having a good time? Having a good time shouldn't be equated with cheating on your boyfriend. Before we made our way away from the bar, the guys who bought us the drinks were upon us.

"Good evening ladies," one of them said with a Southern drawl.

Kendall and I are standing face to face, the guys moved closer, each one standing to our sides.

"Hi," we both replied at the same time.

They are similarly dressed, the one next to Kendall, has clear blue eyes, golden hair, beautiful white teeth, and a deep tan. He spoke first.

"Well ladies, I am Colby Jenkins and this here is my friend Jackson McCoy." His voice was sultry with a thick Southern accent. He put his hand out to shake mine first and then Kendall's.

You couldn't have missed the looks on our faces when the sound of his voice flowed through our ears. Our eyes lit up and smiles came across our faces like the sun rising. I swallowed before I spoke.

"It is nice to meet you both, I am Sydney Stanton, and this is Kendall Martin," I said turning to look at Jackson. He is very striking, deep blue eyes that flickered in the light, dark hair and a smile that was scorching, for lack of a better description. My insides were trembling. What am I doing? Just because Grant is leaving for the summer doesn't mean our relationship is over. I need to get hold of myself. "Don't do something stupid", I kept saying over in my head as I stared up at this handsome stranger.

"Thank you for the drinks, that was very kind," Kendall said. The smile on her face spread from ear to ear as she looked at Colby.

"Would you ladies like to dance?" Colby asked.

Kendall and I exchanged yet another approving glance.

"Yes, that would be nice," Kendall said and we moved to the dance floor, Jackson grabbed my hand and I felt a pinge of excitement spread through me. I looked back at Kendall and she was happier than she'd been in days.

We danced to "Angel Eyes" by Love and Theft, "I do really like this song", I thought to myself as Jackson led me around the dance floor. I was having a wonderful time. We danced to one more song and then Kendall and I excused ourselves to the bathroom.

She and I were laughing as we walked away from the dance floor. Colby and Jackson headed back to the bar.

"Holy cow, they are gorgeous and can seriously move on the dance floor, Southern boys are divine," Kendall giggled to me.

I smiled at her, "I am so happy you are feeling better, now what? Do we hang out with them, or do we thank them and go back to our friends, what do you want to do?"

We were in the bathroom, fixing our hair and make-up. I looked at myself in the mirror and the glow on my face was unmistakable. I hadn't felt this alive in weeks. Maybe I could get through this separation from Grant. At that exact moment, I could feel my pocket vibrate. I pulled out my phone, Grant's name came across the screen. I showed it to Kendall, she smiled and said, "Answer it, you're not doing anything wrong." I shot her a look, knowing she was full of shit.

I took a deep breath, "Hey baby," I said. The bathroom was much quieter than out in the club.

"Hi, how are you? I miss you. What are you up to tonight? I tried to Skype you but you didn't answer." The tone of Grant's voice was very inquisitive.

"Kendall and I are at The Barrelhead tonight with some of our friends."

"Oh, it sounds quiet."

"Well, we are currently in the bathroom." I laughed a little. "Are you ready to leave for your trip?"

"Yeah, I guess. When are you leaving for Jade's wedding?" Grant asked.

"Umm…I think Thursday afternoon, I haven't decided if I am going to fly or drive yet, it is a lot of driving for a weekend."

Kendall was taping her wrist at me, wanting to go back and see if Colby was waiting for her. I laughed a little.

"Grant, I need to go, have a safe trip and call me when you get to your first stop, I miss you tons." My voice cracking, I was trying to control the ache in my heart.

"Are you okay, have you been drinking?"

"I will be fine, I just…I am sad without you." I hate when he questions how much I drank so I didn't answer his question.

"I know, I miss you too. I know you are purposely not answering me about the drinking, you are a big girl, just be careful. I love you,

Sydney Stanton, don't ever forget my words." We hung up a moment later and tears were in my eyes.

"Damn him." Kendall said. "Fix your eyes, you can't go back out looking like you are on the verge of a meltdown."

"I am not having a meltdown…I am dealing with all this the best I can."

"You seemed fine when you were dancing with Jackson!" Kendall said with her eyebrows going up and down.

I smacked her arm, "Stop it!"

"I am doing this for you, I have a boyfriend, you currently do not!"

We both laughed and headed back towards the bar. Jackson and Colby were waiting for us, beers in hand. I turned to Kendall, "Happy?"

Kendall laughed and we spent most of our evening getting to know these two Southerners.

Seems they are in town on business and were told this is a fun place to hang out.

Kendall was having a great time and not seeing her wallow about Matt, made me very happy. I was feeling great, which was probably not a good sign. I didn't feel guilty at all, I shouldn't feel guilty, I wasn't doing anything wrong.

"So, how long are you guys in town for?" Kendall asked.

"Well, we will be here through the weekend and then we have to head back on Sunday for work." Colby told her in his thick Southern accent, which was panty melting.

I looked at her, she seemed a bit sad. Knowing we were leaving for home this weekend for my sister's wedding.

"What are you ladies up to the next few days? Maybe we could hang out together while we are in town?" Jackson asked.

Yet another exchange of glances between Kendall and I, speaking in our ever present silent language.

Kendall piped right up, "Well, we are leaving for California for a wedding, but we will be here tomorrow. Maybe we could meet you guys for lunch or dinner tomorrow?"

I rolled my eyes, she is going to get me in so much trouble. I didn't tell Grant about her and Matt breaking up. I shot her a dirty look while she was talking.

Jackson and Colby were discussing whatever they had going on tomorrow for business, and my mind was off in never-never land worrying about being stupid. I could feel my stomach knotting up knowing Kendall really wanted to hang out with these guys, but also knowing if Grant found out he would flip out. He would have every right to flip out.

"You know it is getting kind of late Kendall. Maybe we should call it a night and get going, don't you think?" I said to her with big eyes bulging out of my head.

"Um, yeah, you are right. Hey Colby, let me give you my cell number and then you can give me a call tomorrow and we can see if we can meet up,." Kendall was in her flirty mode.

"Love that doll," Colby said, he grabbed his phone and Kendall typed it in for him. She handed him back the phone, and he gave her a sweet kiss on the cheek.

I stuck my hand out to both of them and said good night.

"Geez Kendall, I thought I was going to have to drag you out of here, are you kidding me, are you trying to get me into trouble?"

"You didn't do anything wrong, I am not going to tell Grant if you don't. I mean did you see those guys, HOT doesn't even do them justice?" Kendall was blushing.

"Seriously, we are leaving to go to Jade's wedding. I am not getting involved with those guys, you are going to have to go out with Colby by yourself. I don't think it is a good idea for me to go out with you guys."

"Let's see if Colby calls me first, they are only in town for a few days, it is not like I am going to marry the guy."

We got on our bikes and headed home. I was exhausted by the time we made it to our apartment. We said good night and I slept like a rock. I woke up late and headed to the pool for a workout. It was too hot to run, so swimming was my new exercise of choice.

CHAPTER 8

When I walked back into our apartment, I felt invigorated and relaxed from my workout. I headed for my room, to change. I could hear Kendall giggling, I poked my head in her room, she was still under her covers but she was on the phone. I came and sat down on her bed. I quietly asked her who she was talking to.

She mouthed back, pointing at the phone, "It is him!" I rolled my eyes at her and let out a deep breath. Crap, how am I going to get out of this, she is going to cause me so many problems. Kendall being single was not a good thing. She can be very convincing when she wants something.

She was repeating to me whatever Colby was asking her, "Um, today? Well Sydney just got back from working out and I am talking to you, so no, we don't have lunch plans. Yes, we know the hotel, how about we meet you guys at the Chinese restaurant across the street?"

"I don't know the name, but it is right across from the hotel you are staying in, we go there sometimes when our parents are in town, it is really good." Kendall was glowing with excitement.

I was shaking my head, mouthing, "No... I am not going!"

She was on a mission, completely ignoring me. "Yeah, we can meet you guys, how about 12:30?"

I stalked out of her room and went into my room slamming the door. Seriously, I am going to kill her, why does she do this crap to me? I know I will end up caving to her wishes, so I just decided to suck it up. I turned on my shower and hopped into the cold water, hoping it would settle my nerves.

"Sydney, are you mad at me?" Kendall had come into my bathroom.

"Kendall, are you nuts, you are going to get me in trouble with Grant. If he finds out about last night and going to lunch with them today, he will kill me. He won't understand."

"I know you can blame me, please come with me, they are expecting both of us. Please!" She was begging. "I will be your best friend forever if you do this for me," she was laughing as the words came out of her mouth.

I turned off the shower and grabbed my towel to cover myself. I stepped out of the shower and gave her a dirty look.

"First off, that won't work because you are already my best friend forever, and yes I will go with you because you will keep bugging me about it until I give in anyways. But so help me God, if this back fires and Grant finds out, the shit is going to hit the fan."

We packed up our stuff for the weekend so we could head for the airport right after our lunch date. I was wearing a strapless, electric blue summer dress with some strappy sandals and the necklace Grant gave me around my neck. Kendall decided to wear a flowery tank top dress, with wedge heels.

We arrived at the restaurant and found Jackson and Colby had already been seated, the hostess showed us to their table. They both stood as we approached. It was a large oval booth with high backs; the cushions were covered in a deep red fabric, and the table was covered with a white tablecloth.

Jackson and Colby were dressed in business suits, no cowboy hats this time, and wow they looked scrumptious. Seriously, I needed to slap myself. Trouble, you are going to get yourself in to trouble.

"Hi, y'all," they both said at the same time with the same sultry Southern tone from last night.

"Hi, thank you for inviting us to lunch," I said.

I was super nervous, I intended to make it perfectly clear that my only intention here was to be friends, and advise Jackson I was in a committed relationship.

"Sydney, you look darling in this dress." I could feel Jackson's eyes going up and down my body stopping at my breasts, and focusing in on my necklace.

"Sit down," Jackson said.

I slid around the seat, as did Kendall, so we were sitting next to each other and Jackson and Colby were sitting at the ends of the booth. My heart was racing, guilt was spreading through me, this is so wrong...so... so, wrong... to be here... right now.

Colby and Kendall were talking to each other discussing what to order.

"Sydney, you seem, nervous, is everything alright?" Jackson asked very sweetly.

I was running my fingers along my necklace, twisting it a little and biting my bottom lip. My mind was racing as to what to say to him.

"Look Jackson, you are a very nice, and I have to admit, very handsome, but I need to be honest with you about something."

"Yes, you have my full attention, Sydney." He said. Geez, the way my name rolls off his tongue has my breath catching. Crap, no one else has ever made me feel like this except for Grant. This can't be good.

He is waiting for me to finish, but I was incapable of speaking. I swallowed and looked into Jackson's entrancing eyes, I had to shake my head to regain my composure. "You should know, I have a boyfriend and I am not looking for any kind of summer fling." There I said it, I was honest. I felt much better.

"Sydney, is that why you keep running your fingers around your necklace? Did he, your boyfriend, give you the necklace you keep touching, the same one you had on last night?"

I dropped my hand from my necklace not realizing I was still touching it.

"Yes."

"That is fine, we can be friends. I am not looking for any kind of "fling" either," He said.

"Okay, good, I feel better, what do you want to order?"

We looked through the menu and Jackson ordered for the table. He is very confident, with absolutely no air of arrogance at all. We talked non-stop during lunch all about his job, where he was from, his family, and why he was here with Colby on business. They are both 26 years old and from Texas- born and raised.

"Do you know what time it is?" I asked Jackson.

"Almost 2:00. Actually Colby and I need to get back to our meetings."

"Kendall, we need to get going or we will miss our flight."

"Sydney, if we are friends can I call you just to talk?" Jackson very innocently asked me.

"Jackson, you are so sweet, but I don't think that is a good idea. Maybe someday our paths will cross again but for now, I will have to say no."

"Well, I won't push you on this, but we do come in town every few weeks on business, maybe we can all have dinner next time?"

I smiled, this guy is so smooth.

"Sure, Colby has Kendall's number, give us a call next time you are here, and if we are free we can have dinner."

We thanked them for lunch and took off for the airport. Once on the plane we discussed the merits of our lunch.

"Kendall, are you going to keep in touch with Colby?"

"I don't know, maybe. He is nice, they are both nice. But I am not looking to get into another relationship, especially with someone from another state. But they could be fun to hang out with when they come to town, and they are defiantly easy on the eyes." Kendall was smiling at me.

"You are killing me, let's just get through this weekend and get back to school. We have a busy summer ahead of us. We don't need to be distracted by two Southern boys." I firmly said.

Once we got home, my house was in full wedding mode, every moment of every day was filled. I wasn't even in the door and my mom handed me a list of errands to run. I will be gone the rest of the evening, there must be fifteen things to do on it; drycleaners, grocery store, hardware store, liquor store, party supply store, and list went on and on.

I was at the drive-thru picking up something to eat for myself. I heard my phone vibrating in the cup holder of the car. I picked it up to see who was calling; if it was my mom or sister I was not answering as they would just add more stuff to my list of errands.

It was Grant, I smiled like a big dork when I saw his name on the screen.

"Hello handsome!"

"Hey baby, I made it, we are in London. How are you? I miss you." He said.

"I am good, running errands for the wedding, but I wish you were here with me."

"I know, listen I have to go, I just wanted you to know I landed safely and I will be in touch, I love you, and I will talk to you soon." He hung up before I even got to say good-bye. Ugh!

I was too busy all weekend to even notice Grant hadn't called, and to be honest I didn't pick up the phone to call him. It was one event after another, I couldn't wait to leave on Sunday. I said good-bye to everyone who came to town for the wedding. The wedding was beautiful and went off without a hitch. Kendall's dad dropped us off at the airport, and a couple hours later we were back in our apartment.

"This was a busy weekend. I am exhausted. I am glad to be home," I said.

We checked our voicemail, no messages from Grant, but quite a few from Matt. I looked at Kendall with a confused expression.

"Didn't he know we were gone all weekend to the wedding, and why did he leave so many messages, didn't he call your cell?"

"I haven't talked to him. He probably forgot we were out of town. Anyways he is no longer my boyfriend and I don't need to tell him the what, whens and whose of my life anymore." Kendall marched herself into her room and dropped down on her bed.

I just laughed at her and went to my room to wash my face and change. I yelled to her, "I am going for a swim, want to come?"

"No, go ahead without me, I am going to relax."

I didn't believe her, I gave her a skeptical look but went out for a quick swim anyway.

When I came back she was on the phone, I figured she was talking to Matt, but how wrong was I...very. Kendall was chatting it up with Colby who had called her from his home in Texas.

I was relaxing on my bed, Kendall came in and sat down on my bed. I raised my eyebrows at her.

"What is that wild expression on your face?"

"I think I am in deep like with the heavenly Texan," she sighed and giggled at me. I rolled my eyes at her.

"Good, he is very sweet and hot, but he is in Texas."

"That may be, but he will be here in a few weeks and I deserve to have some fun, I am not hanging around waiting for Matt to come around."

"I am not saying you should wait around for him, just be careful. Yes, Colby is adorable, educated, and has a career but he is older, just be careful, is all I am saying."

"Have you heard from Grant?"

"Only the day he landed in London, but I guessed it would be like this. Sporadic calls, if any at all."

"What about Jackson?" She said with a devilish smile.

"What about him? There is nothing. I am with Grant! End of discussion."

"Not end of discussion, Jackson is your fan."

"My fan, what does that mean?"

"It means, he likes you and you were attracted to him."

"You don't know what you are talking about, yet again, I am with Grant."

"Whatever… Colby and Jackson will be back again next month. We'll see," she said as she walked out of my room.

"You are annoying, go to bed!" I yelled to Kendall.

CHAPTER 9

Is it possible that the summer is over, Rush is over, and fall classes are starting in less than a week? It is completely possible. Kendall and I were so busy during the summer, with classes, planning Rush and setting up all the philanthropic events that sometimes we didn't even know what day it was. The days started to run together, never even knowing if it was a Monday or Thursday.

The sad part was that I barely spoke to Grant all summer. The few phone calls we did have were short and the emails he sent were just as short, as well as few and far between. I did have dinner with Grant's parents a few times over the summer but they didn't have any more information about his whereabouts and work than I did - which made me feel better, figuring they were in the same boat as I was. He must have really enjoyed his internship abroad. I wasn't even sure when he would be back in New York, but guessed it would be by the beginning of September, for his classes to start.

If I hadn't been so consumed by summer school, planning sorority Rush and the philanthropic events for the year, I would have lost my mind over Grant's absence from my life. Although I was busy all summer, my heart was in a constant state of flux the entire time. Each time my phone rang, a text came through, or I checked my email, I was desperately hoping for something from Grant. At some point, I just stopped believing in him. I stopped wishing for him to contact me. I just stopped. Each moment was hard, but I faced the hard truth. Each step was devastating and my heart ached for Grant, but at some point I accepted the facts in front of me. Grant was no longer part of my life. He walked away from me, from us...again. I could have called his parents and asked why, but it wasn't their place to tell me...it was Grant's and his track record for being honest was severely lacking.

Colby and Jackson came to town two more times for business trips during the summer. Kendall was more than happy to spend time with them, and eventually I warmed up to the idea. They were very fun to hang around with. Jackson had me laughing every time until my sides hurt. Kendall was in deep like with Colby, and spending time with Jackson was simple, no strings- just friends. Jackson and I had begun keeping in touch on the phone, and sometimes we would Skype. It was nice to have a guy's perspective on my relationship with Grant. I had confided everything to him about Grant. He knew how insecure I was feeling and lost I was.

Jackson was very thoughtful, his words always honest, never sugar coating anything, would put me at ease when I let my imagination run wild concerning Grant. He would tell me, "Don't worry Sydney, he loves you, he will call, he is busy. He is busy with work and that is his focus, when he gets back things will fall in to place, you will see." I would always agree but the nagging feelings in my heart never left.

Kendall and I decided not to move back into the House, we love apartment living, and since we could ride our bikes to school, we were happy. There were so many rules living in the Sorority House, we were not about to give up our freedom. We were already a month into the fall semester and still no word from Grant. I called his phone a few times, sent texts to him, I didn't even bother trying to Skype, what was the point, and he hadn't returned any of my calls and was basically missing in action from my life.

One morning after not sleeping all night, I just decided I'd had enough. I took off my necklace and put it in my jewelry box. Obviously things were not going to be the same. Somewhere over the summer, our relationship had disappeared. When I came out of my room to leave for class, Kendall was packing up her backpack. She looked at me, tilting her head and squinting her eyes at me.

"Hmmm...something is different about you this morning." Kendall was checking me out from head to foot and back again.

"What, do I have something on me?"

"No, actually it is what you don't have on you that is intriguing."

I put my hand on my neck and let out a deep breath.

"It was time, I knew Grant's being in Europe all summer would…well it was time to take off the necklace. I haven't heard from him… in I don't even know how long. As far as I am concerned, it has been over for a long time. I am just now ready to face the facts in front of me, out of sight out of mind, I guess."

"I am sorry, Sydney, I know he was your everything, but you will survive. You made it through the summer without a meltdown and you are being very mature about the situation."

"What I am going to do, I am not going to cry, that won't help. So, I will put one foot in front of the other, and every day will get a little easier."

Easier, easier, am I nuts? I was lying to myself. I wished every day for him to call or knock on my door. I was just not allowing myself to breakdown and have any more pity parties. I would have to deal with my feelings and move on.

Or not deal with my feelings at all.

I couldn't believe my relationship with Grant was over. How could this have happened? Yet again, he walked away from me without a thought to my feelings. Everything he told me over the years had been a lie. He must have found someone else and moved on. He is so selfish. Once again he was unable to be truthful with me, Jason's words came forefront into my mind. "A tiger doesn't change his stripes, he will break your heart…again." Jason's words began to haunt me. How could I be fooled by this man again? I know exactly how, he owned my heart. I could feel my heart , broken in to a million pieces, and my temper flaring inside my body.

"Sydney, does this mean you will be more interested in Jackson now?"

"No," I bit Kendall's head off. "I don't need another long distance relationship, it is too hard. Anyways, Jackson and I are friends, he doesn't see me as any more than a buddy."

Kendall laughed with a snort. She rolled her eyes at me.

"You're delusional, he would love to take it to the next level, you are just too blind to see it."

"Even if what you are saying is true, which it is not, I am not looking for another boyfriend, or fling, or one night stand. I need to focus on school, work, and sorority all of that is enough to keep me busy 24/7, men just complicate my life."

"Have it your way, but they will be here in a few days, why don't you see how you feel when they get to town.

"I have to go, I have class in 30 minutes, bye," I said.

I hopped on my bike. Kendall is crazy, Jackson is my friend, and I don't want to add any more complications to my life. I just want to finish off the next two years of school without any complications. I have classes all day, and need to go to the library in between to do research for a paper. When my classes for the day were over, I pulled out my phone and there were three missed calls from my mom. I listened to my voice mail. Not happy news. I jumped on my bike and headed home.

I called my mom once I was in my apartment. She filled me in on all the details.

"You have a flight leaving tonight, it is a red eye but it is the only flight I could get you on. Your father will pick you up in front of the baggage claim. I love you sweetheart."

Kendall walked in when I finished my call with my mom. I had tears in my eyes.

"God, Sydney, what is it, was that Grant?"

"No, who… Grant doesn't even exist in my world right now. That was my mom, my Grandfather passed away and I am flying out to New York tonight on the red eye."

"I am sorry, is there anything I can do to help?"

"Drive me to the airport?"

"Of course."

"Do you want to get something to eat before I have to leave? I just need to pack a few things and then we can go, okay?"

"Yeah sure, I will be waiting." She said.

I packed a small carryon bag, I didn't need much. I will only be gone for one day. We left our apartment about an hour later and headed to get something to eat.

We were sitting together sharing a small pizza.

"Sydney, are you going to try and see Grant while you are in New York?"

It had already crossed my mind, but I was trying to compartmentalize Grant into a small box of memories tucked far away in my brain. I shrugged, not really knowing what I wanted to do.

"Maybe you should try to see him and get some closure so you can move on, what do you think?" She said as she took a bite of her pizza. Kendall was treading on thin water, my mood becoming frantic.

"I don't know, I mean he hasn't called in months. Do I really want to put myself through more heartache with him? Not calling for months is pretty much the sign of the relationship being over don't you think?" I asked Kendall.

"I am sure you are right but it would be good for you to get closure, and then may be Jackson could take center stage!!!" Kendall's eyes doing the cha-cha at me.

"Really, I am going to a funeral not a fraternity party," I said, laughing at her.

"I know, but damn he is hot."

"You just keep your business on Colby, and what about Matt, what if he saunters back into your life?"

"He won't, we haven't spoken except in passing and anyways, I think he is seeing someone."

"I think you are wrong, but as Jackson would say, things will all fall into place!"

"Hmmm…quoting Jackson, I like it!"

The red eye flight to New York is quiet, at least I could get some sleep. Nothing but business people. Before I fell asleep I could feel my eyes filling with tears and my heartache for Grant. I put my headphones on and fell into a deep sleep. Well, as deep as you can get on a plane. I woke up just in time for the beverage service and a morning snack. I thought about Kendall's idea to see Grant. It would definitely give me closure, but the pain of seeing his face would be brutal.

My dad was circling the airport in a rental car waiting for me when I walked out of the airport. We headed to the hotel, and then we would be going to my aunt's house before the funeral.

"Dad, how far is it on the train from Long Island to the city?"

"I am not sure, maybe 45 minutes by train, why?" He said with annoyance in his voice, and his lips in a grim line.

"Just curious."

"Don't give me that line of bullshit…" Wow, my dad was cussing at me. "Are you considering going to see that rat bastard Grant?"

"Dad…ugh…he is not a rat bastard, why would you say that about him?"

"Did he break your heart? Then he is a rat bastard in my book!"

"Ugh…forget I even brought it up."

"Good."

The funeral is late this afternoon, I could get into the city late tonight or early in the morning and try to meet up with him. I knew Grant wouldn't answer a call from me, since he hadn't answered any of the messages I left. I swallowed my pride and sent him a text.

Thursday, 8:55 am, Sydney to Grant: I am in New York, can we meet up? I will be here for about 24 hours.

I didn't anticipate a response for a very long time, if at all. But I need the closure Kendall spoke of, and this was my opportunity to say a final good-bye to him if he responded. I really didn't know what I would say or how I would feel. I was in my own world when we pulled up to the hotel and my dad got out of the car. I hadn't even noticed we were parked. He came over and knocked on the window.

"Come on space cadet, you can take a nap in your room. Your sister is here, so you two are sharing a room."

"Eew, I don't want to share a room with her and her husband, that is gross."

"Don't be a dork, Eric is not here."

"Oh, then okay, never mind. Yes a nap sounds good."

I took a hot shower and then crawled into bed for a long nap before the funeral. We headed over to my aunt's later in the day. My whole family was in town for my grandfather's funeral. It is sad- I only see these people at weddings and funerals, never just for a visit.

We were preparing for the funeral when I felt my phone vibrate. I pulled it from my back pocket. There was only one message.

Thursday, 2:00 pm: Jackson to Sydney: Kendall told me about your Grandfather, I am so sorry. We will be in town this weekend. I hope you are up for a visit.

Jackson's text brought a smile to my face. I had hoped it would be Grant, but that would have been more wishful thinking. The only closure I was going to get was the closure I gave our relationship myself. I vowed to lock away all thoughts of my love for him, my desire for him, and the bond we had formed, into a small box in the vault of my memories. I vowed to never open myself up so entirely to any man and to keep my feelings and emotions under lock and key.

I never heard from Grant, and as I boarded the plane back to Arizona, it was as if I was finally closing the door on the part of my life which included Grant Montgomery.

Another long flight back to school, well at least all the traveling would be over. And with the schedule I have this term, I have no time to be flying around the country for someone.

I was surprised when I saw my car picking me up at the airport, and more surprised when I saw Mr. Jackson McCoy hopping out of the driver's door to help me with my bag. I started laughing when I saw him.

With my hands on my hips and a grin on my face, I said, "Jackson what are you doing driving my car and picking me up at the airport?"

"Kendall and Colby went out for the evening so I volunteered. I thought you and I could get some dinner, and I believe you need to talk. Am I right?"

"You are so right, and you are so good to me, thank you," I said giving a quick hug and peck on the cheek.

Jackson and I drove towards my apartment and stopped off for a burger and fries. While we were waiting for our order, Jackson placed his hand on mine which was resting on the table.

"Darlin', I am sorry about your grandfather, are you okay?"

"Jackson, you are sweet to worry, but I am fine. Mostly tired, I mean roundtrip to New York in 24 hours is a lot and the emotional strain of the funeral is exhausting. It will be nice to sleep in my own bed tonight." My face was expressionless, Jackson knew there was more, he knows me very well. Which I now find interesting; how well he and I know each other.

"Sydney, what are you not sharing with me?"

"Nothing."

The look on Jackson's face said, "Oh hell no, you are not going to clam up on me now."

I smiled at him, "Fine…Kendall had this crazy idea that I need closure from my defunct relationship with Grant, so she suggested I try to contact him while I was in New York."

"Did you, did you talk to him?" The look on Jacksons face showed concern and maybe a hint of excitement, or maybe something else, but I am not sure what I saw in his eyes.

"I tried, I sent him a text, but of course he failed to respond."

"I see you are not wearing his necklace anymore, what does that mean?" That look was still lingering in his eyes. I touched my neck where the necklace used to rest.

"It means, I took it off and put it away. It means, I am done waiting for him. It means, he is no longer a part of my life. But it doesn't mean I am ready to date. I need time to recover and get over my feelings for him."

I was trying to be nice and gentle with Jackson in case what Kendall had said was true, about Jackson wanting more than friendship from me. I completely changed the subject.

"How long are you in town for this time?"

"We will be here until Monday night and then back to Texas. We have meetings all day tomorrow, and Sunday morning. Do you want to go to The Barrelhead on Sunday night?"

"I would love to go, but I have to study for an exam on Monday morning."

"Oh yeah, I remember those days. How about a late lunch or early dinner, you still have to eat?" I smiled at his adorable face.

"Yes, I think I can fit you in, I do like spending time with you Jackson," laughing a little as I spoke to him. It feels good to laugh.

He drove me home, walked me into my apartment, and put my bag down in my room. Jackson and Colby have been to our apartment on numerous occasions so it was no surprise he felt comfortable here. We sat down on the couch, I could feel my eyelids closing.

"Jackson, I am really tired, would you mind heading back to your hotel so I can go to sleep?" I didn't want to be rude, but honestly I just wanted to go to sleep.

"SureSydney, we will talk Sunday and make plans. Lock the door behind me so I know you are safe and get some rest." Damn he is sweet. He gave me a long hug and a kiss on my forehead before he left.

After I locked the door, I went to my room and changed into my pajamas, and crawled under the covers. I didn't think I had any tears left to cry over Grant, but I was wrong. I cried myself to sleep and didn't wake until late Saturday morning.

Another week flew by at school, which another week I survived without Grant in it. I was running every day to keep me sane. It was really my favorite thing to do, if I missed a day, I became anxious and cranky. The weeks turned into months, and the months went faster and faster, how could time pass so quickly?. One day it was New Year's Eve and the next it was spring break. My junior year of college went by in the blink of an eye.

When we finished our finals after junior year, our lives were in a new phase yet again. Jackson and Colby have become a big part of our lives. We saw them every few weeks when they were in town, and had a blast each time. It is liberating- Kendall and I have no ties to any men at this school. We come and go as we please, we go to formals with whoever we want, or we go with our friends. We are having the time of our lives- just the way college should be.

Summer was going to be fun, we knew exactly what it was going to take to put on the best sorority Rush and get all the philanthropic events planned out before classes started in the fall. Going to summer school has boosted my GPA and is guaranteeing both Kendall and I are going to graduate in May. In a year we would be done, and moving on with our lives. But, first things first, senior year and a summer of pure happiness.

Heather came out to visit us for a few days before she returned to her summer classes at Berkley, and to be with Curt. I tell you those two stunned us all by having a relationship that stood the test of time. Heather started attending Berkley for her junior year of college at Curt's request. They have been together ever since. Kendall and I picked her up at the airport and the first thing she says to us is, "Damn it is hot here!"

We all laughed and made our way back to the apartment.

"It has been a long time since we have all been together," Heather said.

"You guys want to go for a swim and lay out in the sun?" I asked.

"Geez-Sydney, give it a rest with the exercising!" Kendall barked at me.

"What? Are you telling me you don't like how good you look because I make you exercise with me a few days a week? I think Colby likes what he sees when he looks at you," I was cracking myself up.

"Who is Colby? What happened to Matt?" Heather was lost, we never told anyone from home about Colby and Jackson. Of course everyone at school knew about the Southern boys.

"Umm...well Colby is he is a friend that Kendall sees every few weeks when he is in town, and Matt is way out of the picture," I said, trying to be as evasive as possible.

Heather was not buying any of it.

"Spill!" Heather said.

"It is a long story, we will tell you tonight."

"No girls, tell me now. What have you two been up to without me monitoring your activities?" Heather was smiling, she must have known this was a good story.

Kendall told her all about meeting them last summer. How she and Colby had started seeing each other and keeping it light and fun, no long distance commitment.

"Sydney, are you involved with his friend, what did you say his name was- Jackson?"

"We are friends, nothing more than friends, he has been my rock this past year. He keeps me from going insane sometimes. I value his friendship as much as I value ours," I said, but the smile on my face must have shown more than friendship, because Heather gave me a puzzling look.

"Hmmm... that is what you say... but the twinkle in your eye when you speak about him tells me there maybe something else brewing between the two of you." Heather was not easily fooled.

Kendall grunted, "Damn, from your mouth to God's ears, I having been trying to get them together for months." Kendall's arms were crossed with annoyance at me.

"Shut up Kendall, you know Jackson and I are not going to get together. Anyways, I don't want to be in that kind of relationship again."

Heather was amused by the banter between Kendall and I. "What is this about, what kind of relationship?"

Kendall responded before I could even open my mouth. "Jackson adores her, he wants to be with her, but he knows she is gun shy and refuses to have any kind of long distance relationship. As a matter of fact Sydney refuses to have any kind of relationship which will make her open her heart up."

I rolled my eyes and went to get something to drink in the kitchen. Great now the two of them are going to be ganging up on me to move on. I could hear them still talking about it in somewhat hushed tones.

"You two know I am only in the kitchen, I can hear you talking about me and I don't want to talk about it!" I yelled at both of them.

I walked back over, bringing back some iced tea for all of us, handing them each a glass.

"Sydney, you are going to have to move on, let yourself feel again, you are depriving yourself of love, why?" Kendall said.

I was shocked, did I really need to explain to these two why?

"You both know why, I am not going to go over this anymore. I don't want to put myself out there like that, not now and maybe not ever. End of discussion."

Heather and Kendall didn't say anything else about it. They sipped their teas and exchanged knowing glances.

Like everything else in our lives, Heather's visit was over as fast as it started, and she went back to her summer classes -so did we. I didn't bring up Grant nor did Heather bring him up during her visit. What would be the point? I know she knew what the low down was with, him but why make myself crazy? He knows where I am, if he wanted to get in touch with me he would.

CHAPTER 10

Graduation is less than a month away. I have a full thesis to write and my brain is in overload. The thought of moving home after living here on our own for basically four years is daunting, to say the least. Our parents are not about to foot the bill for us to keep living the good life. We were going to have to suck it up, move home, and get, jobs. Between studying for finals and interviewing, Kendall and I are very busy.

We were in our apartment studying when my phone started vibrating on the table. I looked at the screen, Heather was calling, does she know what time it is? It was late, but hell Kendall and I are up cramming for finals.

"Heather, do you know what time it is?" I said laughing as I answered the phone.

"Yes and you are up, get Kendall and put me on speaker phone?"

"Why?"

"Just do it...please?" The obvious excitement in her voice had me intrigued.

"Fine, I am walking to her room..." I knocked on her door so not to scare her. "Kendall...Heather wants to talk to us." I walked into her room and sat down on the bed and pressed the speaker phone icon on my phone.

"Okay Heather, we are together and you are on speaker phone, what is so important?"

"Get Kendall's phone and looked at the picture I just sent her."

"Geez, Heather is this some kind of game? We are cramming for finals here," Kendall said annoyed.

Kendall grabbed her phone and scrolled to open the text from Heather. Kendall's eyes got really wide, and so did her smile.

"What is it?" I asked Kendall, she put the phone in my face, and we exchanged a look.

Heather was giggling on the other end of the phone. I am sorry make that screaming with delight.

"Did you get the picture, do you know what this means…I am getting married! Curt proposed to me tonight!" She started screaming and going on about the proposal. The picture was of a big beautiful 2 carat diamond ring on her hand.

We all started screaming, and Kendall and I congratulated her, but what came next excited us even more.

"So, you are my two best friends in the whole world, I have a couple of questions for you. First, I want you both to be in my wedding. Second, will you be my wedding planners?"

"Of course, we would love to be in the wedding, but Heather neither of us has planned a wedding before." Kendall advised her.

"I know, but you two have put on so many events for your sorority it will be so easy for you, and we want to get married this summer."

"This summer… as in, now?" I asked.

"Yes, Curt is going to medical school in the fall and we don't want to postpone the wedding and have a long engagement. We want to marry in July, move to where ever he ends up, and live happily ever after. Will you guys do it?"

We spent the next hour on the phone with Heather getting all the details of what kind of wedding she wanted, the budget, and where she wanted the wedding to be held. I was exhausted when we were done and it was very, very late.

My head was really in overload with this news. Planning a wedding in two months was going to take some serious work.

Graduation was a bittersweet event. The end of an era for us, and moving back home was not going to be easy. As we drove away for the last time from our apartment, which had become our home, there were more than a few tears in my eyes. The memories were flowing through my brain as I drove home. Kendall was in her car and once again we were caravanning. I was listening to music, country music which I love, but with Colby and Jackson around we listened to it even more. Kendall and I did not realize how much those two traveled for business. We were happy to find out they come to California at least once a month but sometimes more often.

My phone rang, and I pressed the answer button. Kendall's voice was booming through my blue tooth.

"Sydney, we have a lot of work to do for Heather's wedding, do you want to get together with her tomorrow, so we can plan a beautiful wedding?"

"Good idea, it is weird to be driving away from here for the last time." My voice was trembling a bit, a tear in my eye.

"Sydney you're sad, this won't be the last time, we will be back."

"I know, but it will not be the same."

"Syd yeah, I know. I need to ask you something…don't get mad…but you know *he* will be at the wedding, are you prepared for it?"

I knew exactly who she meant when she said *he*, but I played stupid, "*He* who?"

"Seriously, are you playing stupid or was that not the first thing that came to your mind when Heather said she and Curt were getting married? I know you better than you know yourself, and I saw the look of panic on your face."

Crap, she does know me so well. I had put Grant so far in the back of my mind that I kept all my feelings for him wrapped up in a box with a perfect bow tied around, it never to be touched. It had been the first thought, but this isn't about me, it is about Heather and Curt, and I will suck it up for their happiness.

"Damn… you are good. I am trying very hard not to dwell on this fact, but what can I do? He and Curt are cousins and very close. I have no doubt Curt asked him to be in the wedding, which will only complicate the weekend more. Are you going to bring a date?"

"Maybe Colby and Jackson would go with us, and stop avoiding the question about Grant, you need to prepare."

"That is an interesting idea, okay, but first things first, we need to find a place for the wedding and reception, and order invitations."

I completely avoided the topic of Grant, which also had my mind on the fact of his entire family being at the wedding. Knowing his mother who has never given up hope of us being together would try to play matchmaker all weekend. The idea of a date seemed almost a requirement now, not to mention I didn't want Grant to think he was the only man for me.

After a long drive, I parked in the driveway of my family home and looked up at the house. I took a deep soothing breath before entering the house. My dad had left right after my graduation for a business trip. My Mom was back at work. I was home alone, nice and quiet. I started carrying in my stuff from my car. I could feel my phone vibrating in my back pocket.

I grabbed it and hastily said "Hello".

"May I speak with Sydney Stanton?" The voice was professional, and not familiar to me at all.

"This is Sydney speaking."

"Miss Stanton, this is Mrs. Contreras from the Human Resources Department of Yellow Bird Design Group. I received a copy of your resume, would you be available for an interview this week, say tomorrow around 9:00 am?"

My heart was racing, I am so excited, this is the call I have been waiting for. I never in a million years thought they would call, but some wishes can come true.

"Yes, of course, can you give me one minute; I have a huge box in my hands." I put the box down and ran into the house to get a pen and paper.

"I do apologize, can you give me the address?"

"May I call you Sydney?" She politely asked.

"Of course."

"I am sure you are aware we do not have an office in Orange County but I will be down in your area tomorrow and was hoping we could have a more informal interview. How about we meet in the coffee shop at my hotel?"

"That would be fine." I said. She gave me all the pertinent information I needed, and I was jumping for joy when I got off the phone.

I called my mom to tell her and then my next call was to Jackson, I didn't even think twice. I couldn't wait to tell him. He was the one who suggested I submit my resume to them, thinking it was a perfect place for me to work.

I pushed on his name on my phone and listened to it ring.

"Hello, you survived your finals and are now a legitimate college graduate, congratulations." He was laughing and the excitement in his voice only fueled my happiness.

"Guess what?"

"What, darlin'?"

"I have an interview tomorrow with Yellow Bird, can you believe it? You were so right about me sending them my resume. You are the best, thank you."

"It was only my idea, it was your resume that got you the interview, but I can think of another way you can thank me!" He said with his sultry Southern charm.

"Jackson McCoy, you behave yourself. When are you coming to California next, I miss seeing you?"

"You miss me, you never tell me you miss me, are you starting to have feelings for me?" His Southern drawl teasing me.

"I never need to tell you because you are like my period, every three weeks, you show up!" Did I really just say that out loud to him?

"Gross, did you have to use me and your period, in an analogy? That is a definite turn off." He said with a gagging sound.

"Good. Now when are you guys coming out?"

"I am looking at my calendar here, we will be there in a week. What time is your interview tomorrow?"

"9 am and then I am meeting with Kendall and Heather to plan Heather's wedding, which she wants to have in two months."

"What, is she pregnant, what is the rush?"

"You are bad, no she is not pregnant. Her boyfriend, I mean fiancée is starting medical school in the fall and they don't want to wait. Speaking of the wedding, will you be my date?"

Did I just ask Jackson to be my date, I did. I like it, maybe I am ready to move on and move all over his hot body. Geez, get a grip.

"Darlin', are you there?"

"Sorry, lost in my own thoughts for a minute."

"What were you thinking about that had your mind wandering off? I am hoping it was me?" My heart was beating a little faster thinking of his smell and his hands running up and down my back.

"Ummm...the wedding, I don't have the date yet but it will be a Saturday in July, so clear your calendar good lookin' because you are going with me."

"Who is this and what did you do with Sydney...I will save all my Saturdays for you, I would save every day for you if you let me."

Damn him and his seductive voice. I could feel my body, it was getting all excited with the anticipation of my new found craving for him.

"Jackson... I will call you tomorrow after my interview, have a fabulous day."

"I know it will be thanks to this phone call" he said, I giggled and said good-bye.

I must be off my rocker or high on something, I was in full on flirt mode with Jackson, I have never done that with him before. His response was enlightening. Kendall was right he is interested. Maybe I could let some of my feelings out and share something more than friendship with him.

I woke up early to get ready for my interview. I have been on a lot of interviews before graduation but none which excited me as much as working for Yellow Bird. This company has its hands in so many things, but best of all they have their own advertising department. I put on a light summer suit and headed out the door. It took less than 15 minutes to get to the hotel, so I was 30 minutes early. I looked at the clock, it is two hours ahead in Texas, I could call Jackson. No, I shouldn't bother him at work. I am bored, and he is so decadent, his voice so warming and calming to me. Before I could stop myself, I was calling him.

"Well, good morning, I wasn't expecting to hear from you for a few more hours."

"I can hang up and call back later, if you'd rather wait," I said sweetly.

"No, I like the sound of your voice...I thought you have an interview this morning?"

"I do but I am 30 minutes early and well..."

"Well what...you wanted to talk to me?" His voice with the accent just makes my heart pound.

"Yes." Was the only word I could get out.

"Why, we have been talking forever and you have never...what has changed?"

"I am not sure, me I guess. I don't know, I am just having certain feelings lately which are making me...this is embarrassing, I am going to hang up before I say something really stupid." I know he can't see me, but my face is bright red.

"What kind of feelings, should I come visit you this weekend, if you are having those kind of feelings for me?"

"I am not going to stop you."

"Sydney," he said with a long drawl on my name.

"Yeah?" I was totally lost in my thoughts about him.

"It is almost 9 am, you better head in for your interview. Good luck."

I hung up the phone and was flushed with desire for Jackson-crap. I fixed my hair and lipstick in the mirror, grabbed my purse, and headed into the restaurant.

I met with Mrs. Contreras for almost two hours, I had to excuse myself one time to the ladies room because I drank so much coffee. I think the interview went well. She said she would be in touch, I thanked her for her time and headed out to my car.

I left my phone in the car because I didn't want it to interrupt my interview. Kendall had sent me multiple texts wanting to know where I was. Crud, I forgot to call her about my interview. I picked up my phone and called her back.

"Hey, sorry I missed your calls, I was in an interview."

"Awesome, tell me all about it when you get to my house, Heather will be here in about 10 minutes."

"Okay, I need to run home and change, and then I will be over-so in about 30 minutes. Hold on, someone is beeping on the other line." I looked to see who it was…Jackson, my heart zoomed into full hyper speed.

"Umm…Jackson is calling, Kendall I will see you in a little bit."

"You are hanging up on me for Jackson, nice!"

I hung up on Kendall and answered Jacksons call.

"Hi," I said, could he tell my smile is beaming?

"So, how did it go, did she hire you on the spot and tell you they have an office in Texas?" His voice was animated and full of joy.

"No, she didn't hire me on the spot. I think the interview went very well. Do they have an office in Texas?"

"They do."

"Interesting…how is your day at work going?" My voice restrained a little.

"Fine, the usual day, being in the office is good, but I like to travel."

"I know you do…so umm…are you really coming out this weekend?" I was nervous and shy asking him.

"No, I can't I have a softball game on Saturday, and some family thing with my parents on Sunday. Are you disappointed? Tell me you are disappointed."

"Yes, I am disappointed." My heart sank a little, but the guy does have a life and just because all of a sudden my heart is skipping beats for him shouldn't make him change his plans. Remember simple- no strings.

"I will be out the following week, maybe make it a long weekend. Maybe you could stay with me at my hotel, when the conference is over?" Jackson asked with some hesitation in his voice.

"Jackson…I will think about it."

"I have to go, Kendall is going to kick my ass if I am not at her house in a few minutes."

"You sound out of breath, are you running?"

"Yes, I am running up the stairs to my bedroom and changing my clothes."

"Darlin'…umm…what are you changing into or out of?"

Did he want me to describe what I am doing…this is a side of Jackson I have never seen, or in this case heard, before.

"Hold on a second Sydney." I could hear him put his phone down and a door close.

"Okay, go ahead."

"Well, I am slowly unbuttoning my light blue blouse and taking it off. I am shimmying out of my pencil skirt. Now, I am sitting on my bed removing my very high heels and am lifting the silk camisole above my breasts and over my head." My voice was breathless. I could hear Jacksons breathing deepen, and him swallow.

"What are you wearing now?" He asked his voice sexy as hell, and his words were drawn out by his Southern inflection.

"Not much, a cream colored push up bra, and cream colored lacy matching panties."

The tension on the phone line was thick. I could feel myself pushing my thighs together.

"Jackson…What now?"

He was quiet, he softly spoke, "Is your hair up or down?"

"Down and I am sitting on my bed."

I could hear a knock on his door, "Crap darlin', I am sorry I have to go but thank you… you made my day. I will talk to you later."

"Bye," I said completely frustrated.

I flopped back on my bed still holding my phone in my hand. I need a cold shower, but I don't have time. I quickly put on some shorts and a tank top, and headed over to Kendall's.

I was at Kendall's just before she went into a hissy fit about me taking so long. I walked in the door and both Heather and Kendall gave me a dirty look.

"Sorry, it took longer than I thought to get home."

"You are such a liar, you were on the phone with Jackson. Believe me I am not going to complain, I have been waiting for you two to shack up for two years."

"Two years, weren't you still with Grant two year ago?" Heather asked, she seemed almost annoyed.

I looked at Heather, "Are you seriously getting upset at me over Jackson? I have never even kissed the guy, he and I have only been friends until today."

Kendall was jumping up and down and squealing like a little kid.

"What did you do?" Kendall asked smiling from ear to ear and clapping her hands together.

"I was very flirty with him on the phone yesterday and today. He said they are coming out next weekend and asked me to stay with him for a few days, after the conference is over." My smile was rather large across my face. Kendall was thrilled but Heather was not, not happy- not happy at all.

"Okay," I said, "Let's get the task at hand on track. Do you know where you want the wedding and reception? Can they be in the same place, that would be much easier?"

"One place is fine." The tone of Heather's voice was stern, she was not happy with me.

"Do you have a date, what if they can't do it on a Saturday are you willing to do it on a Sunday?" I asked as sweetly as can be.

"No, has to be a Saturday." More sternness from Heather.

"Flowers, candy, doves, what is your problem?" I asked her.

Heather got up from the table, she started pacing the room. Pulling her hair back into a ponytail and then letting it fall again.

Heather was yelling at me, only at me. "Sydney, are you crazy? Why are you getting involved with Jackson? He is all wrong for you. What are you thinking?"

I was completely blown away that Heather is so upset about me wanting to be with Jackson. She doesn't even know him, how could she think he is wrong for me? In Heather's eyes anyone but Grant is wrong for me. Grant left me, not the other way around.

"Heather, do you know how long it has been since I felt this way about someone or allowed myself to have these feelings. They were probably always inside of me just waiting to come out for him, but I wouldn't allow it. I am done depriving myself because I don't want to get hurt again. Jackson is probably the most wonderful man I have met in a very long time and he makes my body tingle with excitement."

Heather was rubbing her face and rolling her eyes at me. Shaking her head, "I don't agree, but you are a big girl and I am not going to tell you what to do."

"Okay, then shall we continue on with the planning of your wedding?"

I gave Kendall a look as if to say, "What the hell was that about?" Kendall shrugged her shoulders at me.

So, we determined the wedding location and secured a date by the end of the day. Heather was heading over to the country club to sign the contract and leave a deposit. We were meeting with the caterer and ordering the invitations in a few minutes. We still needed a florist, photographer, and music.

"Hey Heather, do you want a DJ or band?" Kendall asked before Heather left.

"DJ, no band- they are always unpredictable. Sydney, can I talk to you for a minute?"

I looked up at her, "Yeah."

"I am sorry for my reaction to your interest in Jackson, I just keep holding out hope that you and Grant, well you know. He will be at the wedding and I thought maybe the fire would reignite between you two." Heather's sincerity was overwhelming.

"Heather, I can't go down that road again. He broke my heart and I don't want...I just can't. Is he the best man?"

"No, Curt's brother is the best man, but he is in the wedding. I just have hopes you and Grant will figure this thing out between you two, I know you are meant to be," Heather said to me with worry in her eyes.

"I couldn't choose between you and Kendall, so I picked my cousin to be the maid of honor, I hope you guys aren't mad."

"Don't be silly, we are planning the wedding and are bridesmaids, we are happy to be a part of your big day," I said giving her a hug. "Just do me a favor, make sure Grant and I are not matched up as partners for the wedding. Okay?"

"I will do my best. See you wedding planners later."

After Heather left and I walked back to the kitchen where Kendall was sitting, I turned and looked at Kendall, "You know you are screwed, Heather is going to do everything in her power to make sure you and Grant are matched up at the wedding," she said.

"Yeah, I know. It will be fine. By the way I asked Jackson to escort me to the wedding."

Kendall's head popped right up from her computer, she leaned back in her chair crossing her arms over her chest.

"Sydney Stanton you are in deep like with Jackson, aren't you?"

"I do believe you are correct Miss Martin."

We fell into a laughing fit before we got back to working on the wedding.

CHAPTER 11

Kendall and I were in our element planning Heather's wedding. It was so much easier than any other event we had ever done. We arranged everything for her by the end of the first week. The next items were the wedding gown, bridesmaids' dresses, tuxedos- which Curt was in charge of, and the rehearsal dinner. Curt's parents told us what they wanted for the rehearsal dinner, and we arranged everything for that as well.

The invitations are going to be ready in two days, and we would have them out in the mail the same day, even if we had to spend all night printing the envelopes. Staying up late preparing for an event was nothing new for Kendall and me, we have done it countless times when preparing for Rush or a philanthropic event.

I haven't heard back yet from Yellow Bird, regarding my job interview, but I wasn't giving up hope. Jackson and Colby would be here some time next week, which had me filled with anticipation.

Kendall and I were meeting Heather at the bridal shop in a few minutes. I was waiting for Kendall to pick me up, sitting on the porch swing. I could feel my phone vibrating.

"Hello."

"Hi Sydney, it is Corinne Montgomery." I rolled my eyes.

"Hi Corinne, how are you?"

"I am good, listen dear, I want to congratulate you on your graduation. Kevin and I are very proud of you."

"Thank you."

"I was also calling to see if you would like to join us for our annual Fourth of July party."

"Corinne, you are very kind to invite me, but… I don't think it is a good idea."

"Sydney, we miss you… just come. We would love to spend some time with you."

"I miss all of you very much. I just can't… but we will see each other at the rehearsal dinner and the wedding." Tears were stinging my eyes.

"Grant will be here for the wedding you know?" Corinne's voice was laced with concern.

"I know, I am the wedding planner, I know all about it." I was trying to make light of the situation, but my stomach is beginning to do little flips making me feel sick.

"Sydney, can I ask you something and please don't get mad or offended?"

"Go ahead," I said, my stomach a ball of nerves.

"What happened between you and Grant?" What- she is his mother who knows everything, and she was clueless?

"Corinne, you should ask Grant. I can only give you my perspective. I don't want to go on about it so I will give you my short version. Grant goes to Europe, barely calls, never Skype's, comes home and still never calls, doesn't return my calls, emails, or texts. I fly to New York for a funeral and again, I try to get a hold of him with no response. The end."

"Sydney, I am sorry, I don't know what to say."

"Corinne, it is not your fault. It was bound to happen. The long distance thing, it was too much and him, and being gone for three months to Europe only pushed the break- up along. I just wish he would have had the respect for our relationship to face me, but he always meant more to me than I did to him. It is okay, it took me a long time to get over him, but I did it and moved on." Tears are now dripping down my face.

"Sydney, I am so sorry if I upset you. That was not my intention with this call." Her kindness has always warmed my heart, but hearing her voice making apologies was killing me. "I think you are wrong about how Grant feels about you, you are his life, he would move heaven and earth for you."

"Corinne, why are you using the present tense? I haven't spoken or seen him in two years. I am a different person and well, I have moved on."

"Sydney, what do you mean you have moved on? Are you seeing someone?"

"Corinne, I would rather not get into this with you. I adore you, but you are Grant's mother and it is not appropriate for me to discuss my love life with you. I have to go, Kendall is picking me up, and we are meeting Heather. Thank you so much for calling me, see you at the wedding."

I hung up before she could say anything else. Holy shit, why does she do this stuff to me? Now my eyes are stinging and she is making my feelings over Grant resurface. She does this crap on purpose knowing he and I will be in the same room together in a few weeks. She is a master manipulator. But I am on to her… not this time!

I was staring out the window of Kendall's car and she was going on about I don't know what- something with the florist.

"Hey are you even listening to me, earth to Sydney!" Kendall was almost yelling at me.

"Sorry."

"What is up with you today?"

"You are not going to believe who called me just before you picked me up?"

She was thinking, tapping on her chin.

"I don't know, um Trent?"

"Yuck…not even close, guess again?"

"Hint?"

"Fine, someone's mother?" I had my eyebrows raised way above my eyes, as I said it.

"Someone's mother huh, Heathers? No… are you kidding me… Corinne? What did she want?"

"Yes, the one and only Corinne Montgomery. She called under the pretense of wishing me congratulations for my graduation, and inviting me to their Fourth of July party."

"You are not going to go are you?" Kendall's face was twisted up with disgust over this discussion.

"I told her no. Then she asked what happened between Grant and me. Now, it is truly hard for me to believe she didn't know why it ended. She knows everything. I think she was fishing and then she felt the need to advise me Grant would be at the wedding. As if I

100

hadn't already known. I feel like I have been punched in the stomach." I let out a huge sigh of frustration.

"It will be fine. Jackson will be there to give you whatever support you need, and anything else you are willing to give… or take." I shook my head at her. Kendall was giggling with delight at her comment.

"Who are you? When did you become so free with your sexuality?" I said laughing at her.

"Colby- he brings out the best in me." We both laughed.

We walked into the bridal shop and Heather was tapping her foot at us.

"Calm yourself bridezilla," I said. "We are here, have you looked at any dresses yet?"

"Yes, I have a room full for me, and you two." Great, I can't wait to see what god- awful thing she is going to try to get us to wear.

"Before we step one foot further, Kendall and I have some demands; no floral prints, no dyed shoes, and no long dresses. Okay?"

"Fine, then you might as well look through the bridesmaids dresses over there." Heather said pointing to the other side of the store.

There were only three bridesmaids, including the on for the maid of honor. We ended up choosing a blue dress, called Malibu blue, it is flattering pleating all along the bodice and through the waist, and the neckline is strapless. It is timeless and will look great on all of us. Heather said we could wear any high heeled black strappy sandals we wanted. Heather found her wedding gown and she is set. Her gown is beautiful. It is a white, light shimmering satin, which sweeps across Heather's body draping to accentuate her curves, and strapless on one shoulder. It is embellished with beading around the neckline with a sweeping train. Curt's jaw will hit the floor when she walks down the aisle.

The bridal shop kept all the dresses to be altered, and we went out to lunch.

We were having salads at the café next to the bridal shop. Kendall is talking about the interview she has coming up with a big insurance company. Heather is day dreaming about her wedding and I am dying to know when Yellow Bird will call. Half way through our lunch my phone buzzed.

"Hello?"

"Hi Sydney, this is Mrs. Contreras from Yellow Bird, how are you today?"

"I am good, what can I do for you Mrs. Contreras? I said hoping, to get Kendall and Heather's attention. They both looked up at me holding my phone.

"Sydney, we would like to make you an offer to come work with us," she went on with all the details; salary, hours, benefits. Then she said, "There is only one part of the offer that is not negotiable, you are required to go for training for three to six months. Yellow Bird, will pay all your expenses during your training. We provide an apartment, rental car, food allowance, and your benefits start when you start your training. Are you interested? I hope so, we are eager to have you on board."

"I am, I accept your offer."

"Great Sydney, I will email you all the information."

"Mrs. Contreras, where is the training?"

"Oh, sorry dear, I guess I forgot that part, Texas. Is this a problem for you?"

My eyes were dancing with joy, my heart was beyond happy, and the smile on my face was gleaming.

"No, not a problem at all. When would I need to be there?"

"Two weeks from tomorrow."

"Okay, I just have one condition… I am in a wedding in the middle of July, will it be okay for me to leave for a long weekend?"

"Of course, I will note it in your file. Congratulations Sydney and welcome to the Yellow Bird family."

"Thank you," I said.

I hung up the phone, Kendall's jaw was on the table, and Heather had steam coming out of her ears. I was super excited, clapping my hands together with glee.

"What? You should be happy for me, I have a job, and they made a very nice offer." I am so excited I couldn't wait to share my news with Jackson. Damn, my mind goes straight to him.

Heather spoke first, "When do you have to be where?"

"There is a training program for a few months, I have to be there in two weeks." I said smiling.

Heather's brow was furrowed, "What about my wedding and the wedding plans?"

"Heather, we are almost done, we will have the invitations out in the mail in a few days and everything else is done, except the menu for the rehearsal dinner. Everything will be taken care before I leave, and you heard me ask her about taking a long weekend to come back for the wedding."

Kendall finally closing her jaw, "What do you mean come back, where is the training, oh my gosh… don't even say New York?" The tension in her face was clear.

"No, not New York…way better from my new perspective!" You could have lit up a room with the smile on my face.

"Shut up…damn you are a lucky girl, or maybe Jackson is going to be a man who gets lucky!"

"Yes… Texas!" I said.

Once back at home I called my mom at work and my dad on his trip, to tell them the exciting news. They were both more than overjoyed for me. They are planning another marathon vacation for the entire month of July. They are going to miss Heather's wedding, which is fine with me, I don't need my father going after Grant with a steak knife.

I couldn't wait to call Jackson, I checked the time, he should be off work by now.

"Hello darlin'," his Southern drawl thick as can be.

Damn him, his voice makes me shudder with need.

"Hello to you too, I have some exciting news."

"Yes darlin' do tell."

I had to clear my head for a minute he was distracting me.

"Guess what I got today?"

"A puppy, no- new shoes…darlin' I have no idea."

I started screeching and talking really really fast, "I got the job offer from Yellow Bird, I start in two weeks and the most exciting part is the training, full pay, benefits, but that is not the best part… the training is in …Texas!" I waited for his response, but he was silent.

"Jackson, did you hear me, I am coming to Texas for a couple of months, aren't you happy?" Shit I was wrong, he isn't interested in me in this way, Kendall was way wrong.

"Damn darlin' I am stunned, I didn't know they did their training here. You have no idea how excited I am, I can only imagine how wonderful it will be to see you, maybe on a daily basis. I just…are you sure this is what you want, this job and well… me?"

I was shocked by his candid remark. It took me a minute to respond.

"Jackson, I am sure… about both! So, are you coming here next week?"

"I am, how about when my conference is over instead of staying at the very non-descript business hotel I am forced into for my trips, we head to Palm Springs or the beach for a few days together? Will your parents mind if we go away together?"

"I am a big girl Jackson, and anyways they are leaving next week."

"Great then I will surprise you, I am not telling you which place we are going, just pack what you need for either one. Can we take your car so we don't have to drive around in an ugly rental car?"

"Sure, you let me know where and when to pick you up, okay?" My heart is thudding in my chest from the excitement. I couldn't wait for his hands to be all over me, and mine to roam his scrumptious body.

We ended our call a few moments later. I was elated. I put on a swimsuit and went for a swim in the pool. My mind is racing; a new job, new man, and a new place to live. I have never even been to Texas, having a layover in the airport doesn't count as actually going to there. I am sure it will be very different, good different, and the thought of Jackson at my fingertips sent my body into overdrive. The more laps I swim the less sexually frustrated I am sure I will feel.

I climbed out of the pool and lay down in the sun for some rest and tanning time. I put my headphones on, and listened to my favorite play mix on my iPod. My eyes closed quickly once I relaxed. My mind filled with thoughts of a Southern accent and warm hands rubbing tanning oil on my back. Thoughts of Jackson and me on a secluded patio, his hands brushing over my most sensitive parts, and him slowly untying my bikini. The sound of him breathing heavily in my ear, telling me how much he wants me, and whispering my name. Jackson turning me over onto my back, and pressing his hard body against mine. His lips opening my mouth - our mouths hot with need, his tongue roaming every crevice inside my mouth, and going down my neck…when I was startled out of my dream by loud noises around me. The whirl of a lawn mower and the whooshing sound of a blower had me jumping up from my lounge chair.

Damn it…I was having an amazing dream. How many more days until I am alone with that adorable Texan? I sulked my way into the house and changed in to shorts and a shirt. I looked at my wardrobe, it needs some serious help. This is a problem, better call Kendall for a shopping trip.

"Hey, want to go shopping? I need some more appropriate clothes for my new job." I asked Kendall.

"Speaking of new jobs I have a follow-up interview with the insurance company."

"That is terrific, when?"

"Tomorrow morning, so do you want to go shopping right now?"

"Yep, I will pick you up in 15 minutes, okay?" I told her.

"I will be waiting," Kendall said hanging up her phone.

I finished cleaning myself up, grabbed my phone, purse, and key, and headed to Kendall's. I knew she would be up for a marathon shopping trip. We do a lot of things very well, but shopping is in our blood.

Kendall jumped in my car, almost giddy. "You know Sydney, things are finally falling into place, not the way I would have thought a few years ago. But we are on track to have very happy lives." She kept her smile bright and cheery the rest of the way to the mall.

"So, is Colby coming to the wedding with you?"

"I do believe you are spot-on Miss Stanton."

"Spot on...you're getting so weird."

"What time are the invitations going to be ready tomorrow? Did you finish inputting all the addresses in to the computer so we can just feed the envelopes through and stuff them?" I asked her.

"Yes, umm... you know Grant is back in Arizona?" Kendall said very nonchalantly.

"Why are you telling me this? It is bad enough, I am going to have to deal with his arrogant ass in a few weeks, and now you have to bring him up on the way to go shopping?" I huffed at her.

"I just figured you should know is all, don't shoot the messenger."

"Why should I care? I am getting ready to go away with Jackson for a few days, I don't want Grant on my mind." These people are driving me crazy; Heather, Corinne, and now Kendall, are they trying to give me a nervous breakdown.

"Does Jackson know Grant will be at the wedding and rehearsal dinner?"

"I am not sure, I will have to tell him. I am assuming Jackson and I will fly back here together. I need to talk to him about a bunch of stuff. Are we going to stay in the hotel near the country club or at home?"

"I want to stay at the hotel, especially since Colby will be here, I don't want to have to sneak around at my parents' house," Kendall said.

"I hear ya'sister!" We high- fived each other on that as we walked into the mall.

We shopped until we dropped, I found a bunch of great clothes for work, updated my make-up, found some kick ass shoes and a new purse.

"Oh my gosh, this totally slipped my mind. I forgot, I got the oddest message on my voice mail. I saved the message, listen to this, you are going to die." Kendall was laughing while she grabbed her phone and found the message, she put it on speakphone so we could both hear it.

"Hi, I am looking for Kendall Martin or Sydney Stanton, my name is Belinda Hightower and I got your name from Ray at the 1st Street Florist shop. He said you are the best wedding planners around and I should see how much you would charge to help me plan my daughter's wedding."

The woman went on to leave her phone number and tentative date of the wedding. I looked at Kendall, what the hell?

"You know we always talked about running an event planning service, we could do this you know, on the side, to supplement our incomes. What do you think?" Kendall is definitely excited about this idea. I hadn't seen her this excited in forever, not since we decided to only apply to the same colleges.

"You are out of your mind, I am leaving in 10 days, and what if you get a job offer tomorrow, won't that require you to go for training in Boston?" I was shaking my head at her.

"Sydney, we planned Heather's wedding in less than a week without breaking a sweat, for free no less, I am talking about cold hard cash. We help her with the florist, location, photographer, DJ, and invitations. We tell her we will not be available on the date of the wedding. I think we should do it."

"How do we even know what to charge for our services?" This is a crazy idea, we always talked about this, but I never thought it would be something we would actually do.

"So, I was looking on the internet and we can charge anywhere from 10% to 20% of the wedding budget- depending on what they want us to do as the planners, or as consultants."

"Wow, you are really into this idea, what would we call our company, wait I am getting ahead of myself here, did you already call this woman back? Kendall, tell me you didn't already say yes?" Oh, I could see by the look on her face, she had already agreed to the job.

"Seriously, you get us into all kinds of crazy situations. When is the wedding and when are we meeting with our new client?" I was still shaking my head at her, but cash for the job sounded pretty good.

"So, I advised Belinda that we do this to supplement our income and we are only available in the evenings and weekends for meetings. I also informed in her that my partner Miss Stanton, would be out on an assignment for an undisclosed amount of time. She was fine with it. We are meeting with her tomorrow night."

My eyes were closed and I was rubbing them with my fingers, I could feel the tension coming up my neck.

"I think we need to stop for a drink, are you okay with stopping somewhere?"

"Sure, how about the barbeque place at the next corner?"

"Perfect."

We sat in the bar discussing the small business we were going to have, trying to decide what to call it. After a few drinks we thought of all kinds of stupid names. There was Kendall and Sydney's Events, Greek Goddess Events, We Love Texans, we laughed for ten minutes about that one. We kept on with ideas... Uppercrust Events, Fast Paced Events. Then I was looking at the staircase going to the banquet room of the restaurant.

"How about Uppercase Events? The logo could be the word uppercase in kind of fat short letters above the word events, and the word events would be in long skinny letters below."

"I love it, we have a name...Uppercase Events. We are in business."

CHAPTER 12

Kendall and I met with Mrs. Hightower, she was a bit high-strung about the impending wedding of her daughter. We assured her we could get everything done for her in a few days. She was very happy. She gave us a budget, the date, and the location. She was leaving on a business trip and her daughter was not in to planning. We advised her we could submit everything to her for her approval via email, as long as she responded immediately.

The next day Heather's invitations were ready, we picked them up and went to work; printing all the envelopes, stuffing the envelopes, and getting them weighed and stamped at the post office. It was late when we were done, but the invitations would be in the guests' mailboxes by the end of the week. We were officially done planning Heather's big day, now the countdown begins.

Kendall has been offered the position with the insurance company and is leaving a few days after me. I am leaving in less than a week, and we still have to get everything done for Mrs. Hightower. We met early the next morning and picked out three different invitations, a few centerpiece designs, bouquet designs, and met over the phone with the chef at the hotel where the wedding is to be held. We secured the photographer for the day of her daughter's wedding, as well as the florist. We sent all the information via email to Mrs. Hightower before noon, and then waited for her response.

We are tired.

"Can we take a nap on the couch in the TV room while we wait for Mrs. Hightower's response? I don't think I can keep my eyes open," I said to Kendall, yawning.

"Yes!"

We plopped down on the couch and closed our eyes; we left the lap top open with the email program up so we could hear when a message was received. We were both out cold within minutes. I had fallen asleep with my phone on my stomach. I was awakened by a vibrating and buzzing noise.

I didn't even look at the phone to see who was calling.

"Hello?" I said, my voice scratchy from sleeping.

"Sydney?"

"Yes, this is Sydney." I was still half asleep.

"Hi, it is Corinne. Did I wake you, I am so sorry if I did."

"No, it is fine, I need to get up, I have been swamped, what can I do for you?"

If she badgers me again about Grant I think I am going to scream.

"Well, Heather said you are moving to Texas, is this true?"

"Sort of, just for a few months of training and then I will be back here, based out of the Los Angeles office. Do you need something from me?"

It was never cut and dry with Corinne, she is always planning something.

"Well, Courtney is very upset that both you and Kendall are leaving before the wedding for work, and we just want to make sure you will be here for the wedding."

I am so annoyed with her implication. I sat up, hitting Kendall on the foot so she would wake up and listen to this conversation. She didn't move.

"Corinne... really? Of course we will be here, we may not be here for the rehearsal but we will be back, not to worry. We are Heather's best friends and professional party planners, we would never bail out."

"Oh, you have to be here for the rehearsal, that is the beginning of the great weekend, you can't miss the rehearsal."

I am completely awake now. Corinne is definitely up to something, I could hear it in her voice.

"Corinne, we will do our best to be here for the rehearsal, but we are both starting new jobs and coming by plane, so we will be at the mercy of the airlines and their flight schedules. What is this really about?" She is playing games with me and I am not about to let her get away with it.

"Are you planning on bringing a date to the rehearsal and wedding?" I rolled my eyes at her and hit Kendall in the leg again because she needed to wake up and hear this conversation, and I could see a message from Mrs. Hightower in the email.

"Corinne, do you really want to know, or are you fishing for information for your son?"

"Sydney, of course I am fishing for information but not for Grant. I want to know."

"I don't see why it matters… but yes, I am bringing a date to both events. Why does it matter to you? Grant will find someone else if he hasn't already and she will make you happy and give you more grandchildren. Please Corinne, just let it go, that ship has sailed. What Grant and I had is long gone." My head is hanging down and my heart has a long ache in it.

"It matters to me… it matters to Grant."

I sat straight up and I was starting to get mad, no I am mad.

My voice filled with frustration, "Listen Corinne, I loved him with every ounce of my body and soul, I gave him my heart more than once, and more than once he walked away. Not only walked away, he stomped on my heart, with no remorse. Please stop doing this, I have nothing but respect for you and Kevin, but every time you call me and bring up Grant it reminds me of the loss, and I just can't allow myself…I just need you to stop."

I couldn't handle any more of these conversations with Corinne, she is killing me.

"Sydney, I know I have upset you. I am sorry for Grant's behavior. I just wish…I just wish you would talk to him."

"Talk to him…are you out of your mind? The guy hasn't lifted a finger to call me in two years, and you shouldn't be apologizing for him. He is old enough to apologize for his own behavior. I know what you want to happen but it can't and it won't. I don't want to be rude to you but I need to get off the phone. Take care. Good-bye." I said hanging up my phone.

I am furious, my blood was boiling.

"Kendall, I have to go, I need to go for a run, or swim, or something. I will call you later so you can let me know what our client has decided."

I stormed out of the house and went home. Running will make me feel much better. Once I got home, I changed and headed out for a run. I set my iPod to my favorite mix and set off. When I finally returned home, I was drenched with sweat, I felt better- but not completely. I ripped off my shoes and socks, and started doing laps in the pool in my running clothes. I was wiped out when I was done in the pool, so I dragged myself into the house, and changed out of my wet clothes. My phone started buzzing at me.

I answered in a huff, "What?" I yelled into the phone. Obviously my workouts had not settled my emotions.

"Darlin' are you okay? You sound out of breath and out of sorts." Jackson, my calm in the eye of the storm.

"No, I am not okay. When are we leaving, I need to get out of here? I am turning off my phone, don't even let me answer it while we are gone." My words thick with frustration.

"That is why I am calling, we can leave tomorrow morning, does that work for you, darlin'?" I am beginning to settle down, just from the sound of Jacksons voice caressing my ears.

"Perfect, what time do you want me at the hotel?"

"How about 9:00 am? Listen darlin', I have to go finish up a dinner meeting, but I will see your sweet face tomorrow, and Sydney, you can tell me all about why you are so upset on the drive."

The morning couldn't have arrived fast enough. I spoke with Kendall last night, Mrs. Hightower picked out exactly what we predicted she would, bringing everything to a close. Kendall had ordered the invitations last night and would send the order to the florist today. I reminded her I was leaving with Jackson for a much needed escape.

I was more relaxed today after a good night's sleep. I headed up to Jackson's hotel and was waiting for him outside by the valet, leaning on my car. He came walking out in old faded jeans, which were riding low on his hips showing off his amazing body, his t-shirt, which was tight across his broad shoulders, gave an outline of more muscles. I could feel my body clenching as he stalked towards me. My breathing hitched the closer he came to me. We had been friends for a very long time, it was not that I had never noticed his great physique, or his hotter than hot good looks, but I must have had blinders on, because my body's response to him was terrifying.

"Hi darlin', are you ready to hit the road?" He is very close to me almost nose to nose. Well, he was bending his nose down to my nose. My pulse is racing, I hope he kisses me. I am lost in his eyes as he looks at me. I didn't say anything to him. I was concentrating all my energy on keeping my control. What I really wanted to do was throw my hands around his head and pull him down to me, and kiss his powerful lips.

He grabbed my hand, took my keys from my other hand, popped open the trunk and put his bag inside. He closed the trunk and leaned his back against the now closed trunk, never letting go of my hand. I watched him with big eyes and a smile that wouldn't quit. My breathing is deep as I tried to calm my pulse, but it wasn't working. He pulled me to him by the belt loops on my shorts, and excitement sprang through my body. His lips are hovering over mine, just barely touching. The tension is palpable. My tongue came out of my mouth and slowly licked my bottom lip, my breasts were rising and falling in my little tank top, I could feel his eyes wandering down from my lips to the top of my tank top. I swallowed hard, Jackson leaned in, his lips covering mine and his tongue was wickedly arousing in my mouth. I couldn't move- his kiss shook me to my core. I thought to myself, "This is going to be a great weekend".

We finally broke apart- Jackson led me to the passenger's door and set me in the seat. I was completely entranced by him. He climbed in on the other side of the car and took off down the street getting on the freeway heading out of town.

He reached over and grabbed my hand. I finally came back to earth. I smiled at him.

"Hi," I said to him coyly.

"Well, glad to see you have joined me, are you alright?" His words thick with his Southern drawl.

"Yes, more than alright, that kiss was...delicious," I said with a grin as wide as the Grand Canyon.

He smiled back at me.

"Where are we going?" I asked quietly.

"You will know soon enough. Did you pack a bikini?"

"Yes, two."

"Did you pack a nice dress, like I requested?"

"Yes, two." He smiled at my answer.

"Did you pack any surprises, for me?"

"If I say yes, then it won't be a surprise, will it?" I told him with an air of humor in my voice.

"Are you ready to tell me why you were so upset yesterday?" The worry lines showing on his face, even though he was smiling at me.

"No, I don't want to talk about it and ruin the good… very good mood, I am in."

"Let's just get it over with darlin', get it out of the way so it doesn't resurface over this weekend."

"Okay, well it is a combination of things. First off, I am super excited and nervous about going to Texas for my new job. Second, Kendall has decided she and I are going to keep doing this wedding planning stuff on the side to supplement our incomes. Third, Grant's mom keeps calling me and that is the most annoying part of my annoyance." I looked at Jackson for some kind of reaction. He was driving along, paying attention to the road, but I could see in his eyes his mind is thinking over what I just shared with him.

"Well, let's deal with your annoyances in order. Texas is going to be great, no need for you to worry. You are great, everyone will adore you, and you will be a great success for the advertising department at Yellow Bird. One down, two to go."

"You are sweet. Keep going."

"You and Kendall can do party or event planning in your sleep. I have seen you two do amazing things in less than 24 hours, so planning a wedding, and making some money is a no brainer, just keep on top of it and you guys might end up running the world!"

"Nice, you are good at this!"

Jackson looked a bit uneasy before he started talking about Grant's mom. I mean Grant is my ex-boyfriend, which Jackson knows, and knows every detail about our relationship, since I had confided it all to him over the last few years.

"I know this is a touchy subject for you, and now for us, because we are moving from the friend zone to the more than friend zone." I laughed a little and he kissed my hand, which gave me butterflies in my stomach. "Why don't you just tell me what is going on and then I can help you get through your frustrations."

"Okay, so you know Heather is marrying Curt in a few weeks, and Grant and Curt are cousins, which leads to the obvious point that Grant will be at the wedding." I looked at him for a reaction, he showed no reaction. He must have come to this conclusion on his own already. "Anyways, everyone is making a point to remind me of this on a daily basis, and treating me like a wounded puppy, or a mental patient that might breakdown once I see him. Then his mom has called me twice wanting to talk about him. Both times she asked if I was dating someone."

"What did you tell her, about dating someone?" His eyes were searching my face for a clue.

"The first time I told her my love life was none of her business and she shouldn't be asking, and the second time I said I was bringing a date to both the rehearsal dinner and wedding. I also said, we might not make it to the rehearsal dinner because we would be flying in from Texas. That brought up another issue for her - she tried to imply that Kendall and I are bailing out of the wedding for our jobs. Can you even believe that? I mean really, the woman has some nerve."

"So, how do you feel about seeing Grant again, after not seeing him for what, two years or so?"

"You know what I adore about you, you get right to the point, no pretenses, just go right in for the kill." I said to him.

"It is my killer instinct that makes me a success in business, I can read people, and you my darlin', are an open book."

"What does that mean?"

"It means you are a terrible liar, your facial expressions give away your emotions, and you are as cute as a button. Now stop avoiding my question... Grant, are you worried about seeing him again?"

"Of course I am worried. I am not worried about him trying to get me back. That is not an option. I know him, he will make a scene and try to embarrass me. He will do whatever it takes to upset me, to drive me crazy until he knows he has bothered me so much I want to smack him." My temper was starting to resurface. Grant wasn't even around and I was getting annoyed just thinking of the games he is capable of playing with me.

"Sydney, you tend to over think things. You have no control over his behavior but you have total control over your own behavior. Don't let him push your buttons and you will be fine." I scowled at him.

"Easy for you to say, you are super confident, handsome, and no one can resist your Southern charm." I squeezed his hand. "We have been driving for a long time, wait isn't this the way to Las Vegas, are we going to Las Vegas?" Jackson gave me his panty melting smile and I smiled back at him. I reached down in to my bag and grabbed my phone. Jackson was watching me.

"What are you doing?" He asked.

"I am turning off my phone, I told you the other day, I don't want to be bothered by anyone, so it can go to voice mail, and text messages can wait, this weekend is about us," I said as I put my phone away and grabbed his hand.

A huge smile came across Jackson's face, "Sydney, I will be by your side both nights. I will take care of you and help you keep control over your emotions. The only one I want you to concentrate on is me. After this weekend, and the weeks we have together in Texas, I will have you forgetting about all these so called annoyances." His words making my heart beat faster.

"You are so sweet, I just want to take a lick of you!" I said to him and he laughed at me.

"I like it when you are a little nasty, I can't wait to get to Las Vegas. I really liked when you said "we" are flying in together from Texas, it warms my heart," he said with a smile warming my heart.

"Well, I figure we will be flying together roundtrip from Texas and then back, right? I mean we don't have to if you don't want to." I said, trying to back pedal.

"Sydney, stop second guessing yourself. I was happy to be your friend, I always wanted more, but you were with Grant, and then you were emotionally unavailable. I understood, but we are going to see if the friendship we have created is the foundation for an amazing relationship."

He must have a playbook somewhere because I knew he was smooth, but geez, he is going to talk me out of my clothes in the elevator of the hotel. The drive to Vegas, was easy, and we arrived earlier than expected. We drove down the main strip passing hotel after hotel until we ended up in front of the Bellagio. Jackson, pulled up to the valet, and handed the him the keys to my car, and a bell hop came over to retrieve our bags from the trunk. Jackson took my hand and we walked over to the front desk to check in.

"Good Morning Sir, welcome to the Bellagio, how can we help you today?" The very happy desk clerk said, checking us out from head to toe.

Jackson smiled and in his thick Southern accent said, "Good Morning, we have a reservation under Jackson McCoy."

The clerk tapped on her computer keys.

"Yes, Mr. McCoy, I see your reservation, two nights, is this correct?"

"Yes."

"Unfortunately, you room is not ready yet, if you like we can hold your bags here and you are welcome to spend time by the pool or in the casino, is that okay?" The clerk asked.

Jackson turned to me, we knew we were early, but getting into our room had been a definite goal for us. Maybe waiting a little longer would only make the final consummation of our relationship that much better.

"Darlin', do you want to go to the pool, or head into the casino?" Jackson asked me, his eyes a bit sad.

"Pool sounds good to me."

"Great," the clerk said. "Would you like to take whatever you need from your luggage and then we will store it here? Check back with us in a few hours, and by then your room should be ready."

Jackson and I rifled through our luggage, I grabbed my bikini, and Jackson got his bathing suit. I pushed them both into my handbag along with some sunscreen, and we headed towards the pool. The clerk had given us a special guest pass to allow us access into the pool area and we walked hand in hand. When we arrived we were greeted by a pool attendant. The pool looks amazing, crisp cool water awaits us after the hot drive through the desert. The attendant asked Jackson if we would like a private cabana, we quickly agreed. The cabana is wonderful; fresh fruit, misters, rafts, stocked refrigerator, phone, TV, and anything else you want including a host who would get you anything. We went inside to change behind the curtains, which we closed. I changed into my suit first, while Jackson waited outside, then it was his turn. When he came out I was lying on the comfy lounge chair- in heaven.

"Darlin' your bikini is breathtaking…I mean you in your bikini is breathtaking." His words bringing a smile to my face.

I looked up at him from behind my sunglasses. I motioned for him to come to me. He squatted down next to my chair. I used my index finger to motion for him to come closer. When his lips were next to mine I gently gave him a sweet, seductive kiss. I could hear a deep manly groan come from him.

"Darlin' I am not going to make it if you keep giving me kisses like this," Jackson said, his hands caressing my face. I giggled at his response.

"I think you will make it, but if you feel out of breath I will be happy to give you mouth to mouth resuscitation."

"I like this side of you, all flirty, holding nothing back." Jackson's eyes were filled with delight and anticipation.

"Will you put some sun block on me, I don't want to burn?" I handed him the bottle of sunscreen. He squeezed it to his hands and began massaging the lotion in to my back, shoulders, down my arms, and down the back of my legs and thighs. It was just like my dream, but better because it was real. I must have let out a few soft moans from the touch of his muscular hands, I could hear his sigh as his hands roamed my body. He was massaging the top of my shoulders, saying he missed a spot.

He moved my long hair to the side and was spreading soft kisses along my neck. He whispered in to my ear, "I am so glad you agreed to come away with me this weekend."

I was lying with my hands crisscrossed under my head, my head turned to the side, so he could only see the side of my face. I responded with a huge smile and I blew him a kiss.

Jackson and I had become friends and shared secrets and details of our lives. We had known each other for more than two years and up until this morning, had never even exchanged a kiss. The kiss he gave me when I picked him up at his hotel left me with a longing for more. Seeing him in his bathing suit is heart stopping. I mean we have been swimming together before, but since I only saw him as a friend, his ridiculously sculpted body had not given rise to the feelings I was having now. His upper arms were defined, with round and chiseled muscles, from the top of his shoulders to his forearms. I started drooling from the view of his hard pecs, to the well-defined six pack his abs created. I actually think a little drool escaped my mouth, I took a sharp breath when he stood up next to me. Jackson turned to me when he heard it.

"Sydney, are you alright?" His sultry voice luring me further into my haze.

I am completely lost in the sight of him. His hair is tousled and perfect, his eyes are twinkling from the sun, and his skin is golden brown. His smile is as always warming to my heart.

"Sydney, do you need some water or a drink of some sort?" He is still talking but I am not responding. I could hear him laughing at me.

"I need something, but I don't think it is water!" I said my tone laced with seduction.

His eyebrows shot up and his head tipped back as he bit his lip and started to laugh.

"Damn darlin', you are killing me!"

"You're not the only one!" I said.

We stayed in our cabana most of the day. We ordered lunch and we discussed what we would do this weekend. We decided that tonight we would walk up and down the strip checking out the lights and sights. Tomorrow night we reserved tickets for the Cirque Du Soleil show and planned on checking out the nightclub in the hotel. I am glad I brought two different dresses for the weekend.

Late in the afternoon our very thoughtful cabana host advised us our room was ready, and our bags had already been delivered. He gave us our key cards, and directions to our room. Jackson had made friends with a few people in the pool, and we had played some volleyball with his new friends, which helped pass the time. It also helped keep our minds from wandering into lustville. Eventually, we were done hanging by the pool, and were ready to find our room. Jackson put his shirt on and I covered myself with my crochet cover-up, which really didn't cover anything. Jackson's hand was resting on my lower back as we rode the elevator up to the floor where are room was located.

My heart is racing in the elevator, and my pulse is bouncing off the walls. Jackson's breathing is staggered and his face completely flushed. Neither of us had drunk any alcohol by the pool, so we couldn't attribute any part of the day, or what was inevitably going to happen, to an alcohol induced moment.

We found our room and Jackson inserted the key card into the lock. He pushed open the door to a lovely room.

The room is decorated in rich colors of indigo and platinum. The king size bed rested on a raised surface, which is the central point of the room. There are two large side chairs by the window which give a beautiful view of the city. The bathroom is finished with fine materials, with a separate shower and tub.

As I am standing by the large window looking out at the view when Jackson walks up behind me placing his hands on my shoulders, rubbing his warm hands up and down my arms. Although the room was cooled by the air conditioning, my skin is hot from the hours of being in the sun, and Jackson's touch. I leaned my back against his chest allowing my head to rest on him. My heart is beating faster than it had in a long...I mean a long, time. Jackson leaned down and began kissing my neck with the same soft kisses he had given me earlier by the pool. My body responding with passionate sounds escaping from deep in my core, his hands now wrapped around my waist and resting on my stomach.

Jackson turns me to face him. Our eyes meeting, his mouth coming down and plundering mine, his tongue seeking, circling inside my mouth, I am gasping for breath when we pulled apart.

"Sydney…"

"Yes… Jackson?" I say, as I am barely able to speak.

"I don't want to do anything you are not ready for or wanting," his voice potent with desire and concern. His face tight with worry.

"Jackson, you are over thinking things, sometimes you have to take a risk and go after what you want." I said with playfulness in my tone. The worry lines on his face quickly fading, he lets out a manly chuckle.

He takes my hand and walking backwards, he sits himself down on the edge of the bed. I am standing in between his open legs, my hands around the back of his neck, and his arms are around my waist. His eyes are fixed on mine and my tongue is licking my lips. The heat between us is no longer from the sun, it is strictly body heat resonating from the lust surrounding us. He slowly moves his hands down to the bottom of my cover up, lifting the bottom, pulling it up, I raise my arms, and he tosses it on to the chair behind us.

I am standing before him in just my little bikini which didn't leave much to his imagination. I reach my hands down to the bottom of his shirt and repeat the same steps he did to me, removing his shirt, and tossing it on the chair next to my cover- up. My hands begin to maneuver their way around his upper body, feeling each muscle, each piece of soft yet rugged skin. Jackson's hands are caressing my backside. His shoulders are tense with anticipation, and his breathing is sporadic. With each stroke of our hands, our bodies begin to move together, and our lips are inching closer and closer, until the force of desire pulls us together.

Our mouths are all over each other, no part is untouched. We are still in the same position- him sitting on the edge of the bed and me in between his legs. He unties my bikini top and it falls to the floor. He lifts me up by my waist and turns himself, putting me down on the bed. He strips off his bathing suit and pulls me the rest of the way up the bed. His fingers are tracing around my nipples, followed by the wetness of his tongue. The sounds coming from me and him are enough to get me off. I could feel my wetness pooling in my bikini bottom. His eyes are wandering up and down my body, stopping at certain key points to lick and kiss. First each breast, then my belly button, which he sucks and slurps on, and then back up to my neck. He sucks on each earlobe until my body is completely tortured. He repeats these actions multiple times, until my head is thrashing on the pillow and my hips are grinding on him and arching up to him.

"Jackson, are you enjoying torturing me?" I asked through bated breath.

"It is not torture, I am getting you where you need to be," he said his voice hot with emotion.

It wouldn't take much and I would be over the edge. Just one touch of his hands or fingers inside of me, and I will come. Jackson must have read my mind because his hands are finally seeking out the part of my body which is aching for him. His hand slid under my bikini bottoms.

"I hope you have another bikini, because this one is not going to make it.'"

He rips my bikini bottoms off and his fingers... oh God, they feel so good. First one was inside me, and his palm was resting on my clit, pressing down just enough. My hips are grinding against his hand seeking release. I am there, my breathing picks up, and I begin to moan from the pleasure.

"Don't stop...Jackson, whatever you do...don't stop." I am flying, my hips are uncontrollably grinding and moving from the intense release.

Jackson's fingers keep up the invasion of my body and he is kissing me with such intensity I think I might climax again. He reaches for something from the nightstand, the long forgotten sound of foil ripping makes my body tighten and my excitement pool between my legs. He covers himself with the condom, resting his lengthy erection at my entrance. He looks deep into my eyes, and sees my acceptance of him, my want for him.

His hardness enters me slowly, the penetration is wonderful, and his thrusts into me are mind blowing. He is thrusting inside me, his arms and hands around my head, his chest against my bare breasts. The closeness was staggering. My mind is full of him, and his body... our bodies moving as one.

"God, you are so tight around me, you feel amazing," he says through gritted teeth.

He is relentless, his thrusts not stopping. My nails are digging deep into the back of his shoulders and he is beginning to show signs of reaching his peak. I am holding onto my control, but I am way past the point of control. I come again, with screams of his name and erratic breaths. Once I am flying, Jackson lets loose, the sound of his moans as he comes inside me are earth shattering. His body vibrating from his intense release as he quietly says my name over and over until he collapses on top of me, kissing my lips.

We lay together silent for a few moments, regaining our composure. Jackson is next to me, his hand on my stomach, resting. My thoughts are off in another time and place. I am lost. I never thought I could have this feeling with another man. Grant had taken me to places sexually that I believed only he could get me to, but now Jackson is giving me unbelievable sex. Not just sex- but over the top hot sex. My heart hurts a little with thoughts of Grant coming to the surface.

I turn on my side and look at Jackson who is intently watching me. My eyes are filled with what I believe is deep like for this man.

"Thank you," I said to him, my finger outlining his face.

"I think the feeling is mutual! Are you ready to go again?" He teases.

I smile at him, "Give me five minutes."

His eyebrows go up and down and his smile widens.

"Sydney…" his voice deep and somewhat serious, I look at him as he continues, "You have made me so happy, I have wanted you for so long, and this made the wait all worth it."

"I am sorry. Was it hard for you to be my friend and not touch me?"

"No…yes…sometimes, especially when we would be playing something where we would need to touch, like swimming… or when I tried to teach you to shoot pool. That was by far the worst." He is laughing remembering my pathetic attempt to beat him at pool, not even knowing how to hold the pool stick.

My fingers are running up and down his arm, his lips come over me, and we are kissing again, his fingers moving down under my bottom, and then around to touch my sex.

"Yes," I say telling him, I am ready.

That is all he needs, he grabs another condom and is pulling me on top of him. It didn't take much, me grinding on his full length which is even deeper inside of me with him underneath me. His fingers pressing and fondling my clit, it takes only moments before I am spiraling out of control from my orgasm. Jackson follows right behind me, bucking me with force as his body soars around mine, in a white cloud of ecstasy.

My body is depleted of all strength. Jackson scoots out from under me to dispose of the condoms and use the restroom. I watch him walk back across the room from the bathroom and stop to look out the window. His back is to me...geez...he has a fine back side. Is that a tattoo on his ass? I start to laugh. He comes back with some water, climbing back into the bed with me.

"Are you laughing at me?" He asks with raised eyebrows.

"I am not laughing at you, but what is that on your ass, is that a tattoo? We have known each other forever and you never told me about the tattoo. What gives?"

"I try to forget about it, a drunken night in college, and a dare by my friends. You know stupid guy stuff," he says almost embarrassed.

"Turn over and let me investigate this tattoo." Jackson turns over onto his belly and I climb on the back of his legs to see. On his left cheek is a small capital "A" then a large bold capital "T" and another small capital "M". I start laughing at him. I slap his ass really hard.

"Shit darlin', that hurt," he says jumping up and pulling me under him. I am still cracking up.

"I cannot believe you have the letters for Texas A & M tattooed on your ass. I hope you were really drunk when you did that, but I am glad it is not some girl's name." He is laughing now because I couldn't stop laughing.

"Are you telling me you would be upset if I had branded myself with another woman's name?"

"I would be more than upset, I would be pissed," I say squinting my eyes at him.

"Possessiveness already? We have only had sex twice and you are claiming me, I like it." He says kissing my neck. "Do you have any tattoos?" He asks me.

"Absolutely...NOT! I would never do that to myself, I don't want to be all old and wrinkly with tattoos, that is just gross. Ear piercing is as wild as I get." I tell him.

"So…you are telling me if we fall madly in love, marry and have twenty kids together, you would never brand yourself with my name, even if I asked you too?" I could tell he was joking but his eyes showed some truth in his question.

"Yes, never…I wouldn't care how much you begged or tortured me, no tattoos for this girl!" I was tickling Jackson on his sides as he poked my chest.

"What is our plan, it is late already, do you want to walk the strip or stay in and order room service?" Jackson's eyes were searching mine.

"I vote for staying in, ordering room service, and discovering if you have any more tattoos! I can see everything from the window I need to see of the city."

My desire for Jackson was insatiable as was his need for me.

The next evening we had reserved tickets for the 7:30 performance of Cirque Du Soleil. I am glad I packed a fancy dress. I finished doing my hair and make-up and came out of the bathroom with a towel wrapped around my body.

"Darlin', we are never going to get out of this room if you walk around in a towel all the time."

Jackson grabbed my hand and pulled me on to his lap. His hands were reaching under the towel and he is kissing my jaw. I could feel my sex start to drench for him.

"I want you," I whispered in his ear, my hands roaming down into his boxers.

"Take me then, we can be late to the show… or not go at all," his Southern charm making me move my body to straddle him.

He opened the towel which was covering my naked body. He took one breast in his mouth and sucked so hard I thought I would come right then.

"Jackson, you make me so hot with your mouth." I was clawing to get his boxers off. The sight of his erection made my lust for him uncontrollable.

"Darlin', if you don't hurry up and sooth my fire for you, I am going to pin you to the ground and we will never make it to the show. I promise you that you won't be able to walk when I am done!" His words filled with force and demand.

"I am not stopping you, pin me then." I said looking directly into his eyes with my own demands.

He swiftly picked me up and put me down on the bed, turning me onto my stomach, and pulling my legs back to him.

"I wasn't kidding, you will not be able to walk when I am done ravaging your body." His words shot right through me, I could barely swallow. My heart was pounding out of my chest, my nipples were hard, and my sex was aching for him to enter. Jackson's chest was rising and falling with hard breaths as his enormous length penetrated me. The feeling of demand coming from him was exhilarating. He was hammering me from behind, the sensations coursing through my body were divine, my need for him was like no other. I couldn't get enough of him, his strong hands holding my hips in place, the sweat dripping from his chest on to my back with each thrust.

"Darlin'...oh...God...you feel good..." his words pushing me up to a higher plateau.

My world blew up in front of me, flashes of light and sparks behind my closed eyes. I was pushed so high I didn't even hear my own words coming out of my mouth. Jackson, shuddering behind me with groans of male dominance and bliss. He pulled out of me and picked me up cradling me in his arms on the bed.

"Darlin', what you do to me is beyond my wildest dreams."

I kissed his cheek and then looked over at the clock. I started kissing his mouth and we fell back on to the bed in a tight embrace.

"I think we missed the show," I said. I didn't even care, I wouldn't have been able to make it through the entire show without my hands on him, or his hands on me.

"Are you mad?" Jackson asked.

"Absolutely not, this was a way better way to spend our time then sitting next to each other counting the minutes to taking off each other's clothes again!" I said, as my hands moved along the path of his ridiculously hard stomach.

"Do you want to get dressed and go downstairs to have something to eat, and go into one of the clubs?" I got very excited and jumped up from the bed.

"Yes, that sounds fun, but you have to promise to dance with me."

"It would be my pleasure to dance with you darlin'," Jackson said kissing the top of my head. I went to the closet to find my dress. Jackson went to wash up.

The dress I brought was a light blush color, with a tie halter neck which had a gathered bodice, and layers of swinging fringe which cover the skirt. I put on my strappy shimmering silver high heels, fixed my make-up and was ready to go. The glow on my face would be apparent to even a stranger. Jackson finished dressing in black jeans, crisp black button down shirt, and black loafers, he looks hot.

We walked to the elevators, his hand splayed flat against my lower back, and I am happy- truly happy. I haven't felt this alive in what seems like forever. We stood in the elevator, with his hand still on my back, and when the elevator arrived at the casino floor, Jackson steered me towards one of the quieter bars. We headed in and were seated at a small table. Jackson ordered some appetizers for us to share, a scotch for himself, and a pomegranate martini for me. Jackson was holding my lipstick and ID in his pocket since I didn't bring a purse with me. Of course I was carded by the waitress. I handed him back my ID and he laughed at me.

"Nice picture, how old were you when you had this photo taken?"

I scowled at him, "Sixteen, should I get a new picture done?"

"No, I like it...you are so young...innocent..." Jackson was looking at the picture and then to me.

"What? Don't make fun of me, I was sixteen, give me a break."

"I like the braces...but you haven't changed that much."

"Whatever, so when we are done with our snack, where to?" I asked him. "Dancing I hope."

"Yes dancing, I know you want to get out on the dance floor and move. How about we go to the nightclub here, have you been to it before?"

"No, have you?" I asked, interested to hear his response.

"Of course! Colby and I go dancing together every time we are here for a convention,." He said laughing his ass off.

I took a small sip of my martini, and I gave him the evil eye.

"I am sure you two do many things together, I just didn't know you two got down and dirty like that, but these are modern times and if you go both ways, then that is your choice!" Jackson almost choked on his scotch when he heard my words.

"Not...funny...I only go one way, your way darlin'!" A mischievous grin appeared on his face.

We both laughed. When we were done with our drinks, Jackson signed the bill, charging it to our room, and escorted me to the club.

I excused myself to the ladies room for a moment to fix my hair and lipstick. We walked up towards the club and there was a huge line. I started to get in the line.

Jackson pulled me by the hand, "What are you doing? We are not waiting in line."

I looked at him with a stunned face, "What do you mean, how else are we going to get in the club?"

"Darlin', you know it is not what you know, but who you know, and I know everyone!" he said., I was surprised, by his comment. I mean, I know he is a successful businessman, but I didn't realize he had friends in high places. He sauntered right up to the bouncer at the door, smacked the guy on the back, and they shook hands like old friends. So, I guess they are old friends. "Hey Dirk, good to see ya, how's it goin' tonight?"

"Jackson, nice to see you again man, coming to the club tonight?" The bouncer asked him.

"I was hoping to go in with my girl Sydney," he pulled me close to his side. "Is it slamming busy in there?" Jackson asked the bouncer.

"You know, a couple of bachelor parties, and girls in their short short dresses, it is a guy's wet dream tonight! But you guys are in, just let me see her ID?" Jackson pulled my ID out of his pocket and showed the bouncer that I was over twenty-one.

"Jackson, robbing the cradle...keep an eye on her in there, it is going to get out of control tonight." The bouncer said to him.

"Hey, thanks, see you later." We walked into the club, the music was at a deafening volume. Jackson was holding onto my hand with a tight grasp. He weaved his way towards the bar and ordered us each a shot and a beer, knowing I prefer a beer over another fruity drink. We did our shots and then turned our attention to the dance floor.

Jackson was yelling in my ear, "Finish your beer and then we dance!"

I shook my head no, what was the point in yelling? I was looking around the club. The place was packed. It was hard to tell the décor, because literally there are bodies moving everywhere; servers delivering drinks, people partying, multiple bachelor parties, and people all over the place. The only thing I could make out of the décor is the mood lighting along the floor and above us around the ceiling. What did catch my attention were the loud, and somewhat obnoxious, bachelor parties going on in the club. Did those guys actually have strippers with them? I think they did. I nudged Jackson to look at them. But he didn't have any clue what I was talking about.

We ordered one more shot each, and finished our beers. He took my hand to lead me to the dance floor. I couldn't even tell what song was being played by the DJ. I could feel the beat of the music, the few drinks I had this evening were quickly taking effect, and my inhibitions were quite loose. There was not much room to move on the dance floor, which was fine with me. Having Jackson's hard body pressed against mine is totally arousing.

Jackson tucked me in close to his chest wrapping one arm around my waist as we began to move in unison. Our bodies moving like molten lava, and our eyes are glued together. I turned around to put my back against his chest. He is holding me to him with his hand wide on my stomach. The grinding of our bodies was hypnotic; the rhythm of the music and our hot bodies is captivating. My eyes were closed as we danced, I could feel Jackson's lips pressing on my neck and stimulating my arousal. I could feel beads of sweat beginning to run down my back. I looked back at him, turning my head up to his lips. He stamped his lips on my mine. My hips continued to rub on Jackson, causing I am sure, immense discomfort based on the bulge I could feel in his pants.

I turned around in his strong arms, I pulled his head down and gave him a passionate kiss, then continued to dance with seductive grace. My body was riding his in public and I didn't care. No one was watching us and everyone else on the dance floor is dancing much more provocatively than us.

"Darlin', you are going to make come in my pants if you keep dancing like this," he said in my ear.

I smiled salaciously at him and grabbed his head, pulling his lips to mine. When I finished kissing him, I shouted into his ear, "I am so wet already from your touch."

He slipped his hand under the front of my dress, his eyes got wide with excitement realizing I had no panties on underneath my dress, and he pressed one finger inside of me, my head tilted back and I moaned. Not that anyone could tell, it was a dancing orgy in this club. I wrapped one leg around his waist, I could feel his erection almost breaking through his pants. He removed his hand and licked his finger, which made me ache for him.

"You taste…mmm… good," he said into my ear, his eyes had turned from their normal brown to a lusty black. My ache for him was not going to pass. My leg was still wrapped around his waist and I was panting with desire for him. I felt his hand go back under my dress and this time, two fingers were inside of me, he was making me crazy, he was not going to be happy until I came for him right here in this damn club. I must have drunk much more than I thought because, I didn't care. It was as if we were all alone, I could only see him and the music was background to my need for him.

His fingers and palm were doing a number on me, my breathing was ragged and I could barely stand. He thrust his fingers in and out of my sex until he saw my eyes roll back in my head and I screamed out his name. He removed his hand from under my dress and I lowered my leg. My heart was racing as I watched him suck on both fingers and then kiss me. He pulled me close so my heaving breasts were pressed against his chest.

"Darlin', you are out of this world… hot…if we don't leave this minute I am going to fuck you in the bathroom." I looked up at him with eyes full of lust, and he led me out of the club.

As we were walking out something, or should I say someone, caught my eye in the corner of the club. If I wasn't in a complete drunken stupor and lust filled haze, I could have sworn I saw Curt and Noah, in my peripheral vision. I shook my head and continued to walk behind Jackson. Just before we were out the door of the club, I got the chills as I felt a hand pass over my back. When I turned to look, I only saw a sea of people. But the shivers that went through my body were oddly familiar.

Jackson and I barely made it back to our room without having sex in the elevator and hallway. I thought Jackson was going to break down the door to our room when he tried to unlock the door with the key card. He was so flustered he kept putting the key card in upside down. Sooner or later we got the door open, and he had me pinned to the wall. I pushed him towards the bed. I pushed him down onto the bed and climbed up him, straddling his body.

"What you did to me in the club was…exhilarating, but now you will get my retribution," I said with unwavering nerve. His smile was heart stopping.

"You loved it, you came all over my fingers, I would do it again if you ever let me," his Southern drawl soaking my ears.

I climbed over him kissing him, smothering my mouth over his. I kissed down his neck unbuttoning his shirt. I kissed his hard chest and licked my way down his chiseled stomach, my hands unhooking his belt, then the button on his jeans, and lowering the zipper. Jackson lifted himself up so I could get his jeans off, he toed off his shoes, and I pushed his jeans down to the floor. He was left on the bed clad only in his boxers. I straddled him and began a torturous unrelenting attack on his body. My hips were moving -undulating over his erection. He was moaning and trying to hold me still by my hips. I then took off his boxers, grabbing his ample erection in my hand, and stroked him. I took my tongue and licked the underside of his penis until he was begging for me to stop. I put him inside my mouth, sucking as hard as I could, and stopping every few moments for no other reason than to punish him for his actions in the club.

Ultimately Jackson lost his control, and grabbed me by my upper shoulders. He pulled me over him and pressed me into his chest, flipping me onto my back.

"Enough!" He seethed at me. "I have learned my lesson."

"I wasn't done, yet," I clamored to get back to him. He pushed me down on the bed with his body. He was out of control with desire for me, and pinned my hands above my head with one of his hands.

"Stop," I said. I was thrashing about trying to get out of his grip. Knowing I would not win at this, but I didn't want to give in- I kept up my frustration as a rose.

Jackson grabbed a condom and put it on, I was eyeing him from under my eyelashes. I couldn't wait for him to be inside me again. He pushed my dress up and out of the way. Jackson pushed into me with such force I gasped at the feeling of his heated thrust. He would pull out just enough to make each thrust full of force until I was screaming his name.

"Just do it!" I yelled at him, "I want to come and I want you to make me come right now!"

Jackson smiled at me, "Happy to oblige darlin'." He kept up with fast thrusts, biting my nipples until my sex tightened around him and he felt my nails dig into his shoulders. Then he kept up his pace until his body was quivering from his orgasm. We were in another world, grunting and moaning from the feel of our bodies. He rolled onto the bed not letting go of my body. He kissed my forehead and I swear I heard him mutter something like, "You are the best, I can't live without you."

I am not sure what time it was when we fell asleep in each other's arms. I drifted into dreamland. When we woke in the morning, the light was coming through the window.

"Damn flippin' sun," I heard Jackson cussing and moving into the bathroom.

I stretched my body from the wild night we had together. My body is aching from being bent in different ways. Wild weekend was probably a more appropriate statement. Jackson came out of the bathroom, he looked perfect of course. With his hair tousled, his boxers riding low on his waist. He climbed back into bed with me, kissing my cheek.

"Good morning darlin', are you sore today?" His hands tickling up and down my arm.

"Yes, very sore you sex God," I said snuggling up to him.

"Sex God and sweet enough to lick, the things that come out of your mouth are so cute," he said laughing and pulling me closer to him. "You know you can live with me while you are in Texas? Fort Worth is not very big, you can get to your office from my house in less than 30 minutes, so what do you think?"

It was a fabulous idea, but I am not ready to live with him, I need my own space to be my own person, and I don't want to make the same mistakes I made with Grant. I was running my hands up and down his arms as he held my back to his chest.

"Jackson, thank you for the offer, but I think we should have separate places to live. You have your own life in Fort Worth and I will be busy with training. Now that Kendall has us running "Uppercase Events" I will need space for everything, and you go away on business so often, I would not feel comfortable being in your home without you." I hope I was as nice as possible I didn't want him getting upset, and stomping around mad at me.

"I understand, but if you change your mind my door is open. Is "Uppercase Events" the name of your party planning company?"

"Yeah, do you like it? We came up with it after a few drinks at a bar one night."

"It is catchy… you will be a success at both Yellow Bird and with Uppercase. I am selfish though, I am more excited to have you close to me than about anything else."

"You're so sweet Jackson, how often do you go out of town? I mean, will we be seeing each other everyday or do you leave for weeks at a time?"

"Don't you know my schedule by now, I mean we have practically been dating for two years?"

I looked at him funny, "What do you mean? We just kissed for the first time two days ago."

"Darlin' seriously, we have been talking on the phone almost every day and seeing each other every few weeks for over two years. Call it what you want, but I know you better than any other girl, I mean woman I have ever dated. So, I am saying we have been dating for all this time." His smile was beautiful, he was proud of himself for coming to this conclusion.

"I guess...you are right, I have shared more about myself with you than anybody, you know my dreams, wishes, and sordid past. But if you tell anyone about what happened in the club last night, I will cut you off for a very long time." I gave him a death glare.

Jackson started laughing at me, not afraid of my feeble threat.

"Darlin', it will be our secret and I know you will never cut me off. You want me too much, I see how your eyes drink me in and your thighs press together when I touch you."

"Jackson McCoy, you are nothing but a Southern devil in disguise."

Jackson came over me and took me in his arms, making love to me one more time before we needed to head back.

On our drive home said, "You could have flown back to Texas from Vegas and then I would have just driven home by myself."

"Don't be ridiculous, I wasn't going to let you drive back by yourself, plus it gives us more time together. I know, don't say it...I am sweet."

"Yes, yes you are!"

The weekend together in Vegas was exactly what I needed, and being with Jackson seemed right. I could feel myself slowly allowing my heart and body to feel what I had so long ago put away. Feelings of adoration, comfort, deep like, and very hot sex. I am not even close to going in the love direction. Jackson is amazing on so many levels, but my life is so complicated right now. The thought of giving my heart to him is just not an option right now.

Jackson drove straight to the airport for his flight back to Texas. We were early for his flight, so he pulled into the parking garage.

After parking the car we turned towards each other. He took my hand in his, and looked deep into my eyes. I could feel the depths of his feelings touching the corners of my heart.

"Darlin'…this weekend, well the last few years…what I am trying to say without sounding like a complete idiot is - you mean so much to me. I know we started out as friends, but now we have brought our friendship to a new level. I hope that while you are in Fort Worth you will allow me to show you how great we will be together. Not me just flying in every few weeks and spending 24 hours together rather, a real relationship with commitments to each other."

Commitments, did he say commitments? I am not ready for a commitment, my life is filled with uncertainty and Texas is only for a few months. OH SHIT…I don't want to hurt his feelings or offend him. I really truly like him, but I am not ready for a commitment. Jackson kept talking which was good, because I had no idea how to respond.

"I know what I said is a lot and I know you asked me earlier about my travel schedule but…I have to be honest with you. I travel a lot; once a month to Arizona, two times a month to California, and usually a few trips to Nevada, and all over Texas. So, sometimes I am on the road for more time than I am at home. I know this raises concerns for you, but you will see you won't be neglected." Jackson took a deep breath when he was done.

I looked at him and squeezed his hand. I didn't want to lie or give him false hopes, our relationship has always been based on honesty, and I wasn't going to ruin it by starting to lie.

"Jackson, I adore everything about you, your smile, your good heart, your Southern accent, and how well you know and understand me." He looked at me waiting for the "but".

"But… your schedule and mine are going to complicate what we have. You are so busy with your career and I will be in training, not to mention party planning. Can we take it all on a daily basis and see what happens? I do want to be with you, I just…I am not ready for a commitment, do you understand?"

Jackson tensed at my words, I am sure it was not the response he hoped for especially since we had such an intimate weekend together. I didn't know what life would be like in Texas and I needed to protect myself, my heart… even from Jackson.

"I understand, take it day by day, see how we fit together in our daily lives, right?"

"Exactly, you get me, I am lucky…so I will see you Friday or Saturday when I get to Fort Worth?" I looked into his eyes hoping to see them twinkle a little.

"No, I will be in Arizona until Sunday, I have to check my itinerary." As he finished speaking, I could see he knew what I said was true about our lives being so busy and complicated.

He gave me a long kiss and hug before grabbing his luggage and heading into the airport. I climbed into the driver's seat and decided it was time to turn my phone back on. I sat in the car replaying the weekend in my head. What a weekend, Jackson is the ultimate guy; gorgeous, hot body, smart, sweet, caring, thoughtful, driven, successful, and if I wanted, he could be all mine.

My phone started blowing up. I listened to my voice mail first. Ten messages, geez, no doubt all from Kendall and Heather. Well most of them were from Kendall and Heather wanting to know where Jackson had swept me away to. But there was one interesting message from a friend of Mrs. Hightower's, a Mr. Carlisle.

I would wait to call this Carlisle guy back in the morning. Considering it was a Sunday, they could wait. I pressed Kendall's number and heard the ringing come through the bluetooth before I headed home. I turned the radio on in my car, while I waited for her to answer, "Come Over" by Kenney Chesney was playing softly in the background when Kendall finally answered her phone.

"Damn Sydney, where did Jackson take you to, no cell service there?" She said with an annoyance in her tone.

"Sorry, I turned off my phone, didn't want to be interrupted by my interfering friends."

"So, are you two a couple now or did his hot body not meet your standards?" The sarcasm was more than noticed.

"I don't kiss and tell."

"Yes you do. So is he as good as he looks?" I could almost hear the drool coming out of her mouth as she spoke.

"Kendall seriously, Colby has made you so loose. He is well, more than I could have imagined. This weekend was…well perfect!" There I said it, I admitted it- perfect.

"Interesting, is that all you are going to say about the weekend… it was perfect? Nothing more?"

"Nope, nothing more! So, besides the 5 messages you left on my voice mail, Mrs. Hightower called and wants us to plan a surprise anniversary party for some friend of hers and there was also a message from a Mr. Carlisle. Do you know anything about either of these?" I hoped she had received calls from them both and knew what was going on.

"Yeah, I spoke with Jean, Mrs. Hightower. She wants us to call her Jean now."

"Okay."

"The anniversary party is not for a few months, so we have time but I did secure the location for her and she has given us a budget, as well as an advance, to purchase the invitations and do everything based on her requests. She has basically given us carte blanche to plan the party." I could hear the excitement in Kendall's voice.

"Wow, this is great. Will we need to come home for the party?" I asked, not even sure of the date or where I would be at that time.

"Yes, she has requested we both be there to deal with the vendors. I told her it would cost her, but she didn't care. This woman is going to get our business booming. She has already given our name to half a dozen of her friends. And Sydney, I had business cards printed for us."

"What? You're out of control, I thought this was going to be a once in a while thing, now we have business cards?"

"Well, the florist asked for some, and then I figured all our vendors should have them, and Mrs. Hightower is a walking billboard. That woman knows everyone from San Diego to San Francisco."

"What about this Carlisle guy, do you know anything about him?" I asked her.

"Nope, no clue, call him tomorrow. I have to go, I have stuff to do, call me after you speak to Carlisle." She hung up before I could say anything else.

I was exhausted when I got home to my empty house. I am not complaining but geez, it is so quiet here. I was too tired to call Heather back, I headed upstairs and crashed on my bed.

CHAPTER 13

I woke up early this morning, having a good night sleep does wonders for the body and soul. I took off for a long run, to clear my mind for the long day ahead. I need to call Heather and see what wedding drama she is having. Then I will call back this Carlisle guy. I have a million errands to run before leaving on Friday for Texas, which was scaring the shit out of me in more ways than one. I listened to my favorite artists and tried to keep thoughts of seeing Grant out of my mind. In less than three weeks, we would be in the same room together for the first time in well, what seemed like forever, and no doubt with his mother underfoot, things would get interesting.

Jackson's face was also forefront in my mind as I ran back up the very steep hill to my house. His sweet smile warmed my heart as I pictured him next to me naked in bed. Okay, get off this train of thought before you can't run anymore because of your need for him. I shook off all thoughts, and ran as fast as I could back home. As I was running, I replayed some of the weekend in my mind. I kept going to a certain memory from the club, but I couldn't figure it out, someone had touched me as we left, and the odd feeling of being watched was gnawing at me, but I couldn't reconcile the entire evening.

Tears suddenly sprang into my eyes, it was an odd response, and my heart had a strange ache to it. My feelings for Jackson- are they real or is it just deep lust? I mean yes, the sex was great and he is a wonderful person, but is my heart really in this for the long haul? Is he the one? Or am I trying to convince myself he is the right one for me. Yes, we have been friends for a long time, but I don't see myself having a relationship with him. I shook my head as I entered the house. I need to get my mind on something else before my head begins to hurt or explodes. I took a quick cool shower, and grabbed an apple and some water, and powered up my laptop.

I pressed Heather's number on my phone and looked at the clock- 9 am, she should be up and pacing the house.

"Hello?" a very irritated Heather answered.

"Hi, what's up?"

"Where have you been? I am freaking out over here!" She yelled at me.

"Calm down, what are you freaking out about?"

"All the response cards are coming in and do you realize I am marrying Curt in less than three weeks. Married. I am nuts. I am only 22 years old, and I am marrying this guy."

I was laughing at her, she is definitely freaking out.

"Take a deep breath, don't freak out, Grant is a great guy…you are lucky."

"You said Grant…why did you say Grant…did you talk to him?" I could hear her tone, it is filled with surprise and hopefulness.

"I didn't say Grant and if I did… I meant, Curt, you know they are interchangeable." I was trying to pacify her, but she wouldn't let it go.

"Oh my God…you are still in love with him. What is going on? Is that who you were with this weekend? Is that why no one could get a hold of you?" Heathers obvious pleasure at this crazy idea was annoying the shit out of me to say the least.

"Absolutely not, it was just a slip of the tongue, nothing more nothing less. And if you must know I was with Jackson. Do you hear me? JACKSON, all weekend!" I emphasized his name so she would get it through her thick head that Grant and I were long ago over and Jackson was the man in my life. Shit…who am I trying to convince, her or me?

"Oh… damn," I could hear the disappointment in her voice.

"Stop it. Okay, this is what you need to do with all those response cards. Make a seating chart," I advised her.

"What? No, you do it." Heather hated planning anything so a seating chart would push her over the edge.

"Fine, make a list of who should sit with who based on the guest list and email it to me. Then everytime you get a response card in the mail, email me with the names, and how many guests, and I will do the seating chart and print out the place cards."

"How are you going to do all that in Texas? Do you really have to leave this week, I mean, can't you post-pone your start date until after the wedding?" Her voice filled with desperation for me not to leave.

"Heather, it is going to be fine, everything is ready. I will have my laptop with me, between Kendall and I, everything will get done. Don't worry, we will be back, your wedding will be perfect, and you and Curt will live happily ever after." I hoped my words were giving her the support she needed because I was stressed out enough.

"Listen, I have to go but let's have lunch before I leave. Okay?"

"Okay, how about Wednesday and then we can pick up the dresses from the bridal shop?" She asked me with excitement in her voice.

"Perfect, talk to you later, I have to go call some guy about I don't know what yet."

"See ya."

I finished my water and apple before calling the Carlisle guy back. Did I seriously have a slip of my tongue saying Grant's name? Or was my subconscious rearing its ugly head at me. It has to be the knowledge of seeing him soon which is causing my brain to short circuit. I mean, until the wedding announcement I rarely thought about him. LIAR!

I dialed the number to the Carlisle guy and a woman's voice answered.

"Carlisle, Welch, Seabrook, and…." I don't know what she said, there were so many names. "How may I direct your call today?" She finally asked.

"Yes, Mr. Carlisle please?" I politely asked.

"Yes one moment, may I ask who is calling?" She politely asked me, but with an air of arrogance.

"Of course, my name is Sydney Stanton, I am returning Mr. Carlisle's call."

"Just one moment." I could hear a bunch of clicking sounds and then soft music playing.

"Mr. Carlisle's office," a woman said. What is this the Secret Service?

S.P. Wilcox

"Hi, yes, this is Sydney Stanton, I am returning Mr. Carlisle's call,"
I said again.

"Yes Miss Stanton, Mr. Carlisle has been waiting for your call.
Unfortunately he is in a meeting. He asked me to ask you if you are
available for a meeting with him this afternoon?" This was weird, I
have no idea who this guy is and he wants me to have a meeting with
him?. I pressed my hand on my forehead before I took a deep breath
and spoke.

"Umm…okay. I don't want to embarrass myself, but I am at a
loss here. I have no idea who Mr. Carlisle is, how he got my number
or what this is regarding."

I could hear her laugh a little.

"I am sorry, I didn't mean to laugh…Mr. Carlisle is very
umm…uninformative sometimes. He is interested in hiring you for a
special event, you are one of the partners in Uppercase Events?" I
was flabbergasted!

"Yes, I am. Okay, do you have any more details about what kind
of event?" I asked her.

"No I am sorry, can you make a meeting this afternoon, I could
fit you in for a lunch meeting in his office at noon?"

"Sure, I can be there." I looked at the clock, plenty of time as
long as I didn't have to go to Los Angeles. She gave me the address.
I checked the address on the computer. Oh good not too far away,
Newport Beach, no problem.

I called Kendall and told her about my plans for the day and said
I would call her as soon as I was done with the meeting with this,
hopefully not to pretentious, Mr. Carlisle.

I have no idea what to put on my body, no idea what kind of
company I would be walking in to, or type of person Mr. Carlisle is.
I finally decided on a long light weight navy blue skirt, and striped
gray and white summer sweater, conservative sandals, and left my
hair down flat- no curls. I fixed my make-up, took the directions,
and got in the car. I ran back inside to get my small case which had a
note pad in it. I stopped by Kendall's house to pick up the business
cards she had made for us. They are nice, very professional, and
sophisticated of course, Kendall has impeccable taste.

I pressed Jackson's number as I headed to get on the freeway.
1:30 in Texas, I thought to myself as I looked at the clock.

"Hello darlin', good to hear from you," he said, his accent so
warm to my heart.

138

"Hi…candy man, what are you up to?" I asked my voice filled with flirtation and well… lust. Jackson snorted a little and laughed at my remark.

"Not much, working, thinking about you and the sounds you make just before…" His voice trailed off and I could hear him squirm in his chair.

"Jackson…" I said laughing.

"What are you up to today?"

"Well, I am a busy woman today, I went for a run…"

"Of course you did."

"Don't make fun of me, anyways I called Heather who is freaking out that she is getting married in three weeks, got yelled at by Kendall for leaving all weekend, and now I am on my way to Newport to meet with some Carlisle guy about some event." I was out of breath when I was done.

"Carlisle…is it Steven Carlisle?" Jackson asked, seriously does he know everyone?

"I don't know his first name, he left me a message while I was in Vegas with you and I called him this morning, it is like the Secret Service to get to him. I am having lunch with him in his office at noon. He wants us to plan some event. I have no idea anything about him."

"Darlin', you should have Googled him, he is a big time philanthropist. You should know who he is because of all the philanthropy stuff you did with your sorority." Damn. Jackson is always right, I didn't even think to research him, I was all stressed out about what to wear, I am such a girl.

"Great, who is he?"

"Really, I am not going to do your research for you…you are going to have to learn the hard way, next time Google your client's before you go have lunch with them." He was mad at me…ugh!

"Are you mad at me? For having lunch with a guy I don't know, to plan a party I don't know anything about? Are you *jealous*?" I said with a teasing tone.

"I don't get jealous."

"Uh huh…I think you are, but I will let it go. Don't worry, you are the only candy I want to taste, and when I get to Fort Worth this weekend, I hope you are like rock candy." Thank goodness no one could hear me because that was very nasty.

"Jesus darlin'…if you keep talking to me like this I will have to go home and take care of things because I won't make it to the weekend." His voice low and deep with frustration, I laughed.

"It has only been 24 hours, can't you make it to the weekend?" I asked surprised.

"Not when I can still smell you and think about how good it will be to sink into you again." His sultry voice sent a spasm through my body. If I didn't have two hands on the steering wheel I might have crashed.

"Jackson McCoy, I hope to God, you are alone and no one can hear you saying this to me." At that moment I heard a male chuckle in the background.

"Damn it Jackson, you aren't even alone, and you have me on speaker phone, you are going to pay." I yelled at him.

He was laughing so hard, which only made me more pissed.

"Ugh…I have to go…I am at my destination…I hope this Carlisle guy is young and hot and it annoys you all day wondering what happens in my meeting!" I said in a bitchy voice and then hung up the phone.

Jackson had me fuming; I sat in my car for a minute to calm down. I could see him calling again, but I pressed the button to send his call straight to voice mail. Once my nerves were settled I took a drink of water, got my stuff, and headed up to for my meeting with Mr. Carlisle.

I walked into the lobby of a very large office building. There was a security desk in front of the elevators. I gave my name to the receptionist and she gave me a guest badge and security escorted me to the elevators, pressed the button for the top floor and I was on my way. My heart pounding, I am nervous as hell, this is so over the top. I wish Kendall was here with me, she is way better at this than me. I hate not knowing what I am getting myself into. Jackson was right I should have researched this guy.

The elevator opened to a gorgeous, elegantly decorated lobby, with yet another receptionist. On my approach the young woman said, "Good Afternoon Miss Stanton, Mr. Carlisle is waiting for you in his office." She stood up and opened one side of the frosted double doors for me. "Just go straight ahead and his personal assistant is waiting to escort you to his office."

"Thank you," I said. This place is high powered and I am out of my league. I took two steps and an older woman approached me.

"Miss Stanton, I am Doloris, Mr. Carlisle's assistant, please, follow me, he is eager to meet with you." My eyes must have been wide because she took my hand and said. "Don't worry dear he doesn't bite, well not too hard anyways." I scrunched my eyebrows at her, that was not reassuring at all.

Doloris opened another frosted door for me, I walked into his office, and Mr. Carlisle stood up behind his desk. Doloris closed the door behind me. He walked towards me, extending his hand. He was maybe in his late 40's, dark hair on top, light sprinkles of salt and pepper on the sides, tall- but not as tall as Jackson. Light blue eyes and suntanned skin. Surprisingly he was in casual clothes; conservative khaki colored chinos, a pinstriped blue button down and traditional loafers. A large watch on his left arm sparkled from the sun hitting the metal and he had a large diamond wedding band on his left hand. Thank goodness.

"Miss Stanton, it is nice to meet you, thank you so much for joining me for a lunch meeting on such short notice." His voice was deep, strong, and authoritative.

I extended my hand to shake his. "Yes, thank you I am happy to be here."

"Please let's sit at the table over here, where Doloris has arranged lunch for us. I hope you like chicken Caesar salad?" He asked.

"I do, I must be honest, I am completely lost about this meeting. What kind of event are you interested in having us plan?" I still have no idea, about this man and his company.

"Well, do you know what we do here at Carlisle?" Thank goodness he shortened the name because it was way too long to remember.

"I am embarrassed to say I do not. I didn't get a chance to do any research on your company." I wasn't about explain I had been in Las Vegas when he called having wild sex with Jackson all weekend.

"Well, you and Kendall Martin have made quite a name for yourselves. I have researched the two of you." Researched us, we hadn't even done anything yet. My face giving away my reaction, he chuckled at me.

"May I call you Sydney?"

"Yes, that is fine," I said.

"Your facial expression tells me you are curious about what I know about you two young woman. You see, we, this company, we represent non-profit organizations and your name has popped up on more than one occasion in some of our files. It seems the philanthropic events you and Miss Martin planned for your sorority were very successful and the charities took notice."

Now I was becoming increasingly excited and embarrassed by his praise at the same time. I loved planning the more corporate type of events than weddings and parties, which were fun. But too many personal emotions are tied up in weddings and parties making the client more difficult to deal with. He motioned to eat my lunch, so I did. I was starving since I had only had an apple after my run.

The salad was delicious, no doubt made by a personal chef. I was still lost as to what this meeting was about.

"Thank you so much for your praise, but I am at a loss. What is it you want from Kendall and me? Is there a party you need us to plan?"

"Well yes, I want you to plan our holiday party, and if that goes well then we will consider you for some of our corporate non-profit event planning. Interested?" My jaw dropped open, interested hell yeah, this was our forte. Kendall and I could plan a party in our sleep, no problem. Corporate non-profit, well we thrive on this kind of event planning.

"Of course, I would have to discuss this offer with Kendall. Do you have a date for the holiday party, or any other details you want to discuss?"

"I will have Doloris email you all of our requests; date, location, budget, and once you have reviewed the information, you can send me a contract to sign with your fee disclosure."

Our fee, crap...we would have to figure out how much to charge for this. Just then Doloris' voice came over the intercom on his desk.

"Mr. Carlisle, Mr. Bennett has the information you requested, can he bring it in your office?" Mr. Carlisle jumped up and walked over to his desk, pressing a button on the intercom. "Yes, thank you."

Bennett, couldn't be. Very common last name, the door opened and in walked... unbelievable. He turned and looked at me sitting at the table eating lunch with Mr. Carlisle. Now his jaw dropped open. The exchange of looks and smiles, Mr. Carlisle was well... stunned at my reaction to Matt Bennett. I flew up out of my chair and bounced across the office to him, I could feel Carlisle's eyes watching this interaction.

"Matt!" We exchanged a long embrace.

"Sydney, what are you doing here? Of all places, this is the last place I thought I would run into you." Matt said with a sweet, surprised tone.

Mr. Carlisle chimed in, "Well, I guess you two know each other. Small world, Sydney is here on my request, her company, Uppercase Events, is going to plan our holiday party and maybe more," he said smugly.

"Uppercase Events… nice, I like the name. How are you?" Matt asked, handing Mr. Carlisle a stack of files.

"Great, gosh, do you want to talk for a few minutes when I am done with my meeting? Do you work here?" I asked curious by his presence.

"Sort of, I am an outside consultant, I do web designs. I am currently redesigning all of the websites for the non-profits this company represents."

"Wow, that is great."

"How is Kendall?" He asked with some apprehension. I could see the longing in his eyes, he missed her.

"She is great, um…she and I are partners in this venture, Uppercase Events I mean. You know we do everything together. Listen, give me 30 minutes and Steven and I should be done." Matt raised his eyebrows at me "Steven, huh"! I smacked his arm and gave him a warm hug.

Matt left and I turned my attention back to Mr. Carlisle.

"You don't mind if I call you by your first name, I mean, Mr. Carlisle is so formal?" He laughed a little bit.

"No problem, it is my name. How do you know Matt?"

"Matt and I went to college together and he and Kendall, my partner, used to date. So Steven, what else do I need to know?" My self-confidence showing through.

"Well, we are a large company of over 150 employees, we represent non-profit organizations, and we like to have a good time. Every employee is allowed to bring one guest to our holiday party, so you can anticipate 250-300 people at the party. You will deal directly with me or my assistant Doloris, who is available to answer any questions for you. You are not to exceed the given budget or guidelines we set, understood?" Serious he is very serious.

"Yes, I understand. I do have one question, do you know Jean Hightower?" A pleasant smile came across his face.

"Yes, we are acquainted, why do you ask?"

"Because, something inside me tells me she has something to do with this meeting today," I said smiling back at him.

"Well, I won't lie, your names did come up on our radar many times but it was Jean who... well, encouraged me to contact you. You two have made quite an impression on her. You would be wise to be kind to her, she is your biggest fan and knows everyone." His face serious again.

"Well, I will be sure to thank her, and thank you for your confidence in us, we will not disappoint you!" I said.

"I am sure everything will just fall into place!" I looked at him with a surprised expression.

"Interesting, someone else has said that to me on many occasions!" I extended my hand once again, thanking him for his hospitality. I left his office in search of Matt.

This should be a telling conversation, how much do I divulge about Kendall? Matt was waiting for me in the lobby downstairs. We hugged once again, and took a walk outside, then sat down on a bench under a shady tree.

"So Sydney Stanton, you look great, and based on the smile on your face, I would say your meeting with *Steven* went well." He elbowed me.

"It was better than I could have imagined. I came here having no clue what this was going to be about and walked away with a new contract to plan their holiday party -and the potential for so much more! I am beyond excited, I have to call Kendall."

His face tensed at her name. "Matt what? You can't even hear her name, what is the deal?" He was rubbing his forehead with his hands. It was obvious he still felt something for her.

"Matt tell me? Do you miss her? What is it, you have been broken up for a long time, you are just now figuring out how you feel about her?" I was completely annoyed with him.

"I didn't realize how important she is to me, and when I did she was involved with that guy from Texas. She wouldn't return my calls and now I don't know how to win her back."

"Why don't you try honesty...that might be a place to start. But, she is leaving in ten days for the east coast for her job. So, you might want to get your ass in gear!" He laughed at me.

"Sydney, what is your deal?"

"What do you mean?" I looked at him, my deal, what?

"You look happy, you were so sad for so long, are you back together with Grant?" ARGH!

"No, I am not with Grant, that is over, it has been for a very long time. I am getting ready to move to Fort Worth, Texas for my new job. Kendall has us busy with our new company, and well... then there is Jackson." My smile broad and my face glowing.

"Hmmm...Texan...what is the deal with you and Kendall and the Southern guys?" The tone of his voice screamed annoyance.

"Jackson and I just started seeing each other, otherwise we were only friends. And to be honest he is the first guy since Grant that has me tied up in knots." An idea came to my head. "So, web design huh? Is this your own company or do you work for someone else?"

"I work for a big web design firm...why?"

"Do you do stuff on the side or is that against your company's rules? I am thinking Uppercase Events needs a website, and I believe you are just the man to provide this service for us? What do you think?"

"I will talk to my boss and give you a call, it will cost you though." His eyes filled with delight.

"How much, we don't have a lot of cash on hand yet?"

"I will talk to my boss about the cost, and maybe he will let me do it for nothing, but you have to get me to Kendall."

"No problem, I am leaving Friday, so you will have to work with Kendall on the design of the website. That will give you a lot one on one time, so you will have her swooning in no time." We both laughed knowing it is a great idea.

We hugged good-bye after I gave him my business card.

I basically skipped to my car, this day was going so well. "Jean Hightower is the greatest thing since sliced bread," I thought to myself. Wait until Kendall hears my good news. I started the car and hit Kendall's number, but at the same time my phone began to buzz and vibrate. Jackson...

"Sydney Stanton, owner of Uppercase Events, how can I help you today?" I said arrogantly.

"Sydney, how was your meeting? I expected a call from you a long time ago." Jackson was as nice as could be.

"Well, the meeting took longer than I anticipated and I ran into an old friend so we stopped to talk." My voice was indifferent.

"I see. Are you mad at me?"

"Mad, oh Jackson darlin', now why would I be mad at you? Did you do something to upset me like…put me on speaker phone and allow me to speak suggestively in front of someone else, and then you respond so intimately to me. You didn't do anything as vile as that did you?" I said with a sarcastic sugary sweet tone to my voice.

Really he has some nerve to think what he did was acceptable behavior.

"I am so sorry, you have every right to be mad, will you forgive me?" His voice deep and sultry with regret.

"Jackson, I am not really mad, just embarrassed. Please don't do that again, okay?" I said in my normal happy voice. "I really want to tell you all about my meeting but I have to call Kendall, so can I call you back?"

"Of course darlin', talk to you later."

I called Kendall and told her all about the meeting and how we owe Mrs. Hightower a debt of gratitude. I suggested we should have a website to promote our business, and advised her I met with a web designer. I didn't tell her who the web designer was going to be. I just said we needed to get some ideas together for the website and since I was leaving she would need to meet with him. Matt and I had already scheduled an appointment. They were to meet at a neutral location, where she might feel more comfortable. I would already be gone, so at least she could only yell at me over the phone.

CHAPTER 14

All my clothes were packed, along with my laptop, and I ordered a new wireless printer to be delivered. I was ready to leave for Texas, I would be gone for three to six months and not sure which office I would get sent to after my training. I am hoping to come back to the Los Angeles office, but the company wouldn't give me a guarantee for final placement. I would be back home in two weeks for Heather and Curt's wedding. A shuttle service was picking me up in fifteen minutes. I am so excited, nervous, and ready for another stage of my life.

I was sitting on the steps inside my childhood home waiting for the shuttle. I scrolled through my phone looking at all the names and numbers. Some of the people I didn't even talk to anymore and some I spoke to on a daily basis. I started to delete the names of those who were no longer a part of my life. Starting with A, B, C, D, E, F, G...the only name under G, is Grant. My heart dropped a little, the ache floating up just enough to make my breath catch. My fingers were hovering over the delete key, should I do it...just then I heard the horn of the shuttle honking at me. I jumped up out of my daze and went to open the front door. The driver came and helped me carry my ridiculous amount of luggage to the van.

Once on the plane I stared out the window, it is going to be great, I kept telling myself this over and over in my head. Yellow Bird is an amazing company to work for, this is the opportunity of a lifetime. I was feeling uneasy, maybe I made the wrong choice, maybe I should be putting all my efforts into Uppercase. Maybe I am just nervous; new state, no friends, no family, well only Jackson. Jackson… my mind relaxing, my body sinking into a much needed nap. As the plane cruised through the air destined for Texas, my dreams were filled with Jackson's face, his sweet lips, and his Southern drawl. I could also see someone else not clearly but there was someone else there, just out of reach, not talking only looking at me from afar. Then I could hear voices.

"Miss, would you like a drink or snack?"

I opened my eyes and the flight attendant was waking me up for the beverage service. I smiled at her, but on the inside I was cursing her. Damn, what was I dreaming about, who was in my dream? I couldn't remember all the details, just a fuzzy feeling of unfinished business.

The flight to Fort Worth was quick, only about two and half hours, the company was having a car service pick me up and bring me to the extended stay hotel, not far from the company headquarters. My company car would be waiting for me at the hotel. Jackson is out of town for two more days, so I am on my own to get settled and find my way around. Thank goodness for MapQuest and the GPS on my phone.

I walked out of the baggage claim with the help of a skycap, and the car service picked me up in front of the airport. My first feelings about Fort Worth, Texas…SWAMP ASS HOT! Seriously, I will need a shower every hour to keep cool, running will be out of the question unless I join a gym with an indoor track. A pool, please let the hotel have a pool, my sanity will be safe if the hotel has a pool. Maybe Jackson has a pool, I have never asked him. The driver from the car service was very nice, and waited for me to get my keys and check in at the front desk of the extended stay hotel. I showed him where my room was on the hotel map. He drove me to the room and helped me carry my bags to the door. Once in my new temporary home I looked around. Not bad.

There is a small kitchen right inside the front door, a couch, two side chairs, and a table to eat at with four chairs around it. A flat screen TV, DVD player, and a small desk on the wall by the window. The bedroom is down a short hall, queen size bed, dresser with a mirror, two night stands, and a closet with folding doors. The bathroom has double sinks and a shower tub combination. The entire suite is decorated in browns and blues, the comforter on the bed is striped brown and blue. I walked into the kitchen and found a lovely welcome basket from Yellow Bird, filled with some snacks and drinks. There is a detailed map of the neighborhood outlining the closest grocery store, drug store, dry cleaners, restaurants, gas station and hospital.

I sat down on the couch. Alone. I haven't talked to Jackson, Kendall or my parents. Alone, I am bored. I think I will go in search of the pool, where is the map of this hotel? I found the map on the desk. Looking at the map, pool…pool…where is the pool? "Yes, I am going swimming," I said out loud to myself.

I looked through two suitcases before I found a bathing suit to put on. I changed into my suit, put on some shorts and tank top, grabbed a towel, and headed out for the pool. My phone started to vibrate in my hand as I walked. Not looking at the caller ID, I didn't care who it was, I was desperate for some kind of human interaction.

"Hello?" I said.

"Hey, how is Texas, hot enough for you?"

"Hey Heather, I am so glad you called, I am lonely," I said with a sad tone.

"You haven't even been gone a day, how could you be lonely, and where is Jackson?"

"Jackson won't be back until Sunday from a business trip, I am in desperate need of human interaction. I am heading to the pool."

"Sounds fun, so listen, Curt and I have this idea for our first dance…we want to do one of those crazy dance numbers, what do you think?" Excitement laced her voice.

"Sounds great, you guys should totally do it. You mean where you start out dancing to a love song and then the music changes and you do a wild dance number together, right?"

"Exactly…I am so glad you are on board with the idea because we want the wedding party to participate in the first dance." There was silence on my end of the line. I was stunned, no way am I doing this crazy dance idea.

"Sydney, are you still there? Come on don't crap out on me, it will be fun and take everyone by surprise, the dance instructor says it is better when the wedding party participates…please. Kendall already agreed to it!" She was begging me, desperate for me to agree.

"Absolutely not, there is no way I am doing it." I was adamant about this, I am not getting up in front 200 people and dancing like a crazy person.

"Sydney, make it your wedding present to us, it is such a great number, I will email you the dance number. Please...?"

Seriously!

"Being the wedding planner is your wedding present...I am not doing it!"

"Yes you are, you are going to do it. You can dance with Noah and Kendall will dance with Grant, it will be fine." I took a deep breath, I wasn't going to win, I would eventually give in to her begging.

"Fine...I will do it but you have to promise, I don't have to dance with Grant, right?" I was super serious. I did not want to dance with Grant.

"I promise you will dance with Noah. Okay? You are in. Check your email for the dance number and we will practice the whole thing after the rehearsal dinner, so bring some comfy clothes and your heels to practice in. Thank you so much, I love you, this is going to be great."

We ended our phone call a few minutes later. I finally located the pool, found a chair to put my stuff on, and jumped in. Exactly, what I needed. I swam some laps and then headed back to my room. I hadn't heard from Kendall, so either she was still meeting with Matt or she was so mad at me for setting her up on a blind date/meeting with Matt that she is going to kill me.

It took me a few minutes to open the door to my room, but once inside I plopped down on the couch and booted up my laptop. I immediately went to my email program and found the message from Heather. I opened the file she attached and watched the video. Curt and Heather started out dancing to "Every you Take" by the Police-typical slow first dance at a wedding. Then the music changes to "California Gurls" by Katy Perry, and holy shit, the choreography was... well not what I expected. The people from the dance studio were in the positions for the wedding party. Okay, my body does not move like that, and what is she doing with her hands, oh hell no... then the song changed again...this time to "I Need Something To Do With My Hands" by Thomas Rhett.

Heather and Curt have lost their minds. There is no way I am doing this dance. The moves include the guys sitting in chairs and us dancing around them quite seductively, and then the chairs are moved off the dance floor and the guys run their hands up and down our sides, like going in our pockets, and running their hands through our hair. I hit Heather's number on my phone.

"Hello?" a man's voice said into the phone. I looked at my phone yes I had pressed the correct number.

"Hey, is Heather available?" I asked.

"Hey Sydney it's Curt, what's up can't wait to see you in two weeks."

"Hey, I didn't recognize your voice, where is Heather?"

"She is outside, what's up?"

"Well, to be honest, I was watching the video for the dance number, you know the first wedding dance thing…I can't do it, tell Heather I am backing out." I am the worst friend ever; she is going to be so disappointed in me. "No, never mind, I am still in, can we tone down the bottom smacking and well almost kissing in this dance? I mean really, I can't do half the things your dancers were doing in the video."

Curt was laughing at me. I almost have tears in my eyes, talking to him about dancing.

"Sydney, I have seen you dance and you will have no problem. Anyways we are going to practice together after the rehearsal dinner, you'll be great. It means a lot to Heather and I to have our dearest friends do this with us." He was so sincere, so sweet.

I took a deep breath and relaxed a minute.

"I have one condition which Heather already agreed to… I dance with Noah?" I asked him.

"I know, she told me, you will dance with Noah, don't worry." He was laughing, this is no laughing matter.

"Okay, I have to go, tell her to give me a call, thanks."

I went to change my clothes, realizing I started my period, I needed to go in search of a grocery store. I grabbed the keys to my rental car and headed out. I was completely clueless where I was going. I pulled out the map I found in the kitchen with the highlighted destinations on it. Good thing I remembered to bring the map with me. The grocery store was only a few blocks from the hotel, and the shopping center had everything I need, even a nail salon.

I finished my shopping and went back to the hotel. I carried my two bags of groceries into my new hotel home and began unpacking, I heard my phone buzz. I looked to see who was calling, a smile came across my face Jackson.

"Hello, sexy," I said dragging out the sexy in a super sweet voice.

"Hi darlin', or should I say neighbor, how do you like Texas so far?"

"Well, besides being lonely, and the fact that it is swamp ass hot here, it is just great!" My sarcasm couldn't have been thicker.

"I am sorry, I am not home to welcome you to Fort Worth, but I will be there in a few days and we will go to dinner." The sound of his voice relaxed me and his words made me feel much better.

"So, how is your trip going?"

"Actually, great, I just landed a new client. I have been trying to get this guy to give our company a try for a year and he finally placed a huge order, so I am having a great trip," I could hear the elation in his voice.

"I don't know how anyone resists your Southern charm, but I guess if I was a guy it might not be so hard to resist!" I was completely laughing. "So, check this out, Heather and Curt are doing one of those crazy first dance things, and the wedding party has been summoned to participate. So I am just giving you the heads up to what will be somewhat embarrassing for me, and maybe you."

I could only imagine what was going through Jackson's mind, he already knew Grant was in the wedding and would presume in this dance as well. I was bracing myself for his anger, or jealousy.

"Well, I can't wait to see it, I am sure it will be quite entertaining. Listen I am beat and it is late here, so I am going to say goodnight and I look forward to being with you on Sunday. Darlin', you have a nice day tomorrow."

"Okay, see you Sunday."

Wow, no jealousy, no yelling, Jackson is amazing.

The first week of my new job was great, I met about a million people, and filled out just as much paperwork. Everyday I was called to Human Resources -there seemed to be an endless amount of information needed. The week was crazy; I saw Jackson on Sunday, and then he left again Tuesday for yet another business trip. Kendall was not happy with me, but she was spending more time with Matt than I had anticipated.

Heather was emailing me everday with response card information and each night I stayed up late printing out place cards, not to mention the endless phone messages and texts from her about the wedding. Mrs. Hightower was out of control, she was giving our number to every one she knew. At this pace we would be turning people away.

Another weekend went by without Jackson in town. I don't like this at all. I think I saw him more when I was living in a different state. He promised this was all because of his new client and he wasn't normally gone this much. It was fine though, I really had no spare time for him right now. Between working eight to ten hours a day, and then coming home to work on projects for Uppercase, I was exhausted each night, and would pass out on the couch before getting up to do the same thing over and over again.

Jackson promised to be back to fly with me to California for Heather's wedding on Friday. But when Thursday rolled around and he wasn't back yet, I kind of figured he either would meet me in California, or would miss the wedding all together. This all seems so familiar to me, oh yeah it is, Grant blew me off for Jade's wedding for work too! When I didn't hear from Jackson before I went to bed on Thursday night I knew history was repeating itself.

I requested Friday off, which seemed to be no problem since I was working ten hour days. I was packing my clothes when my phone buzzed.

"This is Sydney." I had stopped answering my phone with just a hello because potential clients were calling for Uppercase Events.

"Hi darlin'," Jackson said with a sweet guilty voice.

I didn't respond, my stomach was already churning. I knew what he was going to say, so I braced myself for the blow off.

"Sydney, you are mad at me and I haven't even said anything yet."

"Just tell me- you are not coming with me this weekend. I already figured that out myself, so just spill it," my disappointment seeping through the phone to him.

"I am so sorry, I am going to try to get a flight out in the morning, but my new client has had some issues with the order, and I have to stay here and figure it out for them. Do you understand?" The truthfulness of his words stung.

"Yeah...I guess...whatever...it will be fine." It wasn't fine, but making him feel guilty wouldn't do either of us any good.

"Darlin' I know you are upset and we have barely seen each other since you moved to Texas, it just can't be helped. I am sorry, I really will try to be there tomorrow," his voice was sincere.

I didn't care though, he told me he would be there with me and now I was going to go to the wedding alone...again! Grant would be so happy to see me alone and gloat while he has some bombshell on his arm. Not to mention his mother, who will be in my business all night. Argh, I just want to scream! I don't even have time for a run or swim. My throat was tightening up and tears were welling up in my eyes.

"Jackson I have to go, I need to leave for the airport. Good luck I hope everything falls into place for you. Bye!"

I hung up, I didn't want his excuses, I needed him and he bailed on me.

CHAPTER 15

I took a hot long shower. Standing with my towel wrapped around me in the bathroom of my parents' house, I looked at myself in the mirror. I looked tired, my eyes were a tad puffy and my skin was pale from being inside an office all day long. I hadn't been on a run or swim for days. Mostly I was…I am not sure…sad, or maybe relieved Jackson isn't here with me. Sick to my stomach about seeing Grant, ecstatic for Heather and Curt, scared to death for this ridiculous dance number I was forced into.

I pushed all my feelings aside. This weekend is about Heather and Curt, you need to make sure everything goes perfectly. I started my beauty ritual. First, a little cooling cream under my eyes to soothe the puffiness. I put hair gel into my hair, brushed it through and then straightened my hair with the blow dryer, then flat-ironed it until it was perfectly straight. My hair was long now, down to the middle of my back. Finally finishing my make-up, I chose to wear a light summer dress and flats. I packed a small bag with my workout clothes and the heels I would be wearing to the wedding tomorrow, per Heather's request. She reminded me at least 100 times about practicing the dance.

I checked myself over one more time before leaving for the wedding rehearsal and dinner at the country club. I look great on the outside but I felt awful. My insides are tied in knots. The anxiety of being in the same room as Grant is pushing me over the edge. I have no idea how to behave in front of him. What if he has a date, what if...too many what ifs...you are going to make yourself crazy. A drink would settle my nerves, as soon as I reach the club I am heading for the bar. I text Kendall to meet me in the bar, ASAP!

I sat in my car for I don't know how long. Confidence... walk into the club with as much confidence as you can muster. Where the hell is Kendall? I thought, I would walk in with her. I need to go inside. Heather is going to freak out any minute, if one of us didn't walk in soon. I opened my car door and started the dreaded walk inside. Geez, stop being so dramatic, what is the worst that could happen tonight? So many things, my mind was filling with them as I opened the large doors to the country club.

Immediately I headed to the bar, but before I could get even close, Courtney, Curt's mom was heading my way. Damn it!

"Sydney!" She yelled from across the room. "I am so glad you are here," she said giving me a huge hug. I hugged her back and plastered on a smile, attempting to cover my nerves.

"Of course, I wouldn't miss this for the world," my voice was trembling.

She stepped back from our embrace and looked at me. My fear must have been plastered across my face. Courtney gave me the sweetest look and grabbed my chin. I could feel the tears coming to my eyes, shit... not now. My heart is already racing and I feel lightheaded.

"Sydney, it is going to be alright, don't worry, be yourself," Courtney's voice was warming.

I couldn't get any words out of my mouth. Kendall walked in just then, and I turned to her, my eyes glossed over. Kendall came right up.

"Oh God, has something happened already?" Kendall asked, concern all over her face.

"No, I think... Sydney, is overwhelmed," Courtney told Kendall as they each held one of my hands.

"I am fine...everything will be fine...I am just tired, give me a minute. Kendall will you go to the bathroom with me before we head out to the gazebo area for the rehearsal? Courtney can you let everyone know will be starting in five minutes, thank you so much," I said my voice cracking.

Kendall and I walked to the bathroom. Once inside she grabbed a tissue and was blotting under my eyes to pick up the wetness from my tears.

"Sydney, are you going to be alright?" Kendall asked.

"I hope so, I don't know what my problem is," I said and began to wash my hands which were super sweaty from my nerves.

"I know what it is, but you don't want to hear it, and anyways I have a bone to pick with you...Matt!" Kendall was leaning on the edge of the sink, changing the subject was a good idea.

"I have no idea, what you are talking about? Do you not like the web designer I hired?" You couldn't miss the sarcasm in my tone.

"We don't have time for this now. We have a long night ahead of us, not to mention the stupid dance you promised Heather we would do." She was as displeased with the idea as me.

"What? She told me you agreed to do it before I did. Oh that girl is in so much trouble." We both laughed.

"Can we get a quick drink at the bar before we go outside? I need some liquid courage?"

We both laughed and headed straight to the bar.

Everyone was already waiting for us by the gazebo and no doubt, Heather was pacing waiting for us. We ordered two shots of Patron and two beers, always the best way to start our evening. Quickly we took our shots, laughing as we drank our liquid courage, grabbed our beers, and made our way outside. Kendall squeezed my hand just before we opened the doors to walk outside.

"You look hot. He will regret every time he broke your heart!" Kendall said to me and I let out a nervous laugh as we walked outside.

As we approached, I could see Heather and Curt standing in the gazebo talking with her cousin, who is the maid of honor, and Curt's brother, Nick, the best man. Heather's parents and Curt's parents were standing off to the side talking. Curt's sister was seated in a chair in front of the gazebo, next to her was Noah and next to Noah... Grant. I took a deep breath and Kendall and I walked right up to Heather and Curt in the Gazebo. My back was to Grant, I could feel the burn of his eyes on the back of my head. I didn't turn around to look at him, it would happen soon enough.

Kendall and I each hugged Curt and Heather. Kendall turned around and looked at me with wide eyes, like... come on this is our show, turn around so we can get this rehearsal started. My heart was pounding out of my chest, the anticipation of seeing his face pulling at me. I decided not to look his way, I focused all my attention on Kendall as she spoke. She directed everyone to the back of the cement walk which lead up to the gazebo. Kendall and I put everyone in the order they would walk down the aisle. Reminding everyone that tomorrow the cement would be covered in white rose petals, so to be sure to hold on to your walking partner's arm so they did not slip.

First, Curt's parents walked, followed by the flower girl and ring bearer, next Noah walked pretending to have a partner, then Grant followed suit, then the maid of honor and best man, Heather's parents walked her down together. I tried so hard not to look Grant in the face, my head stayed down or I looked in the opposite direction. So far we had stood less than five feet apart for the last fifteen minutes and all I had seen was the back of his gorgeous head. My nerves were still all jumbled. Kendall and I took our spots in line as the Justice of the Peace said his spiel about the impending wedding. I traded spots with Kendall because she was in line with Noah which was supposed to my spot. We were bickering about it until Heather shot us a dirty look. Yikes, Kendall and I both flinched and then giggled to each other.

When the rehearsal was over, everyone walked back down the path in the opposite order. Perfect… tomorrow is going to be perfect, well almost anyway. The wedding party headed towards the private room overlooking the garden for dinner. Heather came over to Kendall and I at the bar, which is where we were waiting for another round of drinks. She scowled at us and then we handed her a shot of Patron…all was right with the world.

"Girls, what were you bickering about during the rehearsal?" Heather asked annoyed with us.

"Nothing…Kendall wouldn't change spots, she is supposed to be partnered with Grant, correct?" I asked reminding her of her promise.

"Well, I think it will have to be the other way around, Kendall is not tall enough to walk with Grant even in her heels, it looks odd, the height difference and all," Heather said as if this matters.

I shot her a look but tried to remain calm. It is her wedding.

"Fine!" I said irritated.

The evening was lovely, the food was delicious. Although, I avoided Grant at all costs, moving about the room not wanting to remain in one place for too long, and when he came close, I escaped eye contact and closeness. It was fine until Corinne and Kevin cornered me, I had avoided them like the plague all night. They had been busy talking with family and friends, so it had been somewhat easy. Kendall and I were busy talking over business, we have a lot of parties to plan and a lot of work to do. Since we are in different states, we did everything via Skype and email, which for now was working out. But if we want to land Carlisle's real work, we were going to have step up our game.

"Sydney, you look stunning, you hair is long and you're so fit," Corinne said, giving me her perfect smile and loving eyes. She and Kevin both gave me a hug and kiss on the cheek. "I thought you were bringing someone with you tonight, a date?"

I took a deep breath, I didn't want to be rude and roll my eyes. "He got held up on business, I am hoping he will be here tomorrow," I said glumly.

"Oh-Kevin, did you hear what Sydney said, her friend is not going to make it this weekend?" She looked at her husband with dancing eyes, the same eyes Grant has.

"Yes Corinne, I heard Sydney. Sydney, tell us about Texas?" Kevin requested.

"It is great. I am super busy training with Yellow Bird. But it is so hot and humid there I am not sure how people can live there all the time. I will be happy to get back to California in a few months," I said, not wanting to mention Jackson living only a few miles from me in Texas.

"Oh, so you won't be staying in Texas permanently?" Kevin asked. At the same moment Corinne grabbed Grant's arm as he passed behind them, I had averted my eyes as he walked by, damn her!

I was about to answer him when Corinne pulled Grant right in front of me, and we were standing in the middle of his parents. His eyes searing through me, I swallowed as I looked up at him. My pulse is racing and my breathing is out of control.

"Grant," was all I could get out.

It was as if time was standing still and the room had fallen silent, everyone waiting all night in anticipation of this moment.

"Sydney," he mimicked me with his response. His hand tightly gripped around his beer bottle.

His parents were rolling their eyes at us. I really had no idea what to say. Corinne and Kevin quickly excused themselves, leaving Grant and I standing in the middle of the room, not saying anything to each other. I just stood there looking into his gorgeous eyes, I wanted to touch his face and run my hands through his hair. He is wearing jeans, which hugged him in all the right places, a red Polo shirt, the shirt pulled across his chest showing just enough of his tight muscles underneath. He had obviously been surfing, his skin glowing with a golden tan, his face covered in stubble. Grant looked almost exactly like he did that first summer, my Hot Bonfire Guy just a little more mature, and he smelled divine.

Grant began to run his finger around my neckline making a soft swirling motion on my skin. My lips opened a little and a small gasp escaped. His touch opened a flood gate of sensory memories coursing through my body, and I tensed. Our eyes were still fixed on each other, I could see into his deep chestnut brown eyes, so many questions, longing, and maybe regret.

"You don't wear my necklace? Do you think about me?" He asked his voice deep, but his words soft so only I could hear him.

Think with your brain, not your heart. Don't open the box of feelings which you tucked away so long ago, turn and walk away. I could feel the electricity starting to ignite from our bodies, turn and run away, he will hurt you if you let him in. GO. I listened to my brain. I turned and began to walk away, Grant grabbed my arm.

"Don't walk away," his voice still deep, but his words more stern, more needy.

I didn't look back at him, I removed my arm from his grasp and high- tailed it out of the party. I walked out onto the balcony overlooking the gardens, the same balcony I stood on so long ago when Grant had called me on Heather's phone begging my forgiveness. I could feel him standing in the doorway watching me, I walked down the stairs and made my way to the back of the gardens. Why? I worked so hard to tuck away my feelings for him and with one touch he was opening the box up.

I could feel him, his close proximity making the hair on my neck stand up and my body tingle. I turned towards him as he came up behind me.

"You didn't answer my question, do you think about me?" His words were whirling around my brain.

I didn't answer I just stood looking at him, trying to figure out a response. I didn't want to lie, but I didn't want Grant to think I was pining away for him for the last two years.

Finally my brain and mouth figured out how to work in unison again.

"Of course I thought about you. Did you ever think about me? Did you ever miss me?" I asked, my voice unsteady afraid of his response.

"Sydney…only every other thought is about you." Seriously, he is full of shit.

I crossed my arms, the tears I thought would come turned quickly to anger. How stupid does he think I am? Every other thought…WOW… that is rich, he dropped out of my life more than two years ago… without even a call or explanation and he wants me to believe he was thinking about me in every other thought… I don't think so.

"Huh…every other thought, huh? I find those words hard to swallow. Did you think I would buy that? Did you think you would come here and I would let you back into my arms, my life and my bed with those words? You are an arrogant son of a bitch!" My words were sharp and unforgiving.

"It is the truth," Grant said, walking closer to me.

"Stop…you don't need to be any closer to me than you are right now." I put my hands up to keep him at bay. "You left for Europe, barely called, you didn't return my calls, not even a text… you just walked away. It is so easy for you. You come in and out of my life with no regard for me. You left saying everything would be the same way it was only for a few months. I knew before you left our relationship was over. But I held on, hoping I was wrong, but you proved me right. I guess it was just another wish, that our love was strong enough to keep us together. I was wrong, I guess the saying is true out of sight out of mind!"

He wanted to talk… he was going to hear what I had to say, he wasn't going to walk away from me until I was done! I had kept my pain locked away because he was the one who should hear it, he needed to know how his actions hurt me.

"Sydney, not everything is black and white, there are always shades of gray blurring the truth."

"What the hell are you trying to say, stop with your load of crap. Tell me what made you walk away or did you run? You didn't even have enough respect for me to tell me it was over, you didn't even call when you came back to the states. I came to New York for less than twenty-four hours for my grandfather's funeral, I tried to contact you, but yet again you blew me off." My voice was no longer quiet, I wouldn't say I was yelling, but close to it. Each word which flew out of my mouth was filled with disgust and anger. I just hope we are far enough away from the party not to ruin Heather and Curt's evening.

"You won't understand…," Grant said, running his hands back through his hair, letting out a huge sigh of frustration.

I got right in his face, my teeth were clenched together and my hands were in fists hanging at my sides. "Tell me…tell me, your story…tell me why? Was there someone else? Did you fall in love with someone else?" My words were filled with loathing and anger.

I was so close I could hear him swallow and deep drag for breath.

"God… Sydney…No. There has never been anyone else. You have always been the one. I can't…I don't know how to explain myself to you."

I rolled my eyes at him. My anger was turning to fury, my face red with hate for him.

"You're pathetic…you could never be honest with me. You have always hidden your true self from me. Our whole relationship was a joke, a waste of my time. I have moved on, leave me alone. After tomorrow, we will never see each other again, if it wasn't for this wedding…our paths would not have crossed."

My words cutting like a knife, based on the expression of pain on his face. I don't care, he doesn't deserve my empathy.

I walked past him to go back to the party, thank goodness for the liquid courage I drank earlier in the evening, I finally got my say and the closure. Grant didn't give me his reasons but I had the final word. Now just get through the rest of the weekend and continue my life without him in it.

Once again he grabbed my arm, my back was to him, he whispered into my ear, "I know you feel the fire igniting between us again, don't deny it…I feel it too, we are meant to be together, let me prove it to you?" His voice was deep with determination and passion.

I turned and stood on my tippy toes, looking straight into his eyes, "You had your chance…it was over long ago…we will never be anything more than what we were…we will never be again." My words were cold and calculated, I shrugged my arm away from him and headed back to the party.

He was right on my heels, trying to catch up, I reached the doors to the party. Before I could get them open, Grant put his hands on the door trapping me, not allowing me to open them. My back was to him. I could feel him lean his forehead on the back of my head and take a deep breath. He was so close I could smell his scent, it once again sending my body into sensory overload.

His voice was barely audible, "I am sorry…you will never know how sorry I am…losing you…well it is my biggest regret." I was furious with him, but his words made my heart ache.

"Get out of my way, I don't want to make a bigger spectacle of ourselves in front of everyone, just let me go," I said my voice calmer and forlorn.

The moment I swung open the door, all eyes in the room turned to us. I walked to the bar, where Kendall was standing with Heather. I took a deep breath upon my approach. Heather and Kendall looked shocked. Heather was, I am sure, hopeful we would come back hand in hand, Kendall was more realistic. She knew I wouldn't allow it.

"Who wants a shot, it is early still, bartender three shots of Patron, please?"

While the bartender prepared our shots, Kendall and Heather were waiting for some details. I was completely tense, with a fake smile plastered on my face.

"What did he say? Did you resolve anything?" Heather asked, hoping for some good news.

I furrowed my brow at her, "Resolve, there is nothing to resolve, and no he didn't say anything, couldn't even explain his actions. Two years and couldn't even come up with a good lie or the truth," I said, my anger oozing out.

We each raised our shot glass, I looked at Heather and I said, "To your happiness!"

We downed our shots like experts and smacked the shot glasses on the bar. I threw my head back and let out a nervous laugh.

"Wow, I needed that, when does our secret mission start?" I whispered to Kendall and Heather.

Heather looked at her phone to check the time.

"Any minute, people should be leaving in a few minutes and then we will go downstairs to where the reception is being held to practice."

"Oh good, then we have time for another drink," I said. Kendall and Heather exchanged a glance to each other.

"What? Don't act like I am not standing right in front of you," I said to them both.

"Just take it easy, you don't want to have a hangover and you need to be able to dance," Heather said to me before she left in search of Curt.

I was leaning with my back on the bar watching her talk to Curt. Her arms were crossed and she was relaying my version of the events to Curt. I could read her lips only once, she said; "What is his problem? How stupid is he?" I couldn't see Curt's response. Kendall was watching me watch Heather and Curt.

"So, Grant looks extremely unhappy." She said as she used her chin to make me look at him across the room.

"I don't care, he should be unhappy...actually, miserable would make me happy!" I said, my words fortified with anger.

"Okay then. We should go get our stuff from our cars so we can change and get this dance practice over with and don't drink anymore!" She said pointing her finger at me. "If you want to remain in control of your emotions, don't even have a beer. Do you understand me?"

Damn she is so bossy!

"Fine, let's go get our stuff," I said defeated.

I could feel Grant's eyes following me as I walked across the room. I grabbed my purse to get my keys. Kendall and I walked to the parking lot, the cool air calming my temper. We met Heather in the downstairs locker room to change.

"Wait a minute, how come the maid of honor and best man are not dancing with us?" Kendall asked all irritated.

"My cousin is pregnant and can't move the way she should for the dance and so they are both out," Heather said.

"Oh," Kendall and I said in unison.

When we were done changing, Heather rolled her eyes at me.

"What?" I said irritated by her eye rolling.

"You don't want Grant, but look what you are wearing, he is going to get a hard on when you walk in the room." Heather was smiling at me, she was up to no good.

"You told me to wear something comfortable, easy to move in. This is what I run in. Let him drool for all I care," I put my flip-flops on and carried my heels in my hand.

"Oh, you care alright." Kendall said.

I stuck my tongue out at both of them, "Shut up, I am with Jackson now, Grant is nothing more than an ex-boyfriend."

"You're *with* Jackson...where is Jackson?" Heather asked, I could hear the un-approving tone she gave me.

I grunted and walked out of the room, I could hear them both laughing as the door closed behind me. I stood on the wall waiting for them to come out. We walked to the ballroom together. Curt, Grant, and Noah, were talking with the dance instructors when we approached. There was a table with a bunch of cold of beers and bottled waters for us.

Heather addressed all of us at the same time. Kendall eyed me, reminding me not to drink any more alcohol.

"Curt and I want to thank you for helping us with this special dance for our wedding. We know you will enjoy yourselves. This is RJ and Beth they are going to help us with the dance routine."

RJ and Beth went on to describe how the dance would go. I was sitting on the carpet next to the wooden dance floor, Kendall was to my right side, and Noah and Grant were to my left. They showed us the dance, and then placed us in our positions. Heather and Curt were standing in the middle of the dance floor, dancing. Kendall and I were on opposite sides of the dance floor watching them. Noah and Grant were at the top of the dance floor in front of where the DJ would be set up, there were three chairs placed by them.

"Okay, so Heather and Curt will be dancing to the first song. When the music starts to skip they will break apart, look at each other, then to the DJ. As soon as they look back at each other, the second song will start. Curt will go back up to his chair by Noah and Grant. Kendall and Sydney will come out and stand on each side of Heather. You will grab the waist of the person in front of you and pull yourselves as close together as you can get. Okay, do this part," Beth said.

Kendall and I walked to the middle of the dance floor. We turned our bodies to make a Heather sandwich, facing to the right, our bodies placed back to chest. We were laughing.

"Good, okay. RJ, turn on the music?" Beth asked.

The music started, the chorus played, Katy Perry's voice filled the room, *"You could travel the world but nothing comes close to the golden coast..."*. "Okay, girls I want you to move your bodies like this," Beth continued, while rolling her hips, "as soon as you hear the first word of the song." So, we did as she asked. We could all hear three males, clearing their throats as they watched the three of us moving our bodies to the music.

"Okay, guys when they are doing this you need to quickly bring your chairs right behind them and sit down. Sit in the chair, with one arm over the back and your legs spread out the other hand, resting in between your legs."

RJ turned off the music. All six of us were on the dance floor now.

"Okay, once they guys are seated, you ladies will break apart and turn towards them," Beth said. Noah was behind me, thank goodness!

"You will walk up seductively to them, walk around them, starting on the left and coming around behind them. You will run your hands around their necks and through their hair. When you come to their side, the guys will pull you onto their laps."

Grant cleared his throat, "Um, excuse me Beth, shouldn't we be dancing with our partner from the wedding? I mean, it will look odd to the guests, don't you think?" His smug smile chafing at my nerves.

"Bullshit, I am not dancing with him." I had no problem saying very loudly.

This in turn earned me a nasty look from both Heather and Curt. Crap, another losing battle.

"Okay, yes you are right. For continuity reasons, you should be with the same partner from the wedding," Beth agreed with Grant.

"Damn it…"I sulked over to stand in front of Grant, Heather blew me a kiss and Grant's smug smile is beaming at me. He would have his hands all over me enjoying every moment of this dance fiasco. Kendall was shaking her head and laughing at me.

Grant whispered to me, "Thee who protests too much…" I gave him a dirty look.

"Shut. Up." I said through my gritted teeth to Grant.

"Okay, so they pull you onto their laps and after a tight squeeze and kiss on the cheek you will pop out of their embrace. Put your foot in the middle of the chair and push them away."

I smiled… I like that.

"This will be almost the end of the second song. Then guys, you will need to quickly move the chair back off the dance floor, then come right back up to your girl. The third song will start, the girls will still be standing over here dancing. I want you to move your hands in the air like Katy Perry does, and your bodies to the beat of the music just like you would dance in a club," Beth said to the three of us.

Grant walked up to me and said, "You know how to dance like that, right Sydney? In a club all seductively, like you are about to come on the dance floor!"

I gave him a dirty look, "What is that supposed to mean?" My voice was loud enough for everyone to hear.

"Nothing…just you should be more aware of your surroundings is all." His vague comment reminded me of Jackson, and our actions in Las Vegas.

I squinted my eyes at him. Curt whispered something to Heather, I couldn't make it out but something like, "It is working…" She smiled at him and then over to Grant and I. My temper was starting to flare.

"Let's finish this!" I said to Beth.

"Okay people, keep up with me. Now when the third song's chorus starts, you will do exactly what he says in the song. *"Well I smoke and I fish, But not near enough to satisfy an itch, Of a girl, understand I need something to do with my hands, I don't work, on a car And I'm as bad at pool as I am at throwin' darts And golf, not a fan But I need something to do with my hands So maybe I could stick 'em in your pockets, Run 'em through your hair, And we can get to rockin', There you are and baby, here I am, And I need something to do with my hands."*

"Okay, when he says 'stick em in your pockets', each of you guys, are to take your hands and run your hands up and down the girls sides from just below her hips to just below her breasts and then run your hands through her hair. Got it? Let's run through it. Oh, I almost forgot at the end, "Every Breath You Take," will play again and you are to embrace your dance partner lovingly and hold her tight and finish the song."

"What are we supposed to do while they are coping a feel?" I asked.

Grant snorted at my question, "Shut up asshole," I said.

"Girls you just keep dancing, club style," Beth said.

Grant snorted again and made yet another comment to me, "Easy for you, right Sydney, you are good at it!"

I took a deep breath but didn't respond.

The music started from the beginning, Heather and Curt dancing together, it was going well until Grant pulled me on his lap during "California Gurls" and kissed my cheek, his lips lingering on my cheek a little too long and his hands holding me a little too tight. I pushed his chair so hard he fell backwards. I kept dancing per Beth's request. When Grant came up to do his dance part, he took full advantage, not only running his hands up and down my sides but over my backside and up over my breasts. I turned and smacked his face.

"Ouch, what was that for?" He asked, everyone stopped to see the commotion.

"You know why, keep your hands off my breasts!" I yelled at him. Heather and Curt were smiling at us.

"You didn't mind it when you let that guy touch you in Vegas, you might as well have been having sex on the dance floor with him!" He yelled back to me.

"You were there? Watching me, you sick bastard! I thought I saw Curt and Noah that night. You pervert, did you get off that night thinking about me, knowing you would never get to touch me like that again, were you jealous?"

Oh hell, this was going to hell in a hand basket. "You don't want anyone else to touch me, but you can do whatever you want with God only knows who, I am done with this discussion. Did you think no one else would want me?" My heart was pounding, why did this man infuriate me so? Ugh!

All eyes were on Grant and I. I turned away from him, tears stinging my eyes.

"Okay, then," Beth said. "One more time from the top and then we will be done."

We ran through the dance number two more times and I couldn't wait to get out of there. I basically ran out of the building as soon as we were done. It was so late, my buzz was long gone. Hate and irritation were surging through my body. I ran to my car, but Grant was once again running behind me. He spun me around just as I reached to open my car door. He pinned me to the car, trapping me with his arms.

"Damn it Sydney, don't run away from me," Grant was mad, his words biting at me.

"Why would I run away from you, we are nothing to each other, I am tired and need to get some rest. You are not a part of me anymore," I said, the tone of my voice not convincing at all.

"Stop fooling yourself, give me a chance, you wouldn't be so mad at me if you didn't care," he said.

"Leave it alone Grant, it has taken me a long time get over you and move on and I am not about to step back in to the past. Go find someone you can be honest with. I am sure you have girls falling all over you, pick one marry her and have babies, but leave me alone." I was looking into his eyes and tears were falling down my cheeks.

"Let me go," I said, the ache in my heart growing.

"I can't... you mean everything to me...my life is not full without you in it. I know I screwed it all up again and I don't deserve you but I am lost without you." His eyes were filled with regret, sadness, and desperation.

"You are not lost without me. You have made it all this time without me. You are holding on to what was, the idea of me, but that was a long time ago. I can't do this again, you hurt me too much, I am not willing to be hurt by you again. You have to let me go," I said pushing his arms away so I could get in my car.

"Sydney...walking away was the hardest thing I ever did, but I did it to give you what you needed... freedom. It wasn't fair for me to keep you as my girlfriend when I knew I couldn't give you what you needed. Finishing my MBA, the internship, and making my stand in the business world was what I needed to focus on, and that meant giving you up. I wasn't able to give you the attention you needed from me, and that wasn't fair to you." He said, his words were so raw so honest.

"Leaving me without an explanation wasn't fair to me either. But you did, without batting an eyelash. Why didn't you tell me this back then, why couldn't you be honest with me? At least I would have known why you just dropped out of my world and not left me hanging on to the hopes you would come to me. You should have come clean back then." I was stunned by his admission, I had assumed it was another girl and he was too chicken shitted to tell me the truth.

He looked away from me, pushing his hand through his hair again, and taking another deep breath. "It was the only way, you would have convinced me to stay together, because it was what I wanted, but when I didn't have time for you the break up would have been so much worse. We would have said things we couldn't take back. It was the only way, to walk away without saying a word. I know I don't deserve you. Each time I have ruined it for both of us. Do you think I haven't been walking around miserable all this time?"

"Well, we don't know what would have happened because instead of facing your fears you left me... heartbroken and miserable, always wondering what I did to make you leave me," I was crying out my words to him. "It doesn't matter now…I can't be with you…every time… you end up breaking my heart and I promised myself to never allow that to happen again by you or anyone else." I was attempting to stop crying but my tears just kept flowing. "Your only reason for leaving me high and dry was because of pursuing your dreams? That is the lamest thing you could say to me."

Grant was wiping my tears with his thumbs. He was kissing my cheeks.

"Sydney, if you want to be with me you would allow me into your heart and your life. Don't deny both of us what should be. We should be together. If you don't allow anyone in, how could you let that guy touch you so intimately, who is he?" His voice was colored with possessiveness.

"Did you really think, I wouldn't move on, did you think no one else would want me?"

"No. Of course not. I know other men want you. Just seeing him touch you… like you were having sex with him was unnerving, it made me sick to my stomach," he said his voice low and raspy.

"Grant, it doesn't matter, who he is or who I am with. We are not together. You have to stop. This weekend is…it, after this we will have no more contact, so please, just leave me alone," I said.

"It does matter. I know you don't understand what I did. I know I broke your heart. But it broke my heart too. I think about you all the time," Grant said with tears in his eyes.

"How can you say that to me? If you think about me all the time, why did you never call?" I wasn't yelling at him. I am emotionally tapped out from him and this day.

"I have no excuse, other than I was scared. Scared you would hang up on me, or find out you were in love with someone else, it was easier to avoid it than deal with my feelings for you. I know it was the chicken shitted way to deal with things." His deep strong voice sounded sad like a lost little boys.

I didn't respond to his last statement. I wiped my tears away and I was finally able to get into my car and drive home. I left Grant standing in the middle of the country club parking lot with his hands in his pockets, and his head hanging down.

I was exhausted; the weeks of work, this evening, and my emotions being pulled every which way. I took off my clothes and flopped onto my bed. I was asleep without any effort.

170

CHAPTER 16

I woke early this morning, disoriented by my surroundings. I stretched my body and looked around. I am in my bedroom in my parents' house, my mind quickly reminding me why I am here; Heather's wedding day. I sat up, stretching again. My head hurts, aspirin and water. I walked downstairs, filling a glass with water and opening the aspirin bottle, popped two in my mouth, and swallowed. As I leaned up against the kitchen counter replaying the last few weeks, or maybe it is months, in my mind, everything was crashing into me.

Graduation, moving home, planning Heather's wedding, starting Uppercase, getting my dream job with Yellow Bird, Las Vegas with Jackson, and now seeing Grant again. My brain was in overload, my days were filled with work, my nights filled with event planning, and Jackson- I had barely seen him since I moved to Texas. The house was quiet, I was lost in my thoughts, but I could hear my phone buzz in my bag. I followed the sound of the buzzing until I found my bag by the front door.

"Hello?" It was early, who would call me so early on a Saturday morning?

"Hi darlin', did I wake you?" Jackson's Southern twang thick this morning.

"No, I have been up for a few minutes," I looked at the clock, shouldn't he be on a plane already? "Let me guess, you missed your flight?" I said completely irritated.

"No I didn't miss it, but the plane has some mechanical problems and the airline is trying to fix it or get another plane here. I don't think I am going to make it for the wedding, are you mad?" I could hear the regret in his voice.

The odd thing was it didn't even bother me. I was actually relieved, the idea of having Grant and Jackson in the same room together was giving me more anxiety than I wanted to deal with.

"No, I am disappointed… but I am not mad. It is unfortunate, but not your fault. I will survive, Kendall is solo here too, so we will be solo together."

"Alright darlin', I know you have a busy day ahead and I need to see if I can get on a flight back home. Do you want me to pick you up at the airport tomorrow? What time do you get in?" Jackson asked with his sweet voice.

"I need to look at my ticket, but I parked my car at the airport, so I don't need you to pick me up, but it was kind of you to offer."

"So, will I get to see you this week, I am not traveling?"

"I hope so, I miss spending time with you. I will call you when I get back to Texas."

"You mean, home," he said to me.

"It is only a temporary home…" I said with sadness in my tone.

"Maybe someday you will want it to be a permanent home."

I didn't even know how to respond to his comment. I said goodbye and ended the call.

It was only 8:00 am, I didn't have to pick up Kendall until noon, we were meeting Heather at the hair salon, to prepare for the wedding. I have time for a nice run and maybe even a swim, I would still have time to shower and pick up Kendall. I ran up to my room, grabbed some running clothes and pair of running shoes, and cleaned myself up. I am so glad I left this stuff behind, just in case.

I didn't want to carry my key to the house, so I went out the back door leaving the sliding door unlocked. I came around the side of the house and exited the backyard through the side gate. As I passed the front porch, I could see from the corner of my eye someone sitting on the steps of the porch. I walked up and stopped dead in my tracks.

"Grant, what are you doing here?" My voice filled irritation. He was holding two cups of iced coffee.

He looked up at me with his mouthwatering smile.

"Good morning, I figured you would head out for a run and maybe I could join you, and I brought you coffee in case you needed a pick me up." He stretched out his arm to hand me the coffee.

I gave him an odd look with a hesitant smile.

"That is very thoughtful of you. How did you know I would head out for a run?" I was curious, he and I had never run together before.

"You told me once you run when you have too much on your mind, and I knew you would wake up with a headache and your mind in overload." His confidence seeping through into his words.

Damn him, why did remember everything? What is he up to? I told him last night I didn't want anything to do with him. I looked him up and down, he was in running attire. I put my iced coffee down in the shade, in the corner of the porch. I put on my head phones and began to stretch. I could feel Grant watching me and my body, I looked at him as I bent down arching my back up, he was fidgeting with his shoes, pretending not to be studying me.

"If you're running with me you'd better stretch, I won't slow down if you can't keep up," I said to him my voice cut and dry.

Grant jumped up and began to stretch. The morning was already quite warm. He took off his shirt and tossed it on to the chair on the porch. Damn him, I couldn't help but gaze at his gorgeous upper torso, defined muscles, rippling abs and arms...get a hold of yourself!

"Mmm," slipped out of my mouth at the sight of him as my eyes continued to drink in his body. Shit, did I just make a moaning sound.

I heard a very male chuckle come from Grant, a sensational smile appearing on his face. He inspected me up and down, coming close to me he touched my hip as he passed.

"Mmm, to you too!" He whispered in my ear as he took off running, "We'll see who can't keep up!"

Damn him, he is so distracting to all of my senses. I quickly caught up to him, there is no way he has more stamina than I do for a morning run. I was listening to my party mix just for running. Lost in my own thoughts, I could feel him searching my face trying to catch my eye. He was trying to read my thoughts, and I was not about to give him a free pass into the depths of my soul.

I am still bothered by his admission from last night. Why hadn't he returned my text when I went to New York?

We ran at a steady pace for quite some time, and then I decided to kick into high gear. I purposely quickened my stride.

"Shit," I heard Grant spit out.

I smiled and let out a small giggle. He was keeping up with me, but it wasn't easy for him. I stayed focused on my run, trying to clear my head. I surprised myself not being upset with Jackson for not making the wedding. I was glad because it would give me time with Grant, time I didn't want to admit I wanted with him. I could have a great day with Grant and leave it like that. I thought about what he told me about not having time to devote to our relationship. Was it true, was this the only reason he walked away or was there more, was he involved with someone else? I looked at him keeping pace with me, and returned to my thoughts.

I understood better now what he said last night. Currently, my life was in this same mode. Working an absurd amount of hours for Yellow Bird and trying to keep up with all our events for Uppercase. I had no time for a relationship. The next few months, I would be flying home every weekend to finish up projects for our little business. I didn't even want to think about the party for Carlisle, it was huge, the largest project we had. I was jolted out of my own space when Grant grabbed my hand to make me stop. He was panting, bent over, holding his side.

"Jesus Sydney, do you know how fast you are running? I can't keep up at this pace." He was struggling to catch his breath.

"I didn't ask you to run with me or keep up...this is how I run. Walk back to your car and go home. I will see you later," I said, I was mean to him, but he invaded my private running time and he couldn't keep up... not my fault.

I took off running, leaving Grant. When I turned my head back to him, he was still bent over and he looked like he might vomit. Keep running, he deserves the pain. "When did I become so vindictive?" I thought to myself. I shrugged it off and finished my run. When I came home, I found Grant sitting on the porch. Actually, he was lying flat on his back, with his legs over the steps. I stood over him, letting my sweat drip on to his face.

I was breathing heavily, but I asked him, "Are you alive, do I need to call 9-1-1?"

"No, but you could give me mouth to mouth to help me recuperate!" His wicked tone coming out.

"Ha..Ha..! Up for a swim? Or is the big bad surfer too exhausted?"

"Swim, are you nuts? How much endurance do you have?" He asked all exasperated.

I pulled him up to his feet, "A swim, will help you cool down your aching muscles. It cools down my body from my run."

"Okay hot stuff," He hit my bottom.

I spun around, "Don't do that, we are not together and you...just don't do that again, please," I said.

"Sorry," he said with a shy smile.

We walked through the side gate in to the backyard and headed to the pool. I stripped off my tank top, then my shoes and socks. Grant was watching his mouth gaping at me.

"Aren't you going to change into a bathing suit?" He asked all astonished by my actions.

"No." I was in my sports bra and running shorts.

I walked to the deep end of the pool and dove right in. The water was refreshing, cooling my overheated body; heated from the run, the sun and well, the presence of Grant wasn't helping either. Grant was still standing by the side of the pool when I came up from my dive in the shallow end of the pool. I started to swim laps across the pool. I am not sure when he came in the water, but he was sitting on the steps of the pool watching me swim. I stopped and looked at him.

"I thought you like to swim. Why are you just sitting on the steps?" I asked him.

"I am exhausted, I don't have the energy to swim, your run wiped me out. Anyways, I am enjoying watching you swim." He was being very nice, does he think he can win back my heart in one day...I don't think so. I was cooled down now. I swam up to the steps and sat down beside him to catch my breath. I desperately wanted him to kiss me, to touch me, my pulse was ratcheted up so high and my breathing was uneasy. I had to ask him something before I lost my nerve.

"Why didn't you return my text when I came to New York for my grandfather's funeral?" I couldn't stand not knowing the answer to this question.

Grant didn't answer right away. He just looked at me with sad eyes.

"Another one of my many mistakes, when it comes to dealing with you, I just can't get it right," he said. "Just another thing for me to be sorry about. But I am not sorry I am sitting next to you right now." His voice trembling a bit.

I shook my head at him. This man is such an idiot, I thought to myself. For as much self-confidence as he shows on the outside he is severely lacking it on the inside.

If I didn't know better I would be afraid, Grant and I could be electrocuted by the high powered lightning bolts zipping between us in the water. He turned to me, his body covering mine, pushing my back down into the water of the first step, my head resting on the edge of the pool. His mouth overtaking mine, my lips parting to allow his tongue to plunder inside my mouth, his arms wrapped around my lower back arching my body up to him. My breasts were pressed flush against his hard chest.

My brain was yelling at me to push him away but my body was betraying me. I wrapped my arms around his neck my hands tugging at his hair, I was losing control of my control. His hands didn't move from my back, his kiss filled with passion and longing. I opened my eyes as we finished the kiss, he continued to gently kiss my bottom lip and jaw. He leaned his forehead on mine.

"God, I have missed this so much, you in my arms, and your lips on mine. Please Sydney, don't walk out of my life?" My heart was in my throat, his words were everything I wanted to hear, everything I wanted. I wanted to be with him. I wanted to give all of myself to him again. I missed it too. I pushed him off of me and sat up. My hands were still resting on his chest. I looked him in the eyes.

"Grant, I am sorry, this was a mistake, I shouldn't have let you kiss me. I don't want to lead you on...I can't go down this road with you again." I could feel the tears threatening to escape. I took a deep breath. "I don't want to lie or give you false hopes. Yes, I feel the bolts of lightning between us and we were great together, but that was a long time ago. I am too busy to have a relationship. I am in training, which is a full time job, and Kendall and I are running an event planning company which takes up all of my free time, I just can't give you what you need right now. You should be able to understand what I am saying. I am just being upfront with you, instead of doing what you did to me, just walking away."

"That is a low blow Sydney. If I could do it over, I would have handled it differently. I fucked it up and now you are punishing me for it," Grant said, I could see he was restraining his anger but the tone of his voice was clear.

I could feel my blood starting to boil, "I am not punishing you, I am being honest with you which is more than I can say you ever did for me. I am living in Texas… for I don't know how long and I am not about to start something with you, or anyone else that I can't give one hundred percent of my attention to. If the truth is punishment than, so be it!" Grant must have thought my words were cruel, his face was pale and his hands were in fists.

I walked out of the pool, there were no towels.

"I will go get us some towels, wait here," I said.

I walked into the house dripping wet. Ran upstairs to grab two towels. Grant was running up the stairs behind me.

He pinned me on the hallway wall.

"I am not letting you go this time, I will fight for you to give me another chance. I don't know if you are seeing someone else, or you really are as busy with work as you say, but I am not losing you again." He lowered his head, overtaking my body with his. His kiss this time was earth moving. His lips were relentlessly marking me, reminding me of how wonderful he makes me feel. We were gasping for breath when he finished kissing me.

"I have to get ready to pick up Kendall, you should go. I can't make you any promises Grant, I can't give you my heart. Just being with you today will be nice, can we just have today and not worry about anything else?" I said to him.

I needed him to leave before the kissing got out of control and we ended up in bed together, which would be bad in so many ways.

"I will see you at the wedding, I have to get ready." I walked him downstairs and gave him a kiss on the cheek and then basically pushed him out the door. I double locked the front door and then ran and locked the back door. In case he tried to get back in the house.

Sitting in the salon; my hair was done, my nails and toes were painted, and I was waiting my turn to have my make-up professionally done. It was Heather's gift to Kendall and I - a day of beauty for her wedding. Kendall was sitting in the make-up chair and Heather was off getting her nails done. I was lost in thought about the morning with Grant. Kendall must have spied my far off daze with one eye.

"Where are you? What, or who, are you thinking about?" Kendall asked with an all knowing tone.

"What do you mean? I am right here with you," I said trying to cover my excitement of seeing Grant this afternoon.

"Is Jackson making it to the wedding?" Kendall asked.

"No."

"You don't seem to be upset about him not coming."

"I'm not," I said no feelings either way.

"I thought you were in deep like with him?" Kendall asked her voice probing.

"I do like him and for sure there is a sexual attraction… but I am too busy to be involved right now and he is away on business all the time. I just don't see it going anywhere, you know what I mean?" I asked her, hoping she knew what I was trying to say.

"And Grant?" She asked.

"And Grant… I told him this morning I didn't, or couldn't, allow myself to be with him again," SHIT…did I say this morning.

Kendall popped right up in the make-up chair, the girl doing her make-up got annoyed.

"This morning? Did you guys spend the night together?" She was practically drooling at the mouth for information. Heather came around the corner to join us at this moment.

"What happened this morning?" Heather asked, clueless who or what we were talking about, looking at her nails.

"That is what I am trying to find out… Sydney and Grant spent the morning together!" Kendall informed Heather and they were both next to me wanting more information.

I told them how I found him waiting for me on the steps, and made him go for a torturous run with me, the kiss in the pool, the kiss in the hall and what he said. Heather was more excited about this than me, never giving up hope of us getting back together. Kendall shook her head at me.

"I hope you know what you are doing, you are asking for trouble," Kendall said.

"I told him, he could have today, that was all I could give him. I told him I was too busy to be in a relationship, and wasn't about to get involved in a long distance relationship again. I am not sure he believes me, but if anyone should understand being too busy it is him. Since, he put his career ahead of our relationship, which was his reason for walking away without explaining himself."

"What? That is why he just left, he didn't have time for you?" Kendall said.

"What an ass!" Heather said.

Both of them were obviously surprised by what his reasoning had been.

"Is that really what he said, he stopped calling because he didn't have time for you?" Kendall asked. "I think I might kick his ass tonight, when I see him. What a jerk."

"Look I have been round and round with him, I told him he should have just told me the truth, instead of walking away leaving me out in the cold. I can't change the past and neither can he, I understand now. I don't agree with the way he handled the situation but I get it. I don't have time for anyone right now. Running a business and working full time leaves no free time for a social life."

We discussed Grant in depth until my head hurt analyzing every word, the way females do, and then moved on to Matt. We were in the salon basically all day getting ready. Kendall admitted she was still into Matt and they were going to take things slowly, especially since she was on the other side of the country working. We talked about our meetings for Sunday. Kendall and I have back to back meetings with new clients, and another meeting with Carlisle.

Finally, we left the salon, hair done, make-up done, fingers and toes painted to perfection. We headed to the country club where the three of us would finish dressing before the wedding. We are having pictures done prior to the wedding; first the bridal party, and then groomsmen, separately so Heather and Curt don't see each other until she walks down the aisle.

At last the wedding is only minutes away. We are standing behind a screen with Heather, tears fill our eyes as we hug her for the last time before she becomes Mrs. Curt Wilder. Her parents came up and put their arms around her. Heather looked out of this world beautiful. Her dress is a compliment to her beauty, she is glowing, and everything looks perfect. The ballroom for the reception is completed to our exact specifications, the guests are seated, and it is an unusually cool day for the middle of the summer. The air is cool even though the sun is high in the sky. The music begins and the wedding processional starts.

I stand next to Grant, my heart is racing in his presence. He is beyond handsome in his tuxedo. Everything about him is making me long for what could have been, or what could be, from the look in his eyes, to his smell.

I put my arm through his just before it was our turn to walk down the aisle towards the gazebo.

"You look ravishing tonight, I can't take my eyes off of you," he said and kissed my cheek. I blushed at his words.

"Thank you," I said softly.

I could see his parents looking at us with loving eyes, the smiles on their faces seeing us together warmed my heart. It also made me a little nauseous knowing this happiness is only for today.

The ceremony went off without a hitch. Their vows were moving, bringing me to tears, the love they share, and commitment to each other, is precedent setting. Curt gave Heather a loving kiss at the end of the ceremony, and we all headed back up the aisle.

After many pictures and a few appetizers, the guests were escorted into the ballroom and asked to be seated by the DJ. Music is lightly playing in the background. The wedding party is lined up outside the ballroom with the doors closed. The DJ began announcing everyone in the wedding party; the parents, flower girl, ring bearer. My heart was beating fast, it was only minutes before the first dance.

"What is wrong, you look pale?" Grant asked me.

"Nothing. The stupid first dance is stressing me out," I said with irritation in my voice.

"It will be great, don't worry," he said, and took yet another opportunity to kiss my cheek.

"Stop doing that," I said, furrowing my eyebrows at him.

"No... you said I could have today and I am taking all I can get." His wicked smile making me laugh.

I heard the DJ say, "Please welcome Miss Kendall Martin and Mr. Noah Montgomery."

"Next up, put your hands together for Mr. and Mrs. Grant Montgomery."

I whipped my head around so fast I almost got whiplash. My eyes huge looking at Grant, is he trying to embarrass me?

"Seriously, did you tell him that?" My tone more than irritated.

"Only one day, taking full advantage, it sounds good though, right?" His eyes dancing at me with delight.

"Actually, it could mean anyone is your wife, my name wasn't mentioned, so your wife could be anyone, just not me," I said with annoyance.

"Shit… I should have used your first name. You're the only one I want to be my wife, so whether he said Sydney and Grant Montgomery or Mr. and Mrs., it doesn't matter to me because someday you will be my wife." His declaration was a bombshell to my soul, I could feel the box of feelings I locked away so long ago desperately trying to free itself.

After Heather and Curt Wilder were announced the guests went wild. Everyone was toasting with champagne. Kendall and I ran to the bar for a quick shot of Patron, to give us some needed liquid courage to do the first dance. Grant looked at me and shook his head from across the room.

"What?" I mouthed to him, but he just kept shaking his head from left to right and smiling at me.

The DJ announced Heather and Curt would be starting with the traditional first dance. Most guests were sitting down in their seats.

As the sound of *The Police* filled the room, after about thirty seconds of their slow dance, the music began to skip…I looked over at Kendall and when we heard "California Gurls" start to play, we moved out on to the dance floor. The guests were well, in disbelief by what they were seeing with their eyes. Heather, Kendall and I were moving like one on the dance floor and strutting our stuff, our bodies close together, moving like a flag blowing in the wind. We made our way to fondle the guys as they sat behind us in chairs, and when they pulled us onto their laps, Grant's touch had me gasping. He didn't just give me a kiss on the cheek, he went for a full on open mouth smoldering kiss. I lightly slapped his face and finished my part of the dance.

Grant was not holding back when it was the guys turn to dance. I was well fondled beyond belief, in front of everyone. I don't think anyone could tell but Grant was seducing me in front of everyone. The guests were screaming with glee, while the six of us danced the first dance together. People were hooting and hollering at all of us.

"Every Breath You Take," came back on so we could finish the slow part of the dance. Grant was wrapping his arms around my lower back and my arms were around his neck. My heart was racing from the dancing, and my breasts were heaving up and down. He pulled me close to him in a sensual embrace. This moment was pure bliss for me.

"I love to hold you like this, dancing with you is wonderful." His words making me melt even closer into him. "Will you spend the day with me tomorrow at the beach house?"

He spun me out of his arms and then back to him, pulling me close again.

"I can't," I said, my smile plummeting.

"You can't or you won't?" He asked, his inflection questioning... disbelieving.

"I can't. I would love to spend the day with you, but I have business meetings all day and then I am taking a late flight back to Texas." I was touched by the fact he wanted another day with me, but I didn't have the day to give him. "I told you this morning, I don't have time."

"Can I come visit you in Texas?" He asked.

I pulled away from him and looked into his eyes as we continued to dance.

"I don't think that is a good idea. I told you... you could have today and that was it. I don't have time for a relationship and I don't want to give you false hopes. Let's just have today, nothing more nothing less."

He was not happy, he began to tense and when the song was over, he walked away from me and straight to the bar. I wasn't allowing myself to get caught up in his drama. I gave him today, he could do with it as he pleased. If he chose to get drunk and spend the duration of our time together apart...it was his choice.

I was sitting with Kendall drinking a beer, our feet up on the chairs, music is playing, guests are dancing. Kendall and I are laughing at anything and everything. We were talking non-stop about the upcoming projects we have going with Uppercase.

"Flying back and forth the next few months is going to be exhausting," I told her.

"Yeah, but think of all the business we are getting, maybe soon enough we won't have to work for someone else, maybe our wishes will come true." I didn't get a chance to answer her.

"Oh, I love this song," I said to Kendall. I could hear Tim McGraw's voice singing "It Felt Good On My Lips."

"Sydney, would you like to dance with me? I know this is your favorite song or at least it was at one time," Grant asked very politely, putting out his hand to help me up.

"I would love to dance with you," I said, a smile beaming on my face.

We walked hand in hand to the dance floor, all smiles. His arms wrapped around me, holding me tight as we danced.

"I am sorry, I shouldn't have left you on the dance floor earlier, it was rude," Grant said, his voice filled with shame.

"Are you mad at me, because we can't spend the day together tomorrow?" I asked him. His face was so sad.

"No, I understand. You have a business to run and you only have tomorrow to get things done. What if I drive you to all of your appointments? I will wait for you in the car, would you be willing to let me be your chauffeur?" His voice and face were animated excited by his idea.

I laughed at him, seriously he wants to drive me all over town and wait for me in the car. I wasn't completely against the idea, but really he could be surfing.

"Wouldn't you rather be surfing or something?" I asked, surprised by his request.

"I will be here all week and I only have you for today, and if I can get to be with you tomorrow than I am ahead, what do you think?" His smile was too big and broad to say no to.

"Will it make you happy?"

"Yes… you have no idea, how happy. I just want to be with you and if it means me being your chauffeur, assistant, or sex slave then I am in." He had me laughing at his statement.

"Okay, then you can be my chauffeur, and maybe have lunch with Kendall and Matt after our meeting."

"Matt? When did he come back in the picture?"

"Well, he is our web designer and I plotted to get them into a meeting to work things out, they are meant to be, you know- soul mates," I said, trying to gauge his response to my words.

"Soul mates, huh? They are lucky if they can work it out. I hope someday you and I can work it out to be in the same city for more than a few weeks. I know we could make each other happy for the rest of our lives, if you just give us a chance." Grants word were so sincere and convincing, but I wasn't about to go down this road with him again.

"Grant, stop. We have today and now tomorrow…I can't, please let it go. I will be in Texas and you will be in Arizona, it is just not feasible for us to get involved again."

I leaned my head against his chest and he held me close as we danced.

"I don't want to be with anyone else, only you... it has always been you. Sydney, please let me make you happy? You can run your business from Arizona, quit your other job, I want to take care of you." I could hear his desperate need, but I am not able to give him what he wants.

"Grant, do you want to spend tomorrow with me?"

"Yes, you know I do."

"Then drop it. I am giving you tomorrow, but if you are going to badger me into trying to have a relationship again, then tomorrow is off." My words matter of fact, stern.

"Fine, I won't bring it up again, but this is how I feel and I know you feel the same." He said very presumptuously.

"Grant Montgomery, don't try to tell me you know how I feel. This is the first time we have been in the same room together in more than two years, you don't even know me anymore." My words were heated with annoyance. Really, his arrogance is astounding.

"You haven't changed. You are stubborn, beautiful, smart, sweet, dedicated, and loyal. You are everything to me and you are mine, maybe not today, but you will be my wife someday. When you realize this fact, our lives will be so much easier."

That is it...I am not going to stand here and let him bully me into a relationship with him no matter how much I love him. Damn... I love him. Shit!

"I need some air...I am going outside," I said stomping on to the back patio.

I made my way to the outside bar, I could still hear the music playing. Kendall was in hot pursuit after me. She walked up to me at the bar.

"So, what was all that about, can I kick his ass now?" She asked.

I started laughing, "No. Bartender, two shots of Patron and two beers please."

"Make that three shots," Grant said from behind us.

I rolled my eyes at him and let out a deep breath. He is not going to leave me alone.

Kendall turned to him, "Listen asshole, keep away from her. You break her heart one more time and I am going to personally see to it that you getting your ass kicked." Kendall was in his face poking at his chest.

"Kendall, calm down," I said. "Geez, I am a big girl, the asshole knows where he stands with me. He knows he has to play second fiddle to my career, right?" I said looking at him.

"Hey, I am standing right here, you could use nicer words to describe me, he chastised us.

"No, asshole is a good word to describe you," Kendall said, and we both started cracking up.

"I will remember this conversation when you are in our wedding and making a toast to us!" Grant said to Kendall, now he was laughing.

"Both of you shut up, let's do our shots and then dance the night away!" I said and handed them each a shot.

Well, one shot started a wild night of fun. Soon we had half the wedding doing shots on the patio, including Grant's parents, brother, Heather, and Curt. Grant and I danced almost every dance together. Slow dance or fast dance, he was beside me. He was a gentleman all night.

His mom approached me on my way out of the bathroom.

"Hi Corinne, are you enjoying the reception?" I asked my words partially slurred from all the drinking.

"Sydney, are you having fun? I see you and Grant are having a good time together. Are you going to work things out this time?" I could hear the hopefulness in her voice.

I smiled and gave her a big hug, "Time will tell!" Was my response to her question.

I wasn't fooling myself, I knew once I was back in Texas there was no chance of a continued relationship. Let's get real, I have no time for a boyfriend right now. I told this to Grant repeatedly, but he just didn't want to hear it.

I was pretty much drunk by the end of the night. There was no way I could drive home, I would have to have the club call me a taxi. I went to say good-bye, most of the guests had left for the evening. Kendall's parents were driving her home. Grant's and Curt's families had come together in a limousine. Heather and Curt had a private limousine to take them to the hotel tonight for their wedding night. Tomorrow they are leaving for Hawaii for a ten day honeymoon, thanks to Uncle Kevin and Aunt Corinne.

Grant came walking up to me at the front desk. He wrapped his arms around me and kissed my neck, he was in no shape to drive either.

"I will call you in the morning and see if you still want to play chauffeur," which made me laugh for no other reason than I drank too much.

"No, come home with me, we can pick up your car tomorrow," his voice firm and demanding.

"No…I have to go home…I have meetings all day tomorrow. If I come home with you, you will make me late, or miss them all together. You have no regard for my wishes," I said, annoyed with his tone.

"I am sorry, you're right, can I come home with you?" His eyes lighting up with the prospect.

"No, that is a bad…bad…idea. You know what will happen if you come home with me," I said, kissing his face.

"Miss Stanton, your taxi cab is waiting for you, would you like me to help you to the car?" The front desk attendant asked me.

"No, I think Mr. Montgomery will see me out." I looked at him and smacked his ass to move his hot body along.

"Does this mean you want me to come home with you?" His voice deep and wanton.

"I said you could have me today and tomorrow, it is tomorrow already. You don't want to waste any precious time, do you?" I was being more than forward, but my inhibitions were gone after the third shot of Patron. God I hope I don't get sick tonight.

I laid a big fat kiss on him, hit his ass again, and we climbed into the back of the taxi. I gave the driver the address, which is only five minutes away, but driving ourselves would have been way too dangerous.

Grant paid the driver, once out of the cab, he picked me up, put me over his shoulder, and carried me to the front door. I was giggling the whole time, we probably woke up the neighbors, but I didn't care. I was going to make the most of my time with Grant. I fumbled for the keys, eventually opening the front door.

Once the door was closed, Grant had me pinned to the front door his lips covering mine. The lightning bolts had been coursing between us all night; every touch, each dance, each caress, even the lightest touch had our breathing uneasy. I pulled away from him and raised my eyebrows to him.

I slowly slipped off my high heels. Then I had him unzip the back of my dress, leaving me topless with just a very small thong on.

His breath caught as he began cupping my breasts with his hands and kissing my neck.

Yet again I pulled away from him. I made him follow me to the back door and I opened it, and leading him out to the pool. I took off my thong and dropped it on the pool deck. I dove right in, his jaw dropped at my brazen move. He quickly stripped out of his tuxedo. He jumped in after me. He grabbed me in the water and pushed me up on to the seat in the deep end.

"Damn Sydney, when did you get so reckless, I love it." We were furiously kissing, his hands were all over me.

The yard is dark, I didn't turn on any of the patio lights, or pool lights.

"Life is short…I want to make the most of each moment… no regrets," I said covering my mouth with his again.

"I have missed touching you so much, your body, what it does to me, I have had a hard on for you since last night." I laughed throwing my head back. I looked into his eyes, his eyes were huge brown circles, his desire for me pulsing through him. I could hear my own breathing catch. "Please let me make love to you, let me love you, I want to give you everything," his voice was filled with love and admiration.

I will give him what he wants, what I desperately want, but for today only. Hoping this would be the final closure I need to move on from him. His declaration of love wasn't enough, I was too scared to give him my heart again. I would love him for this weekend only, and then go on with my life.

Grant is kissing my whole body, he sat down on the seat in the deep end of the pool and lowered me on to him, his erection feels divine as he enters me. The feeling of him inside of me was the best feeling I have ever had, I missed him so much. Tears sprang into my eyes. Having him make love to me in the pool is something I have never done… ever. He is sucking on my nipples as I ride him, the water splashing around us like little waves. I am biting my lip from screaming out his name, which I am sure will wake the neighbors.

My body's response to him is undeniable. We fit together so well, each body part coming together as if we are made for each other. I am grinding on him, trying to get him as deep as I could get him inside of me. I finally reached my peak, I could feel his body starting to tense.

"Sydney, look at me…come with me," his words setting me off, and I was gone. The world was exploding around me. This felt so right, but it was destroying me inside, knowing it was only for today. I kept my fears and tears buried beneath the surface of my soul. I could hear Grant groaning out my name, and his body releasing with such intense force.

We kissed for a few more minutes. He lifted me from the pool and carried me to my room. Never breaking apart, we climbed into my bed and made love again. This time it was even better, especially since there was no water splashing around us. He said the sweetest things to me, warming my heart, healing all I thought I lost so long ago. When were done and caught our breaths, I could feel my tears coming out. This time the bond was even greater, as if I was taking a part of him with me.

I couldn't hold on any more. "God, Grant…" I cried into his chest.

"What is it Sydney? Don't you know how much you mean to me? How much I have missed you…how much I love you…I would do anything to change the last few years. I can't change the past, but I can make sure we are happy from this point forward." His words made my heart ache even more, I felt sick. My world was crashing down again around me, I had promised not to let him into my heart, or my bed. I had let him into my bed and my heart, but I would not allow him into my life. After tomorrow, I would walk away, no regrets. No matter how much I love him, I just can't get hurt again.

"Grant, I love you so much, I have wished for this for so long and now, when we are apart, the pain will be even worse. I can't be hurt again…" He kissed me on the forehead. His words were loving, and under any other circumstances, would have been soothing, but not this time. He tried endlessly to convince me we could be together and make it work this time. I listened to everything, but my mind was made up. I would take what I could get from him this weekend and leave for Texas the way I came, alone. We feel asleep wrapped around each other, my tears wetting his chest.

CHAPTER 17

Six weeks ago I was at Heather and Curt's wedding… six weeks ago. Six weeks ago I had given all of the love I had to Grant, given him my body and soul, and walked away. I explained to him I couldn't give him what he wanted. He wouldn't listen, wouldn't take no for an answer. He called all the time, even when I didn't answer, didn't call back, he kept calling. I didn't even have time to shop for food, run an errand, run a mile, let alone have a relationship. I was flying back and forth from Fort Worth to Orange County so much I knew all the flight attendants and pilots by first name. I had racked up enough frequent flyer miles to get me to Hawaii first class, if only I had the time to go.

Uppercase Events was bursting at the seams. Kendall and I are talking about hiring a full time assistant just to handle website requests and answer our calls. I am working full time at Yellow Bird and have been placed in a special advertising group to help do the Super Bowl commercial. To say the least- my world is busy.

Jackson had given up on me shortly after the wedding. He stopped calling once I stopped returning his calls. I was in a constant state of anxiety and stress, and Grant's persistence didn't help. I had to yell at him to stop calling. I had to remind him I gave him the weekend and that was it. It took the six weeks apart for him to finally stop calling. My heart ached for him, but I pushed all the feelings back into the box and moved forward.

Mr. Carlisle was our top priority. I was flying back to Orange County to meet with him at the site of the upcoming holiday party. He wanted me to walk the venue with him before I signed the contract. He wanted to know the lay out of the party, where everything would be placed. I tried to get him to look at the diagram I sent via email but he said he liked to walk the venue and get a feel for it, before he committed. So, I was flying out again on Friday afternoon to meet with him. I had become quite enamored with his assistant Doloris, she was my saving grace on learning to deal with him. She told me about all his quirks, what to do, and what not to do around him. She is the best.

Yellow Bird closed at 3:00 pm every Friday, a special perk for the employees. I was on a 4 pm flight back to California. Carlisle and Doloris are picking me from the airport and driving us straight to the venue. At least on the plane I could get some rest, no emails, texts, or phone calls. I am exhausted. I didn't sleep enough, didn't eat right, and haven't exercised in weeks. I am running on pure adrenaline, and my body is about to give out. I couldn't keep up this pace for much longer.

Before I walked out of the airport, I stopped and got a double shot of espresso, coffee is my best friend. It was late afternoon when I got into the car with Carlisle and Doloris. I really just wanted to lie down and go to sleep. I plastered on a happy Uppercase Events smile and talked about the upcoming party with them. Doloris asked me multiple times if I was okay, I assured her I was fine, but she didn't seem convinced.

"Steven, look at her- she is exhausted, I think we should do this tomorrow," Doloris said to Mr. Carlisle.

"Sydney, are you sure you are up to this? I know you are working very hard, do you want to postpone? We can come back tomorrow?" Steven asked me.

Their concern for me was sweet and kind.

"Don't be silly, let's do it, we are almost at the resort. I will be fine, just exhausted, too much traveling I guess," I said, but really I was not feeling well.

My stomach has been bothering me for days. I guessed bad food or a touch of the flu, who knew? I was on the go so much I couldn't tell if I was coming or going. If I could get through the next hour and check into the closest hotel I would be happy.

We arrived at the venue and walked the grand ballroom, I showed him where each of the activities would be placed; fortune teller, henna tattoos, poker, black jack, roulette, craps, DJ. It was a full blown party, not your normal holiday gathering for a company this large. He wanted to show his employees how much he valued their hard work and dedication.

Steven was walking next to me and Doloris was one step behind us taking notes. Thank goodness, I couldn't have if I tried. I must have stumbled because, I felt Steven's arms around me and then nothing- I blacked out. When I woke up, Steven and Doloris where above me and Doloris was talking with someone on the phone. I grabbed my stomach and began to cry. I could feel panic taking over my body.

Steven was holding my hand, I felt clammy and cold. "Sydney, you're okay, you fainted, we have 9-1-1 on the phone, and they are sending an ambulance to check you out."

I couldn't speak I was in so much pain, but my mind was racing. Doloris was on my other side, and she had a seriously worried look on her face. The pain was ripping through my body.

"Sydney, are you pregnant?" She asked me, my heart dropped in to my stomach. I shook my head no to her.

"Are you sure? Don't panic but there is a lot of blood." I looked over at Steven he is pale as a ghost. He is shaking his head yes to me.

Oh God, pregnant, what the hell, how could that be? I am on the pill, holy hell.

Next thing I know I am in the emergency room, doctors checking me out. Asking a billion questions. Doloris was a godsend, she went in to my wallet and got out all my insurance information, driver's license, and found anything else the hospital needed. I was hooked up to about hundred different devices. I was shivering, my body had given out on me, no way could I be pregnant. I feel like vomiting.

After what seemed like forever, the doctor came in to me and sat down next to the bed on a stool.

"Miss Stanton, I am Dr. Reed. I have gone over all of your blood tests and we have done a vaginal exam. I am sad to tell you... you had a miscarriage today. Do you know how far along you were?" He asked me.

"I...I...didn't even know I was pregnant. I am on the pill, it never even occurred to me that I could be pregnant," I didn't even sound like myself, my voice was cracking and barely audible.

"Were you on any antibiotics lately?"

"No."

"Did you take your pill at the same time every day, or did you forget to take it and then try to double up, or totally forget to take it?" His questions were valid, accusatory... but still valid, how embarrassing.

"I have been so busy with work and traveling it is very possible I forgot to take it, or maybe everything you said, I really don't know." My tears were coming down geez and all this happened in front of my client.

"I understand, these things happen, can I get you anything to help you rest or for the pain?" His bed side manner was wonderful, thoughtful and kind.

"Something to help me sleep would be wonderful," I said.

"We will keep you here for observation for a few hours and then you can be released. I will check in on you a little later." He walked out into the hall.

Steven and Doloris came in a few minutes later. Both of their faces were covered with worry.

"Sydney, we are so sorry, are you okay?" Steven asked me and Doloris held my hand and wiped my tears with a tissue.

"Do you want us to call someone for you?" Doloris asked.

"You are welcome to stay at my home for the weekend. I know my wife would love to take care of you," Steven said. His offer was very kind.

"You are both so kind to take care of me. I am, to say the least, embarrassed by today's events, I hope this will not make you think less of me." I was trying to be mature, but really I wanted to cry my eyes out.

"You have nothing to be embarrassed about, it is part of life. We are just happy you are okay and you will recover from this," Steven's voice is so calm and collected he is a rock in the eye of a storm. My storm.

"My cell phone is in my bag, can you call Heather, she is the only person I know who might be home." My parents are on the east coast and I was not calling my sister.

"No answer," Doloris said.

Damn I would have to call Curt.

"Okay, try Curt?" I asked.

She was scrolling through the phone for the number.

"It is ringing…"

He must have answered.

"Um, this is Sydney's phone, but this is a business associate of hers, is this Curt?"

"Well, Sydney asked me to call you or Heather, she is here, but she is in the hospital."

Doloris walked out of the room to finish the call. She came back a few minutes later.

"He said Heather is gone for the weekend to a trade show… but he is coming to get you."

The tears started to fall again, he would never keep this from Grant. He would run right to him and spill the information. I needed to make him promise to keep the secret. I told Steven and Doloris to go home and said I would talk to them in a few days. I thanked them both over and over for taking care of me. They each gave me a kiss on the forehead.

"Sydney, you call if you need us, and get some rest, no working until you feel better." Steven's words were forbidding like a father's.

I must have fallen asleep, I woke up groggy and disoriented. I could feel someone in the room with me. I turned my head and Curt was sitting in the chair flipping through the channels. I turned to him, and his face was filled with sadness. He scooted the chair closer to me. He took my hand in his.

"Sydney…are you all right? I was so scared when I got the call, do you want me to call Grant?" He asked his voice was trembling when he spoke.

I didn't answer. The tears starting to stream down again.

"God, I am not good at this kind of stuff. What do you want me to do?" He asked.

I laughed a little.

"Did you know you were pregnant?" An acceptable question, but it hurt when he asked me.

"No…no clue. I thought I was over worked, overtired, flu, bad food, never did I think I was pregnant. Curt you have to promise me you won't tell Grant. Please, I am begging you, don't tell him," I begged through my tears.

"Why, why don't you want him to know? He is, or was, the father right? You love him- he should know what you went through."

"Love has nothing to do with it. I just got him to stop calling me. If he finds out about this he will never give up on me. I just can't put myself through any more pain with him, he broke my heart so many times, I promised myself to never be hurt like that again." I was quiet when I was done.

Curt didn't say anything for a few minutes. He looked sad.

"Sydney, I can't tell you what to do, but you are making things harder than they need to be. He loves you, he will understand, it wasn't your fault, it wasn't meant to be this time."

"You are missing the point, I can't be with him. He and I just can't be together, because every time we are... I end up the one with a broken heart and miserable."

"Okay, I won't tell him, it is not my information to tell. But you should know, he is hurting too, he wants you. What about Heather? Do you want me to keep a secret from my wife?" I could hear the uneasiness of his voice.

"No, I will tell her. Can I stay with you for a few days, my flight leaves Sunday?"

"Of course, you can. We are staying at the beach house this weekend and no one is there but us. You can stay upstairs or in um...Grant's room."

"I will stay upstairs," I said. The thought of sleeping in Grant's bed would have my emotions pushed way way over the edge.

I slept the whole way back to the beach house. Curt carried in my bag and helped me upstairs to the guest room. He put my cell phone next to me on the bed.

"I will be right out here studying if you need me, are you hungry or thirsty?" He asked. He is so sweet.

I could feel my tears coming again, "No, I am tired."

"I will get you some water so you can take the antibiotics and sedatives the hospital sent home with you. You will need to eat though. I will order food for later." Curt left me alone only coming back with the water and pill bottles.

I slept the whole night through, when I woke in the morning, I replayed the events of the day before in my mind. I remembered the last time Grant made love to me which only brought out gasping cries from deep inside my body. Curt came running in when he heard me sobbing. He put his arms around me and held me. I am a mess, this was not going to be easy to deal with.

"Sydney, if you tell him he will help you get through this, he is miserable without you. He walks around in a fog and doesn't do anything but work. Stop fighting the connection you have and let him come to be with you." Curt looked into my eyes and wiped away my tears.

"Curt, I can't...I just can't."

"Yes, you can. Pick up the phone and call him I know he would catch the next flight out to be here with you, you are being stubborn," I could hear the frustration in his voice.

"No!" I yelled at him and that was the end of the conversation.

By Sunday afternoon, I was feeling better. Curt took me to the airport.

"Curt, thank you so much for taking care of me, if you hadn't been home to help me, I would have been...well thank you." I gave him a kiss on his cheek.

"Sydney, you are Heather's best friend and like a sister to me, I would do anything for you, but someday you will have to tell him," his words were like a stab in my heart.

I looked at Curt, my eyes glazed with tears and sadness. I gave him a half smile and walked into the terminal.

I wanted to put this incident behind me. I didn't know I was pregnant and it is hard enough for me to comprehend. How could I tell Grant and expect him to understand or even grieve for a child we didn't know about? I wouldn't be able to handle the blame I would see in his eyes for losing our child. It is my fault for this unthinkable event...if I was paying attention to the signals my body was sending me, things might be different. Oh God...why am I doing this to myself? You have to stop- this it is probably the best outcome for this situation. I have quickly learned we can't always control the direction our lives take.

Yet another set of emotions I will tuck into my box of Grant, stored away in the depths of my soul. If I keep all of my love for him in this box, I will be able to move on. No need to have my heart shattered again. No need to wish for what I won't allow myself to need, feel, or want. I have learned on more than one occasion the pain that comes with having him in my life. No more wishing for the fairy tale ending. No more wishing, none at all. I have enough going on in my life. I am leaving all of this in the past and diving into work again.

CHAPTER 18

It has been six months since I left Texas. Three months after coming back to California I resigned from Yellow Bird. Kendall and I are running Uppercase Events on a full time basis. We have an office in an industrial park where the rent is much cheaper than in a high rise, plus we need the warehouse space for props and making designs. We hired a full time receptionist and we each have an assistant. We are seriously busy business woman. We started out doing weddings and parties, which we do on occasion as favors to family, friends, and some personal business associates. Our name has become synonymous with corporate event planning and non-profit events. We handle anything from a corporate retreat to a full scale philanthropic event.

Carlisle was our key to success; he is our fairy godfather. He sings our praises to anyone and everyone. His firm represents so many large philanthropies it is a win- win for all of us. We most recently planned a retreat for Yellow Bird, now that was a coup! Of course to me, Steven Carlisle is a wonderful man; he held my hand during a difficult time and made sure I was in perfect health before letting me continue on with planning his holiday party, or any other event.

All of that was a long time ago. Carlisle and I are meeting today to discuss a new client he has on retainer. It is a conglomerate of some sort, based out of Arizona, with industrial businesses all over the world. This huge company wants to give back to the community it is located in. It has partnered with local businesses and corporations in

Arizona to hold a full scale block party, proceeds from the event are to be given to local charities in the community.

"Sydney, this is a big deal, if you and Kendall can land this account it will make your business more successful than your wildest dreams. You will have to hire a full staff."

I started laughing so hard I almost peed my pants.

"Steven you are so funny…that is a bit of an exaggeration," I said still laughing at him.

"I don't think it is, if you two can get this project, there will other companies who want to do the same thing and will be banging down your door to get you to plan it." His eyes were wide with excitement.

"Why are you doing all this for us, are we your pet project? You have gone above and beyond the call of duty to help Kendall and me become successful. I mean you have more faith in us than our own parents?" I asked giving him a hard time.

"I don't know, you were so excited and full of life the first time you came in to my office. Your successes preceded you here through your sorority, and I felt like you were going to waste your time being in advertising. I wanted to see you both become successful and I get to help you do it… it makes me feel good."

I smiled at him. He is the kindest man I have met in business. He is a success and wants to share his success with others, teach others what he knows. Kendall and I have been thankful for his desire to help us.

"Okay, so what do you think they want us to do?"

"First off, you should know they are very serious about this community block party idea. They have two other event planners coming in to give huge, and I mean huge, presentations. You will need to do a full PowerPoint presentation, so get Matt to help you do all that computer stuff," I giggled at him. "Don't laugh at me."

"I am not laughing at you, keep going," I said.

"The presentation will be in front of the board of directors, as well as some of the other corporate sponsors."

"Do you have a list of the corporate sponsors? I would like to know who is going to be judging us."

"Of course," he beeped Doloris on the intercom. "Before Sydney leaves please give her all the information we have on Lookinglass Industries and the corporate sponsors, thank you."

"Okay, Doloris will copy everything you need from our file for you. You should do your research, and don't slack on this, I know you two think it is so easy, but I think you have your work cut out for you on this one."

I smiled at him, he is such a worrywart. I stood to leave.

"Oh Steven, you are so funny. Have we ever let you down?" I said smiling at him.

"No...well...no, you have never let me down. Sit down for a few more moments. Actually, there is only one thing I don't understand about you," he said, I could feel a lot of questions, or a lecture, coming.

"What?" My tone was less than sweet.

"Kendall and Matt will be married soon, when are you going to find someone and settle down and have some babies?"

"Are you nuts? I am only twenty-two years old. Why do I need to get married and have babies? This project right now is my baby," I said to him, squinting my eyes.

"You know I have quite a few young men who would love to take you out." Steven's face perked up in the hopes I would be willing to get set up on a blind date.

"What? Do you walk around with my picture in your pocket and show it to eligible bachelors in the hopes of finding me a husband?"

"I don't, but Maggie does. She wants to see you married off and give her some pseudo grandchildren."

"You will have your own grandchildren in time when your kids are old enough. I don't have time for a relationship, my company is my life and this new project is my baby. How do you expect me to be successful if I am chasing after a guy all the time?" I asked him, laughing at this silly conversation.

"If Kendall can do it, so can you." I rolled my eyes at him. "Don't roll your eyes at me, what is the problem?" Steven asked me with concern in his eyes.

"There is no problem...I promised myself a long time ago not to get hurt by another man and I don't have time to be hurt, it is that simple," I said, my voice quiet and saddened.

"Nothing is that simple. I don't know who hurt you, but you need to live a little. Sydney, you have to allow your feelings out, you have to take a chance with someone or give *him* another chance." Him, how does he know who *him* is?

I gave Steven and sideways look.

"Who do you think *him* is and why do you assume there is a *him*?" I couldn't believe this, I never said anything about Grant to him.

"I may be older than you, but I know you have loved and lost someone. I don't know the reason, or who it is, but I was there when you found out you miscarried and the look on your face was one of pure devastation. You don't have that look from a one night stand." His eyebrows raised at me. "Sydney, give him, or someone, a chance. Let yourself love, don't deprive yourself any longer."

I stood up as he finished speaking. I had put Grant so far out of my mind this last year, I didn't want to think about him again.

"Steven, I appreciate how much you and Maggie care about me, but I will be fine. I don't need love to be happy." I gave him a kiss on the cheek and left. I stopped by to visit with Doloris before leaving, and to pick up the packet on Lookinglass Industries.

I drove home to the new condo I was renting by the beach, in complete silence. No music, no phone, no nothing. My mind was blank as well. A good run on the beach always perks me up. Kendall and Matt were getting married and I am alone. Tears began to sting my eyes. Then my phone rang and brought me out of my silent meditation.

"Sydney Stanton," I said after answering.

"Hey Sydney, it is Steven. I forgot to tell you the presentation is in Arizona, Labor Day weekend. Lookinglass will put you and Kendall up in a hotel for a few days at their expense. Nice right? Okay, have to go."

I finished my run and was sitting on the balcony drinking some water. I was lost in thought over what Steven had said. Could I have it all? Was it possible to get Grant back after all this time? I didn't have time to think about it. I have only two weeks to get the presentation prepared. I showered, dressed, gathered everything Steven had given me, which I had spread out all over my kitchen table, and headed to our office.

"Good Morning Sydney," our receptionist said as I walked in the doors of our office late in the morning. "Kendall is waiting for you in her office."

"Okay, thank you," I said.

I had a bounce in my step and a smile stretched across my face, I was so excited to tell Kendall about our new project. I stopped in my office to put my purse and bag down, taking the file on Lookinglass with me.

"Hi," I said, walking into Kendall's office.

"Hi yourself, how was your meeting with Steven?" She asked.

I rolled my eyes at her and she laughed, "Another lecture on finding a man to make you happy?"

"Yes, he is worse than my parents. Okay, we have a huge project thanks to our fairy godfather," I giggled as I said the words. "We have to prepare a presentation for this company called Lookinglass, they want to have a block party in the community, all the proceeds raised will go to local charities."

"So, we don't have the job yet?"

"No, we are up against two other event planners local to Arizona. We will have to do a full scale PowerPoint presentation in front of the board of directors and some other corporate sponsors. I am going to split the research up between our assistants, and then we can go over it together."

"Okay," Kendall said. "This is our agenda for the rest of the week…" She went on to list other meetings, lunch dates, and the events we had on the calendar.

"Alright, I will be in my office if you need me."

I walked back and sat down behind my desk, turned on my computer, and grabbed my phone from my bag. I scrolled through the photos on my phone. Stopping on a picture of Grant and I from the first summer together at the beach. We look so happy, tan, smiling in a warm embrace. I could feel the tears stinging my eyes and rolling down my cheeks. Why did my heart still ache for this man? I hadn't heard Kendall come into my office, she was standing next to the door looking at me.

"Call him?" She said, her words making me look up to her, she could see my tears.

I shook my head no.

"Why, the worst he can say is no to you, which he won't…you can have everything… stop being so stubborn. You can have it all, any wish you want, you can have it. I hate seeing you like this Sydney." Kendall walked back down the hall, shaking her head in frustration at me.

I wiped my tears away, took a deep breath, and opened the file on my desk. I looked through the list of corporate sponsors. I knew what I was looking for Yorkshire Properties, I went up and down the list but it wasn't there. Huh? It baffled me a little, I figured the Montgomerys' company would be all over a sponsorship like this. I guess I was wrong. I recognized most of the names. Although there were a few I didn't. I took out a yellow highlighter and covered the names of the unfamiliar companies on the list.

I walked over to my assistant, Mikayla, "Hi, I need you to research only the highlighted companies on this list, I want to know what the company does, who is on the board of directors and/or who the principals are. I want pictures of the people, and I want it all by the end of the day, sorry." I shrugged my shoulders at her. "Kendall and I want to see it up on the flat screen in the conference room, so make it all pretty for us," I said laughing. Mikayla is a very good assistant, she understood our needs, and our odd sense of humor.

I gave Kendall's assistant Becca, a similar job to do on Lookinglass, she was less than thrilled when I walked up and explained the assignment to her. I advised them both we would be working late and bringing in dinner for all of us.

The four of us sat in the conference room eating Chinese food, Becca went first with her part about Lookinglass, we learned more about Lookinglass than we thought imaginable. The photos of the board of directors looked like they are from the 1980's.

"Are these the most current photos of the board of directors?" I asked her.

"Yes," she said laughing.

"Oh geez, should we wear shoulder pads for our presentation?" I asked Kendall, who spit out the food in her mouth, she was laughing so hard.

"Okay Mikayla are you ready?" I asked.

"Yeah, let me wipe my hands," She said. Mikayla pulled up the information on the corporate sponsors.

"So, this first sponsor is a family owned dry cleaners, they have twenty-two storefronts in Arizona, there is no board of directors. The parents are sole proprietors, they have four sons..." Mikayla was going on with all the information I requested, not that I was truly listening. My mind drifted to days long ago, college parties, high school. I looked over at Kendall and couldn't believe we were sitting in a conference room together, living out our dream.

"Ok, the second sponsor you wanted information on is called, Atherton Holdings, it is a.." My phone buzzed, I looked at the caller ID, hmmm, my sister, it was technically after work hours so she probably thought I would be home.

"Excuse me, let me take this call, keep going, I will be back in a minute."

"Hello?" I said answering my sisters' call.

I walked down the hall to talk with Jade, I could hear Kendall say something which vaguely resembled "Holy Crap," from where I was standing. She was tapping on the glass of the conference room to get my attention. I didn't turn around to see what she was freaking out about. My conversation took longer than anticipated and when I went back into the conference room, they had moved on to the third sponsor.

When we finished, Mikayla and Becca went home for the evening, and Kendall and I stayed to finish up some work.

"So, what did Jade want?" Kendall asked, knowing we don't talk very often, since our lives were in different spheres. She was married and stayed home to raise my niece. And I was working eighty hours a week running a business.

"She is pregnant again, due sometime in late spring," my voice was dry, unenthused by the news.

"That is good news, how exciting! You don't seem happy about it?" Kendall's question was right on.

"No, I am happy for them. It is just another reminder of what is missing in my life," I said, gripping for the coming lecture from Kendall.

"I am not going to lecture you, you know what you have to do. Either call him and give in to what you want, or find someone else." That was it- no long rant about opening my heart and taking risks, I was shocked.

I smiled at her, "Wow… that is it? I expected a thirty minute sermon on creating my own happiness and going after what I want."

"I am too tired and you are like talking to a brick wall sometimes!" Kendall said throwing her napkin at me.

We locked up the office and walked to our cars together.

"Hey, when I left to talk to Jade, what was the name of the company, um Atherton something, what do they do?" I asked.

"Um…they…distribute, you know… beverages." Kendall said and jumped into her car smiling.

We worked tirelessly for the next two weeks on the presentation for the block party. Once we perfected it and got all the kinks out, we called Steven and Doloris over to our office for a preview and their opinion.

"Okay girls…ladies I mean, show us what you have prepared. Is our little baby ready to go?" Steven asked.

Kendall and I exchanged big smiles. This was our best presentation and set of ideas we had ever put together. We pulled out all the stops and used every contact we had to design the presentation.

"Yes, sit down and please save your comments until you have seen the entire presentation," Kendall said pointing at Steven.

"Okay!" He said, putting his hands up in the air in defeat.

I started out giving a spiel about being honored to have this opportunity, yadayadayada. Kendall pressed the button on the laptop and the program quickly started the presentation, which took approximately seven minutes to complete. When it was done, Steven and Doloris clapped and said it was wonderful. Steven gave us some suggestions on how to tweak a few things he thought would work better. We happily accepted his advice and thanked them for their help.

We were leaving for Arizona in two days, we decided to fly, neither one of us wanted to drive. Heather had called me a few times, but I had been so busy with the presentation I didn't have a chance to call her back.

We closed the office for a four day weekend, giving our staff Friday off and Monday was Labor day.

When we landed in Arizona the weather is ridiculously hot, not like at home where the weather is beautiful. The sky is blue, the air is warm, and I am excited to lie by the pool, soak up some rays, and relax. The hotel sent a car to pick us up from the airport. The resort is absolutely beautiful, neither of us had stayed in it before, actually it was brand new. The grounds covered in rich vibrant water resistant foliage, rocks were used everywhere, and the green grass swaying from the light winds.

The front lobby was decorated with warm burgundy and gold tones, marble flooring and oversized chairs were placed in a precise manner to indicate privacy and an inviting feeling. The front desk attendant greeted us warmly.

"Hi, we are checking in" Kendall said.

"Yes, Miss Martin and Miss Stanton, welcome to our resort." He knew our names wow, nice touch.

"We were unable to give you adjoining rooms but your rooms are across the hall from each other, I hope this does not create a problem for either of you?" He advised us very politely.

"No, it is fine," we both said at the same time and then let out a giggle.

Once in our rooms, I called Kendall on the hotel phone to let her know I was going for a run, and then to the pool. I would come get her once I changed into my bathing suit. She suggested I bring my suit to her room, and then she would bring it down with her, and we could meet at the pool.

I changed into my running clothes, took the elevator downstairs, and headed out the back doors, passing the pool to the go for my run. I had an odd but strangely familiar feeling as I took off on my run. It nagged at me the whole time. I shrugged it off as butterflies, anxious about the presentation. I ran for some time contemplating my life, should I call Grant while I am here? Should I give in to my buried emotions? Do I tell him about the miscarriage? Too many questions, I picked up my pace, but looked over my shoulder, I felt someone was watching me or following me. It started to give me the creeps so I went back towards the pool at the resort.

I quickly found Kendall lounging by the pool flipping through a magazine and drinking a margarita.

"Hey, how was your run?" She asked from behind her dark movie star sunglasses.

"Fine, you look like you are hiding from the paparazzi, with those big sunglasses on," I was laughing.

She handed me her bag with my bikini and cover up in it.

"I am going to change and take a swim, order me some water and one of those margaritas you are drinking, please and thank you," I said, quickly turning and headed to the bathrooms to change.

I dropped the bag next to her and jumped in the water, it was so refreshing. I swam for a few minutes and then took a seat in the lounge chair next to her.

"Matt, will be here later by dinnertime. Do you want to go out tonight, maybe The Barrelhead?" She asked.

"Aren't we far from campus? How about we find some place walking distance, plus I don't want to drink too much tonight, big presentation tomorrow and all," I said reminding her why we are here.

"Yeah…yeah…did you think I forgot? This resort is awesome, we should plan another visit here. I believe they have condos you can rent for an extended stay."

"Maybe…I am going to rest my eyes for a few minutes." I put my head down on the towel to relax, my drinks arrived just then. I drank the entire glass of water and sipped my margarita. "Mmmm…good margarita."

Kendall and I relaxed by the pool until a rowdy bunch of kids arrived, so we decided to head in for showers.

"Okay, call me when you are ready to go." I said to her, "Are we waiting for Matt or is he going to meet us?"

"I don't know, I need to see how much longer his meeting is going to be, I will call you in a few minutes."

Kendall and I spoke with the concierge about a nice place to eat, that also had entertainment. The resort offered to drive us to the restaurant and pick us up when we were done for the evening, this place is so accommodating.

We ended up at an upscale sushi bar with live music. We sat at the bar and ordered the restaurant's version of a variety plate, a little bit of this and a little bit of that. We each ordered a Japanese beer but no sake, too risky. We finished and stayed to listen to the live music. We moved from the bar to allow other patrons to order. The music was lovely but I was beginning to tire.

"Kendall, I am going to call the resort to pick us up, I am ready to go to sleep."

"Okay, Matt is going to meet me at the resort anyways, we should head back."

It wasn't late, but I hit the sheets and was out like a light, but I didn't sleep well. I tossed and turned all night. When I did fall asleep, my dreams were filled with Grant's eyes gazing into mine, his deep voice reverberating through my dreams. "I love you Sydney, don't leave me, let me make you happy." Over and over in my dreams, until I couldn't take it anymore. I threw the covers off and went to the bathroom to splash cold water on my face.

I looked at my reflection in the mirror, telling myself it was only anxiety about the presentation. I started to say my spiel out loud in front of the mirror. I have it down, ready or not, I was presenting my baby tomorrow in front of a bigger audience than I am accustomed to.

I continued to stare in the mirror, maybe I will call Grant. Maybe, when the presentation is over… yes do it. Don't overthink things like you normally do, just do it, as soon as you finish. I turned on the TV, hoping it would help me relax and fall back to sleep for a few hours. It didn't and I continued to toss and turn. I must have zonked out around 2:00 am, because when the wake- up call came, I was startled and jumped from my bed.

I finished doing my hair and make-up, and put lotion all over my body. I smelled like coconuts. I left my hair down with a slight curl on the bottom. I put on my diamond stud earrings and a chunky bracelet, which matches my dress. I dressed in my teal and gray colorblock shift dress with my favorite Cole Haan, make my legs rockin' pumps. One final check and I was ready. I touched up my lipstick, grabbed my briefcase, laptop, and opened my door only to find Kendall standing in front of it looking hot off the runway. Our tastes are very similar so our outfits coordinated perfectly. We are due downstairs in ten minutes. Matt is meeting us outside the presentation room. We are last up- the two other local event planning companies went first.

Matt met us and took my laptop from me to prepare. We are escorted into the room, which is very dark. I actually like it, I couldn't see the faces of all the people who would be judging us today. Matt sat down at a back table to hook up my laptop to the audio visual system, while we waited by the door.

I was surprised to see Steven Carlisle standing in the front of the room announcing our arrival. He hadn't told us he would be here this weekend. I heard a small sound from the back of the room, like a gasp, as Kendall and I walked up in front of the screen, lights shining brightly on us. I could feel sweat starting to gather on the back of my neck and the same strange tingling feeling I had earlier rolling around my body. I shook it off based on the fear I am having at this moment.

I took a deep soothing breath before starting to speak. Kendall did the same. We introduced ourselves and gave a few examples of our work before beginning our presentation.

"Matt, will you bring up the presentation?" Kendall requested politely of her fiancée.

I started my spiel and then let the PowerPoint presentation speak for itself. When the program finished playing there was a loud round of applause and then a question and answer period. I saw the door open at the back of the room and someone slip out, and then I returned my attention to answer the questions presented by the board of directors and other sponsors in the room. We were in the room being grilled for what seemed like all day.

We finally were able to leave, and we almost passed out from the anxiety and the hundred questions we were asked.

"What do you think, how did we do?" Kendall asked Matt as we rode the elevator up to our rooms.

"I think you did superbly, but I am not objective. I think you guys are great no matter what," he said smiling and hugging Kendall.

"Great, I wonder when they will let us know? The anticipation is going to kill me," I said.

"You are not going for a run," Kendall pointed her finger at me. "We are changing, going to the pool, eating lunch, and celebrating. Even if we don't get the contract, it was a great learning tool and stepping stone for us, right?" Kendall said, her voice filled with reserved enthusiasm.

"Fine no run. Can I swim?" I asked.

"No. No exercising," she said smugly.

"You are seriously a mean person."

"I know!" She said smiling from ear to ear.

"Okay, be ready in ten minutes," I said to both of them.

I went into my room, changed into my bikini and put on my cover up. I pulled my hair up into a pony-tail and donned my favorite sunglasses. Grabbing my iPod I went to meet Kendall and Matt in the hall. I know I said I would call Grant as soon as I was done, but I really need to gather my thoughts before I do that.

The three of us walked, talking and laughing, to the pool, the stress of the morning having dissipated. We found a table and ordered lunch, a round of beers, and one shot each! We toasted to our hopeful success, and relaxed back in our seats waiting for our lunch to arrive. After lunch I took a quick swim to cool off, it is very hot, I wanted to bring my body temperature down a few more degrees from the nervous feeling I was still having.

I lied down on my stomach, putting my headphones on, and let my mind drift, falling into a deep sleep by the pool. I thought I was dreaming, but I could hear my name being called.

"Miss Sydney Stanton, I am looking for Miss Sydney Stanton?" I sat up to see a resort employee walking towards me. Kendall was pointing him in my direction.

"Miss Stanton?" He asked.

"Yes, I am Miss Stanton, how can I help you?" I was puzzled.

"I have an urgent message for you," he said, handing me an envelope.

"A message for me, okay," I said, taking the envelope from his extended hand.

The envelope had the resort's logo on it. It was sealed shut so I used my finger to open the back. I pulled out the card inside and unfolded it. I stared at the card- as I read it again and again.

I see you are enjoying your free time. Shouldn't you be taking care of our baby? I want to talk to you right now come to the bar inside the Resort.

No signature, but "baby", the only baby is our presentation, which we finished. Steven must want to see me. I put on my cover up, fixed my pony-tail and slid my flip-flops back on. I was annoyed by his note, he was at the presentation, what is his problem?

I told Kendall and Matt where I was headed. I was muttering to myself as I went inside, I took off my sunglasses and put them on top of my head, it took my eyes a few minutes to adjust to the light change. I asked the front desk clerk where the bar was, and she pointed down the hall and to the right. I thanked her and made my way to the bar.

I took a deep breath before stepping in to the bar. It was beautifully decorated in mahogany woods, rich golden colors of fabric, and soft music was playing. I scanned the room for Steven, but didn't see him. I took a few more steps inside and saw some booths to the left. Six booths in a row, each divided by high wooden walls with glass on the top. I walked down the aisle looking in each booth until I found him. I stopped at the end of the table, he was seated with Maggie next to him, I didn't look right away to see who else was seated with them.

"Steven, I got your note, what is this about?" I asked, annoyance in my voice.

"Sydney, I didn't send you a note," he said, looking as confused as I felt. "Sydney, please let me introduce you to Kevin and Corinne Montgomery."

My head flipped to the right. My eyes became giant. My world was starting to spin. I was totally shocked that the four of them knew each other. Of course they did!

"Wow, you all know each other?" I asked my voice filled with contempt. My arms crossed over my chest in annoyance.

Steven lowered his eyes at me. "Sydney that bordered on rude. That is not like you, what is wrong?" Maggie asked.

"I apologize, but if you didn't send me this note asking why I wasn't taking care of our *baby*" I used air quotations around the word baby, "then, who did?" I said completely confused by the situation.

Immediately I felt the hairs on the back of my neck stand at attention, the tingling sensation I had been having for the last two days was not butterflies over the presentation…it was Grant. I should have recognized the signs, but as usual I didn't. He is standing behind me- I could feel the tension coming off his body before I even turned around. My body stiffened in response, and I grabbed the table in front of me to steady myself.

"I sent you the note. So tell me Sydney, who is taking care of our baby?" His voice deep with resentment and anger.

I didn't turn around. I could feel the blood drain from my face and the look on Steven's face confirmed my worst fears, Grant knew about the baby. The silence coming from the four people in front of me was scaring the shit out of me. My brain went into overdrive, flee the scene, or face Grant with the truth?

He repeated his question, but this time he twirled me around to face him. His face was taught with anger. His hands were squeezing my shoulders so hard it began to hurt.

"Tell me, were you ever going to tell me we share a child? Is this the real reason you shut me out, tell me?" He began to shake me by my shoulders. His words were so callous, his voice so ugly.

My body began to tremble uncontrollably. I tried to speak but the words they wouldn't come out.

"I…no…you don't know what you are talking about," I said my lips quivering as I spoke.

"Don't lie to me… Curt, told me everything, he spilled your secret, now I want to know what is going on and where my child is?" He demanded.

His parents and the Carlisles were watching this drama unfold in front of them. I could hear Steven whisper something like, "He is the guy?"

"Grant, you don't know what you are talking about…let go of me you are hurting me," I cried to him. "I don't know what Curt said or what you think you heard, but there is no baby, no child. You are confused," I told him begging him to listen to me. My head was down because I couldn't look at him.

"Look at me Sydney, he said something about me not having to change diapers and missing all of the baby stuff. Why would he say that if you didn't have my child?" His tone hadn't changed; still vile, hatred seething through his words.

I still couldn't look at him, I began to cry, tears were streaming down my face. Maggie and Steven jumped up to my side seeing me breakdown. Kevin and Corinne followed.

"I can't...I can't do this." I broke free from Grant's grip and took off out the door.

Grant was yelling at me to stop, Steven was yelling at him, and everyone else was in hot pursuit after us. Grant caught me again by the arm, forcing me stop. We were standing in the middle of the hallway, between the bar and the front lobby.

"I can't talk to you about this when you are so angry. Please," I begged him. I looked at him, his eyes were filled with anger, concern, and maybe loss.

"I almost blew a gasket today when I saw you walk up to do your presentation. I could barely control my anger. I want the truth, NOW...tell me!" He pulled me into his chest hugging me trying to calm my cries and my trembling body.

I willingly went into his embrace. It felt so good after all this time to have his body against mine. I didn't want to lose this feeling...in his arms... it is the only place I wanted to be.

"I...I...I didn't even know... I was pregnant. I was so busy trying to do everything. I just thought I was sick or run down from working so hard," I couldn't get the words out. I was gasping for air. I couldn't continue, the words just wouldn't come out of my mouth. I looked at Corinne and Maggie who were crying.

I felt Steven put his hand on my back before he spoke, "I was there with her Grant, we were walking the venue for a party for my company, Sydney...she, fainted and then...then we called 911 and there was blood, a tremendous amount of blood. An ambulance took her to the hospital. The doctor told her she miscarried."

Grant was still holding me, but I could feel his body tense again. He pushed me away from him to look at my face and into my eyes, to see if the words Steven said were true. My eyes confirmed his words.

"I didn't know and I couldn't tell you," I said through my tears. I stood still as he looked at me.

"Why…why wouldn't you call and tell me? I would have come to help you, taken care of you," his voice was low and distraught.

I buried my face into his chest. My tears not stopping.

I looked up into his eyes, "I begged Curt not to tell you. If I would have called, you would never have left me alone and… I didn't have time to give you the relationship you wanted. It took me so long to get you to stop calling after the wedding and it would have been even worse if you would have known about the miscarriage. How could I ask you to grieve for something neither of us knew about or wanted? You obviously misunderstood what Curt said and thought the worst of me. I would never keep you from a child we shared."

"Sydney, I don't know what to say. I have been steaming about this since last night, when Curt got drunk and spilled the secret," his tone had calmed down. "How long ago did this happen?"

I looked at everyone looking at me for my answer, "About six weeks after Heather and Curt were married."

"So…a year ago?" Grant asked. "Besides Curt and Heather, who else knew about the miscarriage?

I sniffled and wiped my nose on a tissue Maggie had given me. "Steven, Maggie, and Kendall, and Doloris, Steven's assistant."

"Jesus, Sydney, all these people knew and you didn't think I would find out." Grant's temper was rising again.

"I did what I thought was best…there was no reason to get anyone else upset, I told you the weekend of the wedding I didn't have time for you or anyone else. But you wouldn't listen, and when you finally stopped calling I couldn't risk you running to my side." My words were pleading.

"I think we need to go talk…privately," Grant said taking my hand and leading me to a closed door.

We walked away from his parents and the Carlisles. I was going to be sick, my emotions were all over the place. I caught a glimpse of my reflection, not a pretty sight. Grant sat me down in a chair in a big beautiful office, when he closed the door I saw his name stenciled on the outside. What? He works at this resort. My mind is spinning out of control.

Grant is sitting next to me, pushing his hand furiously back through his perfect hair. He looked like he hadn't slept the night before. His beautiful eyes are dark with anger. I still wasn't thinking clearly, my tears had stopped, at least for the moment.

Grant bent down below me holding my hands in his. He looked up into my eyes.

"I blame myself for this mess...if I hadn't walked away from you that summer without giving you my reasons and made you understand what I wanted to achieve, we wouldn't be in this disaster. I would do anything to redo the past." He squeezed my hands kissing my knuckles. "I have been giving you the space you need to pursue your dreams, like I did. I have been waiting for you to come to your senses, but you are so damn stubborn. I am not waiting for you to get your shit together anymore."

I lost it, he was done with me, I was ready to be with him and he was done waiting for me. I started bawling, my body about to convulse from the pain my heart is feeling.

Through a torrent of tears, I gasped out, "I have been punishing myself for losing our baby. It is my fault, I should have been more in tune with my body, I should have taken better care of myself. I am sorry...please...please...Grant...I love you so much...I want to be with you...I want us to be together...please don't give up on me...please say you love me and want me."

Grant pulled me off the chair and onto his lap, his strong arms wrapped around me, cradling me, he rocked me back and forth. We are sitting on the floor. He is kissing me on my temple and wiping away my tears. I bury my head into his neck.

"Sydney, you have been punishing yourself all these months, blaming yourself, you had no control over what happened. I am not going to allow you to punish yourself anymore." Grant kissed the tears on my face. "I have waited so long to hear you say these words, I won't leave you and I do...I love you so much. Let me take care of you, let me love you, I want to be with you forever," Grants words were sweet, loving, and heartfelt.

I looked up into his dark brown eyes filled with love, and my tears still flowing I was on the verge of hyperventilating. I was taking deep breaths trying to calm down.

"Really...you are not mad at me? You understand why I didn't tell you?" I said gasping for breath between words.

"No, I am not mad. I will never understand why you think you have to solve all your problems alone. I would have helped you in any way I could have. But I am not going to dwell over the mistakes we both have made in the past," the honesty in his voice was warming to my aching heart. "I want to be with you, for the good times and the bad, in sickness and in health until death do us part. Please Sydney, let us be together for now and always, can you do this for me?"

I am shaking, is this actually happening, "Yes...I don't want to be apart anymore, I am tired of not having you in my life, will you make me your wife?" I asked him, my smile bigger than the Grand Canyon.

"Nothing would give me more pleasure than to have you be my wife, Mrs. Sydney Montgomery, it just fits you perfectly," He said smiling his gorgeous mouthwatering smile at me.

I looked up at him and he leaned down to kiss me. With his lips pressed on mine I felt my heart mending. We were finally giving in to our wish of loving each other.

I smiled and kissed his lips, whispering, "We fit perfectly together."

CHAPTER 19

Grant led me into a private bathroom in his office. He sat me down on top of the closed toilet seat. Turning on the water to the sink, he took a washcloth and soaked it in under the running water. He bent down beside me to wash my tear stained face, the cooling sensation made the stinging on my cheeks subside. I was overtaken by his gentleness. He continued to clean my face, as I attempted to regain some composure.

"Sydney, I will be right back, don't move," Grant said pointing at me.

I could hear him moving things around in his office. My mind is swirling, I had finally broken down and told him everything. His reaction to the loss of our child was better than I predicted, but still heart wrenching.

What is he doing out there? He is making a racket. He came back into the bathroom and extended his hand to me. I took his hand and he walked me back into his office. He sat me down in his big chair behind his over the top big desk. He got down on one knee. His hands are shaking, his eyes are a deep dark brown, light dancing inside of them.

"Sydney, will you marry me?"

He opened a black ring box, inside was the most incredible engagement ring.

"Yes…I will marry you!" I jumped into his arms. And once again we are sitting together on the floor.

Our kiss is intense, the lightning bolt powering between us at warp speed. He took the ring out of the box and slipped it onto my left ring finger. The ring is off the charts beautiful. It is a full two carat princess cut diamond, encased with smaller diamonds, set in platinum with more diamonds down the sides.

We kissed, cried, and laughed together not letting go of our embrace. When we finally came apart, I wondered when and where he got this ring from. I shouldn't ask but my curiosity is peaked.

"Grant, when did you buy this ring?"

"Well…I didn't buy it…it was my great-grandmother's engagement ring. After our weekend together, the weekend of Curt's wedding, my mom gave it to me. She said she knew it was only a matter of time before we found our way back together. She said she knew we were soul mates and wanted me to have it. I have kept it with me and put it in my office safe, just in case this opportunity came."

My heart is overjoyed by the story he told me. His great-grandmother's ring, it is more special than anything. I will never take it off.

"I love it. I love that it is part of your family. Your office safe, I am so confused. Why is this your office? I thought you work with your family?"

"I do, this is our resort, I am the General Manager."

"What…? I thought your company is called Yorkshire?"

"It was, we bought out another company named Atherton. Their name is bigger, more well known around the world, Dad thought it was a better business move to keep the Atherton name."

"No wonder…I didn't see Yorkshire on the corporate sponsor list for the presentation, I thought it was odd for your family not to be involved in such a huge community project."

"So, you were hoping to see our name?"

"Yes, and disappointed when I didn't. But you know what? I had my assistant research all the companies on the list who were new to us." I shook my head thinking back to the meeting when Mikayla presented the information on Atherton. I started to laugh and mutter about Kendall hiding the information regarding Atherton. "Damn, Kendall is good."

"What?" Grant looked at me confusion marking his face.

"Kendall…she is good. I had to take a call when my assistant was presenting the information about Atherton and when I asked Kendall about it later, to tell me about Atherton, she lied and said it was a distributorship of some kind."

Grant began to laugh. I realized Kendall had plotted to keep me in the dark about Grant's company.

"I thought I couldn't adore Kendall more, but now I am indebted to her, and you have an assistant?"

"Yes, I have an assistant, so does Kendall, and a receptionist. Did you know I was going to be here for the presentation?"

"No, my mom made me sit in on the presentation, convincing me that since Atherton is a corporate sponsor we need representation for our vote. When Carlisle announced your name and I saw you and Kendall walk up in front... my anger...was well uncontrollable...I had to leave the room before I made an ass out of myself and embarrassed you."

"So, you didn't see me until this morning? You didn't see me go for a run yesterday after we checked in?"

"No, I was not here most of the day on Friday. Why?"

"I don't know. I felt like someone was watching me yesterday, I chalked it up to an uneasy feeling and to nerves, but I still had this troubled feeling. It must have been you, the tingling and uneasiness. My body was warning me you were near."

Grant let out a manly chuckle and kissed me again.

"I am sure you are right, no more uneasy feelings. The only tingling sensations I want you to have are happy ones. We should probably go tell everyone our good news. I am sure my mom is pacing the halls."

We both laughed. I cleaned myself up a little more, before exiting his office. He pulled me into his arms and gave me a long hot kiss, which sent my body into a deep need to be alone with him.

His warm hands softly caressed my face, "You're so beautiful, I love you, and no matter what comes our way, I am never letting you go again."

We walked down the hall past a few offices and went out a secure door. We didn't hold hands, I kept my hands in my pockets and my head down. My smile was too big to conceal. Grant walked in front of me, a scowl across his face. We didn't see anyone in the hall, so headed towards the bar. Flashing each other a secret all knowing smile before crossing the opening into the bar, he stopped just inside the entrance and looked around, as I came up behind him. I was not very good at hiding my emotions, no matter how hard I tried.

They were all leaning on the bar. His parents stared at him, the look on their faces filled with alarm. Maggie and Steven turned, looked at me, and their hopeful smiles quickly dropped. Kendall and Matt, had joined this little party. Kendall, she knows me too well, she smiled at me and came running up. The look in my eyes must have given me away.

She hugged me and whispered in my ear, "You know your eyes gave you away, let me see the ring?"

I started to giggle, "Shit…you are so perceptive."

I pulled my hands out of my pockets, she took my left hand and looked at my new old engagement ring. She hugged me again, tears popped up in her eyes, and in mine.

"It is beautiful, I am so happy for you both. You deserve to be happy, to have all your wishes come true!"

Grant put his arm around me, his parents and the Carlisles came up giving us both hugs and kisses. They chastised us for trying to fool them, but the elation amongst us all was one of the best feelings I have ever had. I called my parents to tell them the good news. They were very surprised by our announcement, excited- but very surprised. I didn't talk to them long, they were on some cross country motorhome vacation, and the signal kept going out during our call.

Steven ordered a bottle of champagne, we toasted to our happiness and then sat down at a big round table to accommodate our party. Grant and I did not stop holding hands, we were both bursting with bliss.

"Sydney, I can't believe after all this time you never shared with Maggie and I about Grant. You never mentioned his name to us, I was shocked to find out he is the man you are in love with."

I didn't answer right away, I looked at Grant, his gorgeous eyes looking back at me.

"I could ask you two the same question. We have been working together with our lives intertwined for a couple of years, and you never mentioned knowing the Montgomerys. How do you know each other?"

Corinne spoke up, "We met about ten years ago on vacation, we hit it off and have been friends ever since. Our businesses just now crossed paths, when Steven's company obtained Lookinglass as a client and our name was on the sponsorship list."

It was all coming into perspective now, Corinne, she is a master manipulator, "Did you know Uppercase would be bidding the job?"

The smile on Corinne's face was telling, "Yes, I encouraged Steven to have you and Kendall vie for the project. He was apprehensive at first, knowing how busy you already are, but I persisted until I convinced him to get you two on board."

"Mom, you orchestrated this entire thing?" Grant said eyeing her.

"Yes, I was tired of watching you mope around. I had to do something to get you two in the same room, and it turned out better than I could have dreamed."

"Wait, I am still confused, how did you know about the project to begin with?" I asked Corinne.

She smiled, "I sit on the board of directors for Lookinglass, so when the idea was thrown out to have a community block party hire an event planner to do all the work, it was...well a no brainer for me. Having Steven in my corner helped my cause." Corinne laughed and Kevin squeezed her hand, giving her a loving kiss.

"I love my wife! Speaking of wives, when are you going to make this official? When are you planning to get married?" Grant's dad asked us.

Grant and I looked at each other. We hadn't even talked about the wedding, nothing.

I looked over to Kendall, who smiled at me and said, "Of course, I will help you plan your wedding, just like you have been helping me!"

"We haven't even discussed what we want yet, but I don't want to wait, I want to be married as soon as possible," Grant said and kissed me.

I smiled and squeezed his hand.

"How about a destination wedding?" I said as I looked at him with wide eyes.

"Oooh," the response came from around the table.

Grant smiled, "Interesting, where?"

"Cabo, Cayman Islands, Hawaii, you pick?" I said to him.

"We could be in Vegas by tonight?" Grant responded, eagerly.

Loud, "NO's", came from all the woman at the table, followed by a roar of laughter.

Grant looked over at me, his face a bit flush with embarrassment. I smiled at him and caressed his check. He is so gorgeous and he is going to be mine forever. A small chill went through me.

"So, what did your parents say?"

The table grew quiet when Grant finished asking me the question. I took a deep breath.

"Well, they were surprisingly shocked of course. I could hear my dad in the background saying 'What?' about hundred times. They are going to call me back, something about bad reception from wherever they are on their cross country vacation. But before I forget…Kendall, take a picture of my hand and text it to Heather, I can't wait to hear her reaction."

Kendall took the picture of my left hand with my engagement ring prominently placed on my ring finger. It would take a few minutes before either Kendall's phone or mine started to ring. The conversation continued on regarding the wedding.

"So, when you say as soon as possible, what does that mean?" Kevin asked.

Both Grant and I answered at the same time. He said "three weeks" and I said "three months." Our heads flipped to each other, I repeated his words "three weeks are you nuts?" and he said "three months are you crazy?" Everyone broke into nervous laughter.

Kendall started, "Three weeks is doable!"

"Don't encourage him, we can't plan a destination wedding in three weeks, you know that," I said to Kendall, my eyes wide with worry.

"You are right, but we could plan a wedding here…you could have it here at Atherton. It is close enough so people could drive or fly without too much trouble and it is beautiful. Guests can stay here at the resort and then you two can fly off somewhere for your honeymoon. What do you think?" Kendall's smile showing pure confidence, she knew her idea was perfect.

Corinne and Kevin stood up, Kevin announcing, "Settled then; in three weeks the wedding will be here, now, everyone back to our house for a BBQ to celebrate."

I sat in my seat, watching everything around me unfold; Grant is completely on board with the idea. Three weeks. My phone began to vibrate and buzz on the table; bringing me out of my haze.

"Hello, just so you know, you are on speaker phone."

"What the hell, who's hand is this? I know it is not Kendall's because she has been engaged for two months already. Spill it!" Heather yelled excitedly at me.

"It is my hand."

"And who may I ask, gave you this ring?" I looked up at Grant who was standing behind my chair.

With a strong deep voice, "I did."

Silence…no response….

"I did, and the, "I" being…?"

"If you ask again, you are not coming to our wedding in three weeks," Grant barked at her.

Heather shrieked, "Grant Montgomery, you are not going to keep me from your wedding… wait…did he say three weeks?"

Grant leaned down and gave me a kiss. He whispered in my ear, "I am ready to be alone with you."

"I heard that!" The voice boomed from my phone.

I let out a small laugh.

"Heather, you and Curt meet us at my parents' for a BBQ in about an hour, don't forget to tell my aunt and uncle. Although, I think my mom is already on the phone with my aunt."

There was another round of hugs and everyone dispersed. Kendall handed me my bag from the pool. She and Matt headed up to their room to change. Grant pulled me into his arms, kissing my neck.

Grant was quietly talking to me, "Since, I am the General Manager here it is probably a bad idea for me to start groping you in public. How about we head up to your room for a little one on one time? I don't think I can wait to get back to my house."

I started laughing and my head dropped back, exposing my breast and neck to him. I could hear a very guttural groan come out of him.

"Yes, we better move, before your hands move all over me."

We walked hand in hand to the bank of elevators, employees asking him questions the entire way. He responded to each of them with authority and politeness. Each one received the same answer, "I am taking the rest of the day off, unless this place is burning down, don't call me."

The closer we got to my room, the more my anticipation grew. We hadn't been together since Heather and Curt's wedding weekend, and I hadn't been with anyone since that night. I didn't know about him, but this encounter was long overdue. Grant's breathing was louder, deepening as I opened the door to my room.

"Nice room," he said, closing the door behind me.

I stood with my hands behind my back resting on the chair. My head is tilted ever so slightly. I licked my lips and bit my bottom lip as he stalked across the small space to me. My pulse is racing and little bursts of excitement were running through my body waiting for his touch. I am still in my bathing suit with a cover up and flip-flops. Grant is in nicely pressed grey slacks, a crisp white button down, and loafers. He looks scrumptious.

He came up to me cupped the back of my head with one hand and my chin with the other, raising my face to him. His lips came over mine, engulfing me with more fiery hot passion than I could ever remember. His kisses were long and filled with love. His tongue was swirling in my mouth and then running along my jaw line, and down to my neck, his lips slowly making their way with light kisses to the top of my cover up. He shimmied it down to my feet so I was standing before him in just my small bikini.

The sound of his moans, and the sight of his heavy arousal in his pants had me weak in the knees. I wanted to lunge at him. He had stepped away from me, holding my hand and taking in what he saw. He licked his lips as his eyes drank me in from head to toe and then back up again.

"You are so beautiful, I could stare at you all day, but you are over-dressed in this bikini." His eyes filled with delight and mischief. He came closer to me again, with little effort he removed my top and bottoms. His eyes turned from dark brown to black, his breathing grew heavy. His hands were lightly skimming across my stomach and down to my inner thighs, giving me goose bumps, making my desire for him deepen. I could feel the ache growing inside of me, wanting him to touch me further.

I reached for his shirt, unbuttoning the cuffs, "Now, I believe you are the one who is over-dressed." I kissed his neck as I started on the buttons going down the front of his shirt. He pressed his hands on my ass, pulling me closer to him, I could feel his hardness straining against the inside of his slacks. His hands came around my front, one touching just above my needy sex and the other lifting my breast to his mouth. My head fell back from the sensations.

"Oh…God…your touch feels so good." I rasped out. I pulled his shirt off over his shoulder and he shrugged it to the floor. He continued his attack on my body, circling each nipple with his tongue, back and forth, not wanting to neglect either. I made a move for his pants but he inched back out of my reach.

"Let me get in your pants," I lovingly growled to him.

"Not yet...mmm...I could suck on you all day." His words made the wetness between my legs and my ache to have him inside me spark.

I pulled his head up to make him look in my eyes.

Frustrated, I spat out at him, "You haven't touched me in more months than I can count. I want you inside me, we have a lifetime to take it slow, I want it fast and hard and I want it now!"

His eyes widened from my words and the wicked smile on his face thrilled me. He scooped me up and carried me to the bed. After putting me down, he toed off his shoes, and stripped out of his pants and boxer briefs. I think my tongue was hanging out when I saw his erection. He chuckled at the look on my face.

"I see you still love what you see, do I need to use a condom or are you still on the pill?"

I swallowed really hard, barely able to get any words out because the sight of him naked had me about to have an orgasm.

My words were not coming out, "I...yes...still on pill, but use a condom just to be safe."

"Damn, we are going to be married, does it matter?"

"Well... if it didn't matter why did you ask in the first place? Yes, no babies right now, condom, to be safe."

Where is he going to get a condom right now? I thought to myself, but he reached back down to his pants, pulled out his wallet and guess what, condom!

"I hope this thing is still good," he said, sheathing himself, "It has been in my wallet a long time."

I rolled my eyes at him. Covering up for whatever indiscretions he has had since being together last.

"Did you just roll your eyes at me?"

"Yes, do you want me to believe you haven't needed to use a condom for so long, you forgot this one was in your wallet?"

He didn't respond. He came over me, widening my legs with his knees, he kissed my lips and down my neck. The head of his erection barely pressing on my opening, I let out a small gasp as he started to enter me. The feel of him slowly spreading my walls is tremendous. His thickness touching every part of my nerve endings, finally he is deep inside of me thrusting. His elbows are next to my head, his hips are moving back and forth, my hands are wrapped around the back of his neck, my fingers tugging at his hair.

His chest is pressed firmly against my breasts. Every part of our bodies are touching, the feeling is marvelous. I could feel my climax just out of reach, I could feel him starting to tense with his climax climbing closer. His words making my arousal more intense, "Sydney...God you feel wonderful, you are so tight...you are so beautiful." His words made me purr to him. "Making love to you is the best...having your body wrapped around mine is...heaven." I wasn't going to be able to hold on much longer.

"Grant...oh...don't stop..." I am breathless, my words barely coming out of my mouth.

"Not yet...wait just a few...I want to feel you," Grant whispered lovingly to me.

I could feel my climax coming, arching my back, digging my nails into his shoulders, trying so hard not to let go, he is relentless; his body moved with mine so perfectly, like we are made for each other. I pulled his head to mine giving him a scorching kiss, sucking on his tongue so hard I thought I might pull it from his mouth.

"Open your eyes, look at me," he said, gasping out the words to me, "NOW, come with me, NOW!" I screamed out his name as he did mine, the moment couldn't have been more perfect. Soaring together, our bodies stuck together, sweat pooled in between us, he leaned his forehead on mine, steading his breath. I kissed his lips as his heavy breaths filled me.

"I love you so much Sydney, I am so happy."

My heart is bursting inside from his passion, from his love, from our love.

"Grant...I will spend my life making you happy...but you know I can't cook," I said with a silly smile on my face.

He started laughing and fell to my side, still trying to come down from our high. He leaned over on his side resting his head in his hand, his other hand on my stomach.

"Then if you can't cook we have a problem... you will have to make it up to me in the bedroom, as much as possible. You know if you can't make me three meals a day, I will expect to have you three times a day." His face is serious, but his eyes are dancing with laughter. I punched his arm.

"Not nice," I said.

He laughed some more, dropping on to his back on the bed. He grabbed a tissue from the nightstand removed the condom, wrapping it in another tissue, and dropped it on the floor. I climbed on top of his ridiculously hard body, he wrapped his arms around my back and gave me a peck on my lips.

He smacked my ass as hard as he could, "Listen hot stuff, I don't care if you can't cook, we will learn together, we will learn a lot of things together."

I looked into his eyes, "Three weeks, huh? You really want to be married in three weeks?"

"I would marry you tonight, but you don't want to do the Vegas thing."

"Vegas no. Three weeks is good. My parents are going to freak." I thought to myself, I should probably check my phone to see if they have called back, but I am so comfy lying naked on top of my man, I am not going to move.

"What are you thinking about Mrs. Montgomery?" He said kissing my check.

I giggled. I had my head turned to the side lying flat on his upper chest.

"Um…many things, wedding plans, my parents, my company, my condo, where are we going to live, what about Lookinglass, there are so many things to discuss," I said with a little trepidation in my voice.

Grant smoothed back my hair which was now hanging in my face. He is playing with the ends of my hair.

"One thing at a time, we need to confirm the wedding date and we will live here in my house."

"Your house? I don't want to live with your parents."

"Sydney, I am 26 years old, I don't live with my parents. I have my own house…I mean we have our own home. Do you want to go see it before we go to the BBQ?"

"You're closer to 27… but who is counting. You bought a house? Yes, I want to see it."

We rinsed off in the shower together. We dressed and headed to the garage to get his car and to take a quick detour to his house… our house!

Chapter 19

We drove in his car, a new car, well at least it is new to me. It is a sleek black, BMW, a big four door sedan.

"What did you do with your Jeep?"

"I have it, it is parked in the garage at our house."

Did he say our house, I love that.

"Our house, we aren't even married yet, how far away is *our* house?" I said, with a little giggle in my response.

He smiled at me, catching my use of the "*our*", "Not too far, about thirty minutes or so."

I stared out the window looking at the desert landscape; really I was looking at houses, strip malls, shopping centers, restaurants, etc.

"You know, I heard what you said about the condom in my wallet, and just for the record the woman I was with today is the last woman I was with!" His eyebrows were high above his eyes, awaiting my response.

"Really? Interesting, I would think a hot commodity like 'Grant Montgomery', would have babes lining up at his door for a quickie!" I let out a nervous laugh, hoping his answer was still the same.

"Well, just because they throw themselves at me 24/7, doesn't mean I want them. What I said is the truth, I haven't been with anyone since you."

My heart swelled to full capacity. I am such an idiot, stubborn mule, I wasted so much time.

"Good to know," I said trying to be cool.

He looked at me with his eyebrows still fully erect! I knew he was looking for the same information. I sighed and looked out the window again. If he wants to know let him ask, I wasn't offering up my lack of a social life without him even asking!

"So, tell me, what you do with your free time?" Chicken shit!

"My free time, as if I have any. I work, work some more, and if I am not too tired, I run on the beach."

"So, Uppercase keeps you and Kendall busy full time?" His question was... well rude. Was he trying to imply it was more of a hobby than a full scale business?

I shot him a not very nice look.

"What are you implying? Do you think this is a game or hobby for us, we are not trust fund babies, we work hard at what we do and we are damn good at it! Just because your mom manipulated all of us to get us in the same room doesn't mean Uppercase is not well respected in the community we work in. And another thing, if you think I am going to give up my company and get all bare foot and pregnant you are so wrong...don't you even think I am going to sit home and bake cookies all day...." I was on a rant.

Grant is looking at me like I have two heads coming out of my neck. I believe he is laughing at me based on the smile on his face and his shoulders moving up and down. I couldn't hear any laughter, because I was in his face yelling.

He was laughing at me, "Calm down, Sydney. If I offended you that was not my intention, I was curious how busy you guys are, I am sorry."

I huffed a little and crossed my arms at him. Stupid men, think they are the only ones who can be successful and make money.

"Sydney, stop it…I would never keep you from your business or being a success, but…"

"But… what?" I asked my eyes getting small and squinty at him.

"Nothing, I don't want to fight with you about this, we will have to make decisions about our lives is all. Okay we are here."

I forgot where we were going. Grant had pulled up in front of a beautiful one story home. The outside is landscaped in a lovely desert style. We are parked in the driveway almost at the porch under a portico. The driveway is a half circle in front of the house. The house is painted in strong warming colors of a rich brown leather and fine burgundy wine. The walkway up to the house is flanked with flowers and landscape lighting. We walked across the porch toward the double front doors which are beautiful and made of glass. He opened one door and we walked through, with his hand on my lower back.

The entryway is tiled with beautiful light travertine, which leads in every direction. The house has high ceilings with crown molding. To the left is a lovely sophisticated formal living room, with lots of windows. Warm and inviting, it lurers you to sit down on the luxurious furniture. There are two long couches facing each other, both upholstered in a caramel brown houndstooth pattern. A large coffee table is in between them, and end tables on each side of the couches hold lamps and decorative pieces. My eyes are overwhelmed so far. Grant led me to the kitchen which is just in front of us beyond a doorway.

The kitchen is to die for, granite countertops, beautiful white cabinetry, an island with sink in it. Industrial stove with oven, wine cooler, subzero fridge, I am spinning around in the kitchen and just beyond the peninsula with the main sink, I could see a large kitchen table to seat eight, and full windows from top to bottom. From the kitchen you could see the house is in the shape of a U. In the middle is a sparkling pool with a water fall and water slide, Jacuzzi, and off to the side what looks like a BBQ area. Grant turned on the lights to the yard from a switch by the backdoor. The pool lit up, the yard lit up, and music filled my ears.

He came up behind me as I looked out at the pool, wrapping his arms around my middle and leaning his chin on my shoulder. I turned to him, my eyes filled with tears of joy. He chuckled a little. Grant began to sing along with the song on the speaker system into my ears, *"I wanna wrap you up… wanna kiss your lips… I wanna make you feel wanted and I wanna call you mine… wanna hold your hand forever… never let you forget it…"*

Grant kissed my neck and twirled me around the kitchen and then back into his warm arms. He is holding me tightly against his chest.

"This is the most beautiful home, how long have you lived here?"

"About six months."

"Did you do this all yourself, or did you buy it like this?"

"Most of it was done, well the inside was done, I put in the pool and landscaping. My mom and aunt helped me with the decorating. Do you like it? Let me show you the rest of the house."

He took my hand and guided me to the right of the kitchen into a family room. The house is decorated in the same warm colors as the outside, caramel, burgundy, hunter greens, with splashes of gold or yellow. The family room is anchored by a large sectional couch, a large area rug was underneath the couch, and a beautiful fireplace is in front of it, with a huge flat screen TV, hanging on the wall. We took two steps up to another wing of the house. Down the hallway, is a powder room, an office, and two bedrooms which are connected by a full bath.

We went back the way we came, through the family room, through the kitchen and to the left up two steps, and down a hall. There is a door to the garage, door to the laundry room, and then at the end of the hall is a large opening, double doors left open to the master suite. The entire interior U of the house has windows showing the yard or sliding French doors out to the backyard. He ushered me into the bedroom.

"This is the master suite, this is our room," Grant announced proudly.

I looked around, my mouth open, it is over the top big. There is a large sitting area, beautiful oversized chairs to relax in, both with ottomans, and an armoire which housed a TV. Huge sliding French doors open to the Jacuzzi and pool outside. The king size bed is in the middle of the room, covered of course in a blue striped comforter, night stands on both sides of the bed, a ginormous dresser with mirror on top. The bathroom is the size of a football field. Separate sinks on opposites sides, with separate vanity areas. Walk- in closets on both sides of the bathroom, one filled with Grant's clothing and shoes, the other empty. Mine is the empty one, I walked in and smiled, imagining all my clothes hanging up. Each closet had an island in the middle with drawers and granite tops. There is a beautiful bath tub for two, jets all around it. A huge shower, with seats on each side, two shower heads, and controls for a steam shower.

Grant was standing by the bed when I came out of the bathroom. I ran up to him and pushed him down on the bed, kissing him like a crazy person.

"I love this house, it is exactly what I would have picked, everything about it is perfect!"

"I know," he said with his lips in a perfect smile.

"You know, how do you know?"

"I know you so well, I knew someday we would be together and you would be my wife. I picked this house out based on...well, what I know you like, and a place we could raise our family together," his voice is sweet and loving.

His hand is caressing my face as his voice caresses my brain.

"Family...how many kids do you want to have?"

"As many as you're willing to give me?"

"That is not an answer...2 or 3?"

"Yes, 2 or 3 is good." I laughed at him, "As long as we have 2 or 3 I will be happy," he said, continuing with his kisses.

"If you keep kissing me we won't make it to the BBQ." I told him.

"I know...so, you never told me, have you been with or been seeing anyone, you know dating?" I am like putty in his hands, when he kisses me like this.

"No...I haven't been with anyone since you. Happy?"

"Mmmm...very..." his words trailed off as he continued to kiss down my neck, "I believe we are going to be late to the BBQ."

I could hear my phone buzzing inside my bag. I jumped from his arms to grab it. It might be my parents calling back. I am sure a lecture will be given, about rushing into marriage and so on. I know this is right and nothing my parents say will persuade me otherwise. I have no desire to waste any more time away from the man I love. I know there will be concessions to being together but all marriages have compromises, right?

"Hello?" I mouthed to Grant "my parents."

He flopped back on to his bed and listened to our conversation.

"Hi Sydney, we are finally in an area with good cell reception. Now what is this about you and Grant getting married, we didn't know you two were seeing each other again?" My mom said her voice was nice but hesitant.

"Mom, it is a long story which I don't feel like repeating right now, but he proposed and we want to get married. We have waited so long to get it right and it is finally right. We don't want to wait." I hesitated before telling her the wedding would be in three weeks.

"Sydney, I just think you should wait, why rush it? You have been so busy with work and you two haven't even been dating, you should definitely wait," her tone was pleading.

"I am sorry Mom, I know you don't understand. We are going to be married in three weeks, here in Arizona at the Atherton Resort. Can you come with me to find a dress, fly here from wherever you are, or come home and we can go dress shopping?"

"THREE WEEKS…ARE YOU NUTS…." She was yelling into the phone. "Are you pregnant, tell me you are not pregnant? Why so fast, Christ… Sydney. Your Father is going to freak out when I tell him. Fine you give us the date and we will re-set our itinerary to be in Arizona, but I won't be able to go dress shopping with you," my mom sounded sad, missing out on the preparation for the wedding.

"No, I am not pregnant. Mom, it is what we want, we don't want to wait. We have waited far too long. I wish you could go with me but I understand, I am just happy you will be here for the wedding."

"Sydney, if this is what you really want then we support you one hundred percent. We love you very much."

"I love you to Mom, talk to you soon."

Well that went better than I had anticipated. Hopefully Corinne will want to go shopping for a dress with me, really? Of course she will want to go!

We locked up the house…our house, and went straight to his parents' house, where the BBQ was in full swing. We spent the entire evening planning the wedding. We were in town until Monday, so tomorrow we were shopping for my dress and for the bridesmaids' dresses. I already knew what invitations I wanted, and Grant liked whatever I picked. His only requests were steak for dinner, chocolate cake for the wedding cake, and a traditional first dance. I have no problem with any of those requests.

The guest list was completed, the resort had confirmed the date and set rooms aside for our guests.

"Where are you going to go on your honeymoon?" Kendall and Heather asked.

I shrugged, "I don't know. Will we have time to take a honeymoon? What if we get the Lookinglass account?" I was started to feel a panic attack coming on thinking about everything going on in my life.

"Did I hear someone say, honeymoon? That is the best part of this wedding extravaganza," Grant said licking his lips.

I smacked him in the stomach, "Best part huh, I thought I am the best part?"

"That is a given, you have all the best parts!" His salacious smile showing.

"Gross you guys, we are sitting right next to you." Kendall said, sticking her finger down her throat and making barfing noises.

We all burst out laughing!

"I am planning a surprise honeymoon for us, so don't worry your pretty little party planning heads about it, I am in charge," Grant said with a serious look on his face.

I smiled at him, "Fine, as long as we are not travelling the country from baseball stadium to baseball stadium," I laughed. He raised his eyebrows at me and wiggled them.

CHAPTER 20

On the flight home, my eyes closed and my mind began to spiral with the events of the long weekend. I had come to Arizona for a presentation, had left with a fiancé and an impending wedding…in three weeks! I had spent the entire Sunday wedding dress shopping with my two best friends, soon to be mother in law, and her sister. How did this all happen so fast, don't get me wrong, I was far from unhappy, I am over the moon with happiness, joy, and love. Not in my wildest dreams did I think this would ever happen.

I felt a warm hand wrap his fingers around mine and gently wiggle my engagement ring. I opened my eyes to stare at the most gorgeous loving man sitting next to me, his light kiss grazed my lips, making my smile even bigger. His smile warming my heart, Grant decided to come back home with me for a few days, we had a lot to talk about. Kendall and Matt were sitting across from us on the plane. She was in her own heaven, things were working out for both of us.

We walked to my parked car in the parking structure. Grant looked at the car and then to me. His face was puzzled.

"What?"

"What happened to your cute Jetta?" He looked disappointed.

"Sorry baby, I have a big girls car now." I smiled letting out a silly giggle.

"No, I like it," he said, walking around the car to check it out.

I popped the trunk to put our bags in. Grant went to lift the tailgate. I heard him chuckle.

"What, are you chuckling about?"

"You have a personalized plate? Let me guess you and Kendall have matching cars, your plate says UPPPER and Kendall's says CASE am I correct?" His eyebrows rose at me in speculation.

Kendall and I exchanged glances and started laughing.

"Well yes, is there a problem with that?"

"Absolutely not…you two are just so cute…I can't stand how cute you two are, although I wouldn't want to fight either one of you in a board room."

Matt starting laughing and grasped Grant on the shoulder, "Grant man, I am so glad to have you here. I need all the help I can get to deal with these two megalomaniacs!"

"Hey!" Kendall and I yelled at Matt.

"Are you two going to deny, how controlling and difficult you can be when you set your mind to something. It is the reason your company is so successful, why you two are so successful."

Grant just stood there watching us, he was laughing, his smile big with contentment.

"Get in the car," I said.

The four of us climbed into my white Lexus RX SUV and headed to Matt and Kendall's place. We dropped them off, tomorrow will be another work day for us, hopefully getting some kind of feedback from Lookinglass on our presentation. I only live about ten minutes from Kendall and Matt, so our drive home should be quick.

"By the way Kendall's car is red, so they aren't exactly the same," I said to Grant.

He just smiled at me and nodded his head. He held my hand as we made our way down Pacific Coast Highway to my condo. We pulled up and I opened the garage from a button inside my car and drove into the garage. Grant leaned over, pulling my head to his, and gave me a long kiss.

"I have been waiting to do that all afternoon."

"Mmm…."I smiled at him and hopped out of the car.

Once inside my condo I gave him a quick tour. It was nothing special, the condo was completely dated and in need of a much deserved make over, but I didn't own it and I was hardly ever here, now with the wedding I would probably be giving it up. I only rented it because it was a steal and right on the beach. Grant looked around and gave me a quirky smile.

"It is um…well…not something I see you in, but it is only temporary."

I laughed at him.

"You can say it…it is downright 1980's gone wrong…" I moved closer to him. His eyes began to twinkle. "Let me show you something, the reason I rented this place." I took him outside to the deck, with the stairs leading down to the sand.

He looked down at the beach and smiled back at me, the waves crashing down on the sand and the fresh smell of salt water cleansing our bodies. He pulled me to his side kissing the top of my head.

"I see why you put up with the awful décor, this is all worth it. Do you want to keep this place after we are married? You know you can always stay at our beach house, when you come here on business." There was no hesitation in his statement.

"Hmmm…I hadn't thought about that. Do you think Kendall and I can continue to run our business with me in Arizona and her here?"

"I don't see why not…you can expand and have a satellite office in Arizona and your corporate office here, but if you land the Lookinglass account you will be spending a large quantity of time there anyways and you will need a local office, you can always set up shop at Atherton headquarters, I am sure we can find space for you."

I looked up at him, he is so smart. I hadn't even thought of any of that yet. I was too wrapped up in wedding plans.

"Maybe…I will speak with Kendall tomorrow. What do you want to do the rest of the day, I have no food here? We could go into town and have dinner, take a walk on the beach order pizza, rent a movie?"

Grant only had one thing on his mind. He pulled me into his arms, kissing my neck.

"I think we should go inside, before the beachgoers get a show. I am taking you to the bedroom and well, you know what happens in a bedroom!" I started giggling and threw myself into his arms.

The morning started out wonderfully, waking up in Grant's arms is a feeling I am not ever willing to give up. I laid in bed watching Grant sleep, eventually he stretched and woke up, taking me into his arms for a morning hug.

"Good morning," he said with a groggy voice.

I smiled at him, "Good morning to you boyfriend."

"Boyfriend, how about fiancé?"

"Okay, good morning fiancé," I said smiling.

"What is our plan for the day, do you have to go into the office?" His voice was teasing.

"I do, but first I thought we could talk about what is going to happen."

"Sure, can we have coffee and sit outside to talk?" Grant asked me.

"Great idea, I will make the coffee while you put some clothes on." I smacked his bottom before climbing out of bed.

We sat on the balcony watching the waves crash on the beach, sipping our coffee. I am so happy, my world has finally come together, I could feel contentment all through my body. I haven't been this happy in a very long time.

"What are you thinking about?"

I turned to him, "You and how happy you make me, how happy I am and how excited I am to marry you." I was grinning from ear to ear.

He smiled back at me and took my hand to kiss it.

"So, you said you wanted to talk."

"Yeah, do you think I should keep this place? I mean there is only about three months left on the lease, if I break the lease I will lose my deposit."

"It is up to you but if you are going to pay rent for three more months and not be here we are going to be out the money anyways, so maybe you should just tell the landlord you are moving out."

"Okay, I will call him today. So, I was thinking about what you said about running Uppercase from Arizona and I think I can do it. I will fly back here once a week or on the weekend, depending what events we have planned. And if we land the Lookinglass account I will have to be there anyways, so yes, as long as Kendall is okay with it, then we have no problem. My assistant can still work for me, thank goodness for computers."

"Great, can I come with you to your office? I want to see where the magic happens, then I will head to my parents' house, go surfing, and then pick you up at the end of the day. Okay?"

"Great, I am going to shower and get ready. Although I would much rather stay here alone with you all day!" I said to him and gave him a little wink.

Grant walked behind me into our offices, I introduced him to our receptionist and both of our assistants. I asked Kendall's assistant to have her come to my office when she got in. I closed the door to my office and Grant sat down in a chair across from my desk.

"So, this is where the magic happens?" Grant said looking around my office. "Not much of a view."

I laughed, "Well, we are in an industrial park, so no... no view. Not all of us have offices looking out over the city or golf course."

"I am not making fun of you, you will just like the view better from the Atherton offices."

I sat down at my desk, turning on my computer and checking my emails. I could see a message from Lookinglass Industries. My heart started to pound and I took a deep breath.

"What, is something wrong?" Grant asked me.

"I don't know there is a message with an attachment from Lookinglass, I am going to print it out." I waited for the printer to warm up and then out came the letter.

It was a form letter to all of the event planners, thanking all of us for our wonderful presentations, also advising a decision would be reached within thirty days. I showed Grant the letter. He smiled after reading it and handed it back to me.

"Well, that is definitely a form letter."

"Right, so thirty days from now we will be on our honeymoon. I forgot, where did you say we are going?" I was hoping he would slip up and tell me.

"I didn't say...but nice try. Okay, so I am going to head out, what time do you want me to pick you up?"

I could tell he was ready to go and hit the waves.

"We have a lunch appointment with a new client, so how about around three?" I smiled at him. "Can I trust you to drive my car?"

He laughed at me, came around my desk, and gave me a long loving kiss.

"I am not going to answer that...I will see you my love, at three."

He took my keys, took one more kiss, and left.

I was staring out in dreamland when Kendall came in my office.

"Well good morning. I didn't expect to see you here today," Kendall said with a bright cheery face.

I smiled back at her, "Of course. We received a letter from Lookinglass." Kendall's eyes grew wide.

"And?"

"And...nothing...we will have an answer in thirty days, so while I am on my honeymoon. You promise to call me with the update?

235

That sounds so weird, on my honeymoon, I can't believe I am getting married." I am in the best mood, nothing could bring down from my high.

"I know…it will be great, is Jade going to be your maid of honor?"

"I haven't even talked to her yet, but yes. Are you mad?"

"No, don't be silly. I am just glad you are not making us do a silly dance like at Heather's wedding."

We both laughed and then we needed to discuss the changes ahead.

"So, you know Grant wants me to run a satellite office from Arizona, what do you think?" I asked Kendall, I hope she is on board with this idea. Otherwise I will have to sell her my share of the company because I am not going to live apart from Grant, my soon to be husband.

"Well, not my first choice, but I think it is the only way we can do this and if we get Lookinglass we will be in Arizona so much we will need an office. Plus if Matt gets transferred to Arizona, we will have to move the company anyways."

She said it so fast I almost missed it. I quickly lifted my head up to look at her, my eyes huge.

"I am sorry, can you repeat that please?"

"You heard me. Matt is up for a promotion, which means we would be moving to Arizona, are there any homes for sale on your street?"

I started laughing, smiling, and crying.

"Oh, this is even better…houses for sale I have no idea, we can ask Grant when he comes back to get me. We could keep both offices, fly back and forth for meetings and events. When is Matt going to find out about his promotion?"

"Soon. It seems like our lives are finally falling into place!"

I laughed at her statement, "Yeah, Jackson used to use that phrase all the time, he would say, "Don't worry Sydney everything will fall in to place. I guess he was right!"

"Who's Jackson?" I heard the deep male voice say from behind Kendall.

My body tensed, I hadn't seen Grant come up behind Kendall while we were talking. Kendall ducked out of my office. He came and sat down in the chair across from my desk while I turned off my computer and began gathering my things to head home. His eyebrows were raised at me, waiting for me to answer.

"Um, Jackson was a friend of mine and Kendall's that we met while we were still at school." I tried to play it off, I mean he was a friend and we didn't speak anymore so no big deal. I was fidgeting.

"Oh, I have never heard his name mentioned before is all. Why are you acting so strange?"

"I am not acting strange, let's go get some dinner and head home so we can start packing my stuff up," I said, not wanting to continue this conversation. I took his hand and pulled him up from the chair. "How was surfing?" I asked, changing the subject.

I spent the rest of the week furiously working to finalize my projects before we went back to Arizona. I started packing up my files to take with me, and having my assistant make copies of any necessary documents she would need to keep on clients. I also took letterhead, envelopes, a box of business cards, and a box of Uppercase brochures. Grant dropped me off every day at my office and went to the beach, or just hung out at home. We spent our evenings together packing up my condo and talking about our future.

I was giddy with excitement, as we drove back to Arizona at the end of the week. The wedding is in two weeks...holy crap...I am getting married in two short weeks! My plan is to concentrate on the wedding and only spend a few hours a day working from my home office in our house...our house. I love the sound of that. My parents will be arriving a few days before the wedding, and my very pregnant sister and her family were coming in the day before. I stared at the window twirling my engagement ring on my finger. Grant grabbed my hand giving me a light kiss as we drove away from the beach.

"Are you alright? You seem anxious," he asked.

"I am anxious, not in a bad way. I am just excited to start our life together."

"Are you sad to be leaving the beach, you know we can come out anytime we want to."

I smiled at him, "Sad, no not really, only about not seeing Kendall every day and yes, I know we can come to the beach any time."

"Kendall and Matt will be living here full time in a few months since Matt has been promoted, everything will be great, and you and Kendall will only be separated for a few months. Seriously, I hope you never get in a fight- that will be bad."

"Oh, we fight all the time, we just know there is nothing that can tear us apart. Only once did we not speak for about a month, and that was way back in high school, it was torture." He gave me a perplexed look.

"Do you remember what the fight was about?" He asked.

I did remember but I didn't want to elaborate, bringing up old boyfriends was always a touchy subject.

I hesitated before speaking, "I do, but I'd rather not share, you have a tendency to get jealous, and I don't want to have your mind filled with something that has nothing to do with us."

He looked over at me, I could see in his eyes he desperately wanted to know.

"I can't imagine something that could pull you two apart, I am just so curious."

"Fine, but if you get all annoyed or bring any of this up in a fight, I will never share something about my past with you again."

Grant laughed at my terms.

"I agree, but I don't get jealous anymore."

I chuckled, "We'll see. It was the summer before our senior year of high school and Kendall wanted me to go to a party with her. I didn't want to go, I knew she wanted to hook up with this guy, and wanted me to hook up with his friend."

Grant was smiling as he drove. "Did they go to your school and what does hook up mean?"

I rolled my eyes at him, "This is exactly why I didn't want to tell you, you ask too many questions. No, this was a party from a different high school, and hook up just means kiss...relax."

"Oh, okay, continue." I could see the relief in his eyes.

"Anyways," I said annoyed, "I did go to the party with her, but was less than nice to the friend, which made Kendall mad. I kept leaving him talking to some girls I knew and bugging Kendall to leave. He kept pawing at me, trying to lure me into a room to be alone." I could see Grant's knuckles tightening around the steering wheel. "Stop...this was way before I knew you and nothing happened so why are you getting all upset."

He cleared his throat, "I guess the thought of someone else touching you, whether it was before we knew each other, or when we weren't together makes me... mad." He looked over at me when he finished speaking.

"I know, but we both have a past and we can't change the past," I said with wide eyes. "Anyways, long story short, I was pissed because she wouldn't leave, she was pissed because I wanted to leave, she chose to stay and I left. She had her car, so I called someone to pick me up and bailed. We didn't speak until just before school started. We both apologized and moved on. End of story."

"Why would you think I would be jealous, that is the most ridiculous fight I have ever heard of, who did you call to pick you up?"

I looked at him, I knew he would ask. "Trent."

He flinched at the name, "Were you already dating him, when you went to the party?"

"That was all a long time ago…but no we weren't dating yet, we started dating soon after that night."

"Oh, do you regret dating him?"

Seriously, why does he want to know this again? I told him how much I regretted dating him. "You know, what I regret is not knowing the difference between being truly loved, and wishing you were loved. I was young."

"Yes, you were. You are still young."

I shook my head at him. "Whatever, I can't help it if you are robbing the cradle!"

"What about Jackson, how long did you date him?"

Shit…how did he know I dated Jackson. I really didn't want to discuss him, especially since Jackson had filled a void in my life and helped me put myself back together after Grant left me. I didn't say anything for a few minutes, until he asked me again.

"Sydney, are you going to tell me about Jackson? I don't believe he was only your friend," his tone was prying. I cringed at his words.

I took a deep breath.

"When you left for Europe that awful summer," I gave him a dirty look. "Kendall and Matt broke up about the same time. We, Kendall and I, went out and we met Jackson and his friend Colby one evening. Kendall and Colby started dating but I was, to say the least, not interested in having a relationship with anyone, especially not someone who didn't live close by."

"Oh, he didn't go to ASU?"

"No, they went to school…anyways they had already graduated from college and were working, they only came into town about once a month on business. He and I became friends, he helped me put the pieces of my life back together. He was a good friend to me and then…Do you really want to hear this?"

Grant gave me the look, which said I want to know and if you don't tell me it is going to drive me crazy. I had no choice.

"Fine, but the terms still stand you can't hold any of my honesty against me!"

He chuckled and rolled his eyes at me, "I know."

"Eventually, after a very long time, I was able to put my feelings, broken heart, and pain, which by the way you caused away," I looked at Grant for a reaction, I could see the muscles in his neck tense, I smiled to myself.

"Jackson helped me live again. I had walked around so unhappy and sad for so long I didn't know how to feel for anyone again. Really… that is it, I realized what I felt for him was friendship, not love, actually he made me realize that no matter how locked up my feelings were for you, that no one could fill the space in my heart, except for you. That only you could make me completely happy. I just wish I would have come to this conclusion faster and without so much heartache. Because believe me, the ache in my heart over the last few years has been horrible." I had tears in my eyes when I was done and when I looked at Grant so did he.

"I am so sorry," Grant said his face was grim with remorse.

I smiled at him and took his hand in mine, "We are together and that is what is important, our relationship from the start was not conventional, but in the end we are together. Did you ever think how different our lives would have been if I wouldn't have moved to the beach that summer?"

"Our paths still would have crossed, we were meant to be together. Why else would you have been at that bonfire? Even if you hadn't come to the beach, we would have met through Heather and Curt, and the sparks still would have flown between us." His face was radiating with joy as was mine.

We both laughed, we pulled in to the driveway of our home and stepped out of the car, each of us stretching our bodies from the long drive. Grant handed me the keys.

"Open the door and I will start bringing in our luggage and all your stuff."

"I don't have a key."

"Yes, you do. Look on your key chain." His devilish smile beaming at me.

I found a bright pink key on the key ring and walked to the door to open the lock. I pushed open the door and turned around to find Grant running up behind me as the alarm of the house started to blast.

"Shit…" He yelled and pressed a bunch of numbers into the key pad inside the front door. "Sorry Sydney, I forgot to give you the code to turn off the alarm, we will go over all that later and I will give you a garage door opener too." He smiled and kissed my cheek. "Now move it hot stuff, let's get your stuff into *our* house." He smacked my bottom before he ran back down to the car.

CHAPTER 21

I stood at the top of the aisle with my parents on either side of me. My heart was pounding. This day was finally here, the quick engagement, few short weeks of planning, and the secret honeymoon Grant was planning. The wedding party was already standing at the front, waiting for me to walk down. The music playing was the wedding march, "Rondeau" by Mouret, it sounds lovely.

My wedding gown is made of satin and organza, with wide satin stripes, small applique flowers with rhinestones in the centers adorn my short strapless gown. I have on high sparkly heels to match. My bridesmaids are wearing charcoal colored tulle dresses with a bubble hem with sequins underneath, with a wide grosgrain sash which ties in a large bow in the front. Grant and his groomsmen are wearing black tuxedos. We took pictures separately before the wedding to keep tradition.

The wedding ceremony is being held in a beautiful private garden on the grounds of the Atherton Resort. It is actually the first wedding to be held at Atherton since the opening of the resort a few months ago. I guess it is fitting for the family who owns the resort to have the first wedding at the resort. The walkway to the front of the garden is made of slate and the chairs are lined up in rows, there must be more than 200 people in attendance to see Grant and I finally take the plunge. The gazebo was covered in white roses, the bridesmaids are holding small bouquets of white roses, and my bouquet is the same only larger.

My parents both looking at me said, "Are you ready?" The tears of joy in their eyes made me take a much needed deep breath before we began the short walk to my groom. My father kissed both my cheeks and then lowered my veil. My mother squeezed my hand, and whispered in my ear, "This is the best decision you have ever made, you will be very happy, Grant is a wonderful man. He will be an excellent husband and friend."

We slowly walked down the aisle to the music as the guests began to stand on our approach. I could see Grant's parents smiling adoringly at me, the twinkle in their eyes is definitely a Montgomery trait. Behind them stood Maggie and Steven Carlisle whose smiles were beaming at me. Kendall and Heather were beyond joyful, this would make Heather and I cousins! Who says you can't pick your family!

We reached the end of the aisle, Grant walked up to take my hand, my shaking hand. His gorgeous smile and warm touch calming my nerves. His eyes wide and dancing with joy as he looked at me, we walked hand in hand in to stand in front of the Justice of the Peace.

Grant softly whispered to me, "you look beautiful."

I smiled up to him and mouthed, "thank you."

The Justice of the Peace began talking about how long he has known the Montgomery family and what a delight it is to have me become a part of their family. We turned to each other to recite our vows, Grant put his hands out, palm side up, and I placed my hands in his. Grant went first.

I looked up at him as he began to speak to me, it was as if we were all alone on the pier by the beach, "Sydney, from the first time I saw you sitting in the front row of Biology 101, to the night you looked at me over the flames of the bonfire, I knew you were the one. The way your smile lights up my heart, your kindness gives me joy and your forgiveness gave me you. I will spend my life making you happy and our world together perfect. I love you." His eyes were misted over with tears.

I never took my eyes away from his as he spoke. I took a deep breath and began to recite my vows.

"Grant, the night our eyes met over the flames of the infamous bonfire, a flash of electricity flew through my body sending the hairs on the back of my neck up. I knew then you were special. When you kissed my lips the first time I thought I was floating above the earth and when you told me you loved me I thought it was a dream. When you proposed to me on one knee and told me you wanted to spend the rest of your life with me, I knew it was all real, your gentle touch, your loving heart and warming smile, make me whole. I love you!" We smiled at each other, as my tears of joy slowly rolled down my face, he squeezed my hands.

The Justice of the Peace asked for the rings, Noah handed his to Grant, and Jade handed mine to me. I placed Grant's wedding band on his left finger. I had the band specially made to match mine. Made of platinum with a row of diamonds, engraved on the inside it says, "To my HBG, love Hot Stuff." Grant then slipped my wedding band on my finger and I placed my engagement ring back on. We both repeated after the Justice of the Peace, "With this ring I thee wed." Afterwards, Grant quickly lifted my veil and gave me a long passionate kiss, whispering in my ear, "I love you so much."

Again, I had to wipe my tears of joy from my face as Grant and I pulled apart. The Justice of the Peace said, "Ladies and Gentleman, may I present to you, Mr. and Mrs. Grant and Sydney Montgomery." There was a lot of clapping, we walked up the aisle and headed towards the reception. There were many hugs and joyous words of sentiment. A million pictures were taken and the video guy would not stop filming for anything.

We danced our first dance as husband and wife to "Wanted" by Hunter Hayes. We were quickly joined by our dear friends and family. We danced the night away together and I barely escaped cake being pushed into my face. Grant wrapped me in his arms all night long, we were never apart for more than a few minutes. When the crowd of guests finally became just the family, Grant whispered in my ear, "Mrs. Montgomery, I would like to take you back to the honeymoon suite and make love to you as my wife." His eyebrows were raised and he was licking his bottom lip.

I smiled coyly at him, "Anything for my husband," I said giggling. We said our good-byes and made our way to our suite. Grant carried me over the threshold and kicked the door closed behind him.

CHAPTER 22

After the busy few weeks, wonderful wedding, and hectic lifestyle, fourteen days alone together sounds like heaven. Grant planned an amazing honeymoon for us- two weeks in Greece, island hoping. We started in Santorini, in a beautiful honeymoon suite overlooking the Aegean Sea. The first evening, although we were still tired, we drank champagne and watched the most beautiful sunset from our balcony. We awoke refreshed even though we didn't sleep much during the night.

"So, wife what should we do today?" My handsome husband Grant asked me.

"Well, husband I don't know. I can think of many things to do together. Do we want to leave our suite today or are we talking about staying in all day?" I asked as I raised one eyebrow at him.

His smirk is panty dropping to say the least. He pursed his lips at me.

"Well...wife, how about I surf and you watch me? Sound familiar? But this time you do it from a shaded beach chair with someone serving you a cocktail."

"I like it...can you rent a surfboard?"

"Of course, I have one waiting for me down stairs," he said laughing.

"You are so bad."

"Yes, yes I am... but before we leave our private sanctuary I am going to show you just how bad your husband can be."

I started to laugh as he attacked me jumping over the chairs in our suite and carrying me over his shoulder to the shower. He turned on the shower and removed my camisole and panties. He led me into the warm water pouring shower gel into his hands and massaging every married inch of my body. He whispered the most erotic things in my ears making every part of my body melt for him. His hands are wickedly amazing and that thing he can do with his tongue can make me have an orgasm just dreaming about it. Luckily for me, his tongue is fully engaged on my body at this moment, no need to dream about it.

Once he was done with his relentless but more than satiating attack on my body, it was my turn. I can dish out the torment too. I took his full erection in my hand, it is quite hard and proudly peeking at me, I covered him with my mouth. I could feel his full length touching the back of my throat and the groans emanating from Grant's core almost had me having another orgasm.

"Holy shit Sydney…what are you doing to me?" Grant was barely able to moan to me.

I love the fact that I have full control of his well his…man card when I give him a blow job. He tried to pull me up but I wouldn't let him. I braced down and kept on sucking on him until he came in my mouth, so hard like a wild man. He gripped my hair as his body shuddered from his release, and I could hear a long list of dirty words spilling out of his mouth.

I giggled as I stood up next to him, wiping my mouth, with a ridiculously pleased expression on my face. I rinsed my mouth with the water from the rain shower, my smile still wide across my face. Grant pulled me into his body wrapping his warm arms around me.

"I love you so much," Grant whispered sweetly in to my ear.

"Right back at you hubby, I am a very lucky girl."

"Yes you are, and we are going to have an amazing honeymoon. So, let's get dressed and head out to the beach, don't forget to bring your camera, hot stuff." He smacked my naked ass so hard, for sure I will have a red hand print all day.

"Ouch, that hurt," I griped, but he just smiled at me.

We spent five glorious days in Santorini, and then headed to Crete for five days. Once again, the views are off the charts fabulous, and I am not just talking about the ones out the window. Because the one of my husband's naked ass walking past me is even more fabulous.

The beach in Crete is amazing, no words to describe how spectacular. The crystal clear blue water is breathtaking. Grant, of course, wants to surf on each island we visit. So, he spent I don't know how long with the concierge mapping out his surfing destinations. I think he has more than one reason for picking Greece for our honeymoon. I don't care, as long as we are together and happy, I am more than good.

We did manage to do other things while on our honeymoon besides having sex and surfing. We went out to a few romantic dinners, hiked on many beautiful trails, and even went dancing one evening. Although I do have to say my favorite moments have been when we are wrapped in each other's arms before and after ravishing one another. Our final destination is Athens; can't go to Greece without stopping in Athens.

We took in all the amazing sites starting with the Acropolis, then the Parthenon and The Temple of Poseidon Sounion. It was out of this world historical, everyone should see these sites. We ate gyro's from street vendors, and shopped in the central market. Possibly we drank too much Ouzo, which can be found all over Greece. We had a few bottles of our favorite brand of Ouzo shipped back to the States for us to have at home.

"Do we have to go home? I am enjoying having you all to myself," Grant said with a sad face.

"Yes, we have to go home, but to *our* home. No more living in different states. We have each other forever," I said as I kissed his yummy lips.

"Yes Sydney, we are going to have an amazing, out of this world, knock your socks off, everyone else will be sooo jealous of us life together. Thank you for making me the happiest man on earth." The look in Grant's eyes was heartwarming.

If you would have asked me six months ago if I would have finally given in to my stubbornness and let Grant back into my life, I would have made a grunting noise and avoided the entire conversation. This is the only place for me, hand in hand with my man. No doubt in my mind.

"Well, going home is bittersweet because we have to go back to work and not be able to spend every waking moment together. But we will be together when we wake up and when we go to sleep each night, what could be better than that?" I said to him as a popped my birth control pill into my mouth.

Grant looked at me with a salacious smile. He sauntered my way, "What could be better is if I could keep you next to me, all the time, so I could reach out and touch your sexy body any time of day." He said as he pulled me tight to his chest, locking my arms behind my back.

I started to giggle as he kissed my neck with his luscious lips. "You are out of your mind, but I love the idea, we may have to arrange some special lunch dates."

"Mmm...hmmm...we can arrange anything you want," Grant mumbled out. "When are you going to stop taking your birth control pills? We are married now let's just let nature take its course."

I pulled back from his embrace and the kisses he was smothering me with. As I looked into his eyes I could only see unconditional love.

"Are you serious, you are interested in starting a family already?" My voice came out a bit squeaky.

"Nothing would make me happier than to see you barefoot and pregnant, your belly big and round."

"You are nuts, we have only been married for two short weeks. Let's have some time alone before we bring another person into our family. There is nothing on this earth that would give me more pleasure than to have a baby with you, but I want to have some time alone together. Is that okay with you? Maybe travel a little bit more and if Uppercase gets the Lookinglass account, I will be too busy, and being pregnant would not be a good idea. I am sure I will need to keep my stress level down." I had to be honest with Grant I didn't want to give him false hopes of starting a family right away when I wasn't ready yet.

"I guess I didn't think of it like that. I mean the stress you will be under working. Do you think you will want to continue to work after we do have children? I mean you don't have to work now. I make enough to take care of us," he said it with such confidence and strength.

"I want to be able to be home with our children...I think I will cross that bridge when the time comes, maybe work part time. I don't know, but it helps when you are the owner of the company and your best friend is your partner. As long as Kendall and I are not pregnant at the same time, it should be okay," I started to laugh out loud.

"What are you laughing about?" Grant asked.

"What if Heather, Kendall and I are all pregnant at the same time? I am not sure if that is a good idea or not, but at least you, Matt, and Curt would all be in the same boat! Just the thought of you three guys taking care of three grumpy pregnant women has me laughing." I couldn't help myself the image in my mind had me hysterical.

Grant shook his head at me as I lay on the bed tears streaming down my face as I continued to laugh.

"I wonder if Matt and Kendall made an offer on the corner house. Don't you think it would be awesome to have them living so close to us?" Grant asked me.

"Awesome…yes…very awesome!" I said.

Epilogue

Uppercase Events is now permanently located in Arizona as are Kendall and Matt. Uppercase landed half of the Lookinglass account and is under contract with them to continue on as their in- house event coordinator. Grant has continued on as the General Manager of the Atherton Resort. Although Kevin, Grant's dad has recently been hinting around about semi-retiring. I think Kevin and Corinne want to travel the world and have their children continue the business they created for them. This would mean Grant and Noah would run the business together.

Kendall and Matt moved into their home just prior to their wedding two years ago. Our houses are across the street from each other, and I couldn't be happier. Well yes, I could be if Heather and Curt moved onto our street. Currently they are living with Curt's parents while he finishes his medical residency and their house is done being renovated. They won't be on the same street, but just around the corner.

Grant and I decided each year for our wedding anniversary we would take a one week vacation to celebrate our nuptials. We put a list together of all the places around the world we would want to visit. We printed out the list, cut out the names of the places, folding each piece of paper in half, and placed the folded papers in a jar. Each year we pick one, and that is the place we go.

Just before we left for Maui, Grant suggested I stop taking my birth control pills. I was a tad leery but what the heck, I threw caution to the wind. I am sure no one was surprised when we announced I was eight weeks pregnant at the weekly family dinner. I could see Corinne counting backwards on her fingers.

The smile across Grant's parents' faces couldn't have been mistaken for anything but joy.

"So, I guess this bundle of joy was conceived during your trip to Hawaii?" His mother had asked us.

"You are right, I saw you counting on your fingers," I told his mom.

***

Well that was seven months ago…

"If someone doesn't get me my epidural this instant I am going to scream!" I yelled at my husband.

"Sydney…take a deep breath, the nurse is coming with the anesthesiologist to give you your epidural," Grant sweetly said to me.

I gave him a dirty look.

"Taking a deep breath does not help…get me the drugs. This was your stupid idea, what was I thinking…I am the one who has to deal with all the pain here. You are taking all the middle of the night feedings!" I growled at him.

"Yes, my love, I will do whatever you want me to do," his voice again sweet and calming.

"Your damn right…HOLY SHIT…" I yelled. I grabbed Grant's hand as the pain from the contractions shot through my body and tears pricked my eyes.

Once the Doctor was done giving me my shot, the pain was barely noticeable. I was tired of waiting for this bundle of joy to make its presence known. We had decided not to find out the sex of the baby, we wanted to be surprised. His parents were not happy with our decision but it was our decision to make. The nurse kept coming in to check on me. Every time she wanted to check how dilated I was she asked everyone to leave. This time the nurse's eyes were wide as she checked my cervix and the baby's heart monitor. She rushed out of my room, leaving me in a bit of a panic. Grant took my hand in his, rubbing his thumb over the outside of my hand, and giving me some ice chips to suck on.

The nurse returned with the doctor on staff to check out my situation. I have a situation apparently.

"Mrs. Montgomery, I believe the baby maybe in some distress, I would like to perform an emergency C-section," the doctor's voice was calm but stern.

I looked up at Grant as he squeezed my hand in his. I couldn't even muster the energy to speak. I was scared; tears began to roll down my face.

"If that is what you think is best for the baby and my wife, then that is what we will do," Grant said.

"Okay... we are going to wheel you down to the operating room. Mr. Montgomery you can come as well, you will need to put on scrubs, a nurse will show you where to go, and bring you in to be with your wife. Don't worry everything is going to be fine. I just want to get your little one out into this world with no complications," he said smiling at Grant and me, but our fear was palpable.

I turned my head to look at Grant, he was pale as a ghost. My anxiety had shot through the roof. You could tell because my heart monitor was beeping at a record pace.

"I am sorry..." I began to say.

"Oh love, you have nothing to be sorry for, please don't ever think that you have something to be sorry for. We will go into the operating room as two and come out as three. We are in this together, for better or worse, remember?" He leaned down moving my sweaty hair from around my face and giving me a big kiss. "I love you, Sydney."

"I love you too," I said returning his kiss.

Not much later, the cries of our bundle of joy could be heard in the operating room. Ten fingers, ten toes, two eyes, two ears...perfect. Everything about her is perfect. Olivia Stanton Montgomery, our first born child. Grant kissed my forehead as the nurse placed her in my arms as tears of bliss came down our cheeks.

"Thank you, God, thank you for this perfect day," Grant said as he kissed her cheeks.

The baby and I were released from the hospital a few days later. Grant picked us up in the Jeep, with the car seat securely anchored in the back seat. Once on the road, Grant was driving like an old man. I had to ask him to pick up the pace because there is no reason we should be only going fifteen miles per hour. He advised me that as long as he has precious cargo on board he is not going any faster. Then I reminded him that she would be awake soon and I was not going to be able to nurse her in the back seat of a moving car. I think he started going maybe twenty-five miles per hour. I just laughed and shook my head at him.

We arrived home to find my parents and Grant's parents waiting for us. Our moms had cleaned the house and stocked the refrigerator. While our dads were outside grilling some steaks for dinner. My parents are staying with us in our guest bedroom. I am so grateful to have both of sets of parents here to help.

My mom helped me lie down on the couch, while Corinne rained kisses down on Olivia.

"Mom, stop kissing her, you are going to give her germs," Grant lectured his mother.

"Stop it…I will give our little Olivia more kisses than she will know what to do with," Corinne said in a soft voice to the baby.

I rolled my eyes, good God these people have gone mad. I just want to take a pain killer and take a nap. The hospital is so noisy, nurses coming in and out of my room at all hours of the day and night, you can't get any rest in that place.

"Grant, be a doll and get Sydney a glass of water, so she can take her pain pill?" My mother asked.

Grant handed me the water and my pill, and before I knew it I was in la la land. I was curled up in a ball under a blanket. When Grant picked me up and carried me to our bed, I could feel his hot breath on my neck. I snuggled up next to his warm chest as he carried me.

When I woke the next morning, I was completely discombobulated. Our room is still dark and Grant is holding me tight to his chest. I shot right up in the bed. Then Grant shot up.

"What's wrong?" He asked me.

"The baby, I slept all night…I have to check on her," I said freaking out.

"Your mother is taking care of her so we can get some rest. Please lie back down and close your eyes, you were exhausted last night. Let her take care of Olivia," Grant said as he tickled my arm with soft caresses.

"Well…um…I just want to peek in on her."

"Okay, I will go with you."

We walked down the hall to the nursery and found my mother rocking her in the easy glider chair and giving her a bottle. My mom looked at us as we stood in the doorway. My mom was smiling with so much love for her newest grandchild that I almost lost it watching her. I wrapped my arms around Grants waist and leaned my head on his chest.

"Let's go back to bed, Grandma has it under control," Grant whispered to me.

The next few months were filled with more happy moments. Curt and Heather moved into their home just around the corner from us and announced they would be having a baby in a few months. Kendall had given birth to twin boys just a few weeks after Olivia's arrival.

Life couldn't have been better, surrounded by our dearest friends and family. Olivia was only a few months old and our parents were already asking when we were going to have another. I looked at them in shock. Are these people crazy?

"You people are crazy," I laughed out loud. "I am taking a much needed vacation with my husband to Italy in a few months to celebrate our second anniversary, so if you are all lucky we will come back with more than just photos to share with you."

The End

COMING SOON

Look for the next series of books by S.P.Wilcox, titled My Narrative. This series is written for Young Adults . Hopefully to be released in December 2012 or January 2013. See if you can find the crossover characters from her books, Wishful Thinking and Not Another Wish.

You can visit the authors Facebook page at S.P.Wilcox, or on goodreads, or email her at **s.p.wilcoxauthor@gmail.com** with any questions you have about her books. Look for her website, which is coming soon.